the
Dance

Alison G. Bailey

Editor, Linda Roberts
Cover Design, Murphy Rae Hopkins, Indie Solutions
www.murphyrae.net/
Photography, Abigail Marie, Non'Pareil Photography
nonpareilphotography.com/
Interior Design, Elaine York, www.allusiongraphics.com

ISBN 10: 1533109400
ISBN 13: 978153319408

dedication

To my sister, Kelley. There aren't enough
words to express my love and gratitude.
Thank you for being the best big sister a girl could have.

prologue

I stood in front of the glass wall, mesmerized. The fake sunlight shimmered down through the water, bouncing off the yellow, green, and pink coral. The blue glow of the tank gave the dimly lit nook a mystical dreamy feel.

The prom committee had pulled off an epic feat this year. Instead of having the dance in our gross school gym it was being held at the new state-of-the-art aquarium downtown. Once the student committee agreed, Megan Sims, head cheerleader and overly developed youth, was given the task of presenting the new location idea to the faculty advisor, Mr. Hall. During the meeting, as Megan waxed poetic about riding the waves of hope out into the ocean of the future, she hoisted her massive boobs up to meet Mr. Hall's sightline. Three seconds into Megan's spiel the dude was so titnotized that he would have offered up his first born in order to pay the rental fee.

At first, I had my doubts about spending my final prom at the aquarium. The fishy décor didn't exactly scream romance, but I had to admit, it was pretty cool. The dance was in Ballroom A, which opened up onto a huge deck facing the Charleston harbor. Inside three giant purple octopus chandeliers hung down from the ceiling, casting cool shadows on the walls covered in varying shades of blue. Big white coral sculptures were at the four corners of the room. Tables draped in white linen with candles and seashell centerpieces outlined the room, leaving a huge space in the middle for dancing.

The rules of the night were clear: 1. Proper attire—guys were to wear a jacket and tie, girls were to have their nips and hoo-haws covered at all times. 2. No alcohol. 3. No drugs. 4. No sex of any kind, anywhere. 5. We were only allowed in the designated areas— Ballroom A and the adjacent deck.

My best friend, Sophie, had run off to break rule number four. While Will, my first and only boyfriend, was off breaking rule number two. Deciding hanging out with his football buddies was his preferred way to spend our senior prom. He'd picked me up from home, felt me up in the limo, and then ditched me twenty minutes after we arrived. I was disappointed but not surprised. People loved being around Will and he thrived on the attention, never wanting to let down his parents or his friends. Even though it was hard sharing him with everyone, I had developed an understanding over the two years we'd been together.

Once Will had his fill of his football buddies, he'd come looking for my forgiveness. With his jacket off, his sleeves rolled up, and his muscular forearms flexed, he'd toss his sexy pouty look my way, and I would fall under his spell. I was a sucker for a well-defined muscular arm. Flexed or not, they induced a severe case of amnesia in me. But Will had more going for him than just muscles. At his core he was a good guy. His smile and charm could melt anyone. He'd aimed them at me the beginning of our junior year and I'd been melting ever since.

Each time I looked into his dark brown eyes or ran my fingers through his matching short hair, I knew I was the envy of every girl in school. There was no question in my mind or my heart that Will was my future. We'd had our ups and downs like every couple. But when you loved someone you learned to work through your problems and overlook their less attractive qualities. I just thought tonight being our last prom would be different. Instead, I was spending one of the most romantic nights in a high schooler's life with the cast of Finding Nemo.

After spending a long half hour as a wallflower, I decided to go rogue and break rule number five. I discretely slipped out of the ballroom and snuck down the hallway in search of a quiet place. Turning two corners, I found the perfect spot, the noise and booming music fading into the background. I kicked off my four-inch heels, quieting my screaming feet, and unleashed my long, light brown hair from the nest of pins holding it up. After running my fingers through my hair a few times, I directed my attention to my new date.

My nose hovered just in front of the glass as I stared into beady black eyes. I puckered my lips and puffed out my cheeks, matching the fish blow for blow.

"I can put your blowing skills to much better use." The raspy voice filled the small area.

I stilled, praying to all that was holy on this earth and beyond that those words were a figment of my imagination. The scent of beer and cigarettes drifted toward me. My increased breathing caused my new fish friend to disappear behind the fog. My eyes closed as a deep chuckle swirled in the air. This was real. I'd been caught and there was no way out of it. I turned my head and reluctantly opened my eyes.

Hart Mitchell, Garrison High's resident bad boy, was standing less than a foot away. He had transferred in at the beginning of the year from parts unknown. I had no concrete evidence as to why he'd been dubbed GH's bad boy other than he definitely looked the part.

From day one, rumors flew around school, ranging from the ridiculous to the sublime. One claimed he started coming to GH because of his hot affair with Mrs. Crawford, the very curvy, twenty-five-year-old, redheaded English teacher. No doubt he probably had a crush on her. All the boys did and even some of the girls. Hell, I caught myself a couple of times staring at her ass when she was writing on the dry erase board. The thought of Hart and Mrs. Crawford together formed a knot in my stomach. It was icky. For some reason I wanted that rumor to remain just that, a rumor. The most absurd explanation for Hart's arrival was the one about him being the leader of a motorcycle gang hiding from the Feds. He did ride a motorcycle but who hides from the Feds in high school?

I, along with the rest of the female population at GH, including faculty, noticed the new boy right away. He quietly commanded female attention. He appeared to be a loner. I never saw him hang out with anyone before or after school. In the classes we shared, he always sat behind me in the very back. Several times during the year I resisted the urge to turn around and sneak a peek when I felt his eyes on me. For some unexplained reason he made me nervous.

And then there was the swagger.

The swagger was an entity unto itself. It was confident, purposeful, and a majestic sight to behold. The best parts of my day were after second period biology and fourth period history. Several girls would get into position at their lockers and wait for the swagger to make its way around the corner. Just before it came into view an electric vibration filled the hallway. And when sensation collided with sight . . . no panty was left undropped.

Hart Mitchell was a definite enigma wrapped in hotness.

My gaze moved up his chest and over his sharp angled jaw, finally landing on a pair of piercing eyes. The stretch in my neck indicated that Hart was at least two inches taller than Will. From the few quick glimpses I'd taken of him during class, I thought his eyes were blue but in this light they looked smoky gray.

His gaze dropped to my strapless cream-colored dress. The wisps of hair on the back of my neck bristled. Neither of us said a word. We just stood motionless for . . .

One Mississippi.

My pulse pumped.

Two Mississippi.

My breath stuck.

Three Mississippi.

My head swam.

Four Mississippi.

My fingers tingled.

Five Mississippi.

My knees wobbled.

I needed to look away, take a breather, and focus on something neutral. I lowered my gaze to his smirking lips.

Those weren't neutral.

They were pale pink, plump, and looked really soft like pillows.

I widened my gaze taking in the mixture of light and dark blond scruff peppering his strong jaw and circling around his mouth, accented on either side by perfectly symmetrical deep dimples. My body was having some weird chemical reaction to Hart being this close and looking this intensely at me. I wasn't a big fan of having my personal space invaded by a guy I barely knew no matter how hot he was.

Trying to play it cool and not give in to the wobble in my legs, I slapped my palm against the glass wall to steady myself. Once adequately braced, I took further inventory of Mr. Mitchell.

His hair was long. Not Jesus long but longer than the other boys at school who either sported buzz cuts or overly product styles. Hart's dirty blond locks hit him mid neck, were parted slightly right of center, and tucked behind his ears. The oversized blue and gray plaid shirt he wore made it difficult to see any definition in the chest region but his shoulders were broad. Half of the shirt was tucked into his gravity-defying baggy jeans that hung from his narrow hips.

The corners of my mouth slightly drifted up when I saw the ugly generic black tie draped loosely around his neck. Mrs. Demarco, the algebra teacher, must have gotten to him. She was tonight's fashion police. She monitored each student like a boss. Within a few minutes of arriving, I'd seen her enforce her power. She sent Janice Price and Emma Sloan home for showing too much cleavage. And she had Ricky Bogart scrounging in the bag of ugly ties to go with the equally ugly jacket she made him wear. I wondered if Hart charmed his way out of the jacket.

Leaning one shoulder against the glass wall, his legs crossed at the ankles, he tapped the toe of his tennis shoe on the shiny marble floor and kept staring at me. Since it didn't appear that he was going to start the conversation I took it upon myself to get the ball rolling.

"Hi." The word gushed out of me all breathy like a loud sigh.

Get hold of yourself, Bryson.

His gaze lingered for two Mississippis, before replying, "Hi."

Prickling heat spread over my skin while I waited, hoping he would elaborate. But he just stared and continued to grin. The sensation of a cotton field sprouting in my mouth took over. It was ironic that I was standing in front of a giant tank of water becoming dangerously dehydrated.

Beads of sweat began popping up along my neck.

If I could lick my own neck . . .

Delirium was beginning to set in.

I cleared my throat, hocking up just enough spit to moisten my dry lips. "I'm Bryson Walker."

"I know who you are."

Of course he knew who I was, just like I knew who he was. I mean, we'd been in classes together for the last year. But this was the closest we'd ever been to each other and the first time we'd spoken.

I couldn't figure out what his deal was. After all, he was the one who'd interrupted my alone time with Nemo.

Keeping my palm firmly planted on the wall, I leaned forward, cocked my head to the side, and raised my eyebrows. "Sooo . . . ?"

"Sooo what?" He returned.

I straightened. "What can I do for you?"

The tip of his tongue slid out and rolled over his bottom lip before disappearing from view. "Do you really want me to answer that question?"

"You're very inappropriate."

"You have no idea."

"I mean you show up out of nowhere with your . . . tallness. And decide to clam up."

He leaned back against the wall, reached into his shirt pocket, and pulled out a pack of cigarettes.

Tapping the pack into his palm, he chuckled. "Clam up. Clever. Keeping with the whole sea theme of the night."

"Thank you. I'm quite quick-witted." The tugging at the corners of my mouth caused my serious expression to crumble instantly.

"Obviously." He winked at the same time a cigarette fell from the pack.

I stared as he lifted the cigarette to his mouth. I knew I should have stopped him the second I saw the pack come out of his pocket. I was on the prom committee. It was my responsibility to uphold the rules. Not to mention that smoking was a horrible, nasty, cancer bomb waiting to explode. But honestly, I wanted to see that cigarette slide between those pillow lips.

The click of the lighter brought me out of my thoughts. A tiny flame appeared and frantically flickered up toward the heavens. Just when the tip of the flame was about to meet its mate, my sense of responsibility kicked in.

"Hey, you better not light that. You're not supposed to be smoking in here."

"Who says?"

"I says . . . um . . . I mean, I say."

Looking at me out the corner of his eye, Hart raised the lighter defiantly.

I touched his bicep and tugged.

He's definitely got some bulging going on underneath that plaid.

Squaring my shoulders, I confidently said, "I'm serious. I'm not playing around with you. I'm on the prom committee."

He flipped the top back on the lighter, dousing the flame. With the cigarette dangling from his lips, he leaned toward me. "I wasn't aware you had the power. Would you like to frisk me?" His voice was deep and gravelly and made my body quiver.

"No." I squeaked, offended.

"I'll make a deal with you," he said, backing away.

"What kind of deal?"

"I'll slide my stick back in its package if you put those away." His gaze dropped and stalled for a second before bouncing back up.

"What are you talking about?"

He took the cigarette from his mouth and stuck it in his shirt pocket. "Your nipples. They've been trying to escape since I walked up."

I looked down in horror. My nipples were sticking out so far I couldn't see the tips of my toes. Crisscrossing my arms, I slapped my palms over my high-beams.

"It's c . . . old in here," I stammered as heat flooded my cheeks.

"I'm hot."

Yes he was.

Focused ahead, Hart said, "So you couldn't get a date for tonight?"

"I have a date. My boyfriend is here."

He scanned the empty alcove. "Wow! What have you been smoking?"

With my palms secured to my chest, I raised my elbows and gestured. "I don't mean here, *here*. I mean *here* as in the building."

"Huh."

"What's that supposed to mean?"

"Just huh."

"Will and I are in a committed relationship."

"Huh."

"We don't have to be together 24/7/365. We're not joined at the hip."

"Huh."

"That's what a mature adult relationship is you know."

"Huh."

"Stop already with the huhs!"

The faint sound of piano music trickled down the hall. I didn't recognize the song. It must have been an oldie for all the chaperones to dance to.

Pushing off from the wall, Hart commanded, "Let's dance."

"Huh?"

He took a couple of steps and turned toward me. "Stop already with the huhs. You heard me."

I chuckled. "Where do you get off telling me to dance with you?"

"You know you wanna. I can see it in your . . ."

Nipples. He's going to say, your humungous pointy nipples.

". . . eyes."

Aw, he didn't mention my nipples. Sweet.

"I don't think it's a very good idea. Will, my very real boyfriend, will go ballistic the second he sees us walk into the ballroom."

"Not in there." Hart reached out his hand. "In here."

I stared at his large outstretched hand waiting for mine. I didn't know if it was Hart specifically or that I was getting attention from a new boy that was causing the tingles I was experiencing. Before Will there wasn't exactly a line of guys banging down my door. I was cute by most standards with bright green eyes popping against tan skin and just the right amount of curves on my five-foot-six-inch frame. The thing was, high school boys didn't want cute. They wanted big boobs and open legs. My boobs weren't Megan Sim's size but nice nonetheless. And my legs only opened and will only open for Will Forsyth.

But in this moment, I wanted to know what Hart's hand felt like— warm, cold, soft, rough. I wanted to feel his skin on mine. Hart Mitchell was dangerous territory. The only thing I knew for sure about this guy was that he left me completely off balance. In the only ten minutes we had ever shared, I felt more excited and wanted than I had the entire night.

"What about your date? Where is she?" My voice was shaky.

"At the moment she's standing in front of a fish tank not dancing with me."

I glanced behind me and then back at Hart. He was referring to me. A crooked smile slowly crept across his face when he saw my green eyes light up with recognition. Looking back down at his still waiting hand, I felt fluttering butterflies from head to toe. Hart didn't just want to dance. He wanted to dance with me.

I dropped my arms from around my chest and extended my hand. The touching of our fingertips sent chills ping-ponging to every part of my body.

I should not be chillin' with this boy.

Hart's hand covered mine as he led me to the center of the alcove. I placed my other hand on his upper arm, leaving adequate airspace between us.

His arm wrapped around my waist, pulling me to him. "Come closer."

"Hart . . ."

"We don't want you to have another outbreak of chilly nips."

I giggled. "Yeah, because that happening twice in one night would really be embarrassing."

The area was pitch black except for the bluish glow from the fish tank. No one knew I was in here . . . alone with a boy who was not Will . . . slow dancing. I relaxed, stepped in closer, and rested my cheek on Hart's toned chest. As we swayed his chin pressed against my hair and a deep throaty hum filled my ears.

"You know this song?" I whispered.

"Tony Bennett, "The Way You Look Tonight"."

Closing my eyes, I got lost in the song, the sway, and the sensation of Hart.

One Mississippi.

Two Mississippi.

Three Mississippi.

"Bryson!" The loud shrill whisper of my best friend, Sophie, cut through the air.

I jumped out of Hart's arms and shook the dreaminess from my head. Once cleared, I looked up and saw disappointment in his smoky gray eyes.

"Sophie, I'm in here," I said, pulling my gaze away from him.

A mane of jet black curls appeared as Sophie marched toward me, her bright blue eyes full of panic.

"Thank god I found you."

"What's wrong?"

"Will, he's had too much to drink." She tugged at my arm.

"I'll be there in a second."

Sophie eyed Hart up and down suspiciously.

Swinging her gaze between the two of us, she said, "He's asking for you."

"I said I'll be there in a second."

"Okay but hurry up. I'll wait for you in the hallway." Sophie cut her eyes one last time in Hart's direction before leaving.

I nervously chewed on my lower lip. "Sorry, I have to go."

But I don't want to.

Nodding, he said in a low voice, "It's okay." I turned to leave when his words stopped me. "Bryson . . ." The sound of his raspy voice wrapped around my name caused my insides to flutter. "You're lovely."

My chest caved as all the air rushed from my lungs. "And you're unexpected."

I couldn't tear my gaze away. There was something about this mysterious bad boy using that old-fashioned term that touched my heart. Will admired when I wore my tight pair of jeans or my string bikini. But a lot of times it felt as if he liked the tightness and the skimpiness of the clothing more than the fact that I was in it. Hart didn't say I looked lovely. He said I was lovely.

Sophie's head poked back in as she whispered, "Bryson! Come on! Projectile vomiting is happening."

Keeping my eyes on Hart, I took a deep breath, and stepped backward until I was forced to turn away.

The talk at school on Monday was all about the prom—who wore whom, who got drunk, and who hooked up. I was a bundle of nerves as I headed toward English class. It would be the first time I'd seen Hart since our dance. I thought about our moment the rest of the weekend. I even elaborated on it, imagining what today would be like.

Pausing just outside the door, I took in a few feeble shaky breaths. When I walked into the classroom, Hart was already at his desk, his gaze focused on a piece of paper in his hand. Nonchalantly, I stared at the top of his head, willing him to look up. But he never did. For the remainder of the school year, I waited for him to talk, smile, or just glance in my direction. But he never did. I waited for him to make me feel special like he had that night. But he never did. I considered making the first move. But I never did. My future with Will was so embedded in my mind that the idea of veering off course was not an option. So I lived my life and waited for the memory of Hart and our moment to fade . . . but it never did.

chapter
One

"Suck it in, Bryson!"

"I *am* sucking." The words strained against my throat.

"I'm almost done." Sophie gave one final jerk of the strings, causing me to stumble back, as she cinched the corset tighter.

"Leave room for breathing." I gasped.

She snickered. "You could be your something blue. There. All snug."

"Thanks." I turned around, adjusting and readjusting my boobs.

Looking up, Sophie's big blue eyes were already misting with a mixture of happy and sad tears. Since the age of three we'd been best friends. Sharing every big milestone. We learned to ride bikes together and got our driver's license at the same time. We got our first periods in the same week. Our first date was a double, me with Will and Sophie with Travis Tucker. All through high school and college no matter what, we always had each other's back. Nothing came between girl-time with Sophie. But we weren't kids anymore and things were about to drastically change. After today my number-one priority would be building a future as Mrs. William Grant Forsyth.

Over the past several months instead of focusing on the fact that time together would be limited, we focused on the fun parts—looking for just the right dress, picking out the flowers, and planning the big party. We were in T-minus zero mode now and could no longer avoid it.

"Bryson, you're getting married. Like a grownup."

"I know. Can you believe it?"

Taking in a deep breath, Sophie's expression turned serious. "Promise me one thing."

"Anything."

"Promise me you won't forget your old spinster of a friend."

Laughter flew out of me. "Sophie . . . I don't think you can be considered a spinster at the age of twenty-four. Besides it's impossible to forget you."

"Easy to say that now. But you'll get all caught up in marital bliss, having so much sex your brain goes foggy. Then you'll go all Michelle Dugger on me, popping out babies left and right. Soon the main topic of conversation will be the consistency and frequency of baby poop. You'll fade into the all-consuming world of parenthood where everything is moist and reeks of pizza until the kids hit their teen years. Before you know it I'll only see you at class reunions. Bitterness will have set deep into my bones by then and I'll be forced to talk about how your ass has gotten so large it's beginning to creep around to your front."

"There's a lot going on in your brain. And thanks for all the confidence you have in my ass."

Sophie raised her handsup, shrugging her shoulders, and tilted her head to the side.

Smiling, I placed my hands on her shoulders, and promised. "You have always been and will continue to be a huge part of my life. I will always have time for you. Marriage nor babies will change that."

"What about all the sex?"

"I can't make any guarantees about that." I pulled her into a hug.

Leaning back, Sophie said, "You're such a slut, Bryson."

"True, but as far as my dad and that crowd out there are concerned, I'm as virtuous as the Virgin Mary." We giggled. "I guess its dress time."

Sophie gave me a sweet smile. "It's time."

I found my dream gown the first day I went shopping. The second the crisp white tulle slid over my skin I knew the search was over. The princess dress was aptly named because I felt just like one. The sweetheart neckline and cap sleeves tastefully allowed the right amount of skin to show. Will liked my boobs. I had nice boobs. The tops of them poked out of the fitted flower appliquéd bodice that flowed into the appliquéd full skirt, gathered and secured with a satin bow at the waistline.

As Sophie zipped me up, I caught my reflection in the full-length mirror. It felt as if a stranger was staring back at me. I started planning for today right after Will officially asked me to be his wife a year and a half ago. We'd been a couple since our junior year in high school and we practically lived together during college and graduate school. It was a forgone conclusion that we'd get married soon after graduation.

Will and I wanted a small and elegant wedding much to the disappointment of both our mothers. The ladies tried desperately to talk us into a big lavish event since this would be their only chance.

My older brother, Ryan, at the age of twenty-seven had never even been remotely serious about a girl or a guy for that matter. He repeatedly told my parents that he was never getting married and stood firm in his conviction. Will's older brother, Alex, was the black sheep of the Forsyth family.

Alex had been in and out of rehab three times since I'd known him. It wasn't that Will's parents disowned him but it was close. Will rarely spoke about his brother. It was as if he were an only child. Mr. Forsyth started with nothing, building his construction company until it became one of the largest on the east coast. Unlike Will, Alex didn't fit the image of Forsyth Construction. Will already had a position and generous salary with the company and was on track to take over once his father retired.

My soon-to-be in-laws were so different from my family. Focused on status and image. I had been with Will for eight years and still felt uneasy around them, like I didn't quite measure up to their expectations. As for Alex, I always felt bad for him. He was a nice guy who just couldn't keep it together.

After many guilt-inducing discussions, Will and I compromised, letting our mothers plan the wedding. It was just easier than seeing their sour faces every time the subject came up. Money was no concern when it came to Will's mom. That became very apparent when the bills for the reception started coming in. Since Mrs. Forsyth went overboard on everything, they paid for everything. At first my parents were a bit insulted but decided they weren't going to stand in the way of their little girl's dream wedding. The problem was that it was more Mrs. Forsyth's dream than mine. Not wanting to start off on the wrong foot with the new in-laws, we all acquiesced to Karen Forsyth.

The ceremony was taking place at the historic Saint Mary's Cathedral in downtown Charleston. Our moms made sure that the church was filled to the rafters with three hundred fifty of our closest friends. Will's dad was his best man while Sophie was my maid of honor.

As my gaze traveled down the image in the mirror a tingling sensation spread from my hands up my arms and the room suddenly became very hot. I never doubted that Will was my future. Marriage was simply the natural progression of our relationship. But now that the day was actually here, it felt strange. Draped in this gorgeous gown, my hair pinned up, my mom's antique diamond teardrop earrings dangling from my ears, and my makeup done to perfection, it dawned on me that in a few short minutes I would legally be bound to another person. Bryson Walker would cease to exist.

A knock on the door snapped me out of my wandering thoughts.

The door cracked open and the deep voice of my dad drifted through. "Is it safe to enter?"

"All clear, Mr. Walker." Sophie informed.

When my gaze met Dad's, my throat closed, capturing my breath. The moment of nerves disappeared once I saw the love and pride overflowing from his eyes. It had been a very emotional month for my parents. First, watching me walk down the aisle to accept my MBA degree and now watching me walk down the aisle to my new life.

"Wow! You look beautiful, just like your mother did on our wedding day." Dad gushed as he blinked away tears.

"Daddy, if you cry, I'm going to cry, and my makeup will be a mess. Today is happy, happy."

Taking the handkerchief from his pocket, he wiped a stray tear off his cheek. "I know and it is. You think I'm bad, you should see your mother. We were over at the reception site making sure everything was set. The second she laid eyes on those tiny pies . . .

"You mean quiches?"

"I suppose. She became a blubbering mess. So any uncontrollable wailing during the ceremony is her fault."

"Daddy, I love you."

"I love you too, darlin'. Will is one lucky young man."

Dad leaned in, placing a soft kiss on my forehead. "I'm going to go pull myself together. I'll be right outside the door when you're ready."

"Oh, the feels." Sophie squeaked.

With blurry eyes, I watched my dad slip from the room before his emotions kicked into overdrive.

Frantically fanning one hand in front of my face and the other hand in front of her own, Sophie attempted to dry our tears before they fell, causing a makeup slide down our faces.

"I'm good. You can stop." I sniffled.

Sophie ignored me. "Dry. Dry. Dry. Dry."

Popping her hand away, I cleared my throat and said, "Sophie, knock it off. I've got to finish getting ready."

"Okay, okay. Let's finish."

Sophie brought over the black shoe box that held a special surprise for Will, a pair of four-inch red heels with crisscrossing ankle straps. I couldn't wait to see the look on his face when he saw these babies.

"Here you go, hot momma."

As I slipped into the shoes, another wave of nerves hit my stomach and swirled around my head. I grabbed on to Sophie's arm to steady myself.

"Whoa, are you okay, Bryson?"

"Yeah, I think it's just all the excitement of the day and having to face the big crowd."

"Just picture everyone naked."

"There's some pretty old people out there. Not sure I want that visual on the way down the aisle."

"True. Scratch that. Just picture Will naked."

"You're not helping me."

"Sorry."

"I'll be fine once I see Will."

"I'm going to give your dad a headsup. You got three seconds to pull it together and then its show time."

I nodded.

Sophie walked toward the door then turned to me. "You've got this. You look perfect. I love you."

"I love you, too. Thank you for being my best friend."

I stood alone in the dressing room located in the small building next door to the church, looking at my reflection one last time. Sophie was right, my dress, my makeup, and my hair all looked perfect. I took a few more cleansing breaths. Once I saw Will, my nerves would disappear. He's the love of my life, my rock, and my future.

I picked up the red rose bouquet, opened the door, and stepped into the mid-fall evening. Goosebumps formed as the cool air hit my skin. Dad was waiting for me with a bittersweet smile across his face.

"Ready to give me away?" I asked.

"I'll never be ready for that."

Taking Dad's arm, he led me between the white marbled columns and through the large ornately carved wooden doors.

The inside of the cathedral was majestic and magical. Rows of intricate stained-glass windows decorated the walls. Two rows of dark wood pews flanked either side of the white marble center aisle, which flowed into the brilliant pristine altar at the front of the church. Above the altar hung local Charleston artist John S. Cogdell's painting from the 1800s of the Crucifixion.

As the large pipe organ rumbled to life with Pachelbel's Canon in D, I gave Sophie a slight nod, letting her know it was time. She looked stunning in her black strapless dress with a deep red ribbon around her waist that matched the rose bouquets that we both carried. Since we kept the wedding party small, I was able to splurge on her maid of honor gift, a pair of Tom Ford black patent leather pumps with a tiny gold padlock dangling from the ankle strap. It was unexpected and slightly edgy.

Once Sophie was in position at the altar, the music stopped. Dad placed his hand over the one I had wrapped around his arm and gave it a slight squeeze. Two deep breaths later and my chest vibrated when the sound of *Bach's Suite in D major* hit my ears. The princess transformation was complete.

I had decided awhile back that I didn't want my wedding day to go by in one big blur. I wanted to live in the moment, take every aspect in, no matter how small. But with all the beauty and love surrounding me the only thing I saw was the dark-haired boy waiting for me at the end of the aisle looking incredibly handsome in his classic black tux. When Will's gaze landed on me, his eyebrows rose as his mouth dropped open.

And he hadn't even seen the red heels yet.

As we approached the altar I stole a quick glance at my mom. She was already sobbing into her handkerchief. Dad leaned down, placing a sweet kiss on my cheek before taking his place by Mom.

Father Jacobs motioned for me and Will to step forward. I looked up into the dark brown eyes of my soon-to-be husband.

"Your tits look amazing." Will mouthed inconspicuously.

You would think after eight years with a guy nothing could shock me. I was speechless that he'd made that comment in front of God and everybody.

I just smiled back at him as the music faded and the ceremony began.

"William and Bryson, have you come here freely and without reservation to give yourselves to each other in marriage? Will you love and honor each other as man and wife for the rest of your lives? Will you accept children lovingly from God and bring them up according to the law of Christ and his Church?"

"I do," Will and I said in unison.

"Since it is your intention to enter into marriage, join your right hands, and declare your consent before God and his Church."

My shaky hand slid into Will's steady one.

Clearing his throat, Will began. "I, Will . . . I mean, William, take you, Bryson, to be my wife. I promise to be true to you in good times and in bad, in sickness and in health. I will love you and honor you all the days of my life."

The love and sincerity in his voice was overwhelming, causing my eyes to fill with tears.

I swallowed hard and tried to hold down the emotions that kept trying to bubble to the surface. "I, Bryson, take you, William, to be my husband. I promise to be true to you in good times and in bad, in sickness and in health. I will love you and honor you all the days of my life."

"You have declared your consent before the Church. May the Lord in his goodness strengthen your consent and fill you both with his blessings. What God has joined, men must not divide," Father Jacobs declared.

The crowd responded with a resounding, "Amen."

"May I have the rings?"

Sophie and Mr. Forsyth gave the priest the rings to bless.

"May the Lord bless these rings, which you give to each other as the sign of your love and fidelity."

Looking into my eyes, Will slid the ring on my finger, and said, "Bryson, take this ring as a sign of my love and fidelity. In the name of the Father, and of the Son, and of the Holy Spirit."

I mimicked his movement and words. "William, take this ring as a sign of my love and fidelity. In the name of the Father, and of the Son, and of the Holy Spirit."

I could no longer hold back my tears and Will couldn't hold back taking me in his arms and planting a kiss on my lips.

"By the power vested in me, by the Holy Catholic Church, and the state of South Carolina, I now pronounce you husband and wife. And you obviously know the part about kissing the bride."

A hard constant tapping on the shoulder got my attention. I pulled away from Will's lips to the sound of laughter and the recessional music. Will grabbed my hand and we walked side-by-side as the new Mr. and Mrs. William Grant Forsyth.

After what felt like three hours of nonstop wedding photos, Will and I finally made it to our reception. A few steps into the building, I pulled him into the small office just inside the entrance and shut the door.

Chuckling, he said, "Bryson, what are you doing?"

"I have a surprise for you." I attempted a sexy smile.

"A surprise, huh?" His hands landed on my hips and he spun me around so that my back was against the door. "I'm liking this marriage thing already."

I shoved him back and said, "Not so fast, lover boy."

He followed my gaze down as I slowly lifted my gown, revealing the sexy red heels. Will froze for several seconds. When he lifted his head up to look at me pure desire fired up his eyes.

"God damn, Bryson."

"Shh, Will! We're right next to the church."

"I know . . ."

Extending my foot, I rubbed the side of his leg. "You like?"

"I more than like but there's a problem . . ."

"A problem?" A twinge of humiliation pricked my stomach.

He grabbed my hips and pushed me harder against the door. Will's lips zeroed in on the spot just below my ear that caused me to melt into him every time.

Against my neck, he mumbled, "I have to walk in that reception full of family, friends, and business acquaintances. Be nice and charming. All the while picturing those heels in the air as I fuck you."

Will was never much on the sweet romantic talk. On the surface his words were crude but I knew his heart.

His lips continued their descent toward my chest.

"Will . . ." I giggled, shoving him away. "We have to get in there now or our mothers will send out a search team."

"Mothers. Mood killed." He groaned.

"I know but just think, in a few short hours, all this will be yours." I wiggled as my hands slid down my body.

"You're killing me."

"Come on," I said, grabbing his hand.

As we entered the large hall the breath was sucked from my lungs. The plain empty hall had been transformed into something out of a fairy tale. Both the moms wanted to keep the reception as much as a surprise as possible. They were both so excited so Will and I played along. I'd been privy to a few items, giving my opinion on tablecloths, centerpieces, and flowers. But I never imagined it would turn into the sight before my eyes. The moms had outdone themselves.

Lighted spheres hung at varying heights from the ceiling, cloaking the entire hall in a romantic warm amber glow. To the right of the main entrance was the gift table piled high with boxes wrapped in silver, gold, and white shiny paper. To the left the open bar with every type of drink known to mankind. Next to the bar were long tables, four rows deep, covered in food. Across from the food guest tables were set up draped in tablecloths that matched my dress. Deep red roses in simple clear glass vases served as centerpieces. And a five-piece band was set up in the farthest right corner. But what stole the show for me was the back wall. Black tulle with twinkling amber lights behind it covered the entire area. In front of the wall of lights sat a round table draped in matching tulle and our gorgeous five-tier vanilla bean cake with white buttercream frosting with an elegant scroll design.

Walking a few steps ahead of Will, I said in amazement, "Oh my god!"

He wrapped his meaty arms around my waist, kissed my neck, and whispered, "Does it meet your approval?"

"It looks like a fairy tale."

"Well, you are my princess."

I turned in Will's arms. "And you're my prince."

The day was a little girl's dream come true. I had my tall dark and handsome prince, my gown, and now my kingdom. Everything was perfect.

"I'm knee-deep in sap and ready to hurl." I whipped around to find my brother doubled over, holding a beer with one hand and his stomach with the other.

"Ryan, you're such an ass." I snapped in the typical annoyed younger sister way.

"Better than being a married pussy. Which, by the way, Will, you're already starting to sound like one."

I took a step toward my brother. "Don't insult my husband like that. At least he'll be getting some tonight and every night for the rest of his life."

Raising his drink, Ryan toasted. "My baby sister, ladies and gentleman."

Sophie walked up, holding two glasses of champagne. "Now kids, play nice."

I took one of the glasses from Sophie. "He started it."

"Will, control your woman," Ryan teased.

Will playfully slapped Ryan on the back. "Sorry man, you're on your own. Besides, the more fired up she gets now the hotter she'll be later."

Ryan's face contorted. "Ugh, I gotta go burn my ears off."

My brother was practically sideswiped by Mom as she swooshed past him.

Sophie grabbed my glass of champange as my mom grabbed me by the shoulders and pulled me into a hug. Her eyes already misty. "I can't get over my baby girl is married."

Mom was clutching me so tight I was losing all feeling in my arms. Wiggling my body, I tried to break free with no luck. Finally, Mrs. Forsyth came to my rescue.

Prying us apart, my new mother-in-law said, "Now, Teresa, let the child breathe."

My mom stepped back and sniffled into her silk teal handkerchief that matched her dress. "I'm just so happy." Tilting her head, she gazed at me and Will as more tears threatened. "The two of you look so perfect together."

I took the handkerchief from my mom and dabbed the moisture just below her eyes. "If you don't stop crying we'll have to redo your makeup again."

"Well, you better get the mascara out."

Sensing I needed some help, Sophie placed her arm around Mom's shoulder and led her to the bar. "I bet some Southern Comfort and ginger ale will dry those tears."

Mrs. Forsyth tugged on Will's arm. "Sweetheart, there are some people your father and I want you to meet."

"Mom, Bry and I just walked in."

"It's okay. I need to get used to meeting business associates now that I'm Mrs. William Forsyth." I beamed up at my husband.

"No need for you to come, dear. Go enjoy the party. I'll deliver William back when I'm done showing him off." The smile she sent me wasn't the warm and cozy type. It was more the, I'm the queen bee, back-off type.

The heightened emotions of the day could have been the reason why I heard a bit more sting in my mother-in-law's tone. I decided now was not the time or the place to act like a bridezilla and demand my new husband stay by my side. Besides, the woman had been instrumental in creating this dream reception. I didn't want to appear ungrateful.

"Oh, okay."

"Bry, you sure?" Will asked.

Out the corner of my eye I swore I saw his mother cringe.

"Yeah, I'm fine. Go do what you need to do. I'll come find you for our first dance. I can't wait to try out my new *dancing* shoes." I gave him a wink, hoping that visions of red heels danced in his mind.

Will slapped his hand over his heart and mouthed a groan.

Tugging on his arm, Mrs. Forsyth commanded. "William, come on. Your father is waiting."

For the remainder of the night I saw my new husband sporadically. Will was by my side for the standard reception rituals—first dance, cake cutting, and bouquet/garter toss. But most of his time was spent with his parents or his buddies. Which was fine. It wasn't as if Will and I were a googly-eyed, joined-at-the-hip brand new couple. A certain amount of comfort and routine sets in after so many years together. The wedding was kind of a formality. I kept busy chatting with friends, family, and people I didn't know. After all, Will and I had a lifetime to spend with each other.

chapter Two

Some couples claimed that the first year of marriage was the hardest. The honeymoon period ends and the nittygritty of life takes over. Even if you'd been dating for years the shift in mindset to being legally tied to another person, even one you loved, caused extra stress. Not to mention the little idiosyncratic things that once seemed charming and cute become annoying when exposed to them on a daily basis.

Sure, it took me a little time to learn the basics, like how Will wanted his laundry ironed and folded and that he preferred a homecooked dinner every night at precisely 7 p.m. It surprised me at first that I didn't know these little quirks about him. But I had to admit it was kind of refreshing discovering new things after all these years.

I took pride in making our little starter apartment a warm and cozy home for Will to relax in after a busy day at work. I didn't mind the trail of clothes he'd strip out of as he walked through our place at the end of the day. Picking them up was a small price to pay for the sight of his naked muscular back, ass, and legs as he headed down the hall to our bedroom. When his dark hair covered the bathroom sink after he shaved, I simply wiped it up and went about my day. And I understood the long hours he spent working, both at the office and at home. He was providing for our family's future.

Being Mrs. Will Forsyth kept me busy, at least for the first couple of months. Once my routine was set—dusting, vacuuming, laundry, groceries, and dinner made, I still had plenty of time on my hands.

"So, do you like it?" An antsy smile crossed my face.

Plunging his fork into the Swiss chicken, Will said, "This is awesome. Can't you tell I like it?"

"Well, being that it's your third helping, I had a pretty good idea but it's always nice to hear you say it."

"This is the best thing I've had in my mouth all day." He put his fork down and picked up my hand. His lips skimmed over my knuckles before kissing them. "And later tonight I'll give you the best thing you've had in your mouth all day." He winked and went back to eating.

"We really need to work more on the sweet talk, hon."

"You know I'm not a poet," he mumbled through a mouthful of couscous.

I gave him a weak smile before going back to eating. We ate in silence for several minutes. A couple of weeks before the wedding, Will mentioned how he loved the idea of me being a stay-at-home wife and mother. He was earning more than enough to cover our expenses. His mom never worked outside the home and he wanted our children to have the same experience. Since it seemed so important to him, I agreed. Besides, I had no real aspirations as far as a career.

Once I realized Will would be my future I never gave other options much consideration. I hadn't mapped out any post-graduation plans other than being Will's wife. I went to college because that's what was expected. I chose business as my major because it was general enough to apply to most jobs in case I did get one. When Will decided to continue his education and go for his Master's in business, I decided to follow along.

It wasn't that taking care of Will didn't fulfill me. I enjoyed making sure every night a homemade dinner was on the table waiting when he came home. Watching him devour the food thrilled me and gave me a sense of pride. The dishes started off very simple—meatloaf, spaghetti, chicken and stuffing casserole. I followed the recipes closely, never veering off course. As the year went on I got more comfortable in the kitchen and started to experiment more. I even made up a couple of original dishes. Before I knew it, I discovered not only did I have a talent for cooking but a passion for it as well.

I nervously pushed the green beans around on my plate. "Will, can I talk to you about something?"

"Sure. What's in that pretty head of yours?" He raised his eyebrows, a grin playing across his mouth. "Better?"

He was making an effort with the sweet talk.

I smiled. "Much better."

"So, what's up?"

I inhaled a slow breath, sucking in my nerves. I wasn't sure where they were coming from. I'd never had a problem before talking to Will about anything. But I'd never really discussed anything that was so important to me before.

"What do you think about me going back to school?"

"We just got out of school."

"A year and a half ago."

"You already have a degree," he said.

"I was thinking about taking a few cooking classes."

"You already know how to cook. Three helpings." He pointed to his almost empty plate.

"And I love that you love it. You have no idea what a thrill it is when I see the look of pure pleasure on your face when you're eating something I cooked for you."

He tugged on my wrist. "Come sit in my lap and I'll double thrill you."

"Will, I'm serious."

"Veto." He went back to eating.

"Excuse me?"

"I like having you here when I get home from work."

"It wouldn't interfere with that."

Leaning back in the chair, he blew out a frustrated breath. "Bryson, what about our plans with the house and starting a family?"

Our wedding gift from Will's parents was a piece of land for us to build our dream home on. We were scheduled to meet with the architect next week. Forsyth Construction would do the build with Will overseeing the project.

"Enrolling in culinary school wouldn't . . . ."

He raised his hand. "Hold up. A minute ago it was a few cooking classes and now its culinary school?"

"I thought I could start out with a class or two and if I like it maybe go for a degree," I explained sheepishly.

He leaned forward, taking my hand in his. "Am I not doing a good job as provider and husband?"

"You're a wonderful husband and provider. Me wanting to follow my passion has nothing to do with our marriage." I ran my thumb over his wrist.

"We agreed you'd stay home."

"I know, but . . . I've never really been driven toward anything, career wise. Cooking and creating dishes gives me a sense of accomplishment and pride. And I'm good at it, you said so yourself."

"Bry, I'm glad you get a kick out of doing this stuff. I like your cooking, but shit, I'll eat anything. You know that. Not sure where you got the idea you could make an actual career out of it. It's not like the Food Network is gonna bang down your door. Plus, it would be pretty embarrassing for my wife to be working as a cook in some greasy diner."

My shoulders drooped as I lowered my head, shrinking into my seat. The only sound in the room was the clanking of Will's knife and fork on his plate. After a few minutes, his hand on my forearm came into view.

"I just don't see the point in you taking classes to learn something you're already good at." He was trying to apologize for being an insensitive jerk without saying he was sorry. "We're meeting with the architect next week. Once things get rolling on the house you'll be too busy with that. Bryson, look at me."

I bit my lower lip in an attempt to still the quiver and raised my gaze to meet Will's.

"I'm going to build you the ultimate kitchen. Top of the line appliances, granite countertops, double oven, a wine fridge. Anything you want."

"It sounds incredible. But . . ."

"But nothing. The plan has always been to build our dream house and start a family within the first two years of being married. I don't see any reason to screw things up just because you're a little bored." Pushing his chair back, Will stood, tossed his napkin on the table, and walked into his home office.

End of discussion.

I stayed at the table for a while and sulked until the sting of his words dulled. I didn't have much arsenal to argue my point very effectively.

Everything Will said was true. A year and a half ago I did agree to all the terms he pointed out. But at the time I didn't realize I had a passion for something besides Will.

I grabbed our plates and went into the kitchen. As I rinsed the dishes, Will's words drifted back into my head. Maybe he was right. I'm focusing on the cooking because I'm bored. Once my day got filled with taking care of our family and home, I'd realize how pointless the idea of me going to culinary school really was.

I bent down to load the dishwasher and tried to clear my mind of disappointment. Standing back up I felt the heat of Will's body behind me. I had been so caught up in my own thoughts that I didn't hear him come into the small space. His arms snaked their way around my waist.

Nuzzling my neck, he said, "Don't be mad at me."

"I'm not mad. Just disappointed." I sighed.

"Don't I make you happy?"

I turned, facing him. "Yes you make me happy. It's not about us. It's about me. I've never had a passion for anything."

Will teasingly cocked his brow, making light of what I was saying.

I slapped his chest, annoyed. "I'm not joking. Maybe it is a phase. I don't know. I just don't understand why I can't take a class or two and see what happens."

"Because you taking time away from us to chase a hobby was not the agreement."

From all our years together I knew it was pointless to continue this discussion. Will was stubborn and once he made up his mind that was that.

Will leaned down and nibbled along my jaw as his hands slipped under my shirt. My body stiffened as I gave him a slight shove.

"I'm not in the mood."

He continued nibbling, ignoring my mood. "I thought you weren't mad."

"I need to put the food away and clean the kitchen," I said, dodging his advances, and turned back toward the dishwasher.

Placing his hands on either side of me, Will gripped the edge of the countertop and rubbed his already hard dick against my ass. The thin material of his sweatpants and my yoga pants were flimsy barriers.

"Will, knock it off. I have stuff to do."

He brushed my hair to the side and lowered his lips to the nape of my neck. "Keep doing what you're doing."

Heat radiated throughout my body as my bad mood shifted. I felt incredibly sexy, confident, and powerful knowing I was the only one who affected Will this way. Exciting him to the point of no control. Tilting my head to the side, I wiggled my ass, pushing into his erection. A deep moan rumbled from his chest, causing goosebumps to cover my skin.

"Give me a minute to put the food away and I'll meet you in the bedroom."

"No. I want to fuck you right here and now," he mumbled against my hot skin.

"In the kitchen?"

"Mmmhmm." His hand slipped under my tank top and traveled up my stomach to my chest.

"What about my couscous?"

While one of his hands massaged my breast, Will slid his other hand into my yoga pants and between my legs. I squirmed trying for some friction.

"I love eating your couscous," he said, flicking his index finger over my clit.

Reaching around, I grabbed his hips, and pulled him in closer.

I was getting lost in the moment when suddenly Will ripped my bra down and pinched my nipple hard.

"Ouch!" I yelled.

His voice was husky and low. "Oops."

"It's okay. It just surprised me."

He roughly peeled off my tank and flung it to the side. Will wasted no time in unclasping my bra. I twisted around to face him, needing to put my lips on his body. He stopped me abruptly, spinning me back to face the counter.

His fingers wrapped around my wrist and he placed my hands on the edge of the sink. "Hold on tight."

"Are you sure you want to do this in here?"

The palm of his hand came down hard on the left side of my ass.

"Will!" I yelped.

"Stop talking and just go with it."

"Don't hit me so hard."

Will and I always had a good sex life. I mean, I had nothing to compare it too but it felt pretty good. We were fairly adventurous, having had sex in his car, in my car, and in one of the empty student apartments at college. Like most couples, the sex shifted in intensity. Sometimes it was gentle while other times it was more passionate. Me, being half naked, bent over in the kitchen, was definitely out of the box for us.

My grip tightened with the jostling of my body as Will yanked down my yoga pants and panties at the same time.

"Stick your ass out more." He commanded.

"Will, what are you doing? This is crazy."

"Shut up!"

"Hey, watch it!"

"Just do what I say, Bryson."

I jumped slightly when the tip of his tongue touched the back of my knee. Will's lips licked and sucked up my thigh. My knees buckled as he sunk his teeth into my ass cheek.

"Will, that hurts!"

"It made you soaking wet, though," he mumbled against my lower back.

"What's gotten into you?"

I felt the heat and weight of his body pressed against my back. Reaching around he plunged two fingers inside me, causing my body to convulse. He pumped in and out of me three times before withdrawing his fingers. I felt the back of Will's hand run over my ass.

"Your pussy juice is all over my dick. It's so fucking hard and ready to fuck you in the ass." His hot breath coating my neck and shoulders.

I wasn't a huge fan of dirty talk. Maybe if it were mixed with sweet romantic words I could get on board with it. I knew the point of it was to make things even hotter but it usually made me cringe. Will seemed to be spurred on by the crudeness. For that reason alone, I tried my hand at talking dirty but never quite got the hang of it, so I kept quiet.

A rush of cool air snapped at my skin as Will's body heat disappeared. My next awareness was the sensation of him entering me from behind.

His fingers dug into my hips while he pounded into me hard and fast. Throaty grunts and moans surrounded us. Every nerve ending in my body was lit on fire. My heart pounded against my chest wall. Just as I was about to climax, Will grabbed a fistful of my hair and yanked.

"You're a fucking slut, aren't you?!" He yelled.

I didn't respond, my head spinning with sensation and discomfort.

His hand twisted in my hair, tightening his hold. "Say you're a fucking slut!"

I hesitated. Maybe it was some of the residual effects of the earlier disappointment but a detached feeling washed over me. It wasn't the first time this had happened. Over the years Will and I went through phases. Most of the time I felt our hearts were connected. But there had been instances, like right now, in which I felt more like an object than his partner. I knew he liked dirty talk and I could go along with it for his sake until I felt degraded.

My head snapped back slightly as he tugged. "Say it, goddammit!"

"I'm a slut," I whispered, tears forming in my eyes.

I clenched around Will, causing him to spasm out of control. My body wanted to climax but his words kept swirling in my head. Two more quick jerks and his sweaty body collapsed on top of me.

Placing gentle kisses between my shoulder blades, Will said, "That was incredible."

Before I was able to form words, he withdrew, and stepped away. Suddenly I was freezing, confused, and left hanging. I stayed in position, waiting, and wondering what the hell just happened. I dropped my head, peeking underneath my arm. I was alone, naked, and unsatisfied. After a few seconds I heard the door to the bathroom shut and the shower turn on.

Neither Will nor I brought up what took place in the kitchen that night. After his shower, he went straight to sleep. And I went straight into the bathroom to spend a little quality time with the showerhead. The next morning, he acted normal, not upset or mad. We both went about our days as usual. Even though things went back to normal I couldn't shake the thoughts or weird feeling the night had left in me.

"How about after lunch we catch a chick flick? *Man of Steel* is playing at The Terrace," Sophie said as we walked across the parking lot on the way to yoga class.

The Terrace was a small local retro movie theater that played mostly artsy and old classic films. Occasionally, they'd throw in a new movie. And when I say new, I mean made within the last decade.

"*Man of Steel* isn't a chick flick."

"Maybe not but I'd sure like that Henry Cavill to flick my chick with his *man of steel*." Sophie glanced over for my reaction. "See what I did there?" Raising her eyebrows and smiling.

Pursing my lips, I simply shook my head and rolled my eyes, trying not to encourage her.

"While I'd love nothing more than to watch you drool for two hours, I can't. I'm meeting with my mutha-in-law at three."

"Dum. Dum. Dum." *Ominous music.*

"She's not that bad." I paused. "She can be overbearing. And controlling. And nosey. And fake. But other than that she's an absolute delight to be around."

It was Sophie's turn to purse, shake, and roll. "So, what are you and Witchy Poo up to today?"

"As part of Forsyth wife training, I need to champion a cause . . ."

"Her cause."

I adjusted the strap of my yoga mat on my shoulder. "She's part of some ladies charity that's having some kind of fundraiser to raise money for something at one of the hospitals."

"Wow, you've really got the details of that nailed down."

"If I knew Will's mother genuinely cared and wasn't doing it all for show, I'd get onboard."

Sophie opened the door to the yoga studio and motioned for me to go ahead of her.

"So is married life still blissfully happy?" she asked, as we entered the classroom.

Getting girl time in with my best friend had become increasingly more difficult over the past year. Not only because I got married but because Sophie's job had her traveling a lot. She had taken the position as a project manager at Google. The job required her to travel to lands far and wide several times a year. It was a rare treat that we were able to attend class together.

We walked over to our regular spot. I set my bag and mat down, shrugging my shoulders in response to her question.

Unrolling her mat, Sophie ordered. "Talk to me."

"There's nothing to talk about. Will and I are doing great as always."

"Then what's with the shrugging shoulders?"

I sat down on my mat, extending my legs out in front of me. I reached my arms forward, stretching my back. "It's nothing really. We just had a little disagreement the other night."

Sophie plopped beside me. "About what?"

A few people drifted into the room, one of them being Adele Tannenbaum. Adele was an older woman, in her sixties. Her hair was streaked in varying shades of gray, her face lined with years of living, but her body was sick. I suspected that she'd been doing yoga since its inception. She was a nice enough lady but nosey as hell. She was always trying to find out which instructors were sleeping with clients, who had face lifts and boob jobs. Most of us had carved out a usual spot in class. Not Adele. She liked to change it up, choosing a different area each class in hopes that some fresh juicy gossip would come her way. Today Adele was fishing in my pond.

"Nothing really. It was stupid," I said, keeping my voice low.

"Bryson, you're the most transparent person I know. I can tell by just looking at you it's not nothing. Spill." Sophie ordered.

I glanced over my shoulder to make sure Adele was out of earshot.

Leaning closer to Sophie, I said in a low voice, "I floated the idea of taking a couple of cooking classes by Will. He wasn't exactly a fan of the idea."

"Of course he wasn't. It would take two seconds away from him." Sarcasm coated Sophie's words.

"Will is just old-fashioned. Plus, he knows things are going to get crazy busy with the house being built and we are planning on starting a family soon."

"So what's the problem?"

"After he put the kibosh on the classes, he disappeared into his office. I thought he was pissed off. You know how when we were in school and had a fight, I wouldn't hear from him for a couple of days. Then he'd come back with his sad pouty routine?"

"Yeah and no matter what you'd always forgive him."

A light tap on my shoulder stopped the conversation.

Adele was looking down at me with a fake innocent smile on her face. "Hey girls. I don't mean to interrupt. I'm going to get a towel. Do either of you need one?"

In unison Sophie and I looked down at our towels beside us.

"No, ma'am. We're good," I said, returning her syrupy sweet smile.

As Adele walked away, Sophie muttered, "She's such a sneaky biotch. Continue."

"So he goes into his office. A little while later he comes back into the kitchen while I'm cleaning up after dinner. He comes up behind me and starts touching me. One thing led to another and before I knew it, I'm butt naked in the kitchen."

"Shut up!"

I popped Sophie hard on the upper arm. "Shhh . . ."

"Sorry."

My cheeks heated. "It was kind of hot at first. Then he said some things."

"What things?"

"He wanted me to say I was a fucking slut while he, you know, came in the backdoor."

Sophie stared blankly at me, not saying a word.

"Then after he got his jollies, he left me and went to take a shower. Didn't talk to me for the rest of the night."

Sophie raised her index finger. "One second." She shifted to the side looking over my shoulder. "Did you get that Mrs. Tannenbaum? She had anal in the kitchen."

My head whipped around and spotted an expressionless pale-faced Adele. I could see the word skank floating in her eyes.

I looked back at Sophie, panicked. "Sophie!"

"Don't worry. She doesn't know what that is."

"She knows what an anus is."

"Good morning, everyone. Let's start with a warm-up," Sandy, our yoga instructor, said.

I got to my feet. Out the corner of my eye, I noticed Adele scooting a few inches away from me.

After class Sophie walked me to my car. Not missing a beat, she picked up right where the conversation had left off.

"So, you think the kitchen cockin' was Willie's way of showing you who's boss?"

I opened the driver's side door and tossed my bag and mat across to the passenger's seat. "I don't know."

"Well, did you ask him?"

I shook my head. "No. Neither of us have mentioned it. He's been acting normal since then."

She placed her hands on my shoulders. "I think Will is a spoiled brat but I don't think he'd use his dick as a weapon."

"I don't think he would either but then I keep thinking about the slut remark."

"Maybe you heard him wrong."

"He yelled it out twice."

"Oh." Her lips puckered forming a duck face.

"It's not the first time he's talked to me that way while we were doing things. There was just more of a bite to his tone. It took me off guard."

"Maybe he was just trying it on for size, feeling you out, seeing if you liked it."

"Maybe."

"And maybe he thought you came and when he realized you didn't, he was too embarrassed to say anything."

I chewed on my bottom lip, mulling over her suggestions. "Maybe. He's an incredible guy even though he can be a pain in the ass at times."

"In more ways than one, apparently." Sophie winked.

"That was so bad."

"Sorry. I'm getting loopy. I need food."

"Well, let's get you fed, woman. I have Chicken Piccata with fresh linguine and garlic chives waiting for you back at my place.

"Oh, I think I just found your missing orgasm."

After talking to Sophie more over lunch I realized that I was probably overreacting to the incident in the kitchen. Instead of letting my imagination conjure up all sorts of crazy stuff I needed to focus on the here and now. Will and I were happy and about to embark on an exciting time with the new house and starting our family.

"As you ladies can see the place is extraordinarily pedestrian. I propose we knock down that wall . . ." He dramatically pointed. ". . . Thereby opening up this entire space." He swept one arm out in front of himself. "The walls will be a silky sage green with warm honey hardwood for the flooring. After me and my crew get in here to play, this will be the most deck cafeteria in all the land," said the skinny man in the tight electric-blue suit and red hipster beard.

I'd spent the last hour listening to this hipster kiss the ass of my mother in-law as she soaked up every second of it. Turns out the Junior League, of which she was the current president, would be donating a sizable chunk of money from their annual Twilight Ball fundraiser toward the remodel of the Saint Francis hospital cafeteria. It seemed to be an odd choice when there were so many charities around that could have used the money to help people directly. Although this place was screaming for a makeover.

I didn't know if the ugliness of this cafeteria was the norm for a healthcare facility. I'd been very fortunate in my life, never having to spend any time in a hospital since the day I was born. The lighting was horrible, the walls and floor were slightly yellowed with age, and the tables and chairs looked to be on their last leg. But ever since I could remember, people raved about how incredible the food here tasted. I remember in their later years, my mama and papa would come each Friday to enjoy the cafeteria's fried shrimp platter. By all the happy faces enjoying the food, the praise seemed well deserved.

My gaze scanned the large area as I tried not to appear too bored. Considering the time of day, I was surprised the place was this packed.

The patrons were a mix of doctors, nurses, and other badge-wearing hospital staff. There were a few scattered patients who'd ventured out of their rooms. The rest of the crowd looked to be people who were here just wanting the great food.

"Bryson, what are your thoughts on having a water feature over in that corner?" The soft southern accent of Will's mother drifted into my ears as she tried to include me in the project.

"Which corner?"

Pointing her finger, she said, "Over on the far right wall."

I followed her scrawny finger across the room. When my gaze hit the target a weird buzzing sensation took over my stomach. It had nothing to do with water features or spending too much time with my mother in-law and everything to do with the site of Hart Mitchell. Or some guy who looked exactly like Hart Mitchell. Oh, hell, it was Hart Mitchell. I'd know those color-changing eyes and deep dimples anywhere at any distance. I had spent my entire senior year seeking them out and one unbelievable moment staring into them. The noisy atmosphere disappeared and I got lost in Hart.

"*Bryson.*"

He was sitting at one of the smaller tables with his back to the wall. His golden blond hair was slicked back off his face and shorter than it had been in school, hitting just below his ear. His scruff was now perfectly groomed. I could tell he took time with his appearance but not an overly obnoxious amount.

The way his dark silvery gray dress shirt molded to his upper body, it had to have been tailor made for him. I couldn't see his pants under the table but they were probably black. Black pants would look great with that shirt and tie. With the matching gray tie and large silver watch poking out from under his sleeve, Hart Mitchell could have been a GQ cover model.

"*Bryson, any thoughts?*"

His white teeth and deep dimples kept making appearances as he talked and smiled at the head of blond curls sitting across from him. They didn't appear to be touching. At least I couldn't detect touching. For some reason I didn't want them to be touching.

"*Bryson!*"

The sharp tone of Will's mom pierced my ears, ripping my eyes away from Hart.

"I'm sorry. What?"

She exchanged an annoyed look with hipster guy.

Rolling his hipster eyes, the guy huffed. "Uh . . . the water feature?"

My gaze swung between the two as they stared at me, awaiting my answer. "I think you're spot on with that."

Hipster guy breathed a sigh of relief as he escorted Will's mom away, rattling on about his vision.

Hoping to get a glimpse of the swagger, I turned back toward Hart's table but he was gone. My gaze quickly searched the crowd with no sign of him. I'd looked away only for a brief moment. Where could he have disappeared to so fast? I was about to fan out and go looking for him. I thought it would be fun to catch up on our lives. I stopped myself. There was no point in chasing after Hart. He never made an effort for me during our senior year, even after the moment we shared.

chapter
Three

Building the house took four months longer than expected. Will was meticulous with every single detail, from the earth-tone stones used for the exterior to the nails. Extra special attention was paid to the entrance. My mother-in-law schooled me on the importance of having a proper southern porch. Not everyone will make it past your front door but everyone will see your front porch. It was crucial in her eyes that our porch properly showcased her son's status in the community.

Three deep stone steps led guests up to the large wraparound porch with the intricately carved dark wood door. An Original Charleston bed swing hung at one end while two black lacquered high back rockers were positioned at the other. The furniture popped well against the natural browns, creams, and rusts of the stone exterior. The big front yard was filled with rows of azalea bushes and several moss-covered old oaks. It was a picture right out of a southern fairy tale.

Will had definite ideas and input for the inside but for the most part he left the interior decorating to me. I chose to go with a neutral gray palate for the walls with pops of color coming from the furniture and accent pieces. Dark cherry wood floors covered the downstairs while the upstairs was covered in soft plush heather-gray carpet. Will made good on his promise of giving me the ultimate kitchen. The mixture of browns, blacks, and beiges in the granite countertops and back-splash offset the stainless steel appliances, giving the room a warm cozy feel.

Turned out Will was right about me not having a lot of time once the build on the house got started. The idea of culinary school lingered in the background for the time being as I zeroed in on making us a home and a family.

"How much longer?" Will shifted from one foot to the other with excitement.

"One minute." I flashed a quick smile up at him.

I was sitting at the vanity in our bathroom while Will hovered close by. The past few weeks I hadn't been feeling well. At first I thought it was due to the stress of finishing up the house. But we'd been settled in for more than a month and I still wasn't feeling like myself. The plan had always been to move into our house and then start a family. In my mind that meant live in the house for six months to a year and then start *trying*. Apparently, the powers that be had other plans.

Two months after Will and I started dating, I knew in my heart and mind that he was the one, so I got on the pill. Will continued to wear condoms until three years ago. He hated them. Since I was on the pill and we were going to be married anyway, I was fine with him not wearing them anymore. Besides, I liked the way he felt not all covered up. I was religious when it came to taking my pill and my period was like clockwork. With all the stress and activity of moving, I may have lost track of a few things.

The alarm on Will's phone beeped indicating the minute was up.

Taking in a deep breath, I reached for the pregnancy test.

I stood in front of Will, trying to keep my expression neutral. "Daddy . . ."

"Are you telling me we're having a baby or are you trying to turn me on?"

"We're gonna have a baby!"

Leaping into Will's outstretched arms, I squealed as he spun me around.

I slid down his body until my feet hit the floor. Cupping my face, Will brought our foreheads together. "Thank you."

"Thank you. I couldn't have done it without you."

Will stared down and ran his hand over my stomach. My heart skipped a beat at his gentle touch and the look of wonderment covering his face. It was rare for him to be speechless and even rarer for him to show much emotion. To anyone else, he looked calm and unaffected. But I could feel the excitement and gratitude radiate off his body.

"It's all coming together. Work, the house, and now the baby." He placed a soft kiss on my lips.

"Are you happy?"

"I'm beyond happy. I wouldn't have this life without you. I love you, Bryson."

"I love you . . . for richer or poorer, in sickness and in health, until death do us part."

We stood there in the bathroom, in silence, holding each other for a long time. Neither of us made an attempt to pull away. Finding out that we were pregnant with our first child was a moment we'd never experience again. We wanted to hold on to it for as long as possible. Once we walked out of this room, we both realized life as we knew it would be forever changed.

Over the next few weeks, I spent a lot of time getting used to the changes in my body. During my second trimester the fatigue and nausea were the most difficult. But each time I looked in the mirror at my barely there baby bump, I felt like a complete woman and wife, and it made it all worth it. Will was enjoying that my boobs were growing by leaps and bounds. He swore they got bigger from the time he went to work to the time he got home in the evening.

Although I had no idea whether we'd be welcoming a boy or a girl into our lives, I couldn't help shopping for things all babies needed. The bedroom right next to our room was designated as the nursery. I promised myself I wouldn't decorate until we knew the sex but that didn't stop me from plastering inspiration pictures all over the walls of the room. Will went with me to as many doctor appointments as he could and understood when I was too tired to cook or do anything else. He teased me a lot about buying toys for the baby but I caught him several times sneaking in a stuffed animal or two. With my head in the clouds, I was gliding along living the perfect life. If I'd only looked down maybe I could have avoided the first misstep.

My eyes shot open as a sharp pain stabbed me in the middle of my back. Before the sleepy fog lifted, another piercing sensation took over, causing a loud groan to escape.

Struggling, I rolled over and reached across the bed for Will and found cold empty sheets. The clock on the nightstand read 3:30 a.m.

Another jolt of pain hit me. "Will!"

I swung my legs over the side of the bed, gripped the edge of the mattress, and pushed up on trembling legs. With my palms flat against the wall, I made my way out into the hallway. Taking a firm hold of the banister, I headed downstairs. Halfway down I noticed light coming from underneath Will's office door. Lately, he had been experiencing bouts of sleepless nights. He tried to hide it but I knew he was feeling pressure with more responsibilities at work and the baby coming.

Cradling my stomach, I got to the bottom of the stairs and yelled, "Will!"

The sharp pains had morphed into a dull constant ache. Each time I breathed in it felt as if my throat was closing up. I squeezed my eyes shut as tears filled them.

Where was Will?

My trembling hand let go of the banister and I shuffled across the entryway toward Will's office. Halfway there I noticed my panties felt wet. Looking down, I saw a trail of blood drops.

As I crumbled to the floor, all the air left my body along with a blood-curdling scream. "Will!"

A couple of loud thuds and several footsteps later Will bolted out of the room.

"God, Bryson!" He rushed over, gathering me in his arms.

"I have to get to the hospital." I hiccupped the words as my body convulsed with sobs.

"Okay, baby. Don't move. I'm going to grab my keys and get you in the car."

I clutched his arm. "Will, I'm scared . . . the baby."

Looking straight into my eyes, he said, "Don't panic. I'm here. We're going to the hospital and get you and the baby checked out. Everything's going to be alright. Trust me?"

I nodded and watched through blurry eyes as he ran away.

Eight hours later, Will and I walked through the front door of a place we once called our dream home. In less than a day this house had transformed from a home to the place where I lost my baby. With one arm around my waist, Will guided me past the dried blood on the floor, up the stairs, and into our bedroom.

"Bry, let me help you get into bed."

The second my gaze landed on the bed my pulse raced and I suddenly felt claustrophobic in the large room. "I can't lie on those sheets."

"I'll change them," Will said in a low voice.

I froze at the foot of the bed as he stripped off the comforter and sheets. With each layer removed, my muscles tensed. I forced myself to focus on the stiff tightness, hoping it would distract from the hollow feeling inside. Will balled up the sheets and stuck them on the chair in the corner.

"Get them out of here." I ordered.

"What?"

"I want them out of this room. Out of this house."

Without a word he gathered the mound of material and tossed it in the hallway.

"I need to get out of this nightgown."

Will helped me out of his navy blue hoodie he'd covered me up with before going to the hospital. Taking my hand, he led me into the bathroom, leaving me at the vanity while he turned on the shower. He stood in front of me and gently lifted my pale pink nightgown over my head. I closed my eyes, humiliation washing over me as he peeled back the tabs on the adult diaper the hospital had put me in. It seemed appropriate since I felt like a helpless child at the moment. When I opened my eyes, I saw Will tossing the diaper into the trash can. Holding my hand, he guided me to the shower, reaching in to check the water temperature. He kicked off his sneakers and stripped out of his clothes.

My body jumped at the sound of Will clearing his throat. "I'm sorry." He paused for a second. "A shower will make you feel better."

I didn't feel the warm water wash over me or the touch of Will's hands. Every part of me felt dead. But for Will's sake, I pretended it was all helping. Grabbing the body wash, he poured a drop into the middle of his trembling palm. His hand glided over my body as if he were touching a delicate piece of glass. The air was still and silent except for the splashing of the water against the tiles.

"Do you want me to wash your hair?"

"Yes, please," I whispered.

As his soapy fingers twisted in my hair, I closed my eyes and drifted back into pretend mode. I knew it was important for him to keep focused on an activity. That's how Will handled things. He kept moving.

The sound of running water stopped, replaced by the glass shower door sliding on its track. Will reached out, grabbing a large fluffy towel, and bundled me up in it. He then took a smaller towel and wrapped it around my wet hair.

Helping me out of the shower, he said, "I'm going to take a quick shower while you dry off, okay?"

"Okay."

I sat staring into the vanity mirror covered in towels, thinking the answer might miraculously appear in front of me as to why this happened. After his shower, Will wrapped a towel around his waist and headed into the bedroom. I finally finished towel drying my hair and put on a tank top and pair of lounge pants I had hanging on the back of the bathroom door. By the time I walked in the bedroom, Will was smoothing out the fresh comforter and sheets he'd put on the bed. He was also wearing his work clothes.

My brows squished together as I narrowed my eyes at him. "What are you doing?"

"Finishing making the bed."

"I don't mean that. Why are you dressed?"

He continued smoothing out the comforter, not looking at me. "It's a workday."

"You're going to work?"

He turned in my direction but our eyes didn't meet.

"I have to."

"But you didn't get any sleep last night."

And we just lost our baby.

"I'll down some coffee with a Red Bull chaser." He took my hand. "Let me help you into bed." He pulled the covers up over me. "I called your mom. She's coming over to be with you today."

He placed a soft kiss on my forehead before walking toward the door.

Clutching the covers to my chest, I said, "Will?"

He faced me but still didn't meet my gaze. "Yeah?"

"I'm sorry."

"Me too." He turned and left without another word.

I don't know how long I sat there staring at the door, thinking and hoping Will would walk back through it. We were both in shock that in a matter of hours our little family had been destroyed. Will may have been able to grieve by himself but I needed my husband. The one person who understood exactly how I was feeling.

He didn't even wait for my mom to get here.

Each second that ticked by, my throat thickened with tears. I lay back, pulling the comforter over my head, and let the loneliness consume me.

As days turned into weeks my relationship with Will shifted. He'd been given a lot more responsibility at work and put in charge of a large project. I was proud of him and glad he was thriving at work. But I had my suspicions that he had pushed for the new project in order to keep him at work later. When he did come home at a reasonable time, we'd eat dinner, saying very little, and then he'd head into his office. Many times I didn't see him again until the next day. While Will was apparently moving on, I couldn't get past the night we lost the baby and our connection.

After being together for almost ten years I thought our relationship had a stronger foundation. But it dawned on me one day that until the miscarriage our relationship hadn't been tested, not in any real way. I never wondered how Will and I would handle a difficult time. I assumed we'd tackle it together.

Time seemed to come to a grinding halt after the miscarriage for me. The days bled seamlessly into nights. My doctor gave no real explanation as to why I'd lost my baby other than to say that 10 to 20 percent of pregnancies end in miscarriage with the cause being undetermined. She assured me that there was no medical reason why I couldn't get pregnant again and carry to term. But once you lose a child, a little voice takes up residence in your head saying you're damaged goods.

After three months, I finally forced myself to go into what would have been the nursery to remove the inspiration pictures that lined the walls. I studied the details of each picture until I had committed them to memory. I was so caught up in what could have been I didn't realize Will was standing in the doorway.

"What are you doing?" There was a sternness to his tone.

Not looking at him, I said, "I figured I might as well take the pictures down."

"I'm going to take a quick shower."

"Do you blame me?" The question had been stuck in my throat since the morning we came home from the hospital.

"No. I think the pictures needed to come down."

"I'm not talking about the stupid pictures."

"I have a business dinner tonight."

I whipped around, grabbing his gaze. "Really, Will? Is this how we're going to deal with the first traumatic event in our lives?"

His brown eyes appeared darker than usual. "What do you want me to say?"

"Anything. I want you to look at me for more than a second and say anything."

"I don't know what you're talking about. I've been swamped at work and . . ."

"Bullshit! You blame me for fucking up our well-planned-out perfect life."

"I don't have time for this." He stomped into our bedroom.

I followed, calling out behind him. "Then when will you have time? I'd like to be put on your busy schedule."

Will ripped off his shirt and pants, standing in the middle of our room in only his boxers.

"I've racked my brain trying to figure out what I did wrong. Was it something I ate, did I twist my body a certain way, or am I being punished for something I did in the past?"

"Nothing I can do or say will erase what happened," he said, sounding defeated.

"I know that. I don't expect you to perform some miracle. But I need you. I don't know how to move on from this without you."

"I . . . um . . . I . . ."

I stepped toward him and took his hand in mine. "We can go see a counselor to help us."

He shook his head. "No. I'll do better."

I wanted to believe Will but I had a feeling he was only saying the words he thought I wanted to hear. He caught my gaze for a brief moment and let go of my hand before retreating into the bathroom.

chapter Four

During the months that followed, my relationship with Will ebbed and flowed. We had hopeful moments, though they were fleeting, replaced by long periods of disconnect. I understood people handled grief in many different ways. And you can't dictate to another person the right way to move through their sorrow. I needed the one person in my life who could understand what I was feeling. But he apparently didn't need me. At least not at the moment. I turned to my parents and Sophie, of course, but it wasn't the same. The constant gnawing pain in my heart couldn't be consoled by hugs and a sympathetic gaze.

Will continued to immerse himself in work. Instead of being jealous and angry, I decided that if this was his way of dealing with the loss of our child I had to give him the time and space. Work made him happy and that was important to me. I eventually eased back into some semblance of a routine as I waited for my old self to reappear. A big part of me doubted I'd ever see that girl again. Losing your child changes the atmosphere forever.

We pulled up to the three-story colonial house right across the street from Charleston Harbor in the area of downtown known as The Battery. The beautiful white home was the epitome of old southern charm. Wraparound porches hugged each story complete with quaint rocking chairs welcoming visitors. The house had been in Will's family for four generations. His parents were the current occupants. Alex, being the eldest son, was entitled to be the fifth generation to live there but that would never happen. Alex gave up his birthright the minute he walked out of rehab the first time. Mr. Forsyth made sure to notate in his will that the tradition would skip to his second son instead. One day Will and I would be holding Sunday dinners here with our children.

Before we reached the first step the front door swung open and we were greeted by the open arms of Will's mom. Every time we came over she greeted us as if we hadn't seen one another in years. Will worked side-by-side with his dad every day and we had Sunday dinner with his parents every other week. Whispers had swirled in the local society circle for years about Alex. I assumed Will's mom's grand gesture was more a show for the neighbors. Making sure that those who were within view could see the good son coming home. Thus proving that the majority of her family was indeed perfect despite the one bad apple.

As Mrs. Forsyth waited for her hug, I swear I saw her gaze shift from side-to-side checking for an audience. "There's my handsome boy."

"Hey, Mom." Will kissed his mother on the cheek like any dutiful southern son would do.

"Hey, darling." A pitiful expression crossed her face.

I was well aware of how devastated both sets of parents were when they got the news. Whereas my parents gave me love and support, Will's mom continued to send out subtle signals of hurt and disappointment.

As I climbed the steps, Will walked past his mother and into the house.

With her head tilted in sympathy, a faint smile ghosted across my mother in-law's shriveled bright red lips. "How are you, dear?"

"Pretty good. Thanks. How are you doing?"

She stepped onto the porch, closing the door behind her. "Let's have a little girl chat."

She led me over to the side of the porch toward two large white wicker rockers and motioned for me to sit.

"Bryson, you know I don't like to meddle in my children's lives."

This must be something new she's trying out.

"Will has been coming home with his father a few nights a week."

"Oh really?"

"Yes, for a while, in fact."

I nodded and tried not to show my surprise.

"They grab a couple of beers and sit outside on the patio talking business and life. I've asked Will several times if everything is okay . . . at home. He says yes but a mother knows." With pity in her eyes, she patted my knee. "You'll understand someday . . . I hope and pray."

Karen Forsyth had always been fairly pleasant toward me over the years I dated her youngest son. Granted it, I didn't come in contact with her that much. And with my head being so full of Will, I never noticed her snide subtleties. Since the wedding I'd either become overly sensitive or she had gotten more ballsy. Something had definitely caused her personality to go in a different direction. The words she used weren't offensive on their own. It was the tone of her voice coupled with her steely look that told me in no uncertain terms that she was the queen bee of the Forsyth family. I never confronted her when an insult came out draped in southern sweetness. I remained respectful and let it go in one ear and out the other. But today I wasn't in the mood.

"With all due respect, is there a point coming?" I said as my fingers dug into the armrest.

"I'm concerned about Will. He seems restless. Unsatisfied."

"It's been a rough six months for both of us."

"We were so excited for our first grandchild to arrive." A wistful expression seeped across her crackly over-made-up face. "Gosh, when the ladies at the Junior League heard you were pregnant they immediately started planning two baby showers, one blue and one pink. They were prepared for whatever popped out. Mr. Forsyth and I were simply inconsolable when Will called us with the horrific news. Funny how we place so much hope and joy on a little one even before they enter this world."

"Sorry to disappoint you and the Junior League." My words were clipped.

Waving her hand, she said, "Oh, don't worry about them. It's Will who needs your attention. The doctor has given you the green light to start trying again, correct?"

"Yes, physically she gave me the all clear."

"That's wonderful. Are you making yourself available to Will?"

Squaring my shoulders, I looked directly into her dark brown eyes. "I don't think that's any of your business."

"Will is my son."

"Will is my husband. When and if we decide to try again is our business."

"Y'all don't want to wait too long. How old are you, hon . . . twenty-five, twenty-six?"

"I'll be twenty-six in three months."

"Unfortunately you lost some time but you're still in your prime. You want to have your four children at least two years apart."

"Will and I need to have one child before we even think about a final head count."

She reached over, placing her hand on top of mine. "Why of course. That's completely up to y'all. Four is a wonderful goal to aim for, though. Jonathan and I would be over the moon delighted with whatever number you settle on. It's just we aren't getting any younger. We want to be able to spoil our grandbabies for as long as possible. I know it's difficult but you have to put that little hiccup behind you. Get back up on the horse."

"I will definitely inform Will that his mother suggested I start riding him as soon as possible." I rose abruptly, causing her hand to fall away.

"No need to resort to trashy talk, dear." Keeping her gaze focused on the rippling waves of the harbor, she continued. "My son married you because he wants a child, a family of his own. Someone to carry on the Forsyth name. You've had six months of coddling. It's time to grow up, be a dutiful wife, and give Will what he desires most." She stood facing me with pursed lips. "I'll let you know when dinner is ready."

I held my ground—no words, no expression, no blinking. I stayed frozen in place as the sound of Karen's heels clicking across the wooden slats faded and the front door closed. Staring out into the harbor, I wondered if between all the bitchiness from her there was some truth.

Physically nothing was stopping me and Will from trying to conceive again. But neither of us had brought up the topic. I felt we were still out of sorts. Bringing a new baby into the mix didn't seem like the best choice. In my heart it felt disrespectful to replace our first child so soon after we'd lost him or her. I still couldn't bring myself to read the report letting me know the sex.

After the earful from Will's mother, I wondered if he was truly ready to give it another try. It was possible he'd been waiting for me to bring it up, feeling it was more my call since it was my body. We'd both been wading in grief for so long, finding it hard to see the light at the end of the tunnel. Maybe a bright new glimmer was what Will and I needed to reconnect.

I stayed on the porch until Will came out and got me for dinner. Sitting quietly at the large formal dining table, I pushed the food around my plate, pretending to eat, as I listened to Will and his parents discuss business and people I didn't know. As we said our goodbyes at the front door, Karen pulled me into a slight hug, whispering in my ear to strongly consider her words from earlier. On the drive home I decided to feel Will out on the subject.

I opened my mouth to speak but it suddenly went dry and sticky. I wet my lips while thinking of my opening line.

"Your mother's roast was really moist tonight."

He chuckled. "That sounds wrong on so many levels."

The words ran through my head, causing a chuckle. It felt good to share a light moment for a change.

I twisted and untwisted the strap of my purse around my finger. Glancing over at him, I was taken by how handsome he looked in the dim light of early evening. The sun was just about to disappear but still cast a warm orange glow across Will's chiseled jawline.

"You're so handsome."

Small crinkles appeared in the corners of his eyes as his mouth formed into an appreciative grin.

"You sweet-talker you. Now tell me what's really on your mind."

"What makes you think anything else is on my mind?"

"Because you either ramble or fidget when you're nervous."

I lifted my nose in the air, pretending to be offended. "You think you know me that well, Will Forsyth?"

"Yes. And if you have something to say you better do it now. I have work to do when we get home."

Filling my lungs with oxygen, I started. "I know the first time was a surprise. And things didn't work out like we'd hoped. We really haven't talked specifics about the future. We've both been dealing with a lot. It's been six months." The words were spitting out of me like random bullets. I wasn't even sure if they made any sense.

"Bryson, get to the point."

"I was wondering since Dr. Jamison said it was okay, if you might want to think about trying again?"

The car fell silent. Will's entire upper body seemed to tense.

He stole a quick glance at me and asked, "Are you ready?"

"I think it would be good for us."

"Okay."

That was all Will said on the subject. He didn't act nervous, hesitant, or scared. He also didn't act excited or happy. Even though I was used to Will's lack of emotional displays, his reaction caught me off guard. I assumed once we broached the sensitive topic he'd break from his usual stoic self and emotions would pour out. We rode the rest of the way home in silence.

As we pulled into the driveway butterflies took flight in my stomach. After nine years together the nerves surprised me. Entering the house, it occurred to me that other than a few benign kisses and touches we hadn't been intimate since the miscarriage. At first we couldn't be and then somehow we just weren't.

Standing in the dark entryway, Will and I stared at each other like strangers. I stepped closer toward him, placing my palms flat on his stomach. I ran them over his hard chest while holding his gaze. This was the longest we'd looked at each other in months. Timidly he put his hands on my hips. Even though his expression remained neutral I could feel his nerves radiate off his body. I didn't want him to feel pressured or nervous, but the emotion did give me a sense of comfort. As if we were on the same page.

"I won't break." I assured him.

"I don't know why I'm nervous," he admitted.

"I'm nervous too." I smiled shyly up at him.

He took in a shaky breath and brought his fingertips up to brush away the hair from my face. I took his right hand and placed it flat against my cheek. The feel of his skin on mine caused my eyes to tear up. It had been such a long time since I felt his touch. He brought his left hand up and cupped the other side of my face. His dark eyes stormed with deep emotion.

His gaze dropped to my lips. Just like flipping on a light switch, desire filled the air around us. I gripped his biceps and tugged him to me. Our lips touched and the familiar fire exploded. It didn't take long for the kiss to go from want to need. Tongues swirled wildly as we ripped off clothes. Will pushed me against the wall. Soon we were both blindly groping at underwear.

I pushed him back slightly. "We should go upstairs."

"Why?" He panted.

"Because I don't want our baby to be conceived against a wall."

"True."

Suddenly, he dipped down and slung me over his shoulder. My squeals echoed throughout the house the entire trip up to our bedroom.

Will and I may not have made a baby that night but we definitely made our way back to each other.

One week turned into two weeks, turned into three weeks, turned into a month, then two months and still no baby. Not even a glimmer. And it wasn't for lack of trying. We didn't have this much sex when it was new and shiny.

Dr. Jamison couldn't find any medical reason why we hadn't gotten pregnant yet. Having a baby had always been an important aspect of marriage to me but it wasn't necessarily at the top of my list, at least not until it became out of reach. I quickly got obsessed with all things baby.

My doctor suggested keeping an ovulation chart, so I bought one of those trackers from the drugstore. I was very organized with my charting. I hung large wall calendars in the three rooms I spent the most time in—the bedroom, the bathroom, and the kitchen. I marked the kitchen calendar using a code I made up just in case we had friends and family over. No need for them to know each time I was jumping my husband.

At first tracking my cycle added a new facet to our sex life. Will looked like a deer caught in the headlights when I explained to him how the female cycle worked. I decided to leave out a lot of the technical details. I didn't want him to be in his head too much, concentrating on charts, tracking, and ovulation schedule. Plus, he seemed to enjoy the surprise attacks.

"Well, look what the cat dragged in," Peggy said cheerfully.

Peggy had been with Forsyth Construction since the very beginning as executive assistant. I knew she was around the same age as Will's parents but she looked younger than them. Her features were soft, her figure was slender, and she dressed stylishly even when I saw her in more casual settings.

"Hey, Peggy. Are you behaving yourself?"

"Well, what fun would that be?" She winked. "Let me guess, you're here to see that hubby of yours."

"Am I that easy to read?"

"It's not too hard when you've got the look of love plastered across your face."

My cheeks flushed with heat. If she knew the real reason I was here, I don't think I'd be able to look her in the eye ever again.

"Is he busy?"

"Oh, this is a surprise visit. Fun. He should be in his office. Let me check."

She pressed the button on the intercom. I smiled when I heard the sound of Will's voice come through the speaker. "Yes, Peggy?"

"I was just making sure you were in your office. A special delivery just arrived for you." She tossed me a knowing wink.

"What is it?"

She shook her head. "How should I know? It's for you." She teased.

Peggy was like the cool fun part of the Forsyth family. She showed Will the respect he deserved as her boss but wasn't shy about being honest or joking around with him.

"Okay, send whatever it is in."

"Go right in, special delivery."

"Thanks, Peggy."

My body was already in tingle mode as I walked toward Will's office. I softly knocked on the door, waiting for permission to enter.

"Come in."

He was sitting behind his large dark mahogany desk, concentrating on the blueprints in front of him. I quietly shut the door and turned the lock. Standing in front of the desk, I slipped my phone from my pocket, and scrolled through my pictures. Since men were visual creatures I'd taken a few self-portraits in varying stages of undress recently. I'd send them to Will on the way home from work so he'd be ready once he hit the front door.

I clicked on the newest addition I had taken earlier today—on my back in our bed with over-the-knee black patent leather boots on and nothing else. I slid the phone with the sexy shot across the desk. When the photo came into view Will gripped the pen he was holding and looked up.

"Special delivery for Mr. Forsyth."

"Have I mentioned how excited I am that you've taken up photography?" I giggled.

"Wait until you experience the live show." My hips swayed seductively as I made my way around the desk.

I had on my deep red wrap dress that molded to every curve of my body. My only accessory were the same boots from the picture.

Will twisted his chair toward me. "Bryson, what are you up to?"

Bending over, I placed my hands on the armrest of the chair, caging him in. "It's go time, big guy."

His eyebrows knitted together. "Um . . . right now?"

I slowly nodded.

"Here?"

I continued to nod.

His gaze traveled up and down my body as a sexy grin took over his mouth. "So conceiving our child against a wall is a no-go but my office in the middle of the day is okay."

"Do you know where you were conceived?"

"Even the most remote reference to my parents having sex right now is like dunking my dick in a bucket of ice."

"You're right. Sorry. Get that out of your head. You're hot. I'm hot. We're hot. I got the boots on."

I snatched the phone off the desk and held it up to him.

"And dick is back," Will said.

I tossed the phone onto the desk and crashed my lips into his. We had to get down to business. Peggy knew I was here and if I stayed too long, she'd become suspicious, and we'd become office gossip.

Will ended the kiss but kept his lips on mine. "Where do you want to do it?"

"Right here."

"In the chair?"

"Yeah."

He cupped my ass, squeezing hard. "You got anything on underneath this dress?"

"I'm commando all the way."

"Fuuuck me."

I held his gaze as I stood back and slid my dress up over my hips. Will undid his pants. He was more than ready for me.

I walked toward him and positioned myself in between his legs. He looked down, taking in the boots and my half-naked body. His gaze and hands traveled up the leather until they reached my hot skin.

"Are you sure about the chair, Bryson?"

"Yes." I breathed.

Grabbing my ass he helped me up until I was straddling him. I got right to it, lowering myself down onto him. With our foreheads together, my hips rocked. Will's grip intensified, his fingers digging into my skin.

A guttural moan moved up my throat.

Faster.

"God," I sighed.

"Your pussy is so hot," Will groaned.

"Oh, fuck," I yelped.

Faster.

A muffled deep rumble vibrated from his chest.

"Fuck, Will."

"That's right . . ."

Faster.

"Oooh, fuck, fuck, fuck." My hands griped his shirt.

"Talk dirty to me, baby."

"No."

"Yes," he growled.

"No."

"Yes! It gets me off."

"No, it's my leg. I got a cramp in it. I gotta stretch."

I started to climb off but Will stopped me. Wrapping his arm around my waist, he held on tight and dropped us to the carpet. My legs flew straight into the air.

God, it felt good to stretch.

Frantically pumping in and out of me, Will covered my mouth with his in order to keep the noise to a minimum as we climaxed together.

While still inside me Will and I stared at each other.

"Chair sex looks like a piece of cake in the movies," I said.

"It was hot even with the leg cramp."

After several more attempts with no success the hot spontaneity started to wear off. Sex had become mechanical. When the device indicated that I was ovulating, Will got the call. There was no sweet talk or dirty talk. No foreplay. Sometimes we didn't even get completely undressed. We'd expose the necessary parts and had at it. We no longer made love. There was only one clear and direct purpose for us having sex, to get our lives back on track and have a family. Both Will and I went through additional testing and no physical reasons were found that would keep us from getting pregnant. The doctor's only advice was to relax and keep trying.

With each cycle that passed, insecurities set in. I felt inadequate. There were women all over the world having babies every minute of the day and night. Some on purpose, some by accident, and some who didn't know they were pregnant. I didn't understand what my problem was. It was so easy the first time. The stress was affecting Will as well. He seemed to be retreating into his office more and away from me.

Staring up at the ceiling fan, I counted the repetitions of the blades. Will's face was buried in the crook of my neck as his sweaty body slid over my skin. My eyes shut at the first sensation of him pushing inside of me. Instinctively my hips began to rock. Grunts and hot breath washed down my neck and shoulders. I dug my nails into Will's biceps spurring him on. His hips picked up speed. I was too much in my head to enjoy the physical sensation. I hoped and prayed that at this moment we were making our child. At least that's what I kept telling myself. Another loud grunt filled my ears before Will collapsed on top of me.

He rolled onto his back, draping his arm over his eyes. "Not happening tonight." He snapped.

I grabbed the edge of the sheet and covered myself. "It's okay."

Over the past month there had been times when Will wasn't able to fully perform. I told him we could take a break for a while. He wanted to power through until we made a baby but the stress was getting to be too much to handle.

The silence in the room was broken only by the sound of Will trying to steady his breathing.

In an attempt to lighten the mood, I said, "I'm thinking about getting my hair cut and highlighted like Jennifer Aniston."

Will chuckled sarcastically. "That's not going to turn you into Jennifer Aniston."

He rolled out of bed and headed toward the bathroom.

"I said like Jennifer Aniston."

You moody motherfucker.

Ten minutes later Will came back in the room dressed in his blue T-shirt and gray flannel pajama pants. Looking in the mirror, he ran his fingers through his hair a few times before heading toward the door.

I sat up in bed. "Where are you going?"

"I have some reports to finish for work."

"They can't wait until tomorrow?"

"They're due tomorrow, Bryson."

"Can't you put them off for at least a half hour and just sit with me?"

"I'm dressed. Besides, my head is already in business mode."

"I'm sorry spending non-fucking time with me has become such an inconvenience." My voice cracked.

Other than the time we spent trying to make a baby, Will and I were apart more than together.

"Bryson, don't pull that shit." He huffed.

"Are you kidding me? I'm trying my damnedest to be understanding and patient with you."

"Then get off my back."

"I can't believe you just said that to me. I'm doing everything in my power to be a good wife to you, including trying to give you a child in a certain timeframe."

"And I'm working my ass off to provide for you. How do you think I feel having to perform every time you snap your fingers?"

"Snap my fingers? Do you think I'm looking forward to being sick, tired, and bloated? At least before the sex was enjoyable. Now it's stick it in and hope for the best. What a great way to bring a child into the world."

"Well, maybe we should take a break."

Tears trickled down my cheeks. "Take a break?"

"Yeah, because lately fucking you hasn't been exactly a thrill for me."

"Go to hell!"

He turned and stormed out of the room.

I sat frozen in bed. I didn't know what hurt more, Will's words or the disconnect that filled his eyes. Something had definitely been changing between us and it wasn't all due to the infertility issue or him being busier at work. I thought we were moving past our heartache and gluing our dream back together. But the look he gave me said otherwise. For the first time in our relationship I was scared of what the future held.

Swinging my legs over the side of the bed, I reached for Will's high school football jersey and tugged it down over my body. I wasn't a very patient person. If something was wrong I wanted to deal with it in the here and now rather than letting it fester. I made a bathroom pit stop to splash cool water on my face. Grabbing a pair of wool socks from the dresser, I pulled them on and headed downstairs.

The home office was diagonal to the stairs. Taking in a deep breath, I wrapped my arms around my body. Not only was I nervous to find out what was happening between us, I also knew Will didn't like to be interrupted while working. There was a slight crack in the door. Will was too focused on his work and didn't notice when I pushed the door open enough to peek inside.

The desk was positioned in front of the large bay window that faced the front of the house. The room was dark except for flickering light from the laptop. Will's back was facing me but I was able to see part of the computer screen.

At first I didn't know what I was looking at. My eyes squinted, adjusting to the light. My fuzzy brain cleared and the bottom dropped out of my stomach. A naked blonde filled the screen. Her head was tilted to the side, her eyes filled with the illusion of lust as she looked directly into the camera while sucking on her index finger. Slowly, she drew the wet finger out and slid it down her body and between her open legs. Using her other hand, she pinched and twisted her nipple. With hooded eyes, blond waves fell back as she plunged the finger between her legs and it disappeared inside. Her lips rounded as the finger pumped in and out of her. I saw her mouth forming words but I couldn't hear them. I was no lip reader, though I knew the type of filth she was saying. My gaze shifted to the back of Will's head. He was wearing a headset, enabling him to catch every moan and dirty word. A deep groan rumbled from his chest as his head fell back against the chair.

"Fuck yourself you fucking whore," Will muttered, trying to keep his voice low.

More muffled moans filled the room as he stroked himself while watching the screen skank. Will's body jerked forward then convulsed as he climaxed.

My body and mind went numb. I couldn't believe what was happening in front of me. My husband, who less than thirty minutes ago was unable to come inside of me, exploded in his hand in front of a total stranger.

chapter Five

Gut-wrenching, devastated, hurt, and betrayed are all words I'd attach to the moment I saw my husband having cyber-sex. But I didn't feel any of them as I witnessed the scene in front of me unfold. Novocain replaced the blood in my veins, numbing every inch of my mind and body. It was like watching a movie or TV show and being emotionally detached from the action. Part of me screamed to run away. But the other part of me had my gaze frozen, hoping to convince my heart that somehow I was misinterpreting what was happening.

Playing up her orgasm, the screen skank convulsed as she whipped her head back and forth. Her surgically enhanced chest heaved while she slid the finger out from between her legs. Looking directly into the camera, she smiled and stuck the infamous finger in her mouth.

"Lick it, baby," Will muttered.

Her bright pink overinflated lips moved, eliciting a deep chuckle from Will. It didn't even sound like him. My impulse was to jerk the office chair around to see if in fact the person sitting in it was Will. Nothing about this felt like my life. The numbness began to fade, replaced by waves of nausea churning in my stomach. The sensation of bile rising burned my throat. I couldn't talk or look at Will until my head cleared and the ability to think returned. I needed to get away before he caught me catching him.

Quietly I backed out into the entryway and sprinted to my bedroom. I dove into bed, yanking the covers over my head, and tried to push the images of the last fifteen minutes from my memory. As hard as I tried to refocus, I couldn't un-see what I'd just seen. The images swirled around my head and each second that passed became more and more vivid.

Up to this point no tears had been shed. The nausea had even subsided a little. Suddenly out of nowhere the sharp pain of realization pierced my stomach and spread throughout my body. I'd just discovered the person I thought I knew, the one I let into my heart, didn't exist. Burying my face deep into the pillow, I cried until exhaustion faded into sleep.

The next morning I jolted awake. Rolling onto my back, I peeked from behind the covers over to Will's side of the bed. He wasn't there.

Good.

I didn't know if or when he came to bed last night. It didn't matter. I still wasn't ready to face him. I needed time to process things with a clearer head.

I got out of bed, walked over to the window, and saw that his car wasn't in the driveway.

Another good.

I shuffled into the bathroom and mindlessly locked the door as a precaution. For a split second the action surprised me. Rarely did Will come back home once he left for work. But just in case he did, I didn't want to be caught off guard.

As the hot water drizzled down my body, I tried to look at the situation from all angles. I wasn't that much of a prude or innocent. I grew up with a brother who was openly proud about his *Playboy* collection. And with technology being so integrated into daily life, I knew that porn was just a click away. Guys were visual creatures. Hence, the sexy shots I sent Will. But apparently I needed to upgrade my definition of porn because I was clueless that it had become interactive. And that's the part I couldn't handle. That's the part that felt as if Will had reneged on our marriage vows and cheated on me.

I was to meet Sophie in a half hour for yoga class. I thought about calling it off but felt antsy and needed to get out of this house. I dressed in my black yoga pants, purple T-shirt, and orange and purple Nikes. Standing in front of the dresser mirror, I gathered up my hair into a high ponytail. No reason not to look cute just because my husband was a sex pervert. I was tired of thinking about the fact that a complete stranger, located God knows where, could cause a reaction out of my husband that I'd been unable to achieve. Plus, I knew if I went any further down that rabbit hole my worth as a wife and a woman would be completely obliterated. I needed a mental break and a change of scenery.

As I hit the bottom of the stairs, I turned on my way to the kitchen. My gaze froze on the door to Will's office. I stopped and for a brief moment thought about going in to look around. I wasn't sure what I thought I'd find. He took his laptop with him every day. He never locked the room so obviously he was comfortable with me going in there while he was gone. My phone chirped with a text, pushing the investigation out of my head for the moment.

Sophie: *Hey, chick! How about lunch after class?*

Me: *Sure.*

Sophie: *Awesome. There's a cute new sandwich place I've been wanting to try.*

Me: *Ok.*

Sophie: *Anything wrong?*

Me: *No.*

Sophie: *Are you sure?*

Me: *Why?*

Sophie: *Cause you're texting funny.*

Me: *I'm fine. See you in a bit.*

I certainly wasn't going to ask my best friend's advice about my husband's screen fuck buddy via text. I was already tired of the day and it hadn't even started yet. I needed coffee, pronto.

Sophie kept glancing over at me during our walk across the parking toward the pale blue and green studio but never asked if anything was wrong. She was a great best friend, knowing intuitively when and when not to push me for information. Adele scrunched up her face when she saw the two of us walk in class. She had taken up residence on the opposite side of the room today. I gave her a sideways glance as I unrolled my mat. She was gesturing in my direction and whispering to the middle-aged lady next to her. The lady must have been new because I hadn't seen her here before. No doubt Adele was warning her to stay clear of the anal kitchen queen. She hadn't spoken or come near me for months. I eased down onto my mat and laser-focused on my breathing as I stretched, waiting for class to begin.

The sandwich shop Sophie wanted to have lunch at was right around the corner from the yoga studio. It was early September and the humidity that was a Charleston staple during summer had begun to lift, so we decided to walk to the cafe. We placed our order at the counter, grabbed a couple of bottled waters from the cooler, and found a quiet corner on the outdoor patio. I cracked open my water and took a swig while looking at lunchtime people milling about the downtown market area.

"Okay, spill the beans." Sophie demanded.

"What beans?"

"Something is obviously on your mind. We can play a few rounds of the denial game or we can cut to the chase. You should know, I'm going out of town tomorrow and won't be readily available."

I twisted the top back on the bottle of water. "I'm probably making a bigger deal out of it than I need to. It's probably more normal and natural than I was aware of. I probably should just erase it from my mind."

"Probably. But you can't and won't. Out with it."

A flush of heat crept over my cheeks as my chin dipped down. "I walked in on Will masturbating last night."

My gaze shot up to meet hers. I was both afraid and curious to see her reaction. Sophie's expression remained relaxed.

"So he spent a little time with Palmala and her five sisters."

Narrowing my eyes, I tilted my head to the side. "Who?"

Sophie raised her hand and wiggled her fingers. "Palmala and her five sisters."

"Ew," I said, scrunching up my nose.

"Don't *ew* it till you've tried it."

I was about to respond when the waitress walked up with our order. I couldn't even look at the woman when I mumbled thank you.

Sophie had a lot more experience and kept up to date on things, sexually speaking. I needed to get her gut reaction to the screen skank involvement.

Needing to keep my hands busy, my gaze stayed down as I ripped open the packet of spicy mustard and squirted it over the ham sandwich. "What do you know about cyber-sex?"

I stole a quick glance at her.

Leaning in, she turned her ear toward me. "Come again?"

"Don't look at me."

"Why not?"

"Because I don't want you looking at me when I tell you what I'm about to tell you. Look at your food, look at the ground, look at anything except me."

Sophie scooted her chair away from the table, angling it so she'd be aimed toward the street. "Better?"

"Better. Thanks." I took in a deep breath and cleared my throat. "Last night Will wasn't able to . . . you know, while we were trying to make a baby. We had a big argument and he stormed out."

"Of the house?" she said, looking at me sideways.

"No, he went downstairs to his office. Stop looking at me."

Her gaze shifted back to the street.

"So I felt bad about the fight. We've both been stressed because of the baby thing and he's been working really hard. I went downstairs to his office and found him doing it in front of his laptop with some other woman."

"Can I turn around now?"

"I guess."

Sophie adjusted her chair back to face me. "That slimy motherfucker."

"So you think it's wrong?"

"Goddam right I think it's wrong."

The weight lifted from my chest and sank to my stomach. I was relieved that I wasn't the only one disturbed by it. I was also heartbroken. I bit my lower lip in hopes of keeping the tears that stung my eyes from falling.

"What excuse did he give you?" Sophie said.

"He doesn't know I saw him. I ran upstairs. I don't know if he even came back to bed. He'd already left for work when I got up this morning."

"Did you recognize the slut?"

I shook my head. "No. She looked to be a professional. I feel like he cheated on me." I choked on the last sentence.

Sophie reached over and placed her hand on mine. "I know some ex-Navy Seals. One call. They'll fuck him up." Her head and shoulders swayed like a street-smart tough girl.

"Let's keep that option in the back pocket for now." I paused for a minute to pull myself together. I didn't want to have a complete breakdown in public. "He's been pulling away from me more and more lately."

"I know you guys have been stressing about starting a family."

"It's not that or his work. Something is off between us and I can't figure out what."

"You need to talk. He needs to explain himself."

"I'm scared, Sophie."

She squeezed my hand. "I know. But ignoring it won't solve anything. It will just make things worse."

I knew Sophie was right. Communication and trust were the cornerstones to a mature and successful relationship. Maybe there was a perfectly good reason why Will felt he needed to look elsewhere for his needs. I knew people used porn to get in the mood. I'd even heard that couples sometimes watched those movies together in order to spice up their sex life. But what Will did was the reverse. He didn't use that woman to get in the mood for me. He left me to go be with her.

As we walked back to our cars, Sophie's hands were waving all around while she talked excitedly about how well her job was going. I was thrilled she was so fulfilled in her career. She was an intelligent woman with drive and confidence. She deserved all her success.

Standing between our cars, we said our goodbyes with a hug.

Sophie leaned back, looked me in the eye, and said, "You know I'm here for you. Even if I'm not in town, I'm just a phone call away."

"I know and thank you for always listening to me whine."

"You know you're my favorite whine-o."

We opened our car doors in unison and slid into the seats. Before pulling out of the parking space, I scrolled through my music selection, landing on Colbie Caillat. Her songs always cheered me up when I was in a blah mood. I turned the volume way up on the tune *Dream Life*, then navigated my way out of the parking lot and onto Paul Cantrell Boulevard.

Not more than a half mile down the road, I got stopped by one of the longest traffic lights in town. Waiting, I joined Colbie on the chorus as I played drums on the steering wheel and my head bobbed to the up-tempo beat. My gaze roamed over to the passenger's window. The most magnificent specimen of the male forearm appeared before me. It was muscular, tan, and hanging out the driver's window of the car next to me. Ending my solo performance, I hunched down, trying to get a good look at the entire arm. A small gasp escaped me when the bicep came into view. Even relaxed the muscle was bulging. The black T-shirt hit right at the deep indention of the upper arm, revealing half of a tattoo.

I took a quick glance at the traffic light making sure it was still bright red. Then I stretched my body across the passenger's seat pretending to reach for something on the floorboard. My gaze made one more trip up the arm, moving over the shoulder, before the guy turned in my direction. I froze, staring up at a chiseled jaw covered in golden blond scruff.

Hart Mitchell.

His head poked out the window slightly while his gaze rose along with his eyebrows as something caught his eye down the street. The sunlight lit up his face, allowing me to study his features in the short amount of time. The hint of laugh lines around his eyes and mouth gave him a sexy rugged look. His jawline was more defined and sharper. And that mouth was still mesmerizing. Today it worked a toothpick, sliding it from one corner to the other as it twirled. My eyes remained on Hart as he moved forward, turned in front of me, and rode off. A chorus of car horns filled the air, causing me to look up and realize the light had turned green.

For the rest of the day I kept myself busy. Occasionally, my mind drifted to the Hart sightings. It was so weird and random that I'd seen him again after not laying eyes on him for years. I wondered what type of man he grew into. The only encounter I had with him was at senior prom. Back then he was kind of bossy but sweet.

Pushing off from the wall, Hart commanded, "Let's dance."

"Huh?"

He took a couple of steps and turned toward me. "Stop already with the huhs. You heard me."

I chuckled. "Where do you get off telling me to dance with you?"

"You know you wanna. I can see it in your . . ."

Nipples. He's going to say, your humungous pointy nipples.

. . . eyes."

Aw, he didn't mention my nipples. Sweet.

"*I don't think it's a very good idea. Will, my very real boyfriend, will go ballistic the second he sees us walk into the ballroom.*"

"Not in there." Hart reached out his hand. "In here."

"*What about your date? Where is she?*" My voice was shaky.

"*At the moment she's standing in front of a fish tank not dancing with me.*"

I avoided Will's office completely, retreating to the one place that always gave me comfort, the kitchen. I was more of a foodie than a baker but once in a while I gave it a shot. Besides, I needed to eat my stress away and cake would hit the spot.

Pulling out flour, oil, eggs, and my secret ingredient, vanilla pudding, I focused all my energies on baking. As I cracked each egg into the cranberry red KitchenAid mixer, I imagined dark brown eyes full of slut lust. While the cake baked I stayed busy cleaning the kitchen and then set things up to make the frosting. I flipped the switch on the mixer and watched as the butter, powdered sugar, and cocoa churned together while I figured out what to say to Will. I was so lost in thought that I jumped at the sound of his voice.

"I didn't mean to scare you," Will said.

Flipping off the mixer, I turned around, almost bumping into his chest. Not sure of my reaction I took in a deep breath and braced myself before looking into his chocolate brown eyes. I lifted my eyes and saw the same disconnect I'd seen last night.

My gaze bounced up and down nervously. "Hey, I didn't hear you come in."

"Obviously." He backed away.

I couldn't tell if the tension in the room was a joint effort or my own creation. After all, Will didn't know I saw him last night. Maybe I was sensing the guilt he was experiencing for what he'd done. I stayed silent as he grabbed a beer from the fridge. Leaning back against the counter, he twisted the top off the bottle and took a swig. His gaze aimed in my direction but not at me.

"Did you have a good day at work?" My words sounded forced and trite.

"It was okay." He took another swig of beer.

I came up with at least seven different approaches to bringing up the subject while baking. But every last one of them vanished from my brain now that Will was standing across from me. If he would start with one word or sentence to get the conversation rolling, I could piggyback off of it. I was just too scared to be the first to mention it.

Finally, Will looked at me. "Could you make me a sandwich?"

"For supper?"

"Yeah, I gotta lot of work to do tonight. I'll just eat at my desk."

"But you just got home from work."

"What can I say? Dad's prepping me for when I take over." Pushing off from the counter, he walked toward me. He placed an obligatory kiss on my forehead. "I'm gonna jump in the shower."

As he turned to leave, I momentarily lost my balance. Falling one step back against the counter, my eyes widened as my mouth fell open. Will wasn't the most perceptive when it came to feelings. *Typical guy.* But I was amazed at how clueless he acted. I had a hard time believing he didn't sense the tension in the room.

My chest tightened with a stifled sob as I realized how important it was to me for him to bring up last night. I wanted him to fess up, explain, and ask for forgiveness. Tell me I had nothing to worry about. That it was a one time lapse in judgment. I wanted him to take me in his arms and say how much he loved me. That no woman, cyber or otherwise, could ever take my place. I wanted our connection to be so strong that he intuitively knew something was bothering me. I needed all of that but what I got was the sound of his footsteps heading up the stairs.

Abandoning the frosting for the time being, I took the ingredients for Will's sandwich from the fridge. Out the corner of my eye, I noticed the black bag he carried to work sitting at the end of the counter. In the bag was his laptop.

Will's showers took between fifteen and twenty minutes, depending on his stress level. I'd have plenty of time to check his internet history. Commit a few of the website names to memory and do more investigating on my computer later when I was alone.

I breathed in deeply, my bottom lip captured between my teeth. Curling and uncurling my fingers, they hovered over the black zipper as I contemplated whether or not I wanted to step over this line. With a thumping pulse echoing in my ears, I unzipped the bag and slid the laptop out. Adrenaline pumped through my veins heating up my body. I quickly powered up the laptop and entered the password. It was the play that won Garrison High the football championship our senior year. Will always said it was the best moment of his high school career.

56 89 25

Denied.

A knot formed in my stomach. With my nerves, I could have entered the numbers wrong. I retyped the password slowly, paying close attention to the keys my fingers were landing on.

56 89 24

The screen came to life as I realized I was one number off. The laptop automatically connected to our WiFi network. Before opening the browser I noticed a folder marked *Personal/VL*. I placed the cursor over it and clicked.

Access Denied. Password Required.

I tried to open the folder again.

Click.

Click.

Click.

Click.

Click.

My stomach constricted as beads of sweat popped along my forehead.

Click.

Click.

Click.

Click.

Click.

My finger came down harder and harder each time it landed on the key, thinking somehow that would help me gain access.

Aware of my limited time, I gave up on the folder, opened the browser, and quickly searched the history. With my hand over my mouth, I read the list of websites Will frequented. There were a few construction related but the majority of the sites had the word porn in their address. One address that came up a lot was for a website called Virtual Life. I quickly put two and two together, figuring this was what VL stood for on the folder I couldn't open.

The sound of footsteps and throat clearing jolted me into action. I powered off the computer and put it back in the bag, making sure the bag was exactly as Will left it. I sprinted to the other side of the kitchen and began making a pastrami sandwich. I prayed that by the time Will reached the kitchen any physical evidence of my nerves would be gone.

As Will rounded the corner, I stole a quick glance in his direction. He had changed into his favorite pair of worn jeans and blue T-shirt. I loved when he wore simple causal clothes. Somehow they made him look like the boy I knew in high school.

He'd recently gotten his hair cut. Not quite a buzz cut but close. At first I wasn't sure about the new style but had to admit it looked good along with the scruff peppering his strong jaw. At this moment everything about him looked sexy, cozy, and comfortable. As if on cue, my heart fluttered, brushing away my doubts for the moment.

"Is my sandwich ready?" He asked.

I placed the slice of rye bread on top and cut the sandwich in half. "Yeah. I was just getting ready to dish up some potato salad. Go ahead to your office. I'll bring the food in to you."

Will slid the plate with his sandwich away from me. "That's okay. All I want is the sandwich."

"I'll bring you a piece of cake after I finish frosting it."

He grabbed a napkin and another beer. "Don't worry about it." He tossed the words over his shoulder as he left the room.

I didn't see or hear from Will for the rest of the night. I thought about getting on my laptop and investigating what the Virtual Life site was all about, but decided it was better to do my snooping when Will was out of the house and I was alone. So I cut a big piece of cake, crawled into bed, and flipped through the TV channels trying to find anything that would redirect my thoughts and keep my imagination from running wild.

chapter Six

As soon as Will left for work the next morning I hopped on my computer and searched Virtual Life. From what I could tell, the user created a persona and then role played anywhere on the site. The real person controlled every aspect of their character—the actions, the words, and the feelings. There were different scenes and worlds a character could step into. Since I wasn't a member and didn't plan on becoming one, I had limited access. I did notice there were areas on the VL site marked *adults* only. I decided to do a Google search on cyber-sex. Within seconds I had a screen full of websites, articles, and videos on the subject.

I clicked on a short documentary titled *Wired for Sex*. I watched in disbelief as a husband told the filmmaker how his wife of ten years had ignored him and their two children for months as she developed an intimate relationship with another man through VL. Sometimes spending as much as fourteen hours a day online with this man. A man she had never physically met. The rest of the film showed how these virtual characters can do whatever their creators want them to do, including having full-on graphic sex. The technology was so advanced that the appearance and movements of the characters were extremely realistic. By the time I'd finished my crash course in virtual adultery I felt like I needed to disinfect my eyeballs as well as my body.

I spent the rest of the day with my head in a stagnant fog. As I robotically ran errands to the post office, dry cleaners, and grocery store I tried to figure out my definition of cheating. Was it simply the act of having physical sex? Virtual sex? Or sharing intimate thoughts and feelings?

When I pulled into my driveway that afternoon my mind was made up . . . all of the above.

After putting away the groceries I got started on dinner. Tonight was going to be a quick and easy zucchini pie with a garden salad and cooked apples. I took a mental break while preparing the meal. Two full days had already gone by since I caught Will in his office. Two days of me overthinking. Two days of me searching for just the right words to start the discussion. Two days of me wondering where the man I married went.

I decided to wait until after we ate dinner to talk. I figured that would give Will enough time to decompress from the long work day, putting him in a better frame of mind. As had become the norm, Will got up from the table and headed straight into his office while I cleaned the dishes.

With each step toward the office my mouth dried up, my pulse sped up, and bile traveled up into my throat. Closing my eyes, I took a calming breath and lightly knocked on the door. There was no answer but I could hear tapping on the keyboard. I knocked again.

Will cleared his throat and abruptly said, "Yeah?!"

"Can I come in?"

"Just a second."

Just a second?

My nervousness turned into annoyance with a hint of anger and suspicion. Was he explaining to the screen slut he'd be back in a second? That his wife was waiting for permission to enter a room in her very own house? Gripping the doorknob, I twisted it.

Locked.

Within seconds the lock clicked and the door opened. Will's large frame took up the entire doorway.

He looked down at me, a slight chuckle escaping him. "I don't know why it was locked. I must have hit it by mistake."

"We need to talk."

He glanced over his shoulder. "Now? I have a lot of work to do."

At this point the work excuse was played out.

Pushing past him, I walked into the office. "It's important."

I noticed that his laptop was closed as I crossed the room and sat in the overstuffed burgundy leather chair in the corner. Will swiveled back and forth in his chair. He was trying to come off as nonchalant but I sensed a little nervousness. I rarely bothered him while he was in his office.

"Bryson, can you get to the point? I need to get back to what I was doing."

I looked down at the fidgeting fingers in my lap. "I think we need to go to counseling."

"What kind of counseling?"

I stared at him for a brief moment, not believing he asked that question. "Marriage counseling."

His brows knitted together. "Where's this coming from?"

"You don't think things have changed between us?"

"Of course things have changed, Bryson. It's called being an adult."

"I came in here to have a serious discussion with you about the state of our marriage. You don't need to be snide."

"Is it your time of the month again? You always get so needy during that time."

My neck muscles tensed. "Do not blame this on hormones. Haven't you noticed that we're spending less and less time together?"

"I can't spend every waking minute with you."

"I'm not asking you to. But lately, we basically eat dinner and then you lock yourself in here for the rest of the night doing god knows what."

Will gripped the edge of the armrest. "I'm working my fucking ass off so you don't have to."

"You were the one who didn't want me to work. I could have been working all this time. I'll go get a job right now if you want."

"Doing what?!" His tone was sharp and condescending.

Tears of hurt and anger lurked behind my eyes. "I'm not an idiot, Will."

"I never said you were."

"You may as well have." I choked, determined not to cry.

I waited for him to apologize.

Silence.

"I'm not happy."

Simultaneously, Will huffed and rolled his eyes. "What do you want me to do about it?"

"Give a shit?"

"Each person has to find their own happiness." He sounded cold.

There was no evidence that my words affected him in any way. In fact, he looked annoyed that I was taking up his time.

I inhaled a couple of deep breaths, needing to keep my emotions in check. If I broke down, the conversation would be over. I didn't want that to happen. I wanted to deal with whatever was causing this tear.

"With us. I'm not happy with us, Will."

He didn't react immediately, his gaze drifted down. I was in hopes that my words were sinking in. That he was understanding where I was coming from and realized that we needed to take action before things got worse.

He finally looked over at me. "I think things are good."

My mouth dropped open.

"I need to get back to work." Turning toward the desk, he picked up a pen, and started scribbling something on a piece of paper.

"Is that what you call it?"

"What are you talking about?"

"I know you do more than just work in here," I said.

More scribbling. "I have no idea what you're getting at."

"I saw what you were doing with that woman on the screen." He looked up, his face squished together. He was committed to playing the innocent. "After we had that big argument I felt bad so I came down here to talk with you."

Will dropped his pen, leaned back in the chair, and stared out the window. The air between us was suffocating but I was determined to wait him out.

After what felt like a lifetime, Will said, "I can explain."

I leaned back in my chair. "I'm all ears."

"Guys do stuff like that as a stress reliever. It's no big deal."

"What guys? . . . and it is to me."

"All guys look at porn. It's natural. It's a god-given right, really."

"Really? You have the right to cheat on your wife."

His hands went in the air as he spun the chair around to face me. "Whoa! Hold on a second. I've never cheated on you."

"What was that the other night?"

"Jacking off!"

"You . . . were say . . . ing things to . . . each other," I stammered.

Will flailed his arms. "I wasn't sticking my dick in her!"

"So . . . as long as . . . that . . . doesn't happen . . . everything else is on the table." My voice shook with pain.

"God, Bryson, don't make this into something. It's not a big deal. It's normal."

My lips quivered as a tear rolled down my face. "It didn't look normal to me."

Dropping his chin to his chest, Will slumped forward in the chair.

A second wave of bravery washed over me. "What's Virtual Life?"

Will slowly lifted his head. "What?"

"You go to that site a lot."

"You were on my computer?" he said accusingly.

"You get on mine."

"Because I fucking paid for it and it doesn't have anything important on it. I have sensitive work-related information on mine."

"It's not like you work for the FBI."

"Do you have any idea how bad it would be if you hit one wrong key and deleted a file?"

"I know my way around a computer, Will. We're getting off track."

"Oh, I think we're right on track. I work my ass off day and night for a wife who thinks I'm lying and cheating. Jesus Christ, Bryson, when is it going to be enough for you? I give you everything you want."

Unable to hold them back any longer sobs trickled out of me.

"What's Virtual Life?" I repeated.

Will's brown eyes looked darker than usual.

His voice low and controlled. "It's a gaming site. I get on there when I need to go brain dead for a while. I play war, Knights of the Round Table, cowboys. That's it."

"Open that folder on your computer."

"What folder?"

"The one that requires a password."

He chuckled humorlessly. "No, I'm not going to do that."

"What's the problem if you don't have anything to hide?"

"I can't waste any more time on this. I've got work to do."

We stared at each other, his face blank, mine coated in tears. Will was shutting down and I was drained, so there was no point in continuing tonight. I stood and walked toward the door. Before leaving, I made one last-ditch effort.

"Will, please go to counseling with me, at least one session . . . please." I begged.

"One." He snapped.

As I closed the door, Will fired-up his laptop.

I didn't waste any time setting up the counseling appointment. I wanted to do it before Will changed his mind. The one thing he insisted on was that we kept the fact that we were going to counseling a secret. He didn't want his parents to know or have people whispering about the state of our marriage. I understood his point and agreed. I didn't even tell my parents or brother.

Since my hands were tied, unable to ask friends or family for recommendations, I turned to our church. Will and I were slack when it came to attending Mass each Sunday. We were your typical Chreasters, showing up every Christmas and Easter. But I still receive the church bulletin and that's where I found Joanne Foster.

I'd never been to a counselor before and wasn't exactly sure what to expect. Although I knew Will and I needed to be here, the thought of opening up to a complete stranger was scary. But Joanne was one of those people who radiated peace and calm. Greeting me with a warm smile, she immediately put me at ease.

I sat in her office glancing at the clock on the wall every other second. Joanne had stepped out to take care of something since Will was currently a no-show. My stomach churned with embarrassment.

How could he be late?

I made sure he put the date and time on his calendar. Plus, I'd been reminding him for the past two days. Shoving my hand inside my purse, I grabbed my phone and checked for a text from Will.

Nothing.

I bowed my head, swallowing several times to keep the anger and disappointment from showing. I'd been even more hurt and confused since I confronted Will. I assumed once he was aware that I knew about his extracurricular activities he'd stop. Especially since we'd made plans to see Joanne. Two weeks had passed and he still locked himself away in that damn office every night. Each time the office door shut it felt like a slap in the face. What made it even worse was this woman on the computer was random. She wasn't someone he met and developed true feelings for. Will didn't want to be with her. He just didn't want to be with me.

I flinched when Joanne came walking through the door.

"Bryson, have you heard from Will?"

"Not yet," I said, sheepishly.

She sat down at her desk and looked at the clock. "Would you like to go ahead and start? If he shows up in the meantime he can join us if you like."

"I'm really sorry. Um . . . Will gets very busy at work and . . . um . . ." I could tell she noticed the tremble in my voice.

"It's okay. We all have busy lives and things happen."

I fiddled with the hem of my shirt. "I'm a little nervous. This is my first experience with a counselor. It's me, not you. I'm just not sure what I'm supposed to say, which is odd because it was my idea to come here in the first place."

Leaning back in her chair, she gave me another warm smile. "First things first. Take a deep breath and relax. Anything we discuss stays between you and me. I've been counseling couples for twenty years and there's not much I haven't heard. This is a nonjudgmental safe place."

I nodded and blew out a breath. "Thank you."

"Now, I know from our brief chat on the phone when you made the appointment that you and Will were high school sweethearts."

"Yeah, we met our freshman year. My family moved and it put us in a new school district. I knew a little bit about him before we actually met. He was the star quarterback at Garrison High. He loved playing. Confidence poured off of him when he was out on the field."

My eyes got misty remembering how innocent Will and I were.

"Did he lack confidence off the field?"

"He doubted himself more off the field. But most of us have insecurities at that age."

"Was it Will's confidence that drew you to him initially?"

I paused for a moment and wondered why my answer wasn't immediate. Sure, Will and I had been together for a long time but not so long for me to forget why I was drawn to him.

"I don't know, I guess. I've never given it much thought. For some reason at the beginning of our junior year he asked me out and before I knew it we were officially dating."

"So you were together in high school and what about afterward? Did you attend separate colleges?"

"No, we both went to Newberry."

"Oh, was that planned or just a coincidence?"

"Will got a football scholarship to go there."

"And what about you?" she said.

"I didn't get a scholarship. I was an okay student. I got good grades, just not scholarship material."

"Newberry offered what you were looking for in a college education then?"

"I majored in business and their program was decent. I mean, business is business no matter which college you attend."

"So why did you attend Newberry?"

"Because Will went there."

Joanne slowly nodded her head as if she'd just found what I'd said extremely interesting.

"Tell me about your relationship in college."

"Typical. Nothing really stands out."

"Did you ever break up during this time?"

"We'd have little arguments. Will would pout and not talk to me for a few days."

"What were the arguments about?"

"Like if he was really late or forgot we had a date." I couldn't help my nervous chuckle at the irony. "He did that kind of stuff in high school too. The only person I knew going to Newberry was Will. Since he was part of the football team he had a built-in group of friends the second he got there."

"Did you hang out with him and his friends?"

"Sometimes I'd go to parties with him."

"Any other time, like out to dinner, studying, to movies?"

"Occasionally. Will had a lot of added pressure on him and being around his friends was a stress reliever."

"Added pressure?"

"From his parents. Will has always worked hard not to disappoint them. I think he tries to make up for his brother, Alex, who's a bit of a lost cause. Even now, he's carrying a lot of responsibility at work."

"What do you get out of your relationship with Will?"

"He provides well for us."

"Is that all you get?"

"I don't understand the question."

"Does he give you love, support, and encourage you to follow your passion? Is he a safe place to land when you fall? Can you share all your hopes, dreams, and fears with him?"

I shouldn't have needed time to think how to respond. The answer should have flowed out of my mouth immediately without forethought. But I couldn't answer yes across the board. Why couldn't I answer yes to all of the above?

"Bryson, you don't have to answer if . . ."

"No, he doesn't." Air gushed from my lungs.

It was as if I'd been suffocated by a secret and just saying the words out loud allowed me to breathe. Then panic and shame washed over me.

"Oh my god, I love Will. I don't know why I said . . ."

Joanne reached out and placed her hand on my arm in an attempt to calm me. "Bryson, it's okay. Admitting that you aren't completely fulfilled doesn't make you a bad person. Nor does it mean you don't love Will. You obviously do or you wouldn't be here trying to improve your relationship."

"Will is very old-fashioned. His father worked and his mother stayed at home to raise him and Alex. He wants our children to have the same type of upbringing." I paused and then blurted out, "We lost our baby a little over a year ago."

Sympathetic blue eyes looked at me. "I'm so sorry. Losing a child is one of the most horrific things a parent can go through."

Tears filled my eyes. "After the baby . . . um . . . Will started pulling away. I haven't been able to get pregnant again."

"Has Will been treating you differently since the baby?" Joanne's voice was calm and soothing.

I nodded. "He started getting home later and later. Even when he was home he worked in his office most of the time. I think he looks at me as damaged goods."

The air in the room was stifling. I wanted to tell her about the cyber-sex and what I'd found on Will's computer. I closed my eyes, searching deep inside for the courage to say the words out loud.

"Bryson?"

"I caught Will masturbating in front of his computer."

Joanne remained silent. Not because she was in shock or judging. Now that the floodgates had opened she didn't want to stop the flow."

"The night I saw him, we had a bad argument about not being able to get pregnant. I went to his office to apologize for my part. When I opened the door, I saw a naked woman on the screen touching herself while Will touched himself."

By the end of my admission my entire body was on fire and trembling. Tears coated my face. Plucking several tissues from the box on her desk, Joanne handed them to me, letting me recover for several minutes before speaking.

"Was this a one-time incident or do you think he does it on a regular basis?"

"I don't want to believe he does it on a regular basis. But every time he goes into his office or I see him carry the laptop out the door, I wonder. He admitted to getting on this one website, Virtual Life."

"I'm familiar with it."

"He said he gets on it to play games. But I looked it up and there's more to it than just innocent games."

"Have you noticed a change in your sexual activity?"

I nodded. "He doesn't act that interested and the last few times we've had sex, he's not been able to . . . I thought it was the stress of not being able to conceive."

"Men are visual creatures so it's not unusual for them to be drawn to those sites. With technology making things convenient, they're like kids in a candy story, with access 24/7. Some couples even enjoy watching the occasional movie. And if it's something both partners like then that's their choice. But when one partner engages on a regular basis, especially in secret, then there's a problem. Has he physically had sex with other women?"

"He said he hasn't."

"Do you believe him?"

"I want to but I already feel like he's cheated on me."

"Men and women view this subject very differently." Joanne grabbed my hand, giving it a slight squeeze. "I want you to know this isn't unrepairable. It takes work from both partners but it's doable."

The time with Joanne left me drained but hopeful. It felt good to confide in someone without fear of judgment. She knew how upset and embarrassed I was that Will never showed, but told me to give him the benefit of the doubt until I heard his reasoning.

"I forgot."

Will was in the kitchen making himself a sandwich when I got home from the counseling appointment.

"How could you forget? It was on your calendar. I reminded you for two days. Not to mention the fact that I said, 'See you at the counselor's later today' as you walked out of the house this morning."

He stopped making the sandwich and turned to face me. "I swear to god, I'm sorry." Sincerity filled his eyes. "Dad called me into his office late this afternoon to discuss a big project and the appointment flew out of my head."

Will looked genuinely apologetic. A quality I hadn't seen in a very long time. I was glad Joanne talked me into giving him a chance to explain before I jumped to conclusions and got pissed off. In the end having her all to myself for the hour worked out well.

"I made another appointment for next week, same day and time."

"Okay, I promise I'll be there. I really am sorry, Bryson."

Gee, two sorrys in less than five minutes. That's a new Will record.

"You want me to make you a sandwich?" he said.

I blinked a couple of times, surprised by his offer. Will wasn't a total dick but he'd never been a very thoughtful person. The simple gesture convinced me there was a light at the end of the tunnel. And we'd get to it . . . together.

chapter Seven

During the next week it felt like the old Will and Bryson had moved back into our house. I tried to put into practice what Joanne suggested by not looking at Will through suspicious eyes. After dinner he didn't immediately go into his office and one night we even went out to the movies. When the second appointment day came I walked into Joanne's office with a completely different attitude than I had the week before.

Will was ten minutes late. As usual work was the excuse of choice with traffic being added on for extra emphasis. But I chose to focus on the positive. He kept his promise and made it to the appointment.

"It's nice to have the three us of here," Joanne said through her ever-present warm smile.

A loud ding cut through the tranquil office. Without hesitation Will grabbed his phone and read the text. My gaze darted over to him at the other end of the small sofa we were sitting on. A twinge of suspicion mixed with embarrassment hit my stomach. He was totally oblivious as to how rude he was being.

With a gentle soft tone, Joanne said, "Will is everything okay?"

His eyes stayed focused on his phone. "Yeah, why?"

"We haven't started yet and you seem distracted."

"Just work stuff."

"I understand but I have a rule, cellphones must be turned off during a session."

"I didn't know that. How about I put it on silent?"

"I'm sorry, Will, but I'm going to have to ask you to turn it off completely.

Even on silent the buzzing from texts and voicemails is distracting. It will only be for an hour."

Will looked at Joanne as if she had two heads growing out of her neck. Reluctantly he powered down his phone, cringing as it went dead.

"Thank you, Will. I appreciate you doing that. I want to do a communication exercise with the two of you today. Many times when a couple argues, they get so wrapped up in wanting to get their individual comments out they don't listen to their partner. You'll each have a chance to ask the other one a question. While the person answers you can't comment. You listen and really hear what they have to say. Once they give their answer you're allowed one follow-up comment/question. Understand?"

"Yes," I said.

Will nodded.

"Okay, ladies first. Bryson, what would you like to ask first?"

Without looking directly at Will, I said, "I'd like for him to explain exactly what he does in his office at home."

I knew it was a difficult question to start with but how Will spent his time in that room was a major concern. I'd told him before we got here today that Joanne was aware of what I'd seen.

Joanne turned her gaze on Will.

He cleared his throat. "I work."

A slight huff escaped me at hearing his answer.

"Would you elaborate a little more, please?" Joanne said.

"You really want a detailed description of my job?"

"The point of the exercise is twofold. We want to create an environment in which you feel safe to speak without fear of being interrupted and also give your partner the opportunity to really listen to what you have to say. It's difficult to work on communication if your answers are general and monosyllabic."

Will blew out a deep breath. "I supervise the construction of various projects—working with the client and architect, the budget, the hiring of subcontractors. I also go out and obtain new clientele."

"Bryson, you have one follow-up comment/question?"

"Besides work, how else does he spend his time in that room?"

Joanne and I both looked at Will.

He focused straight ahead. "I don't know what she's asking."

Joanne gave me a slight nod indicating I could ask my question again.

"I want to know what other activities besides work take place in that room?"

"Um . . . I play solitaire . . . and um . . . I don't know . . . occasionally I'll get on a couple of gaming sites, listen to music, or mindlessly surf the net. It helps me destress."

I couldn't believe Will wasn't coming clean on the screen slut incident. He knew I knew. He knew Joanne knew. He knew what a huge problem it was for me. A problem we needed to deal with openly and honestly.

Not wanting to push Will into becoming defensive, Joanne shifted focus.

"Okay, Will, what would you like to ask Bryson?"

"Nothing."

How in the world did he not have at least one question he'd been dying to ask me? Just because the last week seemed like old times, didn't mean things between us were fixed.

"Are you sure?" Joanne asked.

He nodded.

"Okay, Bryson, do you have another question?"

Deep down I knew it was going to be up to me to bring up Will's extracurricular porn activity. I was hoping he'd man up and admit it, save me from the embarrassment and shame of asking the question out loud.

"I'd like to know how often he uses porn to get off."

My insides quivered as I waited for Will to digest my words.

"What the fuck kind of question is that?" There was a bite in his tone.

I focused on the painting of a beach scene that hung above Joanne's desk as I felt Will's gaze burn into me. Was he delusional? He had to know this topic would be brought up.

"I'm not sitting here for this shit," he snapped.

Joanne attempted to diffuse the situation before it escalated further. "Let's stay calm and address this in a reasonable way. Bryson has every right to ask that question. It's obviously something that's been on her mind. Will, I don't want you to feel attacked, though."

"Too late for that. I'm done. I took valuable time out of my work day to come here. And you're accusing me of being some sort of pervert."

"Will, why are you acting this way? You knew we needed to talk about this," I said.

Joanne stepped in. "No one used that word or even implied it. It's not unusual for men or women to seek out those types of sites."

"Okay then . . . I get on porn sites. What of it? I'm a red-blooded male. I've been doing it ever since middle school."

The fact that he'd started getting on these sites at such a young age stunned me.

"Will, do you feel these sites have impacted your marriage?"

"Listen, let's not make this a big deal. You said it yourself, its normal. I'm not going out and having an affair for Christ sake."

Tears began to pool in my eyes. "It feels like you are to me, though."

"Will, look at your wife. What's your reaction?"

"I don't like it when she cries."

"Bryson, what would you like Will to do?"

"Stop looking at porn."

Focusing back on Joanne, he huffed. "Why? I'm not hurting anyone."

"You're hurting me," I whispered.

"Both of you have a responsibility in this relationship. If your actions hurt your partner then it's your job to decide what you're going to do about it."

"Jesus, if it bothers you that much, I'll stop."

Will and I looked at each other. I could see the struggle in his eyes. His hesitation cut right through me.

During the weeks that followed there was a noticeable improvement in the way Will and I interacted. At first it was awkward and at times felt forced. I worked hard on not holding a grudge about the porn. Will vowed to me during each session with Joanne that he was no longer using it to destress. Instead, he'd added a couple more days in the gym. Will explained that at this point in his life it was more the mindlessness of the activity that drew him to the sites and not because our sex life was lacking. As the holiday season came and went, my trust began to grow again. The last four months had been rough but with the new year, it felt like we were finally back on the path toward our fairy tale.

Will had been late for many events over the years—class, football practice, and dates with me. But he'd never been late for work . . . until today. Before the alarm sounded this morning, a familiar and missed nudge woke me from a deep sleep. Before I had a chance to clear my head, Will's fingers hooked around the hem of my T-shirt, pushing it up. The frequency of sex had slowed down considerably. Working on getting our relationship back had caused a kind of formality when it came to being intimate. This morning was the first time in a long time that we acted like a couple in love, each sending nonverbal permission to the other.

I couldn't stop giggling as Will zipped around getting dressed. Like he was making a mad dash out of the room before my overprotective father came in with his shotgun. I never remembered him being so focused and caught up in me that he lost track of time. It made me feel special and loved. Shoving his wallet in his back pocket, Will grabbed his keys and flew out the door. I lay in bed for a few extra minutes enjoying the feel of happiness before getting up and starting my usual routine.

After I showered, I pulled on a pair of jeans and my light blue long sleeve T-shirt along with my gray Nike sneakers. This morning would be spent doing laundry and ironing. Before heading downstairs for breakfast, I gathered up an armful of clothes and dumped them on the bench at the foot of our bed. Will was notorious for leaving things in his pockets. And not normal things like tissue or a piece of paper he used to jot a note on. I'd never forget the time I opened up the washing machine to find our clothes covered with a fine coating of sticky caramel from the handful of Werther's candy. So far my expedition hadn't discovered anything until I picked up the work jeans he'd worn the day before. I reached in and pulled out his dead cellphone. In his rush to leave this morning he'd forgotten it.

I knew there was no way Will would be able to make it through the day without his phone. People needed to be able to reach him especially when he was out on a build site. Since a dead cellphone wouldn't do him any good, I figured I'd let it charge while I did the laundry, then drop it off at his office. I transferred the clothes into the laundry basket and walked over to the nightstand where Will kept his phone charger. I plugged the phone in and within a few seconds it came to life.

As I reached for the laundry basket my gaze inadvertently landed on the lit screen. Will had the basic phone apps—calendar, weather, clock, calculator, music, and a couple construction-related ones. I was tempted to swipe to the next screen to see if there were any porn apps but I stopped myself. There was no way our relationship would survive if I kept doubting his word. Things between us were going too well for my insecurities to jeopardize it.

Suddenly, the main app screen disappeared, replaced by an incoming call. Will must have had the phone on silent. The number that popped up wasn't familiar. But that didn't give me pause. What kept my gaze glued to the screen was the name associated with the number, Val. It was one of those names that could go either way, male or female. As I stood trying to convince myself this Val was probably a *he*, the missed call and voicemail window appeared.

Even if Val was a woman that didn't mean anything. Will dealt with a lot of different people in construction. Granted, the majority seemed to be male but there were women in all aspects of the business. And then there are the assistants of the business associates who'd call for whatever reason. As I stood mesmerized by the name and number, a wave of shame washed over me. Things had been going well between us, Will was making a noticeable effort and then this morning was wonderful. We were finally getting past our bump in the road, so I didn't understand why I was letting my imagination run wild with doubts. My gaze shifted to the text message app, the number twelve hovered just above it indicating Will had some reading to do.

I stared at that number looming over the message bubble for an inappropriate amount of time. Scheming thoughts began to form in my head. It would be easy to tap the screen and open the app. Take a quick look at who was texting Will. Maybe this Val was among the texts. What if Val had some vital information he needed to tell Will as soon as possible? He sent the text and when there was no response he decided to call. It wasn't an invasion of privacy nor a comment on my trusting Will. It was almost mandatory as Will's wife to at least check the list of texts to see if Val's name showed up. If not, then I'd go about my day until the phone was fully charged and I could take it to Will.

It felt as if I'd been standing and staring for a lifetime, weighing out my options. I could twist and turn the reasons for checking the text messages as much as I wanted in order to justify taking a peek, but that didn't make it right. Deep down I knew my only intention for looking through Will's phone was to see if watching porn was his only offense.

The knots in my stomach that had been slowly forming for the past ten minutes tightened as my trembling finger hovered over the message app. I inhaled a sharp deep breath and tapped the screen. It was as if a spotlight came from out of nowhere, shining brightly, leading me right to the name Val. But what shut all my physical systems down was the brief preview of the message—*I miss you.* I looked at the words as if they were written in ancient Arabic. I don't know how long I stood there stuck in space and time before realization slammed into me.

It was like an out-of-body experience. My eyes witnessed my hands trembling before I felt the twitching. I saw my knees buckle before I felt the weakness set in. Instinctively my palm hit flat against the wall in an attempt to keep me from crashing to the floor. I don't remember not breathing, I just remember the sound of gasping when my lungs begged for oxygen.

"Bryson!" The sound of Will's voice floating up the stairs hit my ears.

Joanne taught me that words said in the heat of anger wouldn't accomplish anything. That I should take a few cleansing breaths and calm down. Then I'd be able to express myself in a clear and concise manner.

Fuck that!

Will's fingers wrap around my upper arm as he turned me around. "Babe, is everything okay?"

I jerked my arm from his grasp and stepped away. Looking down, he noticed the phone in my hand. By the time his gaze bounced up to mine, his expression was flat. But he quickly recovered in an attempt to look innocent.

"Thank god you found my phone. I thought I'd lost it," he said matter-of-factly. "I got all the way to work before I realized it wasn't in my pocket."

Will extended his arm waiting for me to place the phone in his palm.

My mouth hung open for a second before my brain ordered it to function. "Who is Val?"

"I'm not following you, babe. Listen, I gotta get back to the office. I just ran in to get my phone."

As I stood there still in shock, Will grabbed his phone and headed toward the door. Another second and he'd be out of sight and on his way back to the office. Somehow I forced my legs into action.

"Who is Val?" My voice sounded stronger and louder than I expected.

Will continued out of the bedroom and down the hallway. Picking up speed, I slipped past and positioned myself directly in front of him. He stopped abruptly.

I looked him in the eye and repeated. "Who. Is. Val?"

His shoulders shrugged nonchalantly as he gave me a relaxed smile. "Babe, I don't have time for twenty questions. Maybe when I get home tonight."

He tried to pass me but I blocked him.

"It's not a game, Will."

His calm expression dropped, replaced by an irritated one. "Nobody important."

"I'm going to need a little more than that."

He hesitated, his gaze scanning the hallway. "Val is a programmer for Virtual Life."

I narrowed my eyes but remained silent, forcing him to elaborate.

"I told you, I get on the site for mindless crap. They assign each user a programmer in case there's a problem."

"And this Val?"

"One of the programmers who helps people with the technical aspects of the site."

"Is Val a she?"

Cocking one brow, he pursed his lips like a smartass teenager. "Yeah, women can be programmers too, you know."

"Why does she have your phone number?"

"You have to give them your contact information. Sometimes it's easier for them to talk you through a problem rather than show you on screen."

"Why does she miss you?"

"What are you talking about?" He still wouldn't make direct eye contact.

"The first line of the text she says she misses you."

"You're going through my phone?" he said, defensively.

I certainly wasn't about to admit to him that I had tapped the texts on purpose. Besides, my snooping wasn't the issue. A strange woman was sending my husband texts telling him how much she missed him. I suddenly remembered the voicemail. Nausea bubbled up in my throat with just the thought of it.

"I accidentally hit the icon and the list opened up."

"Accidentally?" He accused.

"Really, Will? You're going to flip this around on me?"

"I'm not flipping anything. I just don't appreciate being accused of something I didn't do."

"Then let me read the text."

"I don't have time for this shit. I need to go." He tried to get past me again but I blocked him again.

"If you don't have anything to hide then let me read it. I promise not to take long."

"This is ridiculous." He huffed.

We stared at each other, deadlocked in the hallway of the home we'd built together. At this point there was no reason for me to read the text or listen to the voicemail. Will may not have verbally confessed anything but his actions spoke volumes.

"You could end it in a second just by handing me the phone."

"I don't know what else you want from me, Bryson. I work my ass off to provide for you. I put you in a beautiful home and car. I even took time out of my schedule to go to the fucking counselor. And it's still not enough for you. All I ask is for you to take care of the house and our kids. That is if we ever have kids."

I was standing strong until he sucker punched me with the last sentence. No matter how many times I heard the words, "The miscarriage wasn't your fault, Bryson," it never sunk in. There was always a part of me that felt I was the sole cause of losing our child and not being able to get pregnant again. I knew Will blamed me, I could see it in his eyes. He knew what my Achilles' heel was and used it at the first opportunity.

"So you haven't gotten anything out of this deal?" I said.

"I just don't think I've asked for that much in return for what I've given."

"I've supported you, been patient, and have tried to understand the things you've done. I let you touch me this morning and . . ." I choked back a sob. "I did it all because you're my husband and I love you. I never asked for the big house or the fancy car. All I ever wanted was your heart."

He shook his head and chuckled sarcastically. Will disappeared into a blurry haze as tears flowed quietly down my face draining me of all strength. I was on the verge of a complete collapse when he took a step forward trying to escape. Out of nowhere a bolt of energy fueled by hurt and anger took over my body and I snatched the phone from his hand.

"God dammit! Give me the phone back, Bryson!"

"I want to read the text!"

"You have a lot of fucking nerve!"

I tapped on the screen and scrolled through until I saw Val's name. Just as I was about to open the message, Will slapped the phone from my hand. Will and I had had arguments before but never had they come close to physical.

With his jaw clenched, he growled. "Fine! You want to know who Val is? She's a woman I met through VL and we hit it off. She asked for my number and I gave it to her. She has a boyfriend and she knows I'm married. It's just a friendship."

"Then let me read the text," I said through clenched teeth.

"For Christ sake, Bryson! I already told you everything. I haven't been online for a couple of days that's probably what the text is about." He paused for a moment. "I'm not giving you the phone. I haven't done anything to cause you to mistrust me. This is all on you and your insecurities."

Snatching the phone from the floor, he roughly pushed past me, stormed down the stairs, and out the front door. Even from inside the house the screech of the tires in the driveway pierced my ears.

Dazed, I walked back into the room and sat at the foot of the bed.

He promised he'd stop all non-work-related online activity.

I believed him.

He's been lying all this time.

Trying to clear my head and get my thoughts in order, something occurred to me. From the night I caught him in the office until this morning, Will has never actually apologized for any of his actions. He'd justified them and made excuses for them, but never appeared to be remorseful for them. He'd witnessed my tears and heard my gut-wrenching sobs, but neither made an impression on him. I felt like such an idiot thinking he cared about saving our marriage just as much as I did. A committed marriage was about two people coming together to make a life, each putting in the effort even during the times when they didn't feel like it.

These past five months had all been a lie. A façade. An act. Will played the part of the overworked dutiful husband seamlessly. But why? If he truly didn't want to be with me we could end it easy enough. There were no children involved. And after all these years he should know I wasn't a money grubber.

My head swirled with questions as piece after piece of my heart broke. I crawled under the comforter, pulling it over my head, and let the realization that our fairy tale had ended and there was no going back consume me.

chapter Eight

The passage of time ceased to exist while I was barricaded in my comforter cocoon. As I alternated between sobbing and screaming into my pillow, memories flooded my mind. I dissected every part of my history with Will in an attempt to discover any clue that might explain when the first misstep occurred.

Will admitted to having gone on porn sites since he was in middle school, which meant from the very get-go of us it was a part of our relationship, unbeknownst to me. I remembered after we had been dating for several months, Sophie was surprised we hadn't had sex yet. High school boys, especially athletes, have a ton of testosterone flowing through their veins. If they weren't ramming into an opponent on the field then they're ramming into some girl willing to give up that part of herself. Will never pressured me into sleeping with him. At the time I thought I was the luckiest girl around. My boyfriend was patient and sensitive to my needs. Now I'm wondering if that was all an act too. Had the past ten years been for show?

It's hard to put into words the feeling that hits you when you realize that the one person you gave your heart and soul to was an imposter. All at once you question your judgment, your choices, and your worth. After my body was completely drained of sobs the only thing I knew for certain was that I couldn't share any room in this house with this man at this point.

Funny how the mind and body kick into autopilot when your entire world implodes. Eventually, I dragged my tired body out of bed and took the liberty to move all of Will's clothes to the downstairs guestroom. Thank god when dreaming of our home we dreamed big.

I was unaware of how many trips it took me to make my room completely void of any evidence Will existed. I moved robotically between the two bedrooms until I dumped the last armful of clothes into his new sleeping quarters.

I mindlessly headed into the kitchen, turned on the Keurig, pulled out a stool from the breakfast bar, and sat down. Staring out the window across from me, I concentrated on the last leaf hanging from the River Burch tree in the backyard. For some reason I was mesmerized by it. A red robin landed on the branch and pecked a hole in the leaf. The bird flew away but the brown blade didn't let go. I watched as several gusts of wind whipped the leaf around, causing it to spin and twist. Then it snapped, unable to hold on any longer. The leaf swirled in the air, going up and down until finally it crashed to the ground. I could sympathize with that poor leaf.

The click of the Keurig turning off caught my attention but I remained glued to the seat. It was as if I didn't know what to do next, how to function. Like moving Will's clothes had zapped any energy from my body. My brain was drifting into sleep mode and I could feel myself shutting down. Everything moved in slow motion. Time was irrelevant. I didn't feel any sensation. No thoughts took root in my brain. Somehow I managed to climb the stairs to my room, crawl into bed, and pull the covers back over my head. And that's how I spent the rest of the day.

I didn't speak to or look at Will for the next two weeks. It's surprisingly easy to avoid a person who has betrayed you even when living in the same house. Will was gone all day at work and by the time he came home I was tucked away upstairs. Whenever I talked to my parents I acted as if all was normal. Sophie was on a business trip across the country. She sounded like she was having a great time and I didn't want to ruin it with my news. If truth be told, I just wasn't ready to let the world know my marriage was over.

During the two weeks my emotions bounced erratically all over the place. One minute I could be crumpled on the floor heaving with sobs. And the next minute I'd be walking around the house tossing and slamming things in anger. It was like I was beating up my own house. I had no frame of reference for a failed marriage. My parents had been together for twenty-five years and both sets of grandparents celebrated their fiftieth wedding anniversaries. Sophie's parents divorced when we were nine-years-old. To their credit they never put her in the middle of their problems. So I was at a loss as to what direction to go in.

Joanne was incredibly supportive and helpful. She told me to be gentle and allow myself to experience whatever emotions I needed to at the time. She gave me words of encouragement but was honest, saying time and distance were the only two things that would heal a shattered heart. She advised that a strong support system would make things easier but understood I needed to tell my family and friends in my own time. She also helped me make a list of the practical things I needed to consider if I divorced Will, like how would I support myself and where would I live.

Ending a marriage was complicated, both emotionally and financially. With the ebb and flow of my emotions, I still had to consider the practicality of the situation. I basically went from my parents' house to living with my husband, I was twenty-six, never held a job, had an MBA but wasn't really trained for anything. Will was definitely in the driver's seat when it came to money matters. Not only did he earn the sole income but he handled the more involved financial aspects like insurances, investments, and retirement funds. I kept reminding myself I wasn't incapable of learning or handling new things. But when you discover the man you thought you'd spend the rest of your life with doesn't want you, it annihilates your self-esteem and worth.

My pride didn't allow me to want any of Will's money, I just wanted to stay in my home. Every inch of this house was a part of me. I took time and planned the look of each room. And my kitchen was not only the heart of the house but my heart as well. As I went over the logistics and basic numbers of keeping up a house this size on my own I realized it was impossible.

It was nine o'clock at night and I was already in my pink and gray flannel pajamas sitting in bed. With a stack of papers fanned out in front of me, I was going over the monthly budget, attempting one last time to make the numbers do what I wanted them to do. I'd been looking at them for so long my eyes were blurry and my brain scrambled. The only way I'd be able to stay in my home was to stay with Will. Maybe we could live together like we'd been doing for the past two weeks, him downstairs while I took the upstairs.

I leaned back on my pillow and closed my eyes. Was I making too much out of the porn sites and Val text? Was labeling it cheating wrong? My head kept trying to justify what he'd done. My heart wouldn't let me believe what he'd done. But my gut kept telling me what he'd done was cheating. And I wasn't sure if I could get past that feeling and learn to live with it. My stomach growled with hunger, which made me realize I'd not eaten the entire day. Will was already home but my stomach wouldn't shut up. I figured I could dash downstairs, make a sandwich, and get back up here without running into him.

I crept down the stairs trying not to make any noise. I took in a deep breath and forced my legs to move across the floor as quickly as possible. As I passed the hallway that led to the guestroom, I heard his deep voice and laughter. Before I knew what was happening I found myself parked outside of the bedroom door.

"You look fucking hot tonight," Will said.

I didn't hear anyone respond. He was either on his phone or online and using his headsets.

"No, she's still pouting. I kind of like it in the guestroom, though. Means I can spend more time with you uninterrupted." He paused, followed by a chuckle. "I doubt it. She wouldn't be able to support herself." Pause. "I never did, really. She was more my parents' idea than mine. Fit the role."

His words pummeled me in the gut, my stomach taken over by spasms. My knees weakened, almost causing me to fall against the wall. I couldn't think less of Will at the moment but I still didn't want to believe our entire life together was a lie.

"Mmm . . . I wish I could feel you in real life." Pause. "We could meet halfway." Pause. "Don't worry about that, baby. I'll pay for everything."

I slapped my hand over my mouth in an attempt to stifle a gasp. He was actually making plans with this woman. If my heart didn't want to accept Will's cheating before, it sure as hell was being forced to now. Not being able to stomach any more of the one-sided conversation, I walked back upstairs. My growling stomach was quiet and hollow. I couldn't wrap my head around what I'd just eavesdropped on.

Will never loved me?

How could I have been with him for ten years and not felt this? I remembered there being times during our relationship when I was pushed aside, not a priority. I always blamed it on the amount of pressure Will put on himself. I understood and learned to adapt. He always wanted to perform at the highest level possible for his coach and for his parents. But other memories of us as a couple . . . the way he looked at me, smiled at me, made love to me. Those couldn't have all been performances too. Will's parents expected a lot from him, especially since Alex was a lost cause in their eyes. I couldn't believe that my in-laws gave their blessing to our union just because I fit their description of what a daughter-in-law should be.

I shoved all the papers off my bed before climbing under the covers. I rolled onto my side, curling up into the fetal position. My life with Will flashed through my mind like one of those picture flip books. Our first year of dating Will ran so hot and cold. One minute he'd be all over me and the next he was too busy to bother with me. I was so nervous on our wedding day. I never could figure it out but something felt off. At the time I excused it as normal new bride jitters. I didn't know if I'd convinced myself or let others do the job. But looking back, I'm not so sure I chose him.

Time flies when you're reevaluating and readjusting your life. Three months and an entire season had passed. Will and I continued with our unconventional living arrangements. He tried talking to me whenever we were in the common areas—the family room, the kitchen, the entryway, the backyard. The chatter was never about us. He'd talk as if everything was normal. The atmosphere was weird to say the least. Will was keeping up appearances and I went along for the time being. To the outside world, including our families, we were still the perfect couple.

I confided in Sophie, of course. She was extremely supportive, offering me the extra room at her place and helping me get job ready. But fear was an all-consuming irrational monster. It was hard for my best friend to understand why I hadn't left the marriage yet.

"It's pretty cut and dried to me. He's a slimy motherfucker who used you. Leave," she said.

Sophie had kidnaped me one evening for some well overdue girl time. Since she had the next day off and there was drinking involved, I planned on spending the night at her place. We were sitting on her patio enjoying the cool mid-April night air. Each of us snuggled under a lightweight fleece blanket, holding mugs of coffee laced with Bailey's.

"Sophie, it's not that easy."

"Sweetie, I realize you have limited experience in the men department but you can't let that stop you."

Sophie didn't believe in monogamy. She thought it was an unnatural concept. But she did believe in honesty and if you made a commitment you stuck by it.

"The reason I haven't left yet is not because Will is the only man I've been with. It's because Will is the only man I thought I'd ever be with." I paused, swallowing the lump in my throat. "And it doesn't matter what he's done or how much pain he's caused or even if it's all been an act for him. I wasn't acting." Tears welled up in my eyes. "I've thought this way for ten years. I can't stand to be around him but I also can't just flip a switch and let go as if everything had been a lie."

Sophie looked at me blinking back her own tears and said, "I'm so sorry you're hurting but I get where you're coming from. Just know I'm here when you're ready."

I nodded my thanks.

As the night continued we sat sipping more Bailey's than coffee while Sophie told me about her latest business trip adventure. It felt good to hear what was going on in her life and how happy she was in her career. Sophie may not have had a special man whom she wanted to have a future with but she knew who she was and was confident in her abilities. I envied that.

Mid-April soon became mid-May, closely followed by mid-June, July and August. Eight months of living like strangers had passed. I knew something had to give and it had to be me. Will seemed perfectly content with the arrangement. His standing as a good husband and son were still strong in the community and in the eyes of his parents. Plus, he got to spend time screwing his cartoon cunt in the Virtual Life world whenever he wanted to. Not to mention other screen skanks.

With Sophie's encouragement I decided to start looking for a job. I needed to gauge where I was in the market in terms of any usable skill set. I mean, I had an MBA from a respected university. Maybe there was more opportunity out there than I thought.

"So, Mrs. Forsyth, your resume is a bit . . . thin." Mr. Hawkins pointed out.

The pudgy and balding older man sitting behind the desk eyed me up and down. The job was for an administrative assistant at Hawkins Insurance. Not the most exciting job out there but my life had enough excitement in it.

I fidgeted with the strap of my purse, hoping Mr. Hawkins couldn't see over his desk. "Yes, Sir, I realize that. But I'm a quick learner and my computer skills are good."

"I really need someone with more experience or any experience for that matter." He chuckled condescendingly.

"It says here . . ." She pointed to the spot on my resume with her dark blue nail. ". . . That you graduated two years ago from Newberry. Whatcha been doin'?"

My gaze bobbed from her neon pink lips to her yellow hair that was brighter than the sun.

"I got married."

"Uh-huh."

This chick couldn't have been more than nineteen years old and she was already a manager at the cellphone store.

"So were you like taking care of your kid or something for two years?" Her pitch shot sky high on the last two words.

I glanced down as my heart felt a twinge. "No, I wasn't taking care of my child."

She picked up my resume with the tip of her shiny nails and deposited it into the drawer next to her. "I'll let you know if anything opens up that matches your particular skills."

"The ad said you were looking for a sales associate. I have an MBA. I can talk cellphones with people."

"Yeah, we prefer our associates to have some background in sales not basketball. But I'll keep your resume for future reference." She patted the side of the drawer.

"I just need someone to give me a chance."

"It's probably not going to be us, though." Susan, the manager, gave me an apologetic smile.

I thought shifting gears toward something I loved would give me better luck at finding a job. So, I applied at one of Charleston's most popular downtown restaurants, Tommy Condon's.

"I'm sorry, Bryson. It's just the restaurant is so fast-paced that we really need wait staff that know their stuff. Once you get some experience under your belt, please come back and reapply."

At least she was the nicest one to tell me I sucked.

Three days and three 'no thanks' later, I wasn't exactly feeling top notch about my job prospects. I knew it would be hard getting hired since I had no experience. But how the hell was I going to get any if no one wanted to give me the opportunity? After the last no thank you, I decided to head home.

I still had a couple of hours before the threat of Will being here was a problem. I never knew when he'd come strolling in. Some nights he was home at his usual time. But there had been a few nights I heard the front door open and close around midnight. Since the August heat and my week were unbearable, I decided to jump into the pool and a glass of wine.

After changing into my orange bikini, I wrapped a fluffy towel around my body and headed downstairs. I made a pit stop in the kitchen to grab the wine and went out to the backyard. Before plunging into the wine I decided to do a few laps around the pool to cool off. I dropped the towel on the lounge chair and dove in. My skin felt immediate relief from the scorching sun. It was quiet and peaceful under water. If I didn't have to breathe, I'd stay submerged forever. As the water splashed around me, I tried to clear my head of the past three days, the past year, and all the rejection.

Three laps around had tired me out and built up a mighty thirst. I swam up to the edge of the pool where I'd placed the wine glass and bottle. My eyes squinted from the bright afternoon sun as I lifted my face and wiped the water away. Half blinded, I reached for the bottle of High Tide wine from the local Deep Water Vineyard and poured a full glass. The light-bodied red Muscadine flavor tickled the back of my throat as it made its way down. I held the glass between my hands, closed my eyes, and leaned my head back against the pool, soaking in the warm sun.

Glass number one went down pretty quick. Glass number two was almost gone when I realized I probably needed to slow down. I just wanted to get a buzz as quickly as possible and forget how unwanted and lonely I felt. It wasn't until I tried to get out of the pool that I realized how buzzed I'd gotten. I set my glass down, grabbed the rail, and pulled myself up the steps. My body swayed from side-to-side as I headed toward the lounge chair where I'd tossed my towel. As I tried to wrap the towel around me, I lost my balance, stumbling back against a hard surface. I looked down to see two tan muscular arms holding the towel around my body.

"You okay?" The deep voice rumbled in my ear.

I attempted to push off but he didn't let me.

Clearing my throat, I said, "I'm fine. You can let go."

His arms loosened, allowing me to take a step away. When I turned around, my slightly blurry gaze met his dark brown eyes. Will must have had the same idea I had, to end a hot day with a cool swim. He was in his navy and light blue long board shorts, his bare chest already glistening under the sun. My gaze traveled over his broad shoulders, down the planes of his cut chest, to his toned abs. It had been more than eight months since I'd seen his body or anybody's body for that matter. He must have been hitting the gym even more because the indentions were deeper and the ripples were rip-plin'. His hair was cut super short for the summer and a five o'clock shadow was working his chiseled jawline. Will was a rat bastard but a sexy rat bastard.

Swallowing hard, I looked back up and was met by dark brown eyes roaming over my body.

I pulled the towel tighter around my body and said, "You're home early."

"I told my crew to knock off since its Friday and hot as hell."

I blinked a few times trying to clear the fuzz from my brain.

Whipping my head around, I searched for my wine. "I'll get out of your way."

"Don't leave on my account."

"It's okay. I was done."

Found my wine!

I picked up the bottle, clutching it and the towel close to my chest.

"I always liked that orange bikini."

Between the wine, the heat, and the fact that I'd not had a compliment in forever, his words caused a slight tingle in my stomach.

I took a step toward the house but Will shifted, forcing me to stop.

"Thanks," I said, not making eye contact.

This was the closest I'd been to Will in months. He smelled great . . . sweet like black licorice. I needed to remove myself from this situation. I was too buzzed, feeling lonely, and had a sudden craving for candy.

"You're hot." His voice was low and husky.

"Yeah . . . Well, I've been out here for a while."

A throaty chuckle hit my ears, followed by the touch of his fingertips grazing the shell of my left ear. In my foggy head I turned away but in reality I didn't move. I held on to the neck of the wine bottle as if my life depended on it. The back of his hand slid down my neck until it reached the strap of my swimsuit.

"Will, don't."

He leaned down and whispered, "I miss you, Bry."

My eyes squeezed shut as I summoned the memories of all the pain this man had inflicted on me.

The tips of his fingers ran over my strap. "I miss the way you feel underneath me."

I bit down hard on my bottom lip but still didn't move. My head was screaming at me to run and not stop until I was behind the door of my own bedroom. But my heart and body weren't listening. It felt too good to have a strong rough hand glide over my skin and a deep voice in my ear.

"I miss being inside of you, Bry."

Will's fingers continued their trek along my jawline until they found my chin. My eyes opened as he tilted my head back. Slowly he lowered his lips toward mine and hovered, waiting for me to give him permission. Goosebumps pricked at my skin as each pulse point throbbed. It had been so long since I'd felt what it was like to be wanted . . . desired . . . and I missed it.

Wine mixed with licorice filled the air around us as I parted my lips. Once Will got the signal he didn't waste time. His hands cupped my face as his lips and tongue got right to work devouring my mouth. At some point both the bottle and towel I was holding made it to the ground, freeing my hands to wrap around Will's neck. My body was on fire but this time it didn't have anything to do with the Charleston summer.

My legs were like jello and about to give way when I felt my feet come off the ground. Will's large hands had made their way down to my ass. As he lifted me effortlessly, I wrapped my legs around his waist. He walked toward the house. We didn't say a word. We didn't even come up for air. Once inside Will broke the kiss, lowering me to the floor. Within seconds the top of my bathing suit was ripped from my chest, replaced with Will's mouth. He was like a crazed animal sucking the life out of me. It felt incredible having his hands and mouth all over my body.

Will yanked on the two tiny strings that held the bottom half of my bathing suit together. The skimpy material fell to the floor. He quickly stepped out of his board shorts, pushed me down onto our tan soft leather sofa, and fell between my legs. With his head buried in the crook of my neck, his hips rocked. Closing my eyes, I concentrated on the feel of his naked skin gliding across mine. My muscles tensed as my legs tightened around his hips. Grabbing hold of his dick, he pushed inside of me.

Our body heat began to overwhelm me. My lungs struggled for oxygen. I tried to shift and turn my head to get some air but Will's weight had me pinned down. Underneath me the leather was hot and sticky. Above me Will was hot and sticky. He lifted his body off of mine as his thrusts got harder and faster. It had been a long time since I'd been in this position. With the amount of wine I'd consumed, my memory could have been playing tricks on me. But the sensation of Will inside me felt foreign and strange.

I needed to look into his familiar dark brown eyes and see some semblance of the connection I thought we once shared. What we had couldn't all have been an act. My gaze traveled up his bulging biceps as he hovered over me. Sweat beaded along every inch of his torso. His jaw clenched, causing the veins to strain against his skin. I took in a deep breath and looked up into a pair of tightly shut eyes.

Digging my fingers into his arm, I said, "I need to look in your eyes."

He groaned and growled in response but never opened his eyes. In an instant, my mind cleared and my senses returned. All the suspicions, broken vows, disdain, and betrayal of the past several months washed over me. No wonder his dick felt strange inside of me. While I was screwing Will, he was screwing someone else in his head.

Placing my palms flat on his chest, I shoved. "Will, stop!"

He ignored my plea.

I slapped his chest and screamed, "Get off!"

He continued pounding into me, his pace relentless. This was all my fault. Even though I had Sophie and my family if I needed them, the isolation I experienced had been festering since losing the baby. Will and I were drifting apart at that point. And even though he was acting, I missed the deep connection, fake or not. I let my loneliness dictate my actions today. Tears seeped out the corner of my eyes as my body reacted instinctively to the sensation of Will exploding inside of me.

chapter Nine

It was a stupid horrible mistake fueled by alcohol and loneliness. The blame was all mine. After Will collapsed on top of me, I made up the excuse of having to go to the bathroom. Wiggling out from underneath him, I slid off the sofa and ran upstairs to my room. I never went back down to see him and he never came up looking for me.

I was so ashamed that I let things go as far as they did. I sensed something wasn't right the second Will entered my body. When he wouldn't open his eyes and look at me, the lightbulb went off in my head. At this point it had become second nature for me to dissect every little aspect of our relationship. As I lay in bed I racked my brain trying to remember if Will ever looked at me during sex. It's one of those actions that you assume happened but when you start to think on it you can't be sure. Had he been fantasizing about other women our entire relationship?

Next month marked the one year anniversary of the first stumble in my marriage. Emotionally and physically I felt every second of the twelve months and then some. But logically I marveled at the fact an entire year had already passed. A sizable portion of my life had been spent obsessing over a man who clearly couldn't care less about me and my feelings. Will appeared to be content with our current arrangement.

"She was more my parents' idea than mine. Fit the role."

I was still holding on to the last little thread of hope, wanting to believe that the man I'd been with for ten years wanted to be with me. That he did love me and wanted a future with me. That our entire life together wasn't simply to please his parents. But as I took a long hard look at the facts the thread unraveled.

There had been times over the course of our relationship in which I felt Will was happy not spending time with me. But then out of the blue he'd do something super sweet and all would be forgotten and forgiven. He went to a couple of counseling sessions but he didn't take them seriously. He's not made any move to make amends. He's stayed holed up in his office or bedroom continuing to contact women with no regard to how it made me feel.

What a slap in the face.

I tossed and tuned most of the night realizing the time had come for this weird living arrangement to end. Will and I had been floating in limbo long enough. For eleven months I'd been wading through so many confusing emotions too scared to pull the trigger on any solid action. I wanted the life I thought I had back. But you can't have what never really existed.

The next morning I rolled out of bed and slipped my indigo green silk robe over the matching long pajama pants and white T-shirt. I gathered my hair and twisted it into a messy side ponytail before heading downstairs. The scent of coffee drifted out from the kitchen. I knew I hadn't preprogrammed the Keurig to turn on this morning. Will hadn't been thoughtful enough when we were "happily" married to have coffee ready for me in the morning so I doubt he'd set it up to turn on. My stomach churned with the only other possibility. Will hadn't left for work yet.

Shit!

My mind was so preoccupied with my decision that I didn't even consider looking out the bedroom window to see if his car was still in the driveway. In a way, it was good I didn't know he was still home. Otherwise, I would have driven myself crazy the entire day planning what to say. This way I'll just go in there and state very plainly that yesterday was a big mistake. We needed to move on, to legally separate and look into what the divorce process entailed. Beyond that I had no idea what would happen. But I had to move forward even if it was one step at a time.

As I entered the kitchen, I saw Will's silhouette in front of the large over-the-sink window. As I walked farther in I could tell he was leaning back against the counter drinking his coffee. He stopped mid sip when he caught my gaze.

"Good morning," he said, lowering his mug just enough to speak.

I could feel his eyes on me as I walked past to start my coffee. "I didn't know you were still home."

He didn't respond.

Placing my mug under the spout, I popped the K-cup in and pressed the large button. The air was still and quiet except for the buzz of the machine alternating with Will's sipping. I stood focusing on the black liquid dripping into the mug. The click of the machine cutting off startled me. I grabbed the mug, walked across the kitchen to the breakfast bar, and sat down on one of the stools. I needed to feel grounded. I took a long sip of coffee before placing the mug in front of me.

Glancing over at Will, I said, "About yesterday . . ."

He pushed off from the counter and put his mug in the sink. "Yeah, about that . . . I'm glad we're finally getting back on track."

My eyebrows shot into my forehead as my jaw went slack. "Back on track?"

He walked over and stood on the other side of the bar across from me.

Looking down, he smirked. "I knew once you were done pouting, you'd realize how ridiculous you've been."

There were a whole lot of references to me in his sentence. The muscles in my shoulders tensed. I needed to stay calm and not get emotional.

My grip tightened around the mug. "Let's get a couple of things straight. I haven't been pouting and the only thing I've realized is we need to start the divorce process."

He tried to keep his expression neutral but I could see the vein in his forehead was on the verge of throbbing.

Will huffed. "What the fuck are you talking about?"

"Are you kidding me?" I paused, needing to hold my emotions in check. Not wanting to ignite Will's anger and have this conversation spin out of control, my goal was to keep all statements neutral and non-accusatory. I took in a deep calming breath and continued. "Will, we've been having serious issues for a long time. It takes two people to make a marriage work."

He took a step back from the bar, placing one hand on his hip while the other hand massaged his chin. "Give me one good reason why you want a divorce."

His complete denial of our situation was mind-blowing. Like flipping a switch on a nuclear reactor, my anger and frustration soared from zero to a hundred and eighty in two point three seconds flat.

"Jesus, man, are you totally delusional? You've lied and cheated. You don't take the counseling seriously and won't meet me halfway on anything."

His jaw clenched while the forehead vein was in full throb.

Dark brown eyes pierced mine. "For the last fucking time. I. Did. Not. Cheat. Have I talked to a few women online? Yes. Have I texted? Yes. Have I gone on porn sites? Yes. What guy hasn't? You act like I've gone around shoving my dick in every woman on the east coast."

Will's definition of cheating was the polar opposite of mine. And we were both standing firm in our belief. At this point, we'd had this same circular conversation ad nauseam. There was no point in trying to have a mature and civil discussion with this man.

Shoving the stool back, I stood and stomped over to the sink. I turned on the hot water and washed both coffee mugs, giving myself something to do while I calmed my nerves. When I turned back around, Will's back was to me, both palms flat on the countertop, with his head hanging between his shoulders.

Drying my hands with the dish towel, I said, "Why did you marry me?" I was surprised at how small my voice sounded. Almost childish. "Was it all for your parents?"

His head rose but he didn't turn to face me. "Nobody forces me to do anything."

"Then why?"

I heard a deep intake of breath as he hesitated, no doubt wanting to choose his words wisely.

He faced me but didn't make eye contact. "Because I thought it would be mutually beneficial."

His words felt like a direct hit to my soul. I thought after what I'd seen and heard from him prior to today I was more immune to the effect of his words. But I guess there were still a few pieces of my heart that hadn't been shattered.

"Wrong answer," I whispered.

"What do you want from me, Bryson?!"

"I want you to say you married me because you loved me! Because you couldn't imagine living a life without me! I want you to be the man I thought you were!" We locked eyes and I saw the true honest answer. "You never were, were you?"

"I've always taken good care you."

"It's true isn't it? You married me because your parents wanted you to. I was a good girl who came from a good family. Your mother always said we looked perfect together. Beautiful couple would have beautiful children to carry on the well-respected Forsyth name. We completed the perfect family portrait. And what was your prize, Will? What was so fucking enticing to make you give up any hope of truly falling in love with someone?"

His expression was hard and his gaze cold. I was astounded by his lack of emotion. Even if he never loved me, I thought us being intimately connected for all these years would evoke some reaction as he watched the last few pieces of my heart disintegrate. But there was nothing. Not even a subtle gesture of comfort or sorrow.

Then it dawned on me what the tradeoff had been. The deal that his parents had cut with him all those years ago. "You'd inherit the entire company, shutting Alex completely out."

Will opened his mouth to speak several times before forming any words. "I told you, no one forces me into anything. I married you because I wanted to. Yesterday wasn't a mistake. There's obviously still something between us. We can make this work."

Bryson, he didn't deny your theory.

The mind and emotions are tricky beasts. Often they're at odds with each other. One screaming at you to wake up and look at the facts of a situation. The other playing on your weakness, your soft spot, your heart. During my life with Will there were times when my mind tried to shake some sense into me but I allowed my emotions to drown it all out. This past year my emotions worked hard to narrow down the cause of our problems to one singular thing. I fooled myself into believing that our downfall was due to Will's online world and all the lies that accompanied it. But the reality was that every red flag that had been raised over the ten years was only a small symptom. The reason Will and I will never see a future together was because there was never a Will and I.

Beads of sweat appeared along his forehead and upper lip. "I'll give up all the online stuff if it's so damn important to you."

I'd known for months Will didn't want to give up the cyber world he'd created. Up until this moment I thought he was just being stubborn and bratty. But seeing his physical reaction showed me that he relied on that world a lot.

With tears pooling in my eyes, I wrapped my arms around myself, hiding my trembling hands. "I'll pack my things today and stay with Sophie while we figure out the details."

"Don't do this to us, Bryson."

I looked at Will through blurry eyes. "It's already been done."

Balling his hand into a fist, Will pounded it hard against the granite countertop. He spun around and stormed out of the room. Seconds later the walls and windows vibrated in anger with the slamming of the front door. The sound of screeching tires echoed in my ears as Will peeled out of the driveway and down the street.

I was proud of myself for holding it together for as long as I did. For the first time in my life I was listening to what my gut was telling me. The divorce needed to happen. I was terrified to be on my own, embarrassed that my marriage was now a statistic, and sad that a person who'd been a huge part of my life would be gone.

Without warning my knees buckled, sending me crashing to the floor. A sharp pain pierced the pit of my stomach followed by a gush of sobs. Relief mixed with doubts swirled around my head as my new reality forced its way into my life. Determined not to wallow in self-pity, I allowed only five minutes to pass before peeling myself off the floor.

Feeling the need for a little reassurance, I picked up the house phone and called Joanne.

"Hello, Joanne Foster's office. This is Morgan. How may I help you?" I already felt better hearing the sweet voice of Joanne's assistant.

Clearing my throat, I said, "Hey, Morgan, this is Bryson Forsyth."

"Hi, how are you?"

"I've been better." My voice sounded froggy from the sobs. "I was wondering if Joanne had an opening today."

"I'm going to put you on hold while I check."

"Thank you."

There was a click followed by sleep-inducing jazz music. My eyelids were just about to close when Morgan came back on the line.

"Bryson, we had a cancellation. If you can be here in a half hour, it's yours."

"I'll be there. Thank you." I hung up the phone and headed upstairs.

There was no time for a shower, so I ended up just splashing water on my face. I had to multi-task if I were going to make the appointment on time. As I brushed my teeth, I swept blush over my cheeks. Applied a light coat of mascara to my lashes while gliding pale pink gloss over my lips. Rummaging through the closet, I grabbed my dark red leggings and long black boyfriend shirt. While redoing my side ponytail, I stepped into my black flats.

I glanced at the clock and saw I had a couple of minutes before I needed to leave. As I was slipping a few bangles around my wrist my cellphone rang. I wondered if Joanne wasn't able to see me after all. A string of missed calls covered the screen. There were several from an unknown number. Then my mom's name popped up, followed by Sophie's, and Will's mom. All had left voicemails.

I clicked on Sophie's first.

"Bryson, pick up." Her words were clipped.

I clicked my mom's message.

"Sweetheart, you need to call me back as soon as possible. I love you." Mom's voice was shaky.

The first thought that popped into my head was that something had happened to Daddy. My chest tightened, trapping air in my lungs. I didn't even bother checking the other messages. I was gripping the phone so tightly my fingertips had turned white. Sophie sounded the calmest so I chose to get my information from her. I pressed the Call Back button. She answered before the end of the first ring.

"Bryson, thank god you got my message."

"What's going on? Is my dad okay?" I choked back a sob.

"Are you at home?" She blurted out.

"Yes, but what's . . ."

"I'm coming to get you now."

"Sophie?!"

"When no one was able to reach you, your mom called me." She paused taking in a shaky breath. "I didn't want to tell you over the phone."

"Tell me what?"

"Will's been in a car accident."

I didn't know if the phone slipped from my hand or I gently placed it down. All I remembered was the sound of Sophie's fading voice as the blood drained from my body.

chapter
Ten

I swung the door open before Sophie brought the car to a complete stop in front of the emergency room entrance. I had laser focus. Adrenaline propelled me forward as I rushed past the parked ambulances and medics, and through the crowded waiting area to the nurse's station.

Gasping for air, I said, "My husband was in a car accident."

The gray-haired older woman looked up at me with sympathetic eyes. "What's the name, dear?"

"Forsyth. Will Forsyth."

"Bryson!" Mom's voice shot across the waiting area.

The expression on my parents' faces as they walked toward me caused my lungs to deflate. Mom reached me first, wrapping her arms around me in a comforting hug.

"Have they told you anything?" Dad asked.

I shook my head. "No, not yet. The nurse is checking now."

The air around me filled with sobs from Will's mom as she and his dad appeared out of nowhere behind me.

"Thank God someone finally got in touch with you, Bryson." Mrs. Forsyth choked out.

As I turned to face her, she enveloped me in a hug.

Pulling away, I said, "How did everyone find out before me?"

Will's father looked unable to speak at the moment, so Dad explained. "The accident happened in front of the construction offices."

Out the corner of my eye I saw Mr. Forsyth step away from our little crowd followed by his wife.

"Jonathan saw the moment of impact, Bryson." Dad's green eyes were full of fear and sadness. The kind only another parent whose child was in pain could comprehend.

"Oh my god," I whispered.

I was trying like hell to keep my composure. Up until I talked with Sophie, I still felt the aftermath of the argument I'd had with Will. Images of our last moments flashed through my mind. Remembering the screeching tires as he tore out of the driveway, I wondered if the anger he felt was responsible for the accident. The anger caused by my words.

"Mrs. Forsyth," the older nurse said, tearing me from my thoughts.

"Where's my husband? Is he okay?"

"Doctor Bernard will be out in just a few seconds to update you on your husband's condition."

"How can he update me when I don't know anything in the first place? Why can't you at least tell me if he's alive or de . . ." I choked back the word.

I couldn't allow myself to go to that place. Guilt already had a tight grip around my throat. If Will didn't make a full recovery, it would suffocate me.

As the nurse promised, the doctor appeared seconds later.

"Mrs. Forsyth?" He was tall, thin, and looked to be not that much older than Will and I.

Both sets of parents, Sophie, and I crowded around the doctor. I was so caught up in trying to find out information I hadn't even noticed Sophie had joined us.

"I'm Doctor Bernard." He extended his hand to me and we shook.

"How's W . . . ill?" My voice cracked on his name.

"Let's go over to this corner where we can sit and talk."

Doctor Bernard gently touched my elbow, guiding me over to an empty corner of the emergency room.

"Please tell me Will is going to be alright."

The doctor sat next to me as my family and Sophie stood off to the side, close enough to hear.

"Mr. Forsyth . . ."

"Will. His name is Will," I said, tightening my grip on the edge of the arm rest.

"Will has a torn ACL on his right leg." Pursing my lips, my eyes narrowed. "That's the anterior cruciate ligament. He'll need surgery to repair it. He has a mild concussion and multiple contusions as well as cuts on his face, chest, and arms. But no internal injuries."

"He's going to be okay?"

The doctor gave me a smile and nodded. "Will's a lucky man."

A chorus of audible sighs rang out in our corner.

"He'll have some serious rehab ahead of him. But with his age and his good physical condition, I see no reason why he wouldn't make a full recovery."

The flood gates opened and tears of relief rolled out of me. "Can I see him?"

"You'll need to sign consent forms before the surgery, then I'll have the nurse take you back. We have him sedated to make him comfortable until an OR opens up."

Doctor Bernard made his way through the barrage of thank you's as he walked back up to the nurse's station. A moment later a lady dressed in scrubs appeared with a fistful of papers for me to fill out. I probably should have read each form first. I could have been signing my life away for all I knew. It didn't matter. The only thing that mattered was seeing Will and letting him know we were all here for him. The second I signed the last form I jumped out of the chair and took them to the desk where the nurse in scrubs was waiting.

"All set?" She asked, taking the stack of papers from me.

I nodded.

"I'm Lisa, by the way."

"I'm Bryson. Nice to meet you."

Extending her arm, Lisa pointed me in the direction of two large swinging double doors. "Too bad it's not under better circumstances."

"Tell Will I love him very much, Bryson." Mrs. Forsyth called after me as I followed the nurse to the back.

Lisa escorted me into one huge room that was divided into sections. Lining one wall was different types of medical equipment and another nurse's station. The other wall was a series of curtained-off cubbies with patients waiting to be taken back for surgery.

Stopping at the fourth cubby, Lisa pulled back the curtain. Doctor Bernard said Will was banged up pretty severely and he wasn't exaggerating. My head had been in such a tailspin from the moment Sophie called to the moment the doctor said Will would be okay, I hadn't had a chance to think about my reaction once I saw him for the first time.

A slight gasp escaped me when I saw Will lying on the stretcher, flat on his back draped in a white sheet and blanket. I was thankful he was so out of it from the medicines they'd already pumped into him. A large bruise covered almost the entire left side of his face. From the temple to his jaw was a mixture of deep purples and shades of red. The right side of his face was almost untouched, only a reddish patch above his eye was visible along with a cut at the corner of his mouth. Bruises and scrapes ran along both arms. IV lines as well as various cables ran to monitors he was hooked up to.

My vision blurred as my body swayed bumping into Lisa.

She grabbed my arm and kept me from falling. "Are you okay?"

I straightened. "Yeah. I think everything hit me all at once. I'll be fine."

Lisa looked at me with concern. "Are you sure?"

"Yeah, I'm sure. Thank you."

Once I felt stable enough, I walked up beside Will and gently brushed the dark brown hair off his forehead. He didn't resemble the man I'd been married to or the one I'd asked for a divorce from this morning. He looked like the boy I'd fallen for all those years ago at Garrison High. Back then with Will by my side I always felt safe and protected. We were going to walk hand-in-hand into a future full of hope and promise. I just didn't know back then that it was all a big show.

Will turned his head slightly in my direction as his eyelids flickered opened. Dark brown eyes met green watery ones. I gave him a small smile.

"Bry . . . s . . . on," he said groggily.

"Hey."

"I'm so . . ."

"Don't try to talk right now. You need to rest. You're in the hospital. You were in a car accident. They have to do surgery but you're going to be as good as new before you know it."

Even though his eyes were glazed over I could tell he understood. Will turned his left hand over so his palm was facing up on the bed. Glancing down, I saw he still had his wedding ring on. His fingers wiggled and I knew instinctively he wanted me to remove the ring for safe keeping. I slid the ring from his finger and held it in my palm. Placing my hand on top of his, I gave it a reassuring squeeze. No matter how much hurt and disappointment had passed between us, I didn't want any harm to come to Will. I wanted each of us to achieve our dreams even if they weren't together anymore.

The anesthesiologist came into the area and pushed another drug into the IV line that knocked Will out completely. They rolled him away while I returned to the waiting room to update Sophie and the family. As I walked up I was surprised to see a police officer had joined them. All the men stood as I approached.

"Bryson, this is officer Dickson," Dad said.

I took the officer's extended hand and shook it. "I'd say it's nice to meet you but . . ."

The officer chuckled. "I completely understand. I hear your husband is going to make a full recovery."

"Yes, it looks that way. Thank, God."

"I know it's been a rough day but do you mind if I ask you a few questions about the accident?"

"That's fine but I'm not sure what I can tell you."

"I just have some routine questions. Your father-in-law told me pretty much everything I needed to know about the moment it occurred."

"Would you like to fill me in? I haven't had a chance to hear the whole story," I said.

Officer Dickson flipped open his notepad. "Mr. Forsyth was coming out of the offices of his construction company. He heard screeching tires, which made him look up. He saw your husband's car careening around the corner at a speed well over the limit. It then spun out of control and smashed into the side of the brick building across the street. Fortunately, no one else was hurt."

The knot that had been lodged in my stomach all morning twisted even tighter.

"Did your husband ingest any drugs or alcohol before he got in the car?"

"No, it was early in the morning." There was a hint of defensiveness in my tone that I hadn't intended.

"It's routine, ma'am."

"I'm sorry. I didn't mean to sound . . . it's been stressful."

"I understand."

"Barring any mechanical malfunction with the car, can you think of any reason why your husband would be traveling at such an accelerated speed?"

Shaking my head, I answered. "No. Will wasn't a speed junkie."

"Could he have been upset or worried about something causing him to be distracted?"

I glanced over at both sets of parents. Everyone but Sophie was in the dark about mine and Will's marital problems. This wasn't the time or the place to let that cat out of the bag. The idea that the argument could have been the reason for the accident made me nauseous.

"No. It was a normal morning for us. There was nothing out of the ordinary.

"Well, that's all I needed to know. I'm glad your husband will be alright. He's a lucky man to have made it out of that crash and to have so many people care about him." Officer Dickson stood. "Take care."

I gave him an appreciative smile. "Thank you."

He shook the hands of each member of our little group before heading out the door.

Four hours passed before I got word that Will was out of surgery. Doctor Bernard assured me that all went well and he expected a full recovery. Although our relationship was over, I was legally Will's wife so any medical decision making fell on me. Other than running home to shower and change clothes, I was by Will's side. Even for the first few days when he was in and out of sleep and didn't know I was there. But I wasn't going to turn my back on him regardless of how things were between us.

Obviously we hadn't discussed the cause of the accident. The guilt of responsibility was like a dull headache that wouldn't go away. I needed some relief.

By hospital day four, Will's medication fog lifted and he was more coherent and clearheaded. He was flipping through the channels on the

TV while I sat quietly in the corner flipping through a cooking magazine. The sound of sheets rustling caused me to glance up. Will was looking at me.

He cleared his throat and said, "I've been meaning to thank you."

"For what?"

"For being here. I know you're ready to end this." He weakly motioned with his hand, pointing between us.

"It's not just me."

Will's gaze dropped briefly and then bounced back up to mine. "Um . . . I need a favor. Two actually." He paused. "Could we hold off on the separation until I'm back on my feet?"

I closed the magazine as I ran my tongue over my suddenly dry lips. "I don't see a reason to prolong things."

"Christ, Bryson, all I'm asking is for you to stay with me until I'm well. It's the least you could do, don't you think?"

"What's that supposed to mean?"

"The morning you asked me for the divorce . . . I couldn't think straight."

My heart was pounding against my chest. "Is that why you were speeding?"

He didn't say anything. The look he gave me answered my question. Guilt and obligation flooded me in equal parts.

"Okay, I'll stay until you're recovered."

"And let's keep this quiet from everyone, especially our parents. No need for them to know what our plans are right now. Who knows, this may be a blessing in disguise."

Will picked up the remote and returned to flipping through channels. He wanted to keep up appearances for as long as possible. There was no tangible reason why I couldn't play the dutiful wife for a few more weeks while he was recovering. It was a small price to pay to clear a guilty conscience.

I followed closely behind the assistant as she wheeled Will into the brightly lit aquatic therapy room. He had been discharged to one of the best rehab facilities in town. Before we arrived I had a picture in my head of a drab and depressing sterile place. This was the complete opposite. The area we were in was buzzing with activity and laughter.

To the right, large windows lined the upper wall while the bottom half was reserved for equipment. I recognized barbells and exercise bands. Then there were other things that I was clueless about as to their purpose in the water, for example the multicolored belts that hung like a rainbow along one wall. At first glance the pool looked like any other giant pool but on closer inspection it was anything but. The steps were a lot wider, there were more of them sinking into the water, and the railing was a lot thicker than normal. At one end there was a lift that lowered wheelchair-bound patients into the water. Every patient in the pool got the undivided attention of a therapist.

I glanced over at Will to gauge his reaction to how he'd be spending his time for the next several weeks. Somehow he had convinced himself that he was being discharged to home and I'd be hauling him back and forth each day for therapy. He was not happy when he was informed otherwise. He was pouting at the moment, his expression nonexistent as he ignored everything and everyone around him. He'll get over it.

"As you can see we have a pretty aggressive program," said Kim, the therapy assistant giving us the tour.

She whirled the wheelchair around pointing Will toward the pool for him to get a better look. He stared blankly ahead.

"Will, you love swimming, now you'll get to do it every day." I worked hard to sound cheery and optimistic like any good wife.

"We have a pool at home," he grumbled.

Kim plastered an understanding smile across her face. "Well, this concludes the grand tour. I'm sure you're pretty tired and would like to get back to your room." She gave me a sympathetic glance. "Will, would you like to wheel yourself back to the room?"

"Isn't that what they pay you for?"

"Will!" I snapped.

"It's okay. You've both been through a lot lately."

I took my position a few steps behind Kim as she pushed Will's chair toward the exit. As we rounded one corner of the pool a high-pitched squeal caused me to turn around. Another high pitched giggle accompanied by a head tilt came from the very young brunette at the other end of the pool. She was holding two small aquatic barbells and obviously playing up that they were too heavy. I followed her gaze curious to see who her performance was for.

The second I saw her audience I froze. Blinking several times, I tried to clear my vision. But each time I opened my eyes the same figure was still sitting on the side of the pool. Hart Mitchell.

Just like in the hospital cafeteria and at the traffic light, I couldn't help but stare as Hart encouraged the giddy girl to continue with her exercise. He was wearing a fitted black tank with black long board shorts. His hands clutched the edge of the pool causing his muscles to flex. I knew back in school he had some bulging happening underneath that flannel shirt. My gaze landed on the chain tattoo wrapped around his bicep and just above it was a series of numbers etched across his arm I hadn't noticed during the drive by. The time since high school had been really good to Hart. He no longer looked like a bad boy. He looked like a badass.

Before my brain had a chance to catch up with my body, I found myself walking toward him. I was completely clueless as to what I would say. It had been a little over nine years since we last saw each other. Our encounter was so brief, I wondered if he would even remember me.

"Bye, Hart. See you Wednesday," the high pitcher squeaked.

I should've turned around and left. I was still a safe distance and hadn't been noticed. I could leave without him ever knowing I was here. Besides, ambushing Hart this way could be extremely awkward. We shared an incredible moment at the dance. We also never spoke to each other again. My body and mind seemed to be working independently of each other. Because before I knew it I found myself at the point of no return. Hart's head turned in my direction and our gaze locked.

"Hart?"

Shock slapped across his face.

Placing my hand on my chest, I continued. "It's Bryson Walker."

"I know who you are." His expression changed but I couldn't read whether it was good or bad.

I nervously shifted from one foot to another. "I can't believe after all these years. And here of all places."

"Small world." Hart was still a guy of few words.

"What are you doing here? I hope it's nothing serious. God, I can't get over running into you." I was rambling and I needed to be stopped.

"I work here."

"Really? That's a relief. I mean the only other reason you'd be here would be if you were a patient . . ."

"I'm the head of the physical therapy department."

My gaze roamed down his bare arm. "Well, I can certainly see why."

Did I say that out loud?

A deep chuckle rumbled from his chest. "You look very . . . healthy. Why are you here?"

I hesitated for several seconds, debating whether or not to bring up Will. If I didn't I'd look like a perverted creeper who stalked rehab facilities in search of my next victim. "Will. Do you remember Will from school?"

"Barely."

"Well, he's a patient here. Was just admitted today, in fact. He was in a car accident."

"I hope he has a quick recovery."

"He'll be fine."

The sexy dimples that had popped into some of my dreams over the years made an appearance. We stared at each other for several seconds before being interrupted by a deep voice.

"Hart, you have a staff meeting in twenty minutes," said a very cute, very tall dark haired guy.

"Thanks, John. I'll be right there." He looked back at me. "I'm sorry but I have to go."

I frantically flailed my hands. "Oh, yeah, yeah, yeah. You're working. I didn't mean to interrupt."

"I'm glad you did."

My insides got all warm and cozy.

"Me too." I smiled.

"I'll be seeing you around then," he said.

"That would be great."

That was a stupid response.

"I mean, have fun at your meeting." I giggled.

Pivoting, I walked toward the exit as fast as my strappy sandals would carry me before I humiliated myself further. My heart was beating a mile a minute and my stomach felt as if a flock of hummingbirds had taken up residence.

Pull it together, Bryson. You're not a giggly schoolgirl anymore.

Once I got to the door the urge to get one last peek overwhelmed me. Standing just inside the entrance of the therapy room, I grabbed one last eyeful. Seeing Hart again after all these years was shocking but it didn't compare to what was happening in front of me.

John, the cute therapy assistant, pushed an empty wheelchair up to the pool and positioned it directly behind Hart. Flipping two levers, John swung the leg rest to the side, giving Hart clear unobstructed access to the chair. Hart placed his hands on either side of the seat and in one seemingly effortless move he lifted himself into the chair. As Hart finished drying his right leg, John pushed the right leg rest back into place. They repeated the same routine on the left side. Tossing the towel he'd used to John, Hart secured both legs with a strap across his calves. These two guys worked together like a well-oiled machine. Suddenly, the chair swiveled and a bluish gray gaze pierced mine.

One Mississippi.

Two Mississippi.

Three Mississippi.

I tore my gaze away and ducked into the hallway as quickly as I possibly could. But I knew it was too late. Hart had caught me watching him.

chapter Eleven

With one eye on the lookout for Will's room number and the other eye on the lookout for Hart, I walked dazed and confused through the maze of hallways. I didn't want to run into Hart again until I'd had a chance to process what I'd witnessed. The babbling idiot inside me had already made a grand appearance seeing him for the first time. There certainly wasn't a need for an encore performance so soon after finding out about the wheelchair. No telling what inappropriate nonsense would spew from my mouth.

Each time the picture of Hart in the chair flashed through my mind I felt a twinge of guilt. It was irrational and ridiculous but I hated that I wasn't there for him during what had to have been a devastating blow to his life. I mean, we weren't friends back in high school or now. Maybe it was just residual guilt from Will's accident spilling over.

During the days and months after prom Hart Mitchell swirled around my head . . . a lot. Our time together was brief but he'd definitely made an impression on me. I never could put my finger on the reason why. Maybe it was just the mystery of him that intrigued me . . . and his smoky and smoldering blue gray eyes. And his blond scruff . . . and his deep dimples . . . and his lips wrapped around that cigarette . . . and that he said I was lovely.

I remembered being a bundle of excitement and nerves as I walked into English class the Monday morning after the prom. It would be the first time since our moment Hart and I would see each other. God, that moment . . . it was electric and scary and fun and flirty. I didn't want it to end so I kept it alive in my mind that entire weekend. But my teenage fantasies crashed in a heartbeat. As I walked toward my desk, I willed Hart to look up at me but he never did. Although I felt his gaze on me several more times throughout the rest of the school year, I never again got the chance to stare into his eyes.

Hart was the unpredictable unknown. Even though our moment was the most exciting thing I'd ever experienced, it scared the hell out of me. So I went back to swagger watching.

As I turned the corner to go down yet another hallway, I spotted a small group of people milling around outside what appeared to be a conference room. They were all dressed in dark pants and white polo shirts indicating they were part of the physical therapy staff. Kim, our tour guide, explained that other than the doctors and nurses, each therapy department had a different colored shirt—occupational therapy wore red shirts, aquatic therapy wore light blue shirts, and physical therapy wore white shirts. I wondered if this was the meeting Hart was attending. No sooner had the thought crossed my mind when he appeared bringing up the rear of the group.

Hart had changed into black jeans but instead of the white shirt the others wore, his was a royal blue polo. Maybe that color stood for boss man. Even from this distance I could see the color brought out the blue hues in his eyes. The shirt was a perfect fit, melting across his toned chest and falling over his flat stomach. I stared as he gripped the wheels of the chair, rolling himself toward the meeting room. My gaze traveled up to his broad shoulders and continued the climb until . . . Shit! He caught me again.

I started to shift my gaze above him, as if something else down the hall had caught my eye. But at this point the object of my ogling was pretty clear. Having no other options at my disposal, I slowly raised my hand, giving him a little wave and smile. The corners of his mouth twitched into a smirk, causing my cheeks to heat up. Not wanting to embarrass myself further, I spun to leave and crashed directly into the medication cart coming around the corner.

"Ma'am, are you alright?" the nurse asked.

"Oh god. I'm . . . I'm sorry. I didn't see you . . . I was just . . . I'm sorry," I stammered while fumbling my way around the cart.

I didn't look back to see Hart's reaction but there was no way in hell he didn't see my graceful exit.

A few minutes later I finally found Will's room. My brain must have been fuzzy from the events of the day because I could have sworn I'd walked down this hall already. Getting semi lost at least gave me a better lay of the land. The atmosphere throughout the entire place had a positive vibe. Around every corner large windows let in massive amounts of natural light. They did their best to camouflage the medical equipment by having it blend in to the casual but tastefully decorated facility. All the patient rooms were private, which Will liked. Even though there were definite medical elements in the room like the hospital bed and table, the bright light, flat screen TV, and curtains framing the large window made it feel less sterile.

A nurse was coming out of the room as I walked up. We exchanged passing smiles. Will had already transferred from his wheelchair into the bed and was flipping through the TV channels.

"Where the hell did you go?" He snapped.

I placed my purse down on the small corner table, walked over to the recliner next to the bed, and sat.

"I was just exploring your new digs and got turned around. There are a lot of hallways in this place."

"Whatever," he grumbled.

Ignoring his mood, I said, "I thought I'd run home and get a few more of your things— workout clothes, pajamas, and your shaving kit. Is there anything specific you need me to bring back?"

"My laptop and cellphone."

I inadvertently cringed. Even though our problems were due to the fact that the marriage had been a complete lie, I considered my discovery of Will's online addiction to be the beginning of the end. Each time he asked for the laptop or cellphone it reminded me where his priorities had always been and were still. Somehow both things survived the accident with only a few scratches. Will probably threw himself over his beloved computer in order to save it.

"I'll have to ask if you can have them here."

Was I punishing him by exercising that I had control over whether or not to bring him his beloved items? Maybe a little bit.

"I'm not in fucking prison, Bryson."

"I didn't say you were. I said I needed to check first. You'll be having therapy three and a half hours a day. You'll probably be too exhausted. Besides, they have computers in the library here if you're that desperate."

"Just bring my goddam cellphone and laptop!"

"Fine. You don't have to bite my head off."

He blew out a frustrated breath. "Look, I'm sorry. It's just . . . I thought I'd be going home and we'd be able to . . ."

"You need to concentrate on getting well as soon as possible."

He looked over at me and smiled. "Thanks, babe."

Babe?

Wanting to change the mood and subject, I said, "Guess who works here."

"No idea."

"Hart Mitchell."

With pursed lips and narrowed eyes, Will shook his head. "Who?"

"He went to high school with us. Remember, he transferred in senior year. Blonde, about six four, bad boy, loner, rode a motorcycle. You had to have noticed him."

"Apparently not as much as you."

"He's the director of the entire physical therapy department."

"Well, goody for him."

I'd forgotten just how pissy Will could be when he was injured. During junior year he'd sprained his ankle and had to sit out a few games. He was an absolute horror to be around, pouting, bratty, and acting as if his hurt ankle was the worst thing that had ever taken place on God's green earth. We'd only been dating for a couple of months so I was still blinded by puppy love and let his bad mood roll off my back.

Having had my fill of his attitude, I stood abruptly, and announced, "I'm outta here. I'll be back in an hour or so with your stuff."

Before I could step away from the bed, he grabbed my hand. "I really appreciate you helping me. I wouldn't be able to make it through this without you."

"You're a strong and determined person. You can do anything you set your mind to regardless of whether or not I'm in the picture."

Sad dark brown eyes looked up at me. "I still want you in the picture."

I pulled my hand back. "Will, let's not get into this right now."

"I'm not getting into anything. I just want you to know my picture isn't complete unless you're in it."

Oh, dear lord.

"I'll be back in a little while."

The second I stepped out of the room I glanced back and forth down the hallway to make sure the coast was clear of muscular torso and blue-gray gazes.

I only made one wrong turn while on my way to the front entrance. The red exit sign glowed brightly over the door like a beacon guiding me to freedom. I passed several rooms that appeared to be administrative offices. As I walked by the last office I heard a raspy voice call my name.

"Bryson." Of course it was Hart.

Flutter.

Flutter.

I peered around the door into his office. "Hey."

He was behind his desk, a stack of files in front of him, tapping a pen between his thumb and index finger. "Did your friend get settled in?"

It dawned on me that I'd failed to mention Will was my husband . . . technically . . . for now.

Stepping just inside the doorway, I said, "Yeah, he did. Thanks. Everyone has been great."

"Good. Glad to hear it."

My grip tightened around the strap of my purse. "I still can't get over running into you."

I already said that when I first saw him.

"I didn't mean that literally, of course. Obviously, I didn't run into you. I recognized you from across the room and ran over to you. Again, not literally . . . ran. I walked . . . quickly."

For the love of god stop talking.

The pen stopped tapping and Hart dropped it on the desk. "Can I ask you something?"

"You kind of just did." A snicker-snort bubbled out of me.

Earth swallow me whole.

Hart cocked an eyebrow as he bit down on his bottom lip stifling a laugh.

I closed my eyes for a second and prayed I could transport back in time to a few moments earlier. "I'm sorry. It's been a stressful week. I'm usually not this weird and snorty. Um . . . yes, you can ask me something."

"I was just wondering how long it was going to take for you to ask me."

Crossing my arms, I nervously countered. "Ask you what?"

"Pretending to ignore it only shines a spotlight on it, you know."

I started to get the distinct impression that I was being played with.

"I have no clue what you're talking about." The words came out with an unintentional fine sheen of annoyance.

"You haven't noticed that my ass has grown and changed shape since high school?"

I didn't want Hart to think the first thing I noticed about him was the wheelchair. It wasn't my place to pry into something so personal. This guy was barely an acquaintance of mine.

"Listen, none of us look the same as we did in high school. I ran into Maria DelVeccio a few weeks ago. Her ass has its own zip code."

"Ask me, Bryson."

"Why are you so hell bent on me asking?"

"Because you're trying so hard not to."

He wanted to make the moment awkward and me uncomfortable, which pissed me off a little bit.

"You think a lot of yourself, don't you?" I stepped all the way inside his office. "What makes you think I'm even remotely interested in anything about you? I mean, it's been what? Like ten years since I left you in front of that fish tank. You definitely weren't interested enough in speaking to me again back then. So, sorry, I won't be going all Barbara Walters on your ass now."

"Wow, way to hold on to a grudge. I really did a number on you."

"Pfft, you wish you did me."

The realization of what I'd just said set my cheeks on fire. I didn't understand my reaction to this guy. For some reason, I was nervous and comfortable all at the same time when I was around him. I remember how easy the banter was between us that night. It swung from flirty to bickering, back to flirty, and finally sweet.

A deep throaty laugh brought me back to the present. "You still have quite a mouth on you."

Hearing that he remembered my mouth caused a slight tickle in my stomach.

"I didn't mean it that way," I said.

"Really?"

"Of course not."

"Damn, I thought you were flirting with me." He winked.

"I don't make it a habit of flirting with strange men."

"Come on, I know it's been a long time but I'm not a complete stranger."

"I said strange, not stranger." I tossed him a satisfied smile. "Besides, you never know when a girlfriend or wife is lurking around."

I knew I was getting into slightly inappropriate chatter with Hart but I was having fun. It had been a long time since I enjoyed a conversation with a man.

Just then my phone buzzed with a text. I fished it out of my purse while glancing at Hart. "Excuse me for a second."

Will: *Bring the PlayStation. When will you be back here?*

Me: *Ok. Soon. Traffic.*

Guilt made another appearance. I had no reason to feel bad. I wasn't doing anything other than enjoying my time with an old acquaintance. I think I could stay here all day and go at it with Hart but I needed to get back on track.

"I better go. I have errands to do and you have work. I didn't mean to take up so much of your time."

"I called you in here, remember?"

"Oh, yeah." I inched toward the door. "I'll be seeing you around at least for the next few weeks. Have a good rest of the day."

I turned to leave.

"Bryson."

My gaze met his. "Yeah?"

"No one is lurking."

No one is lurking.

I bounced all the way down the hall and out the front entrance beaming. The news that no girl was lurking should not have made me this happy. I was in no position to get involved with anyone. Not that it was a possibility Hart and I would get involved. I had to admit it felt great being a little flirty with a man, especially a sexy one. Hart had obviously been through a lot since high school. As far as his looks, though, the years had been good to him. He looked even better with some age on his face. I realized today that his swagger wasn't defined by his walk. It was working just as much behind his desk as it did down the halls of Garrison High.

My schoolgirl giddiness propelled me across the parking lot and into my car. I'd just put the key in the ignition when my phone buzzed again.

Will: *Bring me something to eat. The stuff they serve here tastes like shit.*

I tossed my phone over to the passenger's seat, came down off my Hart high, and pulled out of the parking lot.

When Will said he wanted me by his side until he recovered, he wasn't kidding. He insisted I come to the rehab every day and stay until the evening. I wanted to keep things as amicable as possible for as long as I could, so I didn't fight him on the issue. Besides, with the way my job search had been going I knew I would need more time to find that one person who would take a chance on me.

As the first week passed I fell into a new routine, arriving at the rehab early each morning toting coffee and some form of pastry for Will's breakfast before he went to his first physical therapy session. Since he refused to eat any of the meals the rehab offered, I packed a cooler every day with enough home-cooked food for him to have for lunch and dinner.

The rest of my day was spent mostly sitting in the room thumbing through my large collection of cookbooks. Occasionally, I'd go with Will and watch as his therapist, Tina, put him through a grueling series of exercises. The program was intense with the ultimate goal being to get the patients up and back to their lives in record time. This gave me hope that Will's recovery wasn't too far away. Once that happened we'd be able to come to an agreement and both move on with our lives.

Although spending my entire day in a rehab center wasn't exactly my idea of fun, I did enjoy the tingles of anticipation that covered my body when I walked into the building, hoping to see Hart. But I wasn't going to go out of my way to look for him. That would be pathetic and might give him the wrong idea. At the most, Hart was a fun distraction while I honored my promise to Will. I'd not seen him since the day outside his office. If I were being completely honest with myself, I felt the pressure of disappointment push down on my chest each evening as I left the building without one of our fun encounters.

Will was focused and working hard during his afternoon therapy session, so I decided to take the opportunity to search for a little something to satisfy my sweet tooth. I slipped from the room unnoticed and made my way up and down the halls. Finally, I struck gold, finding a vending machine tucked away in the staff lounge. Ignoring the *Staff Only* sign, I cracked open the door and peeked inside to make sure no staff was lounging.

I studied the selection for a few seconds before finding what would hit the spot—M&M's with peanuts. I plunked in my coins, pressed the E2 button, and waited for the deliciousness to fall. The machine made a weird whizzing noise before the candy pushed forward, dropped, and snagged on a bag of granola that was sticking out.

Who the hell puts granola in a vending machine?

Since I was alone and in dire need of those M&M's, I gently tapped the side of the machine hoping to set the candy free. No such luck. I banged, shook, and finally kicked the damn thing. But the bag still didn't budge. Squatting down, I stretched my arm up into the machine, trying to flick the bag loose with my fingertips. The only thing that accomplished was the mother of all cramps in my arm.

Needing the unencumbered ability to move freely, I unzipped my black hoodie, peeled it off, and tossed it onto the round table in the center of the room. Since I'd been sitting by Will's side for the past two weeks, I opted for comfort, living in either yoga pants or leggings, a T-shirt, hoodie, and sneakers.

With my position shifted, I bent my knees slightly, lifting my ass in the air. I wiggled my body in an attempt to inch as close to the machine as possible. Scissoring my fingers, I reached up until the tips of my fingers barely made contact with the corner of the bag. One good shove and I should have the object of my desire. Feeling the smooth glossy bag between my fingers, I tugged hard, causing me to lose my balance and stumble back. But I had my candy! I also had two large strong hands gripping either side of my hips. I looked down and saw a wheel. A small wheel like the kind attached to the front of a wheelchair.

"Hello, Bryson," the deep raspy voice said.

Once I regained my balance I stepped away from Hart.

"Hey. Um . . . sorry about that." My thumb shot over my shoulder aimed at the vending machine. "The candy was stuck."

"No problem. It was the highlight of my day."

"You must be having a pretty crappy day."

"Things are looking up now." He winked.

I smiled and swallowed the stupid giggle tickling my throat. Excitement buzzed through my body as my gaze roamed over him. He was wearing a pair of charcoal gray dress pants, a crisp white long sleeve shirt, and solid turquois tie that made the gray in his eyes pop more than the blue.

"You look really nice." The words flew out of mouth before my brain had a chance to filter.

"Thank you. I met with corporate earlier today. Had to look the part."

Suddenly, the door swung open and a cute young brunette dressed in a very tight V-neck purple dress came strolling in carrying a file.

She walked toward Hart completely ignoring me. "I finally found you. You're such a hard guy to track down."

"Well, if I knew you'd been looking for me, I would have stayed put." Hart threw her a flirty wink.

Give me a break.

"What ya need, Erica?" he said.

"I need you . . ." She paused in a lame attempt to be flirty and cute. ". . . To sign a few forms."

Erica gazed at Hart like a lovesick puppy still oblivious to my existence. She opened the file on the round table and indicated where she needed Hart's signature. As she flipped through each form, she leaned in closer until her perky breasts were directly in his line of vision. At one point I thought the back of his hand grazed one of her nipples. The air got thick, hot, and suffocating. Someone needed to teach young Erica proper work etiquette.

The crinkling of the wrapper as I tore into my bag of candy disturbed the little flirt fest going on in front of me. Erica glanced toward me, finally noticing other people did, in fact, roam the earth. Pursing her lips, she surveyed me up and down before returning to the object of her affection.

"Last one." She gathered up the file and clutched it to her chest. "Hey, Hart, did I tell you I'm going to Cabo over Christmas?"

"No. That's awesome. Best scuba diving in the world."

"I've never been scuba diving. I'd be completely lost. I wish I knew someone who could teach me." She dipped her head slightly and looked through her long dark lashes.

"C of C offers beginner classes. I think I have a catalogue in my office. I'll drop it at the front desk for you."

"I'll look into that for sure. Oh, I got the cutest bikini the other day. It's black and the top has these thin white stripes that go from here . . ." She ran her fingers from her collarbone down to her nipple. ". . . To here and the bottom half has white polka dots. I can't wait to wear it."

A cough burst out of me, causing all eyes to shoot in my direction.

Hart's gaze locked with mine. "You okay?"

"Yeah. Just enjoying this riveting conversation," I said, tossing a candy in my mouth.

Erica made this sound that I'm sure if translated into speech would have the words 'fuck' and 'you' in it.

With the flip of her dark waves, she gave a dazzling snowy white smile to Hart. "Well, I better be getting back to my desk. I'll let you know about the scuba. Maybe you could give me some private lessons. I get kind of embarrassed learning new things around a group of people."

Hart didn't give a verbal response, he simply flashed his pearly whites at Erica that had her floating all the way out of the room.

"Unbelievable," I mumbled, tossing another candy in my mouth.

"Excuse me?"

"Not that it's any of my business."

"No, it's not."

"But don't you think that was a bit inappropriate?"

Tilting his head to the side, his eyebrows scrunched together. "There's nothing wrong with a little innocent flirting. You of all people should know that."

141

"That wasn't just innocent flirting. That was giving hope to a clearly delusional child who thought what she was doing in here was sexy. And what exactly do you mean, me of all people?"

"Why do you care?"

"Who says I care?"

"Do you always answer a question with another question?"

"Do I do that? I don't do that." Both his eyebrows un-scrunched. "Not all the time, anyway. You are her superior. I just thought it bordered on the inappropriate."

"No more inappropriate than entering a room clearly marked staff only and molesting a vending machine."

"I needed something sweet."

A dimple-popping smile slowly formed across his face as he extended both arms out to the side.

Laughter flew out of me. God he was fun. Maybe walking by his office a couple of times a week wouldn't appear too pathetic or send the wrong signals. Besides, at the rate Will was progressing he might be discharged sooner than the doctor anticipated. In the meantime, there was nothing wrong with having an occasional moment with Hart and enjoying his friendship.

chapter Twelve

It had become very apparent to me that time was my arch-nemesis. Any encounter I had with Hart, whether for fifteen, ten, or five minutes seemed to disappear in the blink of an eye. Whereas, the rest of the day dragged, especially when I was sitting in Will's room twiddling my thumbs.

Today was moving even slower than usual. It was early evening and I'd been with Will since early morning. To kick off the weekend only morning therapy sessions were scheduled, leaving Friday afternoon wide open. Will wasn't interested in any of the social activities the rehab offered, preferring the company of his true love, the laptop, instead. In order not to go completely bonkers, I walked around the building a couples of times for fresh air and to stretch my legs. Unfortunately, there had been no Hart sighting. Other than my brief stroll I'd been stuck in the room playing my role as one-half of the perfect couple.

I made several attempts to discuss the separation with Will so we could iron out details and make plans for when he was discharged. There wasn't much movement on the topic. I wasn't entirely sure why he was hanging on to this idea that we could still make the marriage work. He never loved me and he was well aware that I'd figured out the game he and his parents were running. I'd been clear that I had no intention of staying in this marriage just to keep up appearances.

We were at a standstill, once again floating in limbo like we'd been doing for a year. But I needed to be patient. Will had been the breadwinner for our entire marriage. If I were going to survive on my own I needed time to find a job and become financially stable. Right now Will was taking up all of my time. I hoped once we got down to the nitty-gritty of the legal separation he'd remember I was here for him and the divorce would go smoothly.

I shoved the cookbook I'd been looking through into my bag, scooted to the edge of the chair, and waited for Will to look in my direction. He didn't. As usual the cyber world held more interest than the real one.

Placing my hands on the arms of the chair, I pushed up. "It's getting dark so I'm going to head out. Do you need anything before I go?"

"No," he said, never taking his eyes off of the screen.

I slung my bag over my shoulder. "Tomorrow I won't be here until later."

He looked up with glazed eyes. "Why?"

"I have some errands to run in the morning and Sophie is coming over for breakfast."

"What about my breakfast?"

"I brought an extra blueberry pastry today and there are apples, oranges, and bananas left in the basket."

Will huffed and shook his head. "It's nice to know you're out having fun while I'm stuck in here."

"Will . . . I'll be here with your lunch by 12:30."

"I realize things between us aren't great. But is it too much to ask for a little sympathy and caring? After all, it was you asking for a divorce that sent me over the edge."

I bit down on the inside of my cheek and focused on the stinging pain instead of his words.

"Why don't you see if your mom will come in the morning and keep you company?"

"Because I want you here."

"I'll be here as soon as I can." I walked toward the door.

"Well, don't rush on my account. I'm certainly not going anywhere." Sarcasm oozed from each word.

Heading down the hallway I tried to clear my thoughts of all things Will related. It was almost 9 p.m. and the overnight staff was quietly going through their routine. For a place so full of life and activity during the day, there was an eerie stillness as the sun set. This was when I felt the saddest for the patients. People should be in the comfort and security of their own homes and beds at night.

I dug in my purse for my keys as I crossed the parking lot. I was almost at my car when I glanced up and saw Hart sitting in his silver and black Honda Element. He revved the engine a couple of times before it went dead. I walked over and tapped on the window. It may have been my imagination but I swear as the glass rolled down his face lit up on seeing me.

"Car trouble?"

"Yeah, I've tried it several times with no luck." He glanced at his watch. "Too late to get anyone out here tonight."

"I can give you a ride home." There was a little too much eagerness in my voice.

Reaching for his cellphone, Hart said, "That's okay. I don't want to put you out. I'll just call my buddy to come get me."

"You're not putting me out. I'm leaving . . ." I dangled my keys in front of him. ". . . And I don't have anywhere I need to be. Besides, no sense in bothering your friend when you have a hot chick offering to give you a ride." I winked.

Creeps, a few days ago I was worried about giving off the wrong signals and now I'm initiating the flirt.

I felt the blush splash across my cheeks. "Wait . . . that didn't sound right. I was just trying to be funny."

A deep throaty laugh vibrated up from Hart's chest. He looked around as if he were trying to find an excuse not to accept my offer. Maybe I'd inadvertently overstepped a boundary. The rehab facility had given us a ton of information when Will was admitted that neither of us read. I wondered if there could be a rule about staff not mingling with patients and families outside the facility.

Blue-gray eyes fell on me. "Where are you parked?"

I pointed to the next row. "Right over there. The red mini coup."

With each word I realized the cause of Hart's apprehension. He wasn't sure if my car would be able to accommodate him or the wheelchair. For the first time, I saw a flash of vulnerability in his expression. It was kind of sweet and sad.

"I guess that would work. Thank you. I really appreciate it," he said, unbuckling his seatbelt.

"Great! I can go throw my junk in the car and drive it around to you if you like. Um . . . do you need help with anything?"

I felt one of my nervous rambles coming. Luckily, Hart nipped it in the bud.

"No, on both counts."

The window rolled up and the driver's door swung opened. Hart twisted, pulling on the handle behind him. The side of the car opened like a set of French doors. Sliding the titanium frame from the backseat, the wheelchair I'd seen him travel the halls in had been completely dismantled. The only things recognizable were the backrest, which folded down over the seat, and the small castor wheels in front. Hart acted like a one-man pit crew assembling the chair before my eyes.

Turning toward the passenger's side, he snatched one of the larger wheels and snapped it on the side of the frame. He repeated the same action with the other wheel. Then positioning the chair, he locked it in place. With one hand gripping the lower part of the steering wheel and his other hand on the chair, Hart slid smoothly into the seat. He grabbed the two foot plates stored behind the driver's seat and attached them. Lifting each leg with his hands, he placed them on the foot plates, securing both with a strap across his calves. With his black bag in his lap, he unlocked the wheels, and pushed away from the car.

"Wow." The word fell from my mouth.

A simple activity that most people did on a daily basis without much forethought for Hart was a meticulously choreographed routine. I was impressed how effortless he made it appear.

My comment was rewarded with an appreciative glance from his piercing eyes.

"Let me get that," I said, stepping around him and shutting the doors.

Laying my hands on the wheelchair push handles, I navigated Hart toward my car.

His hands dropped to the push ring that controlled the large rear wheels of the chair. "Thanks but I've got this."

A hot prickling sensation swept up the back of my neck. My hands popped off the handles as if they were on fire and I stepped to the side. The last thing I ever wanted to do was offend him.

"I'm so sorry. I didn't mean anything by it. I was just . . ."

Wrapping his fingers around my wrist, he looked up with genuine sincerity. "It's okay. Don't worry about it. If I need help I know how to ask for it."

My chest deflated with a long sigh of relief. We locked eyes for . . .

One Mississippi.

Two Mississippi.

Heat radiated from where his skin met mine, quickly spreading to every nook and cranny of my body.

It began to sink in that the car ride would be the longest time I'd spent with Hart. Up to this point, our encounters were brief, teetering between playful banter and innocent flirting. All the other times I was able to step away if my nerves got the better of me. It never happened but knowing the option was there kept me calm. We were getting ready to be in close proximity for an extended period of time with no out. My nerves hopped, skipped, and jumped all over the place.

The sound of a car horn blaring down the street broke the moment, causing Hart to let go of my arm.

We walked and rolled to my car in comfortable silence. Pointing and clicking the keychain, all four door locks popped up. I opened my back door, tossing my bag and purse in the seat before hurrying around to the passenger's side. Hart was already placing his bag on the front floorboard.

I stood off to the side waiting for his instructions. "I'm right here if you need me."

He nodded his response as he rolled up close to the car and locked his brakes. Bracing one hand on the car door while clutching the overhead strap with the other, hart hoisted himself into the seat. As he dismantled the chair I stayed in position, ready to lend a hand. After the first wheel came off, he glanced up at me and smiled.

Giving the wheel one good shove, Hart said, "Mind putting that in the backseat?"

As the large wheel rolled toward me, I lunged, grabbing it before it fell to the ground. Butterflies swirled in my stomach as a huge smile hit my face. He obviously didn't need my help but I was thrilled he'd asked for it. We worked as a team to finish taking the rest of the chair apart. Once it was safely secured in the backseat, I slid into the driver's side.

Fumbling to put the key in the ignition, I glanced out the corner of my eye as Hart was clicking into his seatbelt. He was so close. I took in a deep breath and tried to place his scent. It was a blend of cinnamon, ginger, allspice, cloves, and nutmeg. He smelled like warm pumpkin pie.

"You need some help with that?"

I blinked. "What?"

"The key . . . you need some help with it?" His cheeks popped with those swoony deep dimples.

I jiggled the key and finally got it to go in. "No, I got it. Do you need anything? Are you okay? Are you comfortable?"

"I'm good. Are you okay?" He teased.

I gave him a shy smile. "Sorry."

The car remained quiet while I steered out of the parking lot.

"You want to make a right at the first light. After that you'll keep straight for a few miles." Hart paused for a second before continuing. "So . . . are you going to ask me?"

I knew he meant the wheelchair. He seemed fixated on my reaction to it.

I played it cool. "Ask you what?"

"Oh, I don't know . . . What have I been up to since the last time we saw each other? How long have I been working at the rehab center? Or maybe how my ass turned into a set of wheels?"

I peeked over at him and then back at the road ahead. "So tell me . . . how long have you worked at the rehab center?"

He chuckled. "I've been there a little over two years. One year in the PT director's position."

"We're the same age. How on earth did you snag a job like that?"

"Working my ass off nonstop."

"Impressive. I have no idea what type of training you need for the job. With college and experience, that's a lot to pack into a few years. And - -"

"Sorry, turn left onto Coleman Boulevard. I took some college level classes during my junior and senior years in high school. Gave me a jumpstart."

"Really?" I squeaked.

"Don't be so surprised. I'm more than just a hot bod."

A prickling sensation ran up my arms, neck, and face. Hart Mitchell was definitely full of impressive surprises.

The car fell silent for a few seconds.

"Motorcycle accident. SCI at T5, incomplete," he said in a low voice.

My gaze darted over, catching him staring straight ahead.

"What's SCI?"

"Spinal cord injury."

"When did it happen?"

"A week after we graduated. I spent my summer vacation in the hospital and rehab."

Gripping the steering wheel tighter, I resisted the urge to place my hand on top of his. "I'm sorry."

"Take a right at the next light." He instructed.

We turned down restaurant row. As if on cue my stomach roared to life, reminding me it wanted food on a regular basis. Out the corner of my eye, I saw a set of broad shoulders trembling as Hart tried to suppress a laugh.

"Well, there's no sense in pretending you didn't hear that. You want to grab a bite to eat? We could catch up more," I said, hoping he'd take me up on the offer.

He looked at his stainless steel Fossil watch. "I can't tonight. I have an appointment."

"What kind of an appointment do you have at nine o'clock at night?"

He hesitated for a brief moment. "A business appointment. We don't live in a nine-to-five world anymore, you know."

I chose not to think about what "business appointment" was code for. "Do you mind if I make a quick stop?"

"I'm kind of at your mercy."

"This won't take long," I said, pulling up to the fast food speaker." I rolled down my window. "Do you want anything?"

"No thanks."

Leaning out, I placed my order. "I'll have a double cheeseburger, biggie fries, a small Frosty, and a medium Diet Pepsi, please."

A garbled voice blared from the speaker. "I have a double cheeseburger, biggie fries, a medium Frosty, and regular Pepsi."

"No, a small Frosty and a medium Diet Pepsi." I turned toward Hart and smiled. "It's all about balance."

He chuckled. "Absolutely. That Diet Pepsi should really offset the rest of that junk."

"I don't eat like this often."

His gaze took its time roaming down my body and back up. "I can see that."

A little tickle and tingle in the downtown area caused me to shift in my seat.

After a few minutes the big bag of food followed by my drink and Frosty came through the window. I placed the bag between us, the cups in the cup holder, and drove off.

Burger, cheese, and grease vapors filled the car, making my stomach growl louder and my mouth water.

"Hey, do me a solid. Stick the spoon in the Frosty and hand it to me."

Hart unwrapped the spoon, but before handing it over he loaded it with the cold chocolatey goodness then plunged it into his mouth.

Bold. Aggressive. Shocking. And I liked how comfortable and familiar it felt.

"By all means help yourself." I teased.

He handed me the cup. "I usually do."

Two more turns and we were pulling into a nice older neighborhood in the Mount Pleasant area. Hart directed me to a white ranch-style house with black shutters and a large front porch. He let me help put the wheelchair together and walk him to the door. As I headed up the three steps, Hart went around to the side in order to use the small ramp that led up to the porch. I held the storm door open while he slid his key in the lock. We were quickly becoming a good team.

As soon as the front door swung wide a blur of yellow fur came bounding out onto the porch.

"Hey, girl! I missed you too."

Holding out his hands, the beautiful yellow lab pranced back and forth underneath them, wagging her long tail at lightning speed. Her nails sounded like little firecrackers, clicking and clacking over the wooden slats.

"Sit," Hart commanded.

Without hesitation the dog sat dutifully by his side.

"Bryson, this is Butter. Butter, Bryson."

The fact that Hart named his dog Butter and I loved cooking with *butter* was the ultimate kismet.

Squatting down I scratched behind two big ears.

With my lips puckered, I said in a squeaky voice, "What a beauty. Yes you are. You know how gorgeous you are, don't you?"

Butter leaned her head into my scratch, letting her eyes close in pure unadulterated ecstasy.

"I think you've made a new friend."

"Every girl likes a little ear scratchin' now and then."

"I'll keep that in mind."

I heard the smile in his tone.

"Okay, Butter, you've been spoiled enough for one night. Inside."

Big warm caramel-colored eyes looked up at Hart, begging him to let the scratching continue.

"Inside, girl. Now," he said firmly.

Butter's swishing tail bolted off the porch and bounced inside.

Closing the storm door, Hart's attention turned back on me. "Thank you for the ride."

"No problem. I'm glad I was at the right place at the right time."

"Me too." We locked eyes again. This was becoming a habit. "How's . . . um . . . Will, right?"

"He's fine."

"Is his therapy going well?"

"Oh yeah. The therapy is doing the trick."

I wasn't sure if Hart had already figured out that Will and I were married. At the very least I was sure he knew we were together. I mean, why else would I be showing up at the rehab every day. Even though I'd promised Will I wouldn't tell anyone about our break up just yet, I felt the need to clarify my situation to Hart for some reason. Other than confiding in Sophie, I'd kept my word. But I wanted Hart to know that my relationship with Will wasn't what it looked like.

"Hart, about me and Will . . . we're not . . ."

Suddenly, the click, click, click of heels on the steps echoed behind me. A mane of fire engine red hair whooshed past me and toward Hart. With her hooker heels she stood a good foot taller than me. The skinny jeans painted on the larger than life ass and the fuchsia crop top left nothing to the imagination.

"Hey, baby." She purred as her black painted fingernails combed through Hart's blond locks.

I do not like her.

"Hey, Amber," he said hesitantly, removing her hand from his hair.

She turned, giving me the once over. "Hey, I'm Amber."

My muscles tensed and my eyes narrowed. I struggled to keep my hands from forming into fists. This chick had sex written all over her . . . in neon . . . with a spotlight. She reminded me of the type of women Will gravitated toward online. My shoulders slumped forward with the weight of disappointment. If Amber was a prime example of what men were attracted to, I was doomed to spend the rest of my life alone.

Let the cat collecting commence.

I had no right to feel jealous or let down. It was just . . . whenever Hart and I were together, I felt special. Even though the time was brief, those moments brightened the rest of my day. It was like all of his focus and energies were solely on me and I ate it up. I'd been starving so long for attention and affection. But I didn't realize how hungry I was until the few morsels Hart had fed me were threatened.

My introduction reflected my sullen mood change. "I'm Bryson."

Amber nodded, a slow approving smile creeping over her inflated red lips. "Nice." Keeping her eyes on me, she asked Hart, "Is sweet Bryson joining us tonight?"

"No! She was just leaving," Hart blurted out. "Amber, go inside." The tone in his voice was the same as when he gave his dog commands.

Amber huffed then tossed me a wink before disappearing into the house.

My arms crossed, complementing my arched eyebrow. "A business meeting?"

"A business meeting."

"Huh."

I wanted Hart to give some sign that he'd rather stay out on the porch with me than go in and conduct business with Amber. But it quickly became awkward and obvious that I was the third wheel that needed to go.

Avoiding direct eye contact, I said, "I guess I better leave so you can get down to business."

"Thanks again for the ride."

Not wanting to leave on a down note, I made an attempt at a joke. "Oh, you're talking to me. I thought you were giving Amber a little pat on the back."

A flash flood of heat washed over my entire body. I knew as word number three was flying out of my mouth I needed to stop. But it appeared that whenever I was around Hart my mind and body worked independently of each other.

"Bryson, are you okay?"

I looked up and was met by a serious expression. Hart didn't seem mad, but genuinely concerned at my snotty childish outburst regarding Amber.

"Sorry . . . I shouldn't have said . . . It was my lame stab at a joke." I took a step back. "You're welcome." I took another step back, waving my hand in the air. "Have fun with all dat biz-nass."

I turned and rushed down the steps.

"Bryson." His deep tone hit my ears.

My entire body whipped around. "Yeah?"

"You're even lovelier than you were back in school." He treated me to a new smile, a sweet smile, before heading into the house.

Standing at the bottom of the steps, I stared at the door for several seconds. There was no point. Hart wasn't going to make a sudden change in plans and come back out.

I was almost at my car when the booming bass of Flo Rida's "GDFR" song rumbled from the house. My head was already in mid-twist as my inner Peeping Tom surfaced. The front curtain-covered window filled with the silhouette of Amber seductively swaying her hips while her hands lifted up her flaming mane of hair.

Doesn't anyone use blinds anymore?

I froze in place, my gaze following the path of her hands as they made their way down her body. Her fingers hooked around the top of her crop top and slowly peeled it away from her large chest. The hips stayed in perpetual motion while her hair whipped from side to side. She continued enjoying the feel of her own body, paying extra attention to her nippular area.

The outline of Hart came into view. The Frosty from earlier bubbled and churned in my stomach. I needed to leave. I'd seen too much already. But my legs were currently ignoring my commands, forcing me to watch Hart pull Amber toward him and bury his face deep between her tits.

"Are you lost, dear?"

A gasp of epic proportion shot out of me. The small crackly voice had me jumping twenty miles out of my skin. Turning around, I was met by a gray-haired little lady, holding a cane in one hand and a leash in the other. At the end of the leash was a tiny white puff.

"Are you okay? Your face is bright red. Do you have a fever?" Concern was evident in her tone.

As inconspicuously as possible, I side stepped away from the peepshow, trying to distract the little lady's sweet brown eyes. "Oh ... uh ... yeah. I'm fine. I was just heading home."

"You're a friend of Hart's?"

My gaze darted between the window display and the old lady. "Yes, ma'am. We actually went to high school together."

"That's nice. He's such a sweet boy. Always checks on me. He brings me fried chicken from work every time they fix it for dinner." The old lady closed her eyes and puckered her lips as if she had just taken a delicious bite of the fried bird. "Oooh . . . they make the best buttermilk fried chicken. Have you had it?"

I shook my head.

"Hart piles so much on my plate that I have enough for the entire week. I'm Polly by the way. What's your name, hun?"

"Bryson." I smiled and relaxed a little, realizing she wasn't able to hear the booming music.

"What a lovely name. It's nice to meet you, Bryson."

"Nice to meet you too."

"I'm sure I'll be seeing more of you. Maybe you could come for fried chicken next time."

"That would be great."

Looking down at the white puff, she said, "Come on, Honeybun. Time for bed."

A pair of beady black eyes poked out from behind the fur and looked up at Polly. "Goodnight, Bryson."

"Goodnight," I called after her as she waddled off down the sidewalk.

I watched the little old lady and Honeybun head into the house right next door to Hart's. Forcing my gaze to stay straight ahead, I got into my car. My eyes had been tainted enough for one night. Besides, as I drove home I preferred to fill my head with thoughts of the Hart who brought his elderly neighbor fried chicken rather than the Hart who was banging Slutty McMasterson.

chapter
Thirteen

About a mile down the road the fried chicken flew the coup and my thoughts drifted back to the old bump and grind. I gripped the steering wheel tighter with one hand while the other hand shoved fries in my mouth. Hart and Amber didn't even look as if they had anything in common. Not that I had an idea of what either of their interests were or hobbies . . . nor did I care . . . nor was it any of my business.

As I pulled into my driveway, it occurred to me that I was working a little too hard at trying to convince myself how much I didn't care about the Hart and Amber show. More than likely it was just the newness of the subject matter. For months all of my thoughts and energies had been concentrated on my failed marriage. My mind just needed a little break. A simple diversion. Everyone needs a little mindless fluff now and again to break up the pain in life.

The next morning I groggily dragged myself out of bed having spent the entire night tossing and turning. Every time my eyes were about to close visions of Amber's big sugar plums with Hart's face buried between them danced in my head. I decided to get up early and get a few things done around the house before Sophie showed up for breakfast.

Once out of the shower, I applied light makeup and gathered my hair into a messy bun. I'd been living in yoga pants, T-shirts, and tennis shoes for weeks and needed a change. I pulled on a pair of olive green capri pants and a plain white tank. I topped off the casual look with gold hoop earrings, my collection of bangles, a lightweight tan denim jacket, and brown wedge sandals.

I was on my second cup of coffee while sitting at the breakfast bar paying bills online when my phone buzzed with a text. I cringed, hoping it wasn't Will already. This was the first morning in three weeks that I'd had to myself. I was thrilled when I saw Sophie's name pop up. Since Will's accident we haven't had much girl time.

Sophie: *Hey girlie! Open up. I brought breakfast.*

Me: *Yay! Walking to door now.*

I opened the door to find my best friend holding a bag of cinnamon buns from my favorite local bakery, The Bake House Café.

"I love you more than words can express," I said, eyeing the bag of goodies.

"I'm no fool. You only love me for my buns."

I could smell the warm pastries as Sophie walked past me heading toward the kitchen.

"They are mighty sweet buns." I followed.

Knowing she was going to bring breakfast, I had already set out two small plates and napkins. While I grabbed our coffee, Sophie plated the gooey goodness.

Sitting, she took a sip of coffee and said, "Talk."

"So much for pleasantries," I said sarcastically, pulling out a stool.

"Well, our time is limited since Prince William has you at his beck and call."

"Sophie."

"What? I'm sorry. Am I out of the loop? Has he stopped laying a guilt trip on you?" She tore off a piece of the blueberry pastry, tossing it in her mouth.

"He has his moments. But I've been very clear. He knows once he's recovered we have things to deal with."

Her violet eyes were filled with concern. "I hope so."

I hoped so too.

I took a bite of sugary warm dough. "Mmm . . . These are better than sex."

"With the crew I've been screwing lately, I'd have to agree."

"You need to be more selective with whom you share your buns." I smiled, pausing a second to take another bite. "With things being so crazy lately I forgot to tell you . . ."

That was a little white lie. Sophie had been in and out of town sporadically since Will was admitted to rehab. I started to text her several times about running into Hart. But decided to keep it my little secret until we were together.

"Guess who works at the rehab place?"

"You know I'm no good at guessing games. Cut to the chase." She took a sip of coffee.

"Hart Mitchell."

Sophie's face scrunched up in confusion. "Doesn't ring a bell."

"Are you kidding me? Hart Mitchell, tall, blond, mysterious bad boy."

"That dude from prom? He was hot."

"Yes! He's the director of the entire physical therapy department. I saw him the day Will was admitted. One of the nurses was giving us a tour of the facility. We were at the pool . . ."

"Pool? What is this place, some sort of spa?"

"They do aquatic therapy. Anyway, he was sitting on the side of the pool. I recognized him immediately. I wasn't sure he'd even remember me but he did, last name and everything. His hair is a little shorter. He still has the scruff and the dimples. We've run into each other a few times. We chat. He's really fun."

Setting her coffee down, Sophie's eyes narrowed as she pointed her manicured finger at me and wiggled it. "What's going on here? What's happening?"

"I'm telling you about running into an old classmate." My gaze dropped to my fidgeting fingers.

"No. No you're not. You're telling me about a guy . . . a guy you're hot for."

I choked on a gasp, coughs pouring out of me.

Sophie rushed to my side and vigorously patted me on the back. "You okay?"

"I'm fine." A couple of faint residual coughs escaped as she sat back down. "And I'm not hot for anyone. I don't even know him."

"Bryson, being hot for someone is a pure chemical reaction. It has nothing to do with whether you know the person. You could pass some random guy on the street who gets your juices flowin'."

My nose crinkled.

"I mean, if I had a dime for every guy my hoo-haw heated up for on any given day . . . Well, I'd have a pocket full of change."

"Rest assured, there's no heating of hoo-haws happening."

Completely ignoring my last statement, her eyes brightened with excitement. "This is perfect if you think about it. While Slimy Bastard is laid up you could be doing a little rehabbing of your own. This Hart dude could be your transition guy."

"My what?"

"Transition guy . . . he fills in the gap between serious relationships. You have fun and a lot of sex. He helps you forget the old guy and clears the way for the new one. A cleansing of the vajayjay, if you will."

"I'm not ready for any of that. I'm still married."

Reaching across the table, Sophie placed her hand on mine. "Things between the two of you have been bad for a long time and you've basically been living apart for months. You're getting a divorce. You have no kids. No one will get hurt by you having a little fun."

I'd be lying if I said Hart hadn't appeared in a few of my dreams lately. The idea of being with someone other than Will terrified me. I'd never even been kissed by another guy. Then there was Hart's disability. My mind hadn't gone to how that affected his love life.

I shook my head Etch-A-Sketch style in hopes of erasing the silly notion of me and Hart together.

"I don't exactly know his situation. Besides, I gotta look at his type and I'm nowhere near it."

With her elbows on the table, Sophie rested her chin in her hands. "Do tell."

"He was having car trouble last night so I gave him a ride home."

"Listen at you prowling the rehab parking lot."

"We were on his front porch when this Amber creature showed up. Fake from top to bottom."

"Girlfriend?"

"I don't think so. He hinted that there was no girlfriend or wife. He likes to tease me a lot, so he could have been playing around. What's weird is he referred to it as a business appointment."

Sophie leaned back, her brows rising up her forehead. "Oh my god! Maybe he's a dom and she's his submissive."

"Ugh . . . you and your erotic books. It wouldn't hurt to pick up a Jane Austin once in a while."

Gathering the remnants of our breakfast, Sophie said, "Maybe I need to pay a little visit to Slimy Bastard and check out Mr. Mitchell."

"Don't you dare!"

A mischievous smile crept over her perfect rose bud lips as she slid from the stool and threw our trash away.

"Sophie, I mean it."

"Relax. But I think you're missing out on a prime opportunity. You're obviously attracted to him."

I huffed. "What makes you think that? I never said anything about being attracted to him. I was simply letting you know he's alive and well and working at the rehab." The word shot out of my mouth like a bullet at warped speed.

"Man, the sugar and caffeine combo has you all wound up. Or is it a certain bad boy therapist?" She walked over to where I sat and draped her arm around my shoulders. "Bryson, I've known you for most of my life. And I've become quite adept at spotting your bullshit. All I'm saying is, if he's willing and able, treat yourself to a little fun."

It occurred to me that I hadn't told Sophie about Hart being in a wheelchair. It wasn't that I was trying to hide it from her. It was nothing to be ashamed of. So he was in a wheelchair. After the initial shock wore off, I never saw the chair again. I just saw Hart.

"But I'm still technically married and if Will ever found out he could make things . . ." I jumped off the stool waving my hands. "This is all a moot point. Nothing is going to happen with Hart."

Sophie moved in front of me, placed her hands on my shoulders, and looked me directly in the eye. "All I'm saying is pass the idea by the guy. If he's into it, just keep things on the down low. Besides, I don't believe for one second that Slimy Bastard limited his slimy dick to just his own hands."

A slight tremor ran through my body at her words. Finding out Will never truly loved me, along with his online activity, and texting other women devastated me. It may have been a protective shield of denial I held in front of me, but I'd always chosen to believe him when he said he'd never physically been with another woman. I knew I was being naïve and gullible. I just needed to hold on to one tiny thread of hope and pretend it was real.

Tears pooled in my eyes.

"I didn't mean to make you cry." Her eyes were misting.

"I know you didn't. You're probably right about Will. It's so stupid that I'm even getting upset. I don't love him and haven't for a while. I guess I'm having a hard time saying goodbye to ten years of my life even if it was all a lie."

Sophie pulled me into a tight hug. "I don't see how you are able to sit in the same room with him."

"I have to for the time being."

She pulled away from me and with her thumb wiped the couple of tears that had trickled down my cheek. "Please, seriously consider having a little mindless fun. You deserve it."

I nodded in agreement to appease my best friend. I had no intention nor the guts to ask Hart to serve as my play thing while I mended my broken heart. I was completely satisfied with our occasional chats and my daydreams.

After Sophie left I packed the cooler with Will's lunch. He still refused to eat the food the rehab facility provided. He was such a brat. Mrs. Tanner, the head dietician, was very understanding, allowing me to come in the kitchen to reheat food if needed. We were both foodies, so I think that helped in persuading her. The only thing she asked of me was to keep a tight lip. If others knew she had made an exception for me then everyone would bombard her with requests.

Will was in a particularly pissy mood when I arrived at his room. He'd already been to his morning therapy session and was sitting in the recliner when I walked in.

"Where the hell have you been?" He snapped.

"Well, hello, Sunshine." I placed the cooler at the foot of the bed, tossing my purse beside it.

He shifted in the chair, wincing in pain. "I've been pushing that fucking call button forever and still no nurse."

"What do you need?"

"A pain pill. Damn Jackie almost killed me today." He squeezed the call button again. "Where the fuck is that stupid nurse?"

"Will, keep your voice down and don't be so ugly toward the staff."

"This is what happens when you're off having a fun morning. Bryson, I need you to be here every day, all day. They stick me in bed or this fucking chair and ignore me." He was gripping the call button so tightly that his knuckles were changing color.

"I have to have some time to run errands and make your meals. The outside world is still revolving." I needed to reign in my sarcasm. "I know it's difficult when you're in pain but you're not the only patient."

"I'm starving."

I started unpacking the containers from the cooler.

"I made my famous chicken salad, sourdough bread, and pecan pie," I said, trying hard to sound cheery.

"Yum," Angie, Will's day nurse, said, as she walked in the room.

"It's about time," he growled.

"Will!"

"Oh, it's okay. He's more bark than bite." She handed him the little white cup that had his pain pill in it along with a cup of water. "Here, that should hold you for a while."

"Angie, would you like a piece of pie? I brought three."

"I'd love one but my waistline wouldn't."

Angie was a very attractive woman, maybe in her early forties. She had long blond hair that was always in a bun whenever I saw her. She was a little taller than me and curvy. I'd never seen her without a sweet warm smile. I admired that. Her job could not be easy.

"Well, just let me know if you change your mind."

"Thanks." She directed her attention to Will. "You behave yourself and buzz me if you need anything."

"Should I start buzzing you now for my four o'clock meds? Maybe I'd actually get them on time."

"Angie, I'm sorry."

She raised her hand, waving off my apology. "It's the feisty ones that get better quicker."

As she walked toward the door, I gave Will a dirty look.

"Y'all enjoy your lunch."

"Thanks," I said.

I opened up the container of chicken salad and placed it on the hospital table in front of Will.

He huffed. "I'm not in the mood for chicken. Would you go across the street and get me a burger?"

"Are you kidding me?"

"No."

"I went to all this trouble. Why didn't you text me this morning and tell me to get you a burger?"

"I didn't know you were bringing chicken," he grumbled.

"You knew you wanted a hamburger."

"Bryson, get off my back. I'm in enough pain without having to listen to your whining."

I inhaled a deep breath and tried to tamp down my anger. Will could be a manipulative son of a bitch. After dating for a while I began to notice how he'd say hurtful things just to see my reaction. Once he got what he was going for, he'd swoop in all sweet. At first I didn't argue, chalking it up to teenage angst. I had my moody days too. As we got older I challenged him on occasion. He'd back-pedal, claiming he never meant the harsh words the way I took them. As the marriage crumbled I knew this was his way of inducing guilt and making me feel even worse. I'd been working very hard not to take the bait.

I put the lid back on the container of salad and packed up. Grabbing the cooler and my purse, I turned on my heels and headed toward the door.

"Bryson, wait." I stopped and waited for an apology. "I'd like fries too."

As I closed the door, my middle finger levitated on its own volition as I muttered, "Asshole."

I stomped down the hallway and out the main entrance. As I rounded the corner of the building where my car was parked, I passed the courtyard. It was a quaint little area with shade trees, azalea bushes, a couple of benches, and picnic tables. I'd come out here before when I needed a breather from Will's attitude.

The courtyard was deserted except for one person. Hart was sitting at one of the picnic tables, soaking up the warmth of the sun and reading. The corners of my mouth curled up and all the anger and annoyance from earlier disappeared. Without consulting my brain, my legs moved me forward until I was standing next to him.

"Whatcha reading?"

He looked up with squinted eyes. A slow grin formed across his mouth, causing butterflies to swarm in my belly.

"*Reading Is Sexy: A Guide to Picking Up Hot Women.* It's working great so far."

I gave him a shy smile. "Have you had lunch yet?"

"Nope."

"Do you like chicken salad?"

"Yep."

I placed the cooler on the table and unpacked it. "Today's your lucky day."

Hart watched in amazement as I pulled out the food, paper plates, and utensils, setting it all in front of him.

"What's all this?"

"Will wasn't in the mood for chicken today."

He closed his book and put it aside. "You do know we have a fully staffed dining room, right?"

"He doesn't like what they serve."

"So you bring him food every day?"

I nodded, then cringed remembering the promise I'd made. "Please, don't get Mrs. Tanner in trouble. She's been wonderful and understanding."

Hart gave a subtle head shake and tried to hide an eye roll, unsuccessfully. "My lips are sealed."

A sigh of relief drifted out of me.

"Thank you. Well, enjoy." I started to walk away.

"Whoa. You can't leave me here to eat alone."

I knew he was just being nice. After all, I'd laid a feast before him. But I had to admit his words made my head a little floaty. I was more excited than I probably should have been to spend more time in his company. Hart had positioned himself at the end of the table. Without protest, I sat next to him.

I scooped three large spoonfuls of salad onto a plate and handed it to him.

"Don't forget the bread." I slid the plate of already sliced bread across the table.

"Looks like you thought of everything," he said.

"I didn't bring anything to drink."

He raised his bottled water. "I'll share my water."

My cheeks flushed thinking about my lips touching the same bottle as his touched.

I sounded like a Hallmark movie.

Hart plunged his fork into the salad and brought it up to his mouth. I got a little dizzy staring as he chewed and swallowed. When he stopped chewing I noticed the corners of his mouth twitching into a slight grin. I darted my eyes away but it was too late. He'd solidly caught me.

"Bryson, this is incredible. Where'd you get it from?"

"I made it."

"You're kidding." He sounded surprised.

"I made the bread and the pie too."

"What's in this salad?"

"You really want to know?"

He nodded his head, eating another forkful, appearing genuinely interested.

"Well, chicken, of course. Red grapes, walnuts, celery, celery seed, salt, pepper, mayo, and my secret ingredient."

Grabbing a piece of bread, he flirted. "What's your secret, Bryson?"

"If I told you that it would take all the mystery out of our relationship."

"I think there's enough to spare." He tore off a small piece of bread and popped it into his mouth. "Damn, this melts in your mouth."

My cheeks were hurting from the smile glued to my face. I was beside myself with excitement from Hart enjoying my food so much.

"Okay. I'll tell you but you're sworn to secrecy."

"I'll take it to the grave."

I placed my forearms on the table and leaned forward. "I add two tablespoons of Durkee's."

"I have no idea what language you're speaking." He continued to eat, alternating between the salad and bread.

Chuckling, I said, "Durkee's famous sauce."

Hart shrugged his shoulders, still having no clue what I was referring to.

"It's a mustardy, vinegary, mayonnaise-based concoction."

"Why didn't you say that in the first place? I'm a simple man. You gotta use simple words."

"I'll remember that the next time we eat together."

"So, there's going to be a next time? Man, that book really does work."

My entire body heated and blushed. This was the happiest I'd felt in a long time and all it took were a few kind words from the right person.

"What restaurant are you the head chef at?" He lifted another forkful to his mouth.

My eyebrows furrowed. "In my kitchen at home."

"You mean this isn't your career?"

I simply shook my head in response.

"You're kidding." He swirled the last piece of bread around his plate collecting every little salad remnant. "Damn, woman, it should be."

Beaming, I dished out the biggest piece of pecan pie and slid it toward him. "You think so?"

"Absolutely." He twisted the top off of his bottled water and took a swig. "Where did you go to culinary school?"

"Nowhere." My gaze dropped. For some reason I felt embarrassed to admit that fact.

"So, this is all natural talent."

The biggest smile split across my face.

"At one point, I thought about going to culinary school. Maybe opening up my own catering business. But, you know, other priorities come into play and force you to choose. It was a silly idea anyway."

Hart put his fork down and held my gaze. "Your heart's passion is never silly. If you follow it, it will steer you in the right direction."

My throat tightened with the hint of a sob.

Hart was oblivious to the impact his words had on me. He was only the second person I'd shared my dream with, of running my own catering business. But he was the first person to encourage me to reach for it. He was a nice guy being nice. I needed to remind myself to take it at face value and not read anything more into it. As I stared into his smoky eyes, it was becoming clear to me that I craved our time together no matter how brief. I wanted him in my life in some capacity for as long as possible.

My body vibrated with anticipation as he brought the golden-pie-filled fork to his mouth. His expression relaxed into pure pleasure. I couldn't help the laugh that bubbled up and out of me. As he devoured the rest of the pie, fully enjoying each mouthful, tears played at the back of my eyes.

Oh my god! What is wrong with me? I cannot let him see me cry. He'll think I'm a nut case.

I looked away, blinking back the tears as I kept busy packing up what was left of lunch.

The touch of a warm hand on my forearm stilled me. "Hey, you okay?"

I looked down at Hart's skin touching mine before my gaze bounced up to his.

Pursing my lips, I nodded. "Must be allergies."

The second he removed his hand, a twinge of emptiness hit me.

"Thank you for lunch. It was amazing."

"I'm glad you enjoyed it."

"It was the second best thing that happened to me today." He winked.

I wasn't sure if he was implying the first best thing was spending time with me. I wasn't going to ask for clarification. So I smiled, kept my big mouth shut, and finished packing the cooler.

"We could do it again sometime if you'd like," I said.

"I'd like that."

A rush of adrenaline zipped through my body.

"Great. Let me know some of your favorite foods and I'll work around them." My insides cringed with how eager I sounded.

"Oh no. Next time it's my treat."

"You cook?"

"Um . . . no. But I order a mean pizza." We exchanged smiles. "That is if you think it won't cause trouble between you and Will. Is he okay with you sharing your talents with an old friend?"

"Will and I are married." The words catapulted from my mouth.

My eyes doubled in size as I stared at Hart with my mouth hanging wide open.

"Oh god. I'm sorry. I don't know where that came from. I didn't mean to blurt it out that way. I just felt I needed to . . ."

Hart reached over and grabbed my hand putting a halt to my rambling. "It's okay. I knew already."

My features scrunched up in confusion.

"I have access to patients' records."

I couldn't deny the goosebumps popping up along my arms knowing Hart had checked on my availability. Maybe he was enjoying our time together as much as I was.

"So, you did a little snooping?" My tone was a lot flirtier than I intended.

His gaze dropped. "I review every patient's chart on admission and periodically throughout their stay. The married box was marked and you're listed as Will's emergency contact."

My stomach dropped with disappointment and embarrassment. Hart must think I'm some desperate housewife looking to cheat on her poor incapacitated husband. I needed to make a quick exit before I made an even bigger fool of myself. I grabbed the cooler and was about to stand when Hart's fingers circled around my wrist.

"Bryson, what just happened that has you bolting out of here?"

Without going into a lot of detail, I wanted Hart to know that Will and I weren't as we appeared.

I took in a deep breath and lowered myself onto the seat. I noticed Hart didn't let go of my wrist. "Will and I . . . it's complicated." I hesitated. Other than Sophie, no one knew Will and I had argued the morning of the car wreck. "I asked Will for a divorce the same day as the accident. While he was in the hospital, he asked me to stay with him during his recovery."

Hart removed his hand from my arm and nodded. "I think I understand."

"But that shouldn't stop two old friends from sharing a meal on occasion. At least I hope it doesn't."

I focused on the red cooler in front of me, not wanting to see Hart's reaction. My stomach twisted in knots. I knew that this was probably the last moment we would share. Even though we were becoming just friends, there was no way he'd want to invite the drama of a divorcing couple into his life. And I couldn't blame him.

After what felt like an hour of silence, Hart said, "What do you like on your pizza?"

Whipping my head in his direction, our gaze locked for . . .

One Mississippi.

Two Mississippi.

Three Mississippi.

My phone buzzed with a text, startling me. I kept my eyes on Hart as I pulled my phone from my purse, looking away at the last possible minute.

Will: *Where the hell are you? I'm starving.*

Shit! I forgot about his hamburger.

Me: *Traffic. Be there shortly.*

"Sorry. I better go." I grabbed the cooler and my purse.

Hart nodded in understanding.

"Catch you later." He threw me a wink and a grin.

I took a few steps backward. "Black olives, extra cheese, and spicy Italian sausage."

We exchanged one last smile before I turned and headed to my car.

chapter Fourteen

"What's the deal with you?" Will said, pulling the T-shirt over his head.

I was putting away some of his clothes I had taken home earlier to wash. "I don't know what you're talking about."

"You're all dressed up." I could hear the smile in his voice.

It was the end of September and even though the calendar claimed autumn had begun the thermostats all over Charleston begged to differ. The heat waned a bit as the sun went down but the rising temperature during the day leaned more toward feeling like summer. I was anxious for the season to transition from the stifling humidity to the crispness of fall. It was by far my favorite season. When I got up this morning and felt the cool snap in the air, I immediately rummaged through my fall wardrobe. I knew in all likelihood I'd probably be burning up later but I didn't care.

Mom had invited me to lunch at 82 Queen, nestled in downtown's historic French Quarter. The restaurant was upscale casual and one of the oldest and best in Charleston. Yoga pants and a T-shirt wouldn't do.

I squatted down to put some T-shirts in the bottom drawer. "I had lunch with mom today. It's just jeans and a sweater, Will. Nothing special."

"Like hell it isn't. Your ass looks mouthwatering in those jeans."

I paired my dark jeans with a beige cashmere sweater and over-the-knee boots. My hair was down and my makeup simple. I wasn't a big jewelry person but I had a few pieces that meant a lot to me. The long gold leaf pendant necklace that hung around my neck had been last year's birthday present from my parents, as well as the gold hoop earrings.

The click-clack of crutches came up behind me as I continued to put away the clothes. Hot breath brushed the back of my neck. A steady quiver permeated my insides. I blew out a series of short breaths, trying to stay calm as his nearness closed in around me. Without warning a gasp pushed from my lungs when his hand cupped the denim covering my ass.

"The black boots are a nice touch." His voice was low and husky.

I abruptly straightened and stepped to the side. "Will, stop it!"

"What?! You come in looking all hot and don't expect me to react?" He moved toward me.

Raising my hand, I stopped him in his tracks. "Nothing has changed between us. You understand that, right?"

Will's broad shoulders slumped forward as he walked back over to the bed and sat. "Why are you so quick to give up on us?"

My hands automatically curled into fists. "Give up on us?"

"I know we have some problems but things could be worse. I mean, I never hit you, Bryson."

"So, as long as there's no blunt trauma everything else should be acceptable?"

"All I'm saying is life with me isn't exactly horrible."

"What about all the lies?"

Placing his crutches to the side, he raised his dark brown eyes filled with all the sorrow he could muster. "I never intentionally lied to you."

I stood shocked in place. But it wasn't Will's blatant denial of any wrongdoing that surprised me. It was my reaction. The twinge of anger I felt just a few seconds ago had dissipated and was replaced by apathy. Over the last twelve months I'd obsessed over each aspect of my marriage.

At the beginning, I sobbed every hour on the hour. My stomach twisted in a constant state of knots. I was consumed by schizophrenic emotions. One minute convulsing in pain and the next screaming in intense anger. Not too long ago I teared up while talking with Sophie about moving on from my marriage.

But as I listened to Will watering down our problems and his part in them, I didn't feel angry, or hurt, or the threat of tears. I felt removed. Indifference had settled in my heart and I knew we were over.

I decided to ignore his manipulative attempt. There was no point rehashing our years together.

"Is there anything you need me to get before I head out?"

He narrowed his eyes and huffed. "You've not been here for most of the day and you're leaving already?"

I arrived at the rehab early this morning with breakfast in hand as usual. Since Mom and I were going to lunch, I took the rest of the afternoon off from my babysitting job. To avoid an argument earlier, I promised Will I'd come back before the day was over.

"It's past nine and I'm tired."

Will slapped his crutches to the floor and pushed himself farther up the bed. "Fine."

Without commenting, I walked over, picked up his crutches, and leaned them against the wall next to the bed. As I moved to grab my purse, Will reached for my arm.

"Bryson, wait." His voice had softened but his expression was tight. "I thought you wore those jeans for me."

I faced him. "Why are you doing this?"

"Doing what?"

Looking into his eyes I couldn't tell if Will was completely delusional or playing me. I knew the last thing he wanted to do was admit to his parents that he wasn't the perfect son they always dubbed him to be. He would suffer a slight chink in his armor but the embarrassment of our failed marriage would eventually subside. And I was sure his parents would once again raise him up to heights only mere mortals dreamed of achieving.

"We're done. You never loved me and I don't love you."

I held his gaze for several seconds, hoping he'd realize the seriousness of my conviction before I turned and walked away. Just as I was about to cross over the threshold it dawned on me. Will wasn't scared to tell his parents about the divorce. He was terrified of me telling them the reasons for it.

I made my way down the quiet hallway, very aware of my accelerated pace as I neared Hart's office. I didn't know the reason for my speed. It was Saturday and Hart didn't work on the weekends. At least I hadn't seen him around the three weekends I'd been here. Plus, it was way past his normal hours.

I was three doors away when I noticed the light on in the office. My pulse pushed against each pressure point of my body. The prickle of excitement skidded across my skin. I slowed my pace as I approached the open door, hoping Hart would look up at the very second I became visible. As I passed the door the sound that flew out of the office wasn't the deep raspy voice I craved. Instead, the high pitch of a drawn-out whistle pierced my ears.

I was shocked and thrilled at the same time. Hart was definitely not shy when it came to playful flirting. But he'd never been so openly bold.

I liked it.

After the tense moment with Will I was ready for a little fun. I furrowed my eyebrows and set my lips in a straight line, pretending to be offended. Slapping my hand on the doorframe, I leaned back and poked my head inside the office. All the blood gushed from my body as four pairs of eyes zeroed in on me.

Hart was sitting behind his desk with two guys occupying the chairs in front. My gaze darted to a third guy perched on the conference table leering at me. I realized then Hart had not been the whistler.

"Hey," Hart said, an awkward mixture of surprise and hesitation in his voice.

Other than Miss Polly and Amber . . .

God, Amber.

I'd not been privy to much of Hart's private life. I basically stumbled on those two women the night I took him home. Considering the day and time, I assumed these guys were friends. There was definite hesitation in his voice with just the one word. Maybe he was a stickler for keeping his private life and work life completely separate. And right now I fell more into his work life than private.

Tightly gripping the strap of my purse, I straightened and moved inside the doorframe. "Hey, what are you doing here on a Saturday night?"

Hart tapped his finger on the papers in front of him. "Uh . . . quick paperwork."

We exchanged smiles.

Hart's gaze moved down my body, causing flash fires to ignite from head to toe. No doubt my cheeks and red purse matched. I would have turned away to hide my reaction but I enjoyed watching him watch me. We both snapped from our haze at the cacophony of throat clearing that filled the room.

Hart tore his gaze from mine and gestured toward his friends. "Bryson, these three stooges are my friends, Colin . . ."

Colin was one of the guys across from Hart. Even though he was sitting I could tell he had a lean athletic build like a swimmer. His jet black hair complimented his tan skin perfectly. As our bright green eyes met he raised his chin, giving me a sweet smile.

"Ronnie . . ."

Ronnie sat beside Colin. He was husky and boxy. No doubt a current or ex-football player. The dark short beard that peppered his slightly rounded jawline was the only hair on his head.

As his long legs pushed him up in the chair, Ronnie said, "Nice to meet you, Bryson."

"And that's Doug."

A big smile crept across Doug's face as he slid off the conference table and walked toward me. "Well, hello there, Bryson."

"Back off, Doug!" Hart snapped.

Ronnie shifted in the chair. "Yeah, I'm sure Bryson likes to breathe in fresh air."

"I took a shower." Doug fired back, his gold hazel gaze drifting down my sweater.

"What year?" Colin asked sarcastically.

It was obvious these guys had been buddies for a long time.

Placing one hand on the doorframe, Doug ran the other hand through his sandy blond short hair. "Don't listen to these guys. I'm minty fresh."

I shifted away from Mr. Minty and moved closer toward Hart. "So what do you fellas have planned for tonight?"

"We're gonna go have a few drinks," Colin said.

I startled as the hot minty breath of Doug hit the side of my cheek and neck. *When the hell did he get that close?* "Hey, Bryson, why don't you come with us?"

"Yeah, come with us," Ronnie chimed in.

Colin agreed. "It'll be a blast."

"Come with us, Bryson," the three guys said in unison.

I looked over at Hart trying to gauge his reaction.

Once again I felt the heat of his smoky blue-gray eyes over my body.

"Bryson looks like she has other plans, guys." His gaze ended its trip back at mine. "I'm sorry. Don't pay these guys any attention."

Colin leaned forward in his chair. "Do you have any plans tonight, Bryson?"

"Yeah, Bryson do you?" Ronnie asked.

"Come with us, Bryson." Doug felt even closer.

"I don't have any plans. Not sure if I'm dressed appropriately though."

The guys all wore dark jeans and different colored dress shirts, untucked with rolled-up sleeves. Against the silvery gray of Hart's shirt his eyes popped brighter than I'd ever seen. I figured I was okay in the wardrobe department but wanted to give Hart another out. I didn't want him to feel pressured by his friends to have me tag along.

"You look hot." Doug breathed.

Clenching his jaw, Hart warned. "Doug, knock it off."

It was obvious Hart didn't want me to go.

"Listen, thank you but I don't want to intrude on guy's night out. Y'all have a good time."

As I turned to leave the peanut gallery piped up again, shouting, "Bryson, pleeeassse come with us!"

And then the only voice I wanted to hear found my ears. "Bryson, please come out with us."

I turned toward Hart, beaming with excitement. "Really? I won't cramp your style?"

"Being that none of us have any style, there's nothing for you to cramp." He winked.

"Give me two seconds to run a brush through my hair, throw on some more lip gloss, and I'll meet you guys outside."

Doug inched even closer to me. "Low maintenance. I like that. Exactly how low do you go?"

Hart abruptly shoved away from his desk as his eyes seared into Doug.

"I'll be back in a few minutes," I said, turning to leave.

Going out with these guys was probably not the smartest way to spend my Saturday night. But I didn't seem to think logically or with any forethought when it came to Hart. I liked how he made me feel whether it was intentional on his part or just a side effect of him being a nice guy. All I knew was I wanted to spend as much time with him as I could.

Once out in the hallway I heard Hart's deep growl. "If you don't stop saying shit like that to her your ass can sit this night out."

"I'm just having a little fun, man. What's your problem? Do you lurve her?"

"I mean it, Doug. Don't fuck with me on this one."

"Okay guys, cool it. We all know Doug's a douche so let's not let that ruin things." I couldn't be sure but it sounded like Colin was the voice of reason.

"That's right, Hart. I'm a douche."

Warmth spread throughout my chest at Hart's protectiveness. Other than the time I gave him a ride home, the only experience I'd had with Hart was within the confines of the rehab facility. I was excited and touched that he was opening up the friendship door by allowing me into his private world.

A shuffling noise coming from the office caused me to jump to attention. I quickly headed down the hall to the bathroom before I got caught.

Once I freshened up I headed outside, seeing my dates for the evening standing by Hart's car.

"Hart's the designated driver for the night," Ronnie said.

I craned my neck, looking past the guys at the car. "Are we all going to fit?"

Hart was already in the driver's seat, dismantling his chair, handing off each part to Colin to store in the rear of the car. "It will be a tight fit but we'll make it work."

"I like it tight." Doug winked at me.

Hart shot a death glare at Doug. "Bryson, you'll be upfront with me."

The guys and I piled into the car and we headed out of the parking lot.

"So where exactly are we going?" I asked.

"A bar." Colin offered up.

"I figured that. I meant what's the name of the bar?"

I glanced over at Hart, the streetlights casting shadows over his chiseled face.

Doug's voice drifted from the back seat. "The kind that serves adult beverages."

It was the first thing out of his mouth that didn't sound lewd.

Since I wasn't having any success getting a straight answer out of these guys, I shifted my focus out the window with the occasional inconspicuous peek at Hart.

At one point, I acted like I was just checking out the scenery as my gaze roamed over to Hart's side. His confidence was radioactive. I didn't know if it was his protectiveness from earlier or his quiet strength that had my body buzzing. I jerked my gaze away the few times he'd caught me but not before witnessing a big grin break out across his face.

I was in the midst of a good long look when suddenly the car stopped.

"Everybody out!" Hart announced.

The guys tumbled out into the parking lot. Doug and Ronnie hovered around the front of the car while Colin headed toward the back.

I turned to Hart. "Do you need my help with anything?"

"Nah, Colin will get the parts from the back."

"Okay."

I twisted in the seat and placed my hand on the door handle.

"Bryson, wait for me by the car." Hart's tone was firm and adamant.

"Okay."

I slid from the passenger seat and closed the door. As I rounded the front of the car, I caught a glimpse of the building in front of me.

"Um . . . whoa . . . whoa . . . whoa . . . this is a strip club." My pitch reached heights only dogs could hear.

Hart was attaching the second wheel to his chair. The blinking neon sign lit his face just enough for me to see the corners of his mouth twitch in a poor attempt to hide his amusement.

"Hell, yeah, it is!" Doug shouted.

"I thought we were going to a bar for drinks."

Colin walked up next to me. "There's a bar inside."

"Um . . . there are a ton of . . . um . . . regular bars in town. Why this one?" I stammered.

Doug draped his arm over Ronnie's shoulder. "Cause it's our boy's final moments of freedom."

I whipped my head toward Ronnie. "You're getting married?"

He grinned from ear-to-ear. "Yeah, next weekend."

Standing firm with hands on hips, I said, "You guys didn't tell me this was a bachelor party."

Colin tilted his head, trying to look all innocent. "Didn't we mention that?"

Looking at each other feigning confusion, Ronnie and Doug mumbled and muttered.

"I thought we mentioned it." Ronnie piped up.

Doug agreed. "I'm positive we said something."

My head shook back and forth so quickly I could hear my brain rattling along with my nerves. "I can't go in there."

"You're over twenty-one, right?" Ronnie joked.

I nodded blankly.

Colin draped his arm loosely around my shoulders. "If we're lucky it might be open pole night."

My jaw went slack as my eyes stretched wide. "Open pole night? What's that?"

Doug positioned himself directly in front of me. "It's when they let the lady customers ride the pole." He gyrated his hips while his eyebrows danced.

Hart's booming voice startled us all. "God dammit, Doug! I warned you!"

Doug threw his hands in the air and backed away. "Just having a little innocent fun with the princess."

Hart slid from the driver's seat into his chair. "Y'all go ahead. Bryson and I will catch up."

The guys quickly headed toward the giant lady-shaped sign with the flashing neon nipples.

The crunch of the gravel echoed in my ears as Hart rolled up beside me. "I can take you back to your car. No problem."

I didn't want to go back to my car. And I didn't particularly want to go in the strip club. But I wanted more time with Hart.

"That's not necessary. I don't want to ruin your night. I'm fine. I've seen naked women before. I get naked every day . . . obviously not out in public with a pole between my legs . . ."

"Bryson . . ."

"Girls gotta make a living though. Right? Who am I to judge . . .?"

I felt the touch of his large warm hand grab mine. "I promise I won't let anything bad happen to you. Just say the word and I'll whisk you away."

Gazing at his sincere expression, I felt safe.

"Okay," I whispered.

I took a deep breath before Hart and I headed into the club.

My only frame of reference in regards to a strip club was from TV and movies. I expected the inside to be seedy and full of middle-aged men in ugly leisure suits with comb-overs. To my surprise there were several female customers, some looked to be part of bachelorette parties and others were there with men. The clientele looked normal and not creepy at all. Tall leggy topless women constantly circled the large dimly light room carrying trays of drinks. The loud pulsating music pushed on my chest.

Hart and I weaved through the dense crowd until we spotted the guys sitting at a table a few feet back from the main stage. I did as Hart had told me and stayed close by his side until we reached our table. Smiling up at me, Doug patted the empty seat beside him. I hesitated for several seconds until I saw Hart take the spot on the other side of the chair. Relaxing a little, I positioned myself between the two guys. I was beginning to feel overwhelmed with the flashing lights, the crowd, and the naked women. Hart must have sensed my anxiety. Placing his warm hand over mine, he gave it a slight squeeze.

With my attention aimed forward, the large stage suddenly went dark. The crowd erupted into whistles, hollers, and the occasional bark. The song *Earned It* by The Weekend seductively surrounded the room. The stage lights slowly brightened, revealing the silhouette of a tall curvy female. She swayed her way into the light toward the pole at center stage. My brows furrowed as I took in what she was wearing, sparkly pasties with matching thong and killer heels. For a stripper, there was very little on her to strip down to.

"How ya doing?" I was so focused on the show, I almost jumped out of my skin at the sound of Hart's voice in my ear.

I turned to face him, putting us only an inch apart. My eyes closed slightly as the scent of warm pumpkin pie wafted over me.

"Bryson?"

My eyes shot open to a grinning Hart. "Trying to take it all in."

Neither of us moved for . . .

One Mississippi.

Two Mississippi.

Hart blinked, pulled away, and fished his phone from the front pocket of his jeans.

After reading what I assumed was a text, his eyes met mine. "I'll be right back."

"You're leaving?" The panic obvious in my voice.

"Just for a few minutes. Don't move."

I slowly nodded, my gaze staying glued to Hart as he left my side.

The clank of a glass being placed in front of me caused my head to snap forward. I looked down at a shot glass full of amber liquid.

Twisting my head to the right, I saw all three guys smiling my way with their own shots ready to be chugged. "Hey, I didn't order this."

Colin raised his glass. "First round's on me."

"Maybe we should wait until Hart comes back," I yelled over the music.

Lifting his glass, Doug nodded in the direction Hart went. "By the looks of things our boy won't be coming back for a while. That a boy, Hart!" he shouted.

A huge lump formed in the middle of my throat. Hart was over in the corner near the side of the stage talking with Amber. They were too far away and the place too dark for me to make out a lot of details. She was wearing boy shorts, a barely there bikini top, and the tallest heels I'd ever seen. She was in front of Hart, her chest practically shoved in his face. Images of the window display popped in my head.

I grabbed the shot glass, clamped my eyes shut, and downed the drink. The second the whiskey hit the back of my throat a fire erupted. Coughs flew out of me as I slammed the shot glass back down on the table.

Doug patted me on the back. "You okay, princess?"

The patting quickly morphed into slow deep circular rubs moving lower and lower. I backhanded Doug in the chest as the coughing fit died down.

He leaned in close and whispered in my ear. "How'd you know I liked it rough?"

Turning toward him, I let the final cough slap him in the face. He leaned back with a toothy grin, unfazed.

"The first shot's a real ass kicker," Ronnie said.

"How long has that been going on?" I tilted my head toward Hart and Amber.

Colin was the only one to answer. "Awhile."

Another shot magically appeared.

Doug sat up taller with his glass held high. "A toast to the man of the hour! To Ronnie!"

All four of us raised our glasses and in unison yelled, "To Ronnie!"

One-by-one shot glasses hit the table.

Whack.

Whack.

Whack

Whack.

The boys and I were like a synchronized swim team.

My lips and tongue tingled from the spicy hot cinnamon flavor. Other than wine, I wasn't a big fan of the harder stuff. But these shots reminded me of red hot candies and were delicious.

My gaze drifted over to where Hart and Amber were still talking. "Is it slerious?"

"Doubt it." Doug waved his hand in the air. Seconds later another round and a pair of bare breasts popped into my sightline.

I tried not to look but the bedazzled nipple art was hard to ignore. I couldn't get over how high this chick's breasts were without the aid of a bra.

"Bottoms up!" Ronnie shouted.

Leaning in close, Doug brought his face within an inch of mine. "Bry . . . son. Brys . . . on. Did I ever tell you how much I like your name? Cause, I do like it. I like it a lot."

It may have been the alcohol but I don't remember Doug having a British accent.

"What exactly is your stitchuation?"

I blinked a few times trying to bring him into focus. "I'm in transizon . . . transition."

He jerked back and gasped. "Holy shit! You're a dude?!"

"No!" I leaned forward. "Do I look like a dude?"

Moving closer, he said, "You look like a hot piece of ass."

The comment was rude and crude, but it made me smile inside.

"I'm in the prob . . . cess of ending a long-term relatiationship."

"You're getting a divorce?"

I nodded.

"Whew! Now where were we?" He was so close the tips of our noses were almost touching.

Suddenly, Doug was yanked back as if a giant vacuum were sucking him away. Then my body vibrated from what was quickly becoming my favorite sound.

"Doug, back the fuck off!" Hart growled.

My head whipped around, smashing into intense blue-gray eyes. *Tingles.*

"Hart's back!" I yelled.

"Bryson, are you drunk?" Hart's lips were sexy forming the words.

"Nope." I popped the p.

"God dammit, guys. I was gone for less than ten minutes. What the hell did y'all give her?

"Calm down! We just had a few shots of Fireball." Ronnie sounded unaffected by the alcohol.

"She's fine. Just having some fun," said Colin. Sweet adorable Colin, the peacemaker.

My head began to swim as my body swayed from side-to-side and back and forth. Grabbing my shoulders, Hart steadied me before I fell out of my seat.

"Bryson, you're not much of a drinker, are you?" Hart was so close if I stuck my tongue out I'd be able to lick his sexy lips.

"Nope." Once again I popped the p and smiled.

Through gritted teeth, Hart scolded. "Nice going, guys. She's plastered."

"Sorry."

"Sorry."

"Sorry."

I looked in the air searching for the source of the shower of apologies falling all around me.

"Bryson . . . Bryson . . ." My gaze swung to Hart. "I'm going to take you home, okay."

I leaned toward him. "What about big tits?"

I was woozy and unfocused but a definitely laugh came out of that sexy man.

"Colin, help me get her to the car."

My eyes doubled in size as Hart began to shrink right in front of me. "Hey, what's happening?"

"Back up a little more, Hart." Colin instructed, as he tugged me to my feet and wrapped his arm around my waist.

The strip club and the boys got really fuzzy after I stood. The next thing I remembered was the sound of Hart's voice saying my name.

chapter Fifteen

"Bryson."

My eyes squinted open for a brief second before closing again.

"Wake up."

A soft moan drifted over my lips at the sound of his deep gravelly voice.

"You can't sleep in my car." There was a slight tug on my arm. "Come on. It'll be over soon."

My eyes stayed closed as I was helped to an upright position. A large warm hand slid under my right knee and then my left, lifting and twisting until my feet fell out of the car.

"Bryson, open our eyes. I need your help."

Slowly my lids cracked open to blurry blue-gray eyes.

Hart brushed the hair away from my face. "Can you stand for me?"

On my head if you wanted me to.

My arms rose as if working independently from the rest of my body. Suddenly, the sensation of hard broad shoulders hit my palms.

"Bryson, I'm going to stand you up then lean you against the car so I can close the door. Okay?"

"Okay." My pitch squeaked so high it startled me.

The pressure of a powerful grip pressed on either side of my hips. I bent forward as Hart lifted me out of the car, my fingers digging into his shoulders for support. Shifting sideways my back hit the cold hard side of the car. The next thing I was aware of was Hart's fingers wrapping around my wrists as he gently pulled me forward and down onto his lap.

"You okay?" His warm breath glided over my lips.

Mmm . . . pumpkin pie.

"I'm more than okay." I sighed.

"Put your arms around my neck and hold on."

Soft hair tickled the back of my hands as they slid behind his neck. We were so close I

felt his ever present scruff bristle across my cheek. I took in a deep breath and melted against his toned chest.

My foggy gaze floated down, then up, then down, and finally back up over his gorgeous

face. "Your eyes are ama-a-azing."

Tiny crinkles appeared at the corners of his eyes. "Thank you."

"Those lips of yours are so splexy . . . splippy . . . sexy lippy."

The vibration of a deep chuckle migrated from his chest to mine. "I appreciate that."

"And don't even get me started on those dimples." My right hand slipped from behind Hart's neck, feeling its way down his jaw. "They're so deep I could take a bubble bath in them." I waved my right hand in the air, tipping back slightly. "I'd just lay back and lux-ur-i-ate."

Hart grabbed my arm and flung it back over his shoulder. "Whoa! We need to get some coffee in you."

A gentle breeze blew through my hair as my body began to lightly bounce. "Hey, we're moving."

Hart rolled us up to his front door and stopped. A couple of clicks later and we were heading inside. The lights flipped on, causing my eyes to clamp shut and my face to dive into the crook of Hart's neck. The collar of his shirt was the only thing separating my lips from his skin. I couldn't tell whose chest stopped moving. All I knew was for a brief moment one of us wasn't breathing.

We glided across the floor then stopped abruptly. My body jostled at the jerk of Hart's arm. A loud clank, like keys hitting the counter, rang in my ears. Out of nowhere a persistent force began to nudge my elbow.

"Butter, sit." Hart's chest vibrated with the command.

The prodding quit and we were on the move again. I swayed a little as we swiveled back and forth, coming to a complete stop. Familiar strong hands returned to my hips.

"Bryson, you have to let me go."

I did ten years ago and it was the biggest mistake of my life.

My head lifted reluctantly as Hart peeled my arms from around his neck. Placing his hands on my waist, he picked me up, and moved me to the sofa.

"You stay put and I'll go make the coffee."

"Okie dokie," I said, flopping back against the cushion, my gaze scanning the room.

Hart's place was nice. Blurry at the moment but nice. The décor was sleek and modern with a lot of whites, blacks, and grays. From my vantage point, I could see the dining room, kitchen, and what looked to be a home office in the far corner. A set of large French doors and windows lined most of the back wall.

The more my gaze moved around the room the woozier I got. Beads of sweat popped up across my forehead. Muffled gurgles emanated from my stomach. The air and my throat got thick. I closed my eyes a second before the first wave of nausea hit.

"Hart!" I groaned.

"Down the hall, first door on the left."

Slapping my hand over my mouth, I bolted off the sofa and ran to pay my penance.

I made it to the bathroom just in time to see everything I had consumed over the past month spew forth. I held on to the toilet for dear life as I violently convulsed, echoes of my humiliation ricocheting off the porcelain. Cool air hit my neck as the curtain of hair on either side of my face was pulled back and lifted away. For a brief moment I prayed that a merciful hand would crawl up from the toilet, grab me, and flush me into oblivion.

After my stomach was completely emptied, I remained motionless with my face buried in the toilet. I was afraid any sudden movement would have my insides flipping and flopping again.

"Ju-u-ust let me know when you're ready," Hart said, his voice calm and soothing with a hint of amusement.

Unable to stand the taste of the ghost from meals past any longer, I slowly lifted my head and sat down on the floor with my legs stretched out in front of me. My gaze darted up to a damp washcloth waiting for me. I quickly grabbed it and covered my blotchy face.

"I'm so sorry," I mumbled through the terrycloth.

"Don't worry about it. We've all been there."

"Oh god. I only had three shots." I moaned.

"You downed three shots of sixty-six proof whiskey in a little under ten minutes. That'd kick most people on their ass."

"Ugh . . . I don't know what I was thinking."

"Give me the washcloth and I'll warm it back up."

I lowered my face and handed the cooled cloth to Hart.

Moments later he returned with the rewarmed washcloth. I took it, quickly putting it back in place over my face.

"Listen, if you'd call Uber, I'll get out of your hair." The material puffed in and out as I spoke.

"You're not going anywhere in this condition. You're spending the night here."

His tone was so commanding and final.

Poking one eye out from behind the washcloth, I said, "I can't stay here."

"Why not?"

"I've already ruined most of your night. I'll go home and you go back to the strip club. I'm sure Amber is waiting."

Ignoring me, he said, "Towels and washcloths are on the shelf over there. I'll get you a T-shirt and a pair of boxers."

"Hart . . ."

"I'm gonna grab those things and your coffee."

"Hart . . ."

"Cream? Sugar? Both?"

Realizing I wasn't going to win this argument, I caved.

"Two sugars and a splash of cream."

Without warning, he moved closer to me and reached down. "First, give me your foot."

"Excuse me?"

"Those boots need to come off."

"I can manage, thanks."

He didn't move. He was waiting for me to prove that I was indeed capable of removing my own boots. As I leaned forward, I got dizzy and everything blurred. My hand flew up, clutching the side of the toilet to keep me upright. When the slickness of the porcelain met my sweaty palm, I knew I was done for. My grip loosened, causing my hand to slide and me to sink back against the wall.

Hart's fingers wiggled at the end of his outstretched arm. "Come on. Give it up."

Feeling completely helpless and defeated, I placed my booted foot into his hand. Hart cradled my left ankle, using his other hand to gently push the soft leather over my knee and down my calf. A chill ran through my body as his fingertips grazed the back of my knee. My fuzzy brain could have been playing tricks on me, but I thought I heard a sharp intake of air as his bottom lip disappeared into his mouth.

Placing the boot to the side, Hart repeated the action with my right leg. My entire body buzzed and it had nothing to do with the alcohol. I became very aware of my position on the floor with Hart hovering above. The corners of my mouth involuntarily drifted up.

Hart was wiggling and pulling the heel when he noticed my expression. "What are you smiling at?"

I pointed to where he was holding my leg. "It's like a reverse Cinderella."

"I'm all about the fairy tale." He winked, slipped off my boot, and extended his hand. "Let me help you up."

Waving it off, I said, "I got this."

"You sure?"

I nodded.

No need to be an overachiever in the embarrassment and humiliation category. I knew getting off the floor would not be a graceful maneuver. Hart swiveled his chair toward the door and rolled out of the bathroom, leaving me alone with my frayed dignity.

As predicted, the rise from the gray slate tiles was not pretty. In fact, it took three attempts before I was able to hoist myself onto the closed toilet. As my first ass cheek hit the seat, Hart reappeared with a T-shirt and a pair of boxers slung over his shoulder and a cup of coffee in one hand. It was amazing how he could maneuver the wheelchair using only one hand and shifting his weight.

Wanting to relieve him of one less thing to carry, I placed my hands on either side of the seat and leaned forward, attempting to stand. Less than an inch up, the room began to spin, forcing me back on my ass.

"Whoa. Aftershocks."

Hart placed the mug of coffee and my new pajamas on the counter.

Turning toward me, he lifted a bottled water he had tucked beside him, cracked the seal, and handed it to me. "Something to rinse your mouth out with."

"Thanks," I said, taking the bottle.

My cotton mouth soaked up the cold water immediately. I whooshed it around a few seconds then realized I had to dispose of it somehow. The way I saw it I had two options. Spit or swallow.

Hart sensed my dilemma. "Need a little help to the sink?"

I nodded, my cheeks bloated with water.

My hand seemed so tiny compared to Hart's as our palms met. He held me steady while I shuffled toward the sink. I gripped the edge of the countertop and was just about to spit when I remembered I had an audience. Looking at Hart's reflection in the mirror, I twirled my index finger in the air, motioning for him to turn around. He shook his head, chuckled, and then complied.

"Blak!" The noise shot out of me.

Real dainty, Bryson.

"Feel free to use the mouthwash."

I grabbed the bottle, unscrewed the cap, and looked around for a cup to pour the minty liquid into.

"Just throw it back, Bryson. We're all friends here." I definitely detected a little too much pleasure in his voice.

I chugged, swooshed, and repeated the same embarrassing noise as before. "Blak!"

"Feel better?"

"Well, my mouth is cool and refreshed."

"Drink some more water before tackling the coffee."

I inched my way back to the toilet seat on steadier legs. Hart's hands were at the ready just in case I wobbled.

I sat and took another swig of water. "Has anyone ever told you how bossy you are?"

"Yep." He handed me the mug.

The room fell silent for a few seconds as I sipped the coffee. Closing my eyes, I enjoyed how soothing the warmth felt trickling down my throat.

"Maybe I should stay in here while you shower."

My eyes shot open. "Excuse me?"

"Just to make sure you don't fall."

"I . . . um . . . I."

"I'm not looking for a peep show, Bryson."

"I didn't say you were. Why you would want to peep at me when you have . . . um . . ."

Hart's eyebrows rose. "Big tits?"

My cheeks flushed with heat. "Did I call her that?"

A huge grin broke across his face. "Yes you did."

"I'm sorry. I had no right to . . ."

"It's okay. She does have big tits."

We both tried to stifle our laughter but were ultimately unsuccessful.

"If you're sure you'll be okay, I'll leave. Just put your jeans outside the door."

"What for?" I asked.

"I'll throw them in the washer."

"You've already done more than enough for me."

Holding my gaze, Hart said, "No problem."

"You don't need to wash my clothes."

"I think I do."

"No, really, it's too much . . ."

"Bryson, you have vomit on your jeans."

Hello, dignity? Where are you?

"Oh . . . okay." I hid my embarrassment behind the mug and took another sip of coffee. "Hart, thanks again for taking care of me."

"Best time I've had all day." He moved toward the door then stopped. "Oh, Bryson."

"Yeah?"

"I'll cover up the peephole in the door."

I tugged a hand towel down from the rack above me and threw it at him. Staying put a little longer, I sipped my coffee, enjoying the sound of Hart's deep laughter as it faded behind the closed door.

My head had cleared enough that I felt confident in my legs. I headed over to the shower and turned it on. While waiting for the water to heat up, I finished my coffee and looked around. The bathroom was huge and from what I could tell fell in line with the modern feel of the rest of the place. On the same wall as the door, hung two small brightly colored abstract paintings that were in stark contrast to the rest of the monochromatic palate.

Once steam filled the air, I pulled the sweater over my head and shimmied out of my jeans. Standing in just my pale pink lace bra and matching panties, I quietly inched the door open enough to push my arm through and let the jeans fall from my fingers. They didn't fall far. They were caught mid-float before hitting the floor.

I fumbled to shut the door, forgetting all about my arm, which was still hanging out in the hallway. "Ow!"

"Jesus, are you okay?" Hart said, concern evident in his tone.

I cracked the door open enough to free my arm. "I'm good, thanks."

Shutting the door, I pressed my back against it and let out a deep sigh. Even with my throbbing arm, the sound of Hart's deep rasp coupled with the fact I was standing merely inches away practically naked had my body humming. This was not good. Not good at all. Sure, Hart flirted with me but I got the impression this was his MO with most women. I was lonely and he was being a friend. That's all it was and will be. I didn't need to read any more into it.

Before pushing off from the door, I glanced down, gasping in horror. My nipples looked like a couple of B cup missiles ready for launch. And this was just from the sound of his voice.

Not good. Not good at all.

I unhooked my bra, let my panties drop to the floor, and stepped into the shower. The hot water poured over me, warming the Hart induced chills. I spotted the shampoo and body wash and quickly got to work.

Stepping out of the shower, I grabbed one of the large fluffy black towels and wrapped it around my body. It wasn't until standing in front of the mirror towel-drying my hair that I realized my purse with my brush was in the living room.

Dammit!

I did the best I could, running my fingers through the tangled mess a few times. I didn't want to scare Hart any more than I had already. I pulled on my panties and the black and white plaid boxers.

Hart definitely had signature colors.

Since the gray long sleeve T-shirt was made of thicker material, I decided it'd be safe to go braless. I didn't like to keep the girls confined at night. As I slipped it over my head I breathed in, hoping to catch a hint of his scent.

I needed to pull myself together before I went out there. This was just a silly little crush I was experiencing. Nothing more. Hart was showing me attention, being sweet and flirty, taking care of me. We were becoming friends, that's all. He had Amber and I sure as hell didn't need to get involved with anyone at this point in time.

I walked down the hall repeating the little pep talk to myself. As I approached the living room I was met by a pair of big caramel eyes and a wagging tail.

Excited to have a visitor, Butter circled around me several times, finally landing when I squatted down and did some ear scratching. "Hey, sweet girl."

Hart was rounding the kitchen island carrying a plate in his lap with what looked to be a grilled cheese sandwich.

He stopped and stared at me for a brief moment, his gaze causing my body to heat up again. "Feeling better?"

"Much. Thanks." I stood and scanned the room for my purse. "Do you know where my purse is?"

Butter's nose shot into the air as she followed Hart to the coffee table. "I put it on the sofa."

I quickly retrieved my brush and ran it through my damp hair.

"Sit and eat." Hart commanded.

Butter and I both sat.

My attention turned to the coffee table. Along with the sandwich was a fresh cup of coffee, another bottled water, and Tylenol.

I fidgeted with the bottom of the long sleeves. "I'm not hungry."

"Doesn't matter. You need to eat. You'll feel better. I promise."

I wasn't used to this type of care and attention.

I picked up the sandwich and took a small bite. Then another. And another and another until the entire thing was gone. Seeing that the sandwich had disappeared, Butter slunk back to her bed and curled up.

"Glad you weren't hungry." He teased

"It was delicious. Thank you."

"Sorry it wasn't gourmet."

I gave him a shy smile. "It was just what I needed."

"I only know how to cook two things."

"What's the second thing?"

"If I told you it would take all the mystery out of our relationship." He teased, repeating my own words back to me.

"With the events of tonight, I'd say there's very little mystery left."

"Before I forget. Do you like toasted Pop Tarts for breakfast?"

I picked up my coffee with both hands and scooted farther back on the sofa. "I could teach you how to cook."

"Why would I need to learn how to cook when I have a lovely lunch lady visit me every day?"

My cheeks flushed. There was that word again. "Come on. Man cannot live on grilled cheese and toaster pastries alone."

"I'll let you attempt to teach me on one condition."

"Name it."

"That I don't lose my lunch lady visits."

I answered in a low voice. "You won't."

Our gaze locked. Hart and I both knew once Will was released that the daily lunches would come to an end. My life was a mess at the moment and I knew it was unfair to bring Hart into it even as a friend. But I was quickly realizing how much our time together meant to me and I didn't want to give it up.

Breaking the moment, I said, "When would you like your first lesson?"

"I'm wide open."

"How about tomorrow?"

"I already have plans." *With Amber?* "Besides, you probably won't feel like doing much of anything."

"I'm feeling better already."

He hesitated for a second. "Okay. Weekends are best for me."

"Next weekend?"

He cocked an eyebrow. "Are you sure it won't cause trouble?"

I took a stab at sounding confident. "Why would it cause any trouble? It's just one friend helping out another friend."

He slowly nodded. "True."

There was a slight twinge of disappointment in my stomach. I was so confused. One minute I thought Hart felt the same pull as I did. Then he'd say something that had me crashing back down to reality. It was becoming very obvious that my instincts were out of whack. I mean, I thought Will loved me for all these years and I was way off the mark with that one. I suddenly wished I'd taken Sophie's advice and played the field some when I was younger. Even a little frame of reference would help at the moment.

"So next weekend it is. That will give me enough time to plan and shop for lesson one."

Grinning, Hart tipped his chin up a little. "Oh, there's going to be multiple lessons?"

"Eh, if you're a good student one might do the trick."

"Then I'll make sure to be bad." His expression went flat, as if he were shocked by the degree of his flirting.

I took another sip of coffee and hid my blush.

Clearing his throat, Hart asked, "How about some more coffee?"

"I'm good, thanks."

"I'm gonna get a refill."

While he headed toward the kitchen, it gave me a chance to get a better, less blurred view of the main part of the house. A collection of sports magazines and books lined the black bookshelves that were on the opposite wall from the large flat screen TV. Along the wall in the dining room, gallery, shelves held up pictures of varying sizes. Some were art pieces, like sketches and paintings while others were photos. I couldn't quite make out who all was in the shots, so I headed over there, my curiosity getting the best of me.

The photos were predominantly of Hart, Colin, Ronnie, and Doug from childhood up to adulthood. My heart sank seeing pictures of a younger Hart standing. It made me feel good knowing he had such great friends by his side when he needed them the most. There were several photos of him playing sports post-wheelchair—basketball, snow skiing, water volleyball. Hart certainly didn't let his disability slow him down.

"See anything you like?" The raspy tone hit my ears, letting me know I'd been caught snooping.

"I was just admiring your photos and artwork. Did you paint these?"

Shaking his head, he said, "My mom was the artist."

"And the paintings in the bathroom?"

"Hers too. Any artwork you see around here was done by her."

"It's gorgeous work. I'd love to meet her someday."

"You're about eleven years too late. She passed away from ovarian cancer my junior year in high school."

Clutching the back of a dining room chair, my gaze dropped. "That's terrible." I paused for a few seconds then looked back at him. "I'm so sorry."

My heart ached at the thought of Hart losing his mom at such a young age. This must have been the reason he had to move in with his dad and transfer to Garrison.

"It was a long time ago and life goes on. Right?"

His tone was flat but I could tell in his eyes he was as affected by this mother's death today as when it happened.

Not wanting to upset him I redirected. "You and the three stooges have been friends for a long time?"

We both eyed a picture of the four friends at what looked to be a ski resort.

"Colin and I grew up together. We met Ronnie and Doug in middle school and couldn't get rid of them."

"Old friends are special. I have Sophie. Not sure if you remember her."

"She's the one who took you away from me."

Comments like that made my body hum and my head swirl. "So, no pictures of the rest of your family?"

"Not much of a family."

"And no pictures of your girl?"

I knew I was a glutton for punishment by wading in Amber waters.

"I don't have a girl." He turned abruptly and headed toward the living room.

I hesitated for a moment and then followed.

"I'm sorry. I just assumed that you and Amber . . ."

"You assumed wrong." He interrupted.

I lowered myself back onto the sofa. Grabbing the Tylenol, I popped two in my mouth and chased them with a swig of water.

Rubbing the back of his neck, Hart said, "Bryson, I'm sorry. I didn't mean to sound like an ass."

"Perfectly okay. I shouldn't have pried into your personal life."

He looked directly at me. "I don't have anything to hide. Amber and I have a business arrangement. Period."

I pushed back on the sofa as an awkward silence settled in the air. This was the first of its kind between me and Hart. Our friendship or whatever this was developing into was foreign territory for me. Besides Sophie, I didn't have a lot of my own friends, especially male ones. The couples Will and I hung out with were made up of his friends and their wives.

My encounters with Hart had been light and breezy for the most part. A tug of war was taking place in my head. Part of me wanted some details about Amber but the other part wanted to stay ignorant. I decided the best thing would be to get us back to light and breezy, so I joked my way out of the awkwardness.

Waggling my eyebrows, I teased. "Exactly what kind of business of yours is she arranging?"

"You really want to know?"

Shit, he's actually going to answer my question?

"Dying." The word fell out of my mouth before I realized it.

His expression was serious as his blue-gray eyes held me in place. "I pay her to have sex with me."

Everything dropped—my mouth, my heart, my stomach. I stared wide-eyed at him. From what I'd witnessed at the rehab, Hart didn't want for female attention. I didn't understand why he paid for something that any number of women would gladly give him free of charge.

He didn't look away or say another word. He was waiting for me to make the next move. Hart's honesty opened a floodgate of questions. But did I want to go further down this rabbit hole?

"Why?"

Damn my curiosity!

"Uncomplicated, unattached, and unemotional."

"Wow, that's a sad way to have a relationship."

"It's not a relationship."

I couldn't tell if he was just spouting the information like he would to anyone else or he wanted to make sure I was clear about the arrangement.

"Semantics," I said.

"I don't do relationships."

I didn't try to hide my eye roll. "What does that even mean? You don't do relationships. You just haven't found anyone you wanted to do it with."

Cocking an eyebrow Hart said, "Oh, I've found a lot of anyones to *do* it with."

The direction of this conversation had blindsided me.

I huffed. "Not allowing yourself to fall in love with another person is a very empty existence."

"Bullshit. My existence is quite full, thank you. Besides, no woman wants damaged goods."

I shifted in my seat. "I didn't mean . . . you're the strongest and most confident person I know. It's obvious you don't let anything hold you back. And as far as women are concerned . . . don't you see the blushing cheeks and the smiles they give you?" My tone turned more teasing. "And the giggles at your flirty comments that are sophomoric at best."

"I'll have you know I'm a master flirts-man." His expression remained serious but I detected a mischievous twinkle in his eye. "You fell in love and look where it got you . . . divorced before the age of thirty." His words were biting but his tone wasn't harsh.

Squaring my shoulders, I sat up straight. "It doesn't mean I stopped believing in true love."

His expression softened a bit. "Why?"

"Why what?"

"Why did you marry him? Why didn't you go to culinary school? Why aren't you a chef or running your own catering business?"

"Why are you being such a dick?"

"I'm not trying to be a dick."

"So it's a natural talent?"

His entire face lit up with enjoyment. "You obviously have a passion for creating edible art. Yet you've spent the last ten years not following it. That to me is an empty existence."

Touché.

I loved how our conversations flowed seamlessly from fun to serious and back without missing a beat. If I'd had a similar conversation with Will it would have ended in an argument. Will's tone was always condescending and dismissive. He never really cared what I had to say on any subject. Always talking at me instead of with me. Not only did Hart talk with me, he listened and paid attention. He was honest, forthright, and interested in my opinion.

Taking a cue from my silence, Hart leaned forward, gathering up the grilled cheese aftermath. "It's getting late. I need to get you in bed."

With wide eyes, my head jerked in his direction. "What?"

He headed into the kitchen and loaded the dishes into the dishwasher. "You need to go sleep off the rest of your whiskey haze."

I scooted to the edge of the sofa. "I'm feeling okay. I think it's pretty much out of my system."

He moved toward me. "Come on, I'll show you my bedroom."

"I'm fine on the sofa."

"Bryson. My bedroom. Now." He made a sharp turn.

A warm buzz spread to all my key areas. There was definitely something different when Hart spouted out an order. I felt secure and cared for, like he was putting me at the top of his priority list.

"Hart . . ."

He hovered at the end of the hallway. "Haven't you learned by now? There's no need to argue. I always win. Now get your sweet little ass up and follow me."

Swallowing hard, I stood on shaky legs, grabbed my purse, and followed him down the hall.

Hart's room was more elegant than I imagined it would be. Not that I had been fantasizing about his bedroom. The walls were a darker gray than the rest of the house. His king-size bed sat front and center on the long wall covered in a light gray comforter with a silver striped design. All the furniture was sleek and black. He rolled over to the dresser and grabbed his pajamas before snatching a pillow from the bed.

"Hart, I wish you'd let me sleep on the sofa."

"It'd be a little crowded with the two of us out there. If you need me, I'll be right outside the door."

He was right, there was no need to argue.

"Thank you, again, for everything," I said.

He moved toward the door and turned to face me. "Goodnight, Bryson."

"Goodnight, Hart."

As I stood in the middle of the room a strange sense of peace and contentment washed over me, knowing I'd start the next day seeing him.

chapter Sixteen

Bang.

Bang.

Bang.

Despite the great care I received last night, the loud pounding was incessant. Ignoring my throbbing temples, I pulled the comforter over my head, attempting to sink back into oblivious sleep.

Tap.

Tap.

Tap.

"Bryson, are you awake?"

I shot straight up, the covers tumbling and pooling at my hips. Even with the vice around my head tightening, the smooth deep rasp of Hart's voice first thing in the morning gave me chills.

Tossing off the comforter, I swung my legs across the bed and let my feet drop. My hands landed on either side of my hips, gripping the mattress as I let my feet get used to the floor beneath. Once I felt confident in my leg's ability to hold me up, I pushed off from the bed and stood. Other than my aching head it appeared the rest of me was no worse for wear.

Tap.

Tap.

Tap.

I headed toward the door and cracked it open. A familiar flutter in my stomach took over when I lay eyes on Hart's sexy half face.

"Come in at your own risk," I grumbled, pushing the door wide open.

Hart had already showered and dressed. He was in a pair of black sweat pants, a white and blue basketball jersey with Steelers stretched across his chest, and Nikes. His hair was still damp and slicked back off his face. Apparently, his scuff was a constant presence in his life. He had it even when we were in school. I remembered being mesmerized by the contrast of his baby face being covered with the manly beard. For a second I wondered what a clean-shaven Hart would look like but quickly realized he wouldn't look like himself without his trademark.

"I come bearing gifts." He moved farther into the room holding a mug of coffee in his right hand.

His muscles rippled beneath his skin with each push of the wheel. As he rolled past me, I got a good look at the tattoos on his left arm. I was curious to know what relevance they had in his life.

Turning toward me, he stared for a couple of seconds before clearing his throat and speaking. "How ya feeling this morning?"

"Jury's still out." I took the coffee and climbed back in bed.

I sipped and caught Hart staring, his Adam's apple slowly making its way down his neck.

He was checking out my ass.

I took another sip, enjoying the hypnotic effect my ass had on him for

. . .

One Mississippi.

Two Mississippi.

Three Mississippi.

Four Mississippi.

"So what else you got for me?"

Hart snapped out of his daze at the sound of my voice. "Excuse me?"

"You said gifts with an s."

He tilted his chin up in recognition and held up a blueberry Pop Tart.

"Once you get a couple of cooking lessons under your belt you're gonna make an actual tart your bitch."

He moved in closer, handing me the cellophane-covered chemically enhanced pastry. "I thought I was doing that already."

I was in no mood to start the day with an Amber reference. Narrowing my eyes, I snatched my breakfast out of his hand, tore into the paper, and bit off a chunk. I ran my tongue across my bottom lip, licking off the crumbs. When lazy tingles spread over my body, I knew Hart's eyes were on me.

I inhaled a deep breath. "So what's with the get up?"

He swallowed hard as his gaze met mine. "I have a game in an hour."

Staying put, I took another bite of Pop Tart.

More staring accompanied by comfortable silence.

Like a bolt of lightning zapping me in the head, I suddenly clued in that he was trying to usher me along in the nicest way possible. I held the half-eaten pastry between my lips, kicked off the covers, and jumped out of bed.

Handing off my mug to Hart, I dashed around the room, grabbing my sweater and purse.

"I'm an idiot. You told me last night you had plans," I mumbled out the corner of my mouth.

Whipping my head back and forth, I scanned the room for my jeans and boots as I swallowed what was left of my breakfast. "Any idea where my jeans ended up?"

When I got no response, I glanced over at Hart staring at me *again*.

I ran my hand over my face, praying that nothing was hanging or dangling. "Is something wrong?"

Slowly shaking his head, Hart said, "No, nothing's wrong." He paused. "You look really pretty in the morning."

As inconspicuously as possible, I brought my knees together and squeezed.

He shot his thumb over his shoulder. "I'll see you out there."

"Good deal." I sighed.

Hart was almost out the door when I remembered the mystery of my jeans had not been solved. "Um . . . my jeans?"

"In the dryer," he yelled, as he left the room, never looking back.

Since my jeans were still drying, I had some time to do a quick freshen up. The master bath was even larger than the one from last night with similar décor. My gaze roamed as I set my purse and sweater beside the sink. It looked like a regular bathroom with only a few exceptions to accommodate the wheelchair. The tub/shower combo had a door allowing

Hart to roll right into it. Everything was lower—towel racks, mirror, and shelves. There was no cabinet under the sink and brushed metal grip bars were strategically placed to aid in mobility.

I turned on the faucet and let the water warm up. As I filled my cupped hands with warm water, my thoughts drifted back to last night. It felt so natural and comfortable with Hart. When the conversation turned serious it didn't derail into an argument. He gave up his night with the guys to take care of me. And then this morning . . . the look in his eyes . . . I wanted to believe that look was reserved for only me. I splashed the handful of water in my face and shook off the daydreaming.

After putting on my bra and sweater, I ran the brush through my hair and gathered it up into a high ponytail using the spare scrunchy I always kept in my purse. Poking my head in the bedroom, I saw no sign of Hart or my jeans.

With more time to kill, I went ahead and folded Hart's shirt and boxers. The psychotic single white female part of me wanted to take them home. But I suppressed the urge and placed them on the top of his dresser. I then sat on the side of the bed and pulled on my beige wool socks. Then I made the bed. Then I sat on the bed, fingering the owl pendant around my neck while my foot wiggled back and forth. I thought about dusting but the room was spotless.

The longer I waited for my clothes the more anxious I got for some reason. Maybe because for the first time in my life I was half naked in a man's bedroom. A man that I was attracted to. A man I didn't want to say goodbye to. Unable to sit still any longer, I hopped up and walked around the room, admiring the artwork created by Hart's mother.

Over the bed hung a giant abstract oil done predominantly in shades of blue. The wavy strokes swirled around and down the canvas, resembling waves churning to the bottom of the ocean. At the very top, streaks of bright red, yellow, green, and orange broke through, streaming down the canvas. There was something very familiar about this painting. Last night too many things were filling my head for me to have noticed any of the artwork in the room. I wracked my brain trying to remember if I'd seen this exact painting or a similar one at some point. I liked art and certainly appreciated it but I wasn't exactly an art buff.

Glancing at the clock I realized while I was getting lost in the paintings a chunk of time had slipped away. But Hart still hadn't returned with my jeans. Not wanting to make him late, I decided my only option was to go searching for the rest of my outfit. My sweater hit me mid-thigh but for added security I tugged the hem a little lower. I realized Hart had seen me in his boxers and it wasn't like I was naked. But a girl could never be too careful when it came to a potential hoo-haw flash.

With my purse slung over my shoulder, I cracked open the bedroom door and listened for noise.

Silence.

I quietly tiptoed across the dark hardwood until I reached the end of the hallway. Craning my neck around the corner, I scanned the living room and kitchen areas.

Empty.

I spotted a door just past the kitchen. Figuring that had to be the laundry room, I headed toward it. Just as I reached for the doorknob, the door flew open and Butter came barreling through. Unable to contain her excitement, she circled me several times, her propeller tail tickling the backs of my knees.

"Shh, Butter. You gotta calm down." The words came out between giggles.

With each repetition, I reached for her collar with no luck.

"Butter. Sit." Hart's voice caused Butter's tail to drop to the floor and my head to pop up.

I grabbed the hem of my sweater and tugged. "Hi."

His gaze roamed the length of my body before landing back on my eyes.

With an innocent expression, he asked, "Looking for these?"

No doubt the heat coursing through me had my blush blushing.

"I knew you had to leave soon and I didn't want to make you late."

"I still have time." He took another look-see while holding my pants.

As a cool draft crawled up my leg, I caught something in those blue-gray eyes that told me Hart was in the mood to play. He knew I wanted my pants. He knew I needed my pants. He wanted to see how long it would take for me to ask for my pants. What he didn't know was, I was up for the challenge.

Sliding my purse off my shoulder, I placed it on the countertop and met his gaze. "So-o-o . . . this basketball game is pretty serious."

"Pretty serious." His eyes lit up, knowing exactly what I was up to. "It's the league championship."

"How long have you been playing?"

"Six years."

Goosebumps popped up on my thighs but I be damned if they were going to take me down.

"Where do you play?"

"College of Charleston."

"I'd love to come watch you sometime."

"You'll have to wait until next season. Today is the finals."

It was like we were playing in a verbal tennis match.

"The cooking lesson still a go for next Saturday?"

"Looking forward to it." He smiled.

I shivered. "Hart . . ."

"Bryson . . ."

"Give me my pants."

Dammit!

Holding my jeans in front of me, he smugly said, "All you had to do was ask."

I snatched the pants out of his hands. "You think you're pretty cute, don't you?"

"I've been told." His gaze stayed glued to me.

As I stepped into my jeans, I kept glancing up and was met by piercing eyes each time. I could stay here all day and play with Hart.

He cleared his throat. "I need to take you to your car. You feel okay to drive, right?"

I buttoned, zipped, and replied, "I'm good. I'll just go grab . . ." Halfway through the sentence I realized I had no idea where my boots landed. ". . . My boots?"

He tilted his chin up. "Next to the sofa."

While Hart put Butter out in the backyard to enjoy the beautiful sunny day, I slipped into my found boots.

The majority of the ride back to my car was done in comfortable silence. We each swapped the occasional sneak peek at the other. Each time I caught a glimpse of Hart's hand I wanted it to reach over and touch my hand, or my knee, or my thigh. Anything. As the rehab parking lot came into view a twinge of regret pinched my heart. I didn't want to say goodbye just yet.

Hart pulled up alongside my car. The air around us shifted. He stared straight ahead not saying a word, his hands gripping the steering wheel.

I waited for a second, not sure if I should just hop out. Finally, I broke the deafening silence.

I turned toward him. "Thank you again."

He nodded.

Okay.

I hadn't been around Hart enough to be able to read all the subtle nuances of his expressions or moods. The atmosphere in the car had been great up until we pulled into the parking lot. If I'd learned anything in my life it was not to walk away from a situation when you cared.

"Hart, is everything okay?"

His eyes met mine. "Yeah, everything's fine."

There was an odd tone in his voice. We were acting as if we weren't going to see each other again.

"I already have the menu planned out in my head."

"What?"

"For your lesson next weekend," I said, the reassuring words for his benefit as much as mine.

My hand rested on the door handle as I lingered for another second. "Good luck with the game."

"Thanks."

Unless I wanted to own up to the fact that I didn't want to say goodbye just yet, I needed to leave. I took in a deep breath and without another word opened the door and hopped out. Immediately after the door shut I heard the buzz of the window lowering.

"Hey, Bryson."

I bent down and looked inside the car. "Yeah?"

"I had a great time with you." He gave me the sweetest most sincere smile.

Thank god the car was between us, hiding my buckling knees and helping me stay upright. There was something about his choice of words that sent electric shocks through my body. Hart was direct, firm, and specific with his words. His statements weren't general. He didn't just have a great time. He had a great time with me.

"It was a lot of fun even with all the throwing up and . . ." My eyebrows squished together as a vague memory flashed in my head. "Did I say something about taking a bubble bath in your dimple last night?"

"Yeah you did." He grinned from ear to ear, emphasizing the aforementioned dimples.

My eyes closed as I shook my head, hoping to transport back in time to a few minutes earlier. When I opened my eyes Hart was still staring, his tongue gliding across his lower lip.

"I had a great time with you too." I tossed a shy smile his way. "I better let you go so you're not late for the game."

"See ya, Bryson."

"See ya, Hart."

I could feel Hart's eyes on me as I walked away. I didn't know if I was feeding off his vibe, but I definitely felt more confident in that moment than I had in . . . never. My back straightened, my shoulders pushed back, and my hips moved with a little extra sway.

Once at my car, I fumbled with my keys and dropped them.

Smooth, Bryson.

Sticking my ass out, I exaggerated bending over and reached for the keys. Before standing back up, I peeked under my arm to find Hart looking and laughing.

He gets my silliness.

I slid into the driver's seat and tossed my purse next to me. Once Hart saw I was safe in my car, he gave me a smile and a wave before pulling away. As I watched his car leave the parking lot, I knew I didn't want to wait until tomorrow or next weekend to see him. Shoving my hand in my purse, I grabbed my cellphone.

Dead.

It never crossed my mind last night to ask Hart if he had a charger I could have used. I grabbed the extra one from the glove compartment and plugged in my phone. The screen came to life with a ton of missed calls and texts, mostly from Will.

Will: *What are you doing?*

I'm sorry for the way things were left between us.

What time are you coming tomorrow?

Where are you?

I'm starving.

You promised to help me, Bryson.

I didn't even bother listening to the ten-plus voicemails he left. I looked toward the rehab center. Will was only a few yards away and it would be easy to head to his room as usual. But I knew if I did the happiness I was currently experiencing would disappear. I wasn't ready to say goodbye to it just like I wasn't ready to say goodbye to Hart.

Me: *Sorry. Got sick during the night. Stomach bug. Don't think it's a good idea to come today. Don't want to get you or anyone else sick. Will update you tomorrow.*

I hit the send button and buckled up for the guilt trip. Almost immediately, Will responded.

Will: *I guess I'll just twiddle my thumbs and listen to my stomach growl. Sorry you're sick.*

I refused to let his pouting spoil my great mood. I thought about my fun exchange with Hart in the kitchen this morning. Warmth radiated throughout my body. Glancing in the mirror, I discovered a smile had crept across my lips, my cheeks appeared rosier, and my eyes had a twinkle in them I'd not seen before. God, I missed him already.

I picked up my phone, dialed Sophie, and prayed she was still in town.

"Hey, chick! What's up?" The sound of her voice made my smile widen.

"Hey!"

"Wow, you sound inebriated."

"Shut up." I scolded. "I'm just having a great day."

"Oh do tell."

"Later. Are you in town?"

"I am."

"Any plans for the day?"

"Nope. I'm free as a bird."

"How about lunch?"

"Sounds delicious."

"Great. Meet me at home in forty-five minutes?"

"See ya then. Oh, Bryson."

"Yeah?"

"You will divulge the cause of your audible happiness . . . no?"

"See you in forty-five."

I pressed the end button, disconnecting the call. As I drove home my mind worked overtime figuring out how to talk Sophie into taking part in my plan.

Once home, I hit the front door running and didn't stop until I was in my bedroom. There was no time for a shower. I figured that was okay since I took one right after the spew fest last night. My necklace and earrings were already in my hand and heading toward the top of the dresser when I entered the room. Flopping on the bed, I simultaneously slid off my boots and socks, and pulled my sweater over my head. I ran to the dresser, shoving my jeans and underwear down along the way. Bras and panties flew from the top drawer as I rummaged around for the perfect combo.

After seeing his place it was obvious Hart was a big fan of the basic colors, so the black push-up bra with matching lace boy shorts was a no-brainer. Not that he was going to see my underwear. Just knowing I was wearing his favorite color gave me a thrill and a little extra umph in my step. I slipped my arms through the straps and hooked the bra. Heading toward the closet, I hopped and stumbled as I stepped into my panties.

The frenzy of activity continued in the closet as I pulled on my black skinny jeans along with a plain black short-sleeve shirt. I topped off the look with my long gray cashmere sweater jacket and black leather short boots. On my way to the bathroom I glanced at the clock. I had just enough time to do makeup and hair before Sophie came knocking.

I attempted a subtle smoky-eye effect with light mascara. Dusty rose blush and pale pink lip gloss was the last bit in the makeup routine. As I picked up the silver teardrop earrings, I noticed my wedding ring. For the past ten years it had been a part of me and I hadn't thought about removing it. Staring down at the princess-cut diamond and band, I hesitated.

Each step away from my marriage was filled with mixed emotions. I was positive I didn't love Will or want to be with him. But I also hadn't been able to picture my life without him in it. Except during the time I spent with Hart, I felt married. It was hard to disengage when I was going through the motions—being by Will's side every day at the rehab, doing Will's laundry, and cooking for Will. My life stilled revolved around being Will's wife. The ring was another outward lie that Will and I were the perfect happy couple.

Several weeks ago I had every intention of following through with the promise I made to Will. It seemed simple and doable at the time. Now it felt like the promise was wrapped tight around my neck, strangling any effort to move forward. Taking in a deep breath, I slid the ring off my finger and placed it beside the sink. It was a small step but at least it was in the right direction.

Before I had the chance to reconsider, I heard the dulcet tones of Sophie coming from downstairs. I loosened my ponytail and ran the brush through my hair several times, deciding to leave it down. I grabbed the bottle of mouthwash, chugged a mouthful, swished, and spit. I checked my makeup in the mirror one last time. No lip gloss on the teeth. And I was good to go.

When I got downstairs, Sophie was sitting at the kitchen counter and had helped herself to a glass of wine.

With the glass hovering at her lips, she said, "You're the designated driver."

"No problem."

"Well, look at you, sexy lady. Damn. You didn't have to get all done up for little 'ol me. What's the deal?"

"No deal. Why does there always have to be a deal? It's nice dressing nice. It makes me feel . . ."

"Nice?" she said with a hint of snark in her tone. "How about Angel Fish for lunch? I could really go for their fried green tomato burger."

I double-checked directions and the time of the game. "I have a new place in mind."

"What place?"

"It's a surprise." I looked up at her. "We need to go or we'll be late."

"Late? Do we have a reservation?" She threw back the rest of her wine like it was a shot of tequila.

"Um . . . kind of." Slipping my purse on my shoulder, I quickly headed toward the front door. "I'll meet you in the car."

"Creeps, slow down! I'm coming!"

The click of Sophie's heels echoed in the entryway as she followed me out the door.

chapter
Seventeen

I took a left on Calhoun, the first right onto Saint Phillips Street, and pulled into the parking lot.

"Bryson, what the hell are we doing here?"

Trying to sound cheery and excited, I said, "Going to a basketball game."

Ignorance was bliss when it came to Sophie attending an athletic event. Her idea of being a sports fan was to see how many football, baseball, basketball, and hockey players she could get her hands on. In high school the only time I was able to get her to go to a game was if she was crushing on someone on either our team or the opposing one. If I had mentioned earlier about my plan to attend the basketball tournament she wouldn't have gotten in the car. And I needed her by my side today.

"I thought we were going to lunch." The tone in her voice moved from confusion to annoyance. And if I knew my friend, pissed off, was just around the corner.

I circled the crowded parking lot searching for a spot to land. "They have concessions inside."

"I'm not in the mood for a greasy hotdog and cotton candy."

"The food choices have come a long way since the last time you went to a game," I said, working hard to amp up the excitement so she'd climb onboard. "And cute guys in shorts will be running . . . will be around."

"Correction. I'm not in the mood for greasy hotdogs, cotton candy, or inexperienced prepubescent tally whackers."

I gave her a sideways glance. "It'll be fun. Besides, it's not college boys playing. "

At least I assumed all the players would be around our age. But what did I know. Up until this morning, I wasn't even aware that a wheelchair basketball league existed.

"You're shitting me, right? This is one of your weird little jokes." I pulled into a spot, turned off the car, and took the key out of the ignition. "Oh! My! God! You're serious! We're actually going inside!"

"You need to open your mind to new experiences," I said, getting out of the car.

Sophie was closing the door as I walked up to her.

"I'll have you know my mind is plenty open to new experiences. Just last week I let a guy fuck me hanging upside down in a pair of gravity boots."

Sophie and I had been friends since childhood. You'd think nothing she said or did would shock me at this point.

Wrong!

"I stand corrected. You're wide open. Who wore the boots?"

Tilting her chin in the air, her eyes narrowed. "We each had a go at it."

I pivoted and walked toward the coliseum. The crunch of gravel got louder as Sophie caught up with me. I glanced over at her walking on wobbly legs. As usual she looked stunning in her burgundy sweater dress and matching three-inch heels. Maybe I should have given her a little warning.

Clutching my upper arm for dear life, she grumbled, "You could at least have given me a slight heads-up about this little swit-cha-roo. My heels weren't exactly made for rock climbing."

Sophie complained incoherently all the way across the parking lot. As we approached the ticket window I was surprised to see such a long line. Hart told me this was the final day of the tournament. I just didn't realize the fan base was so big. Luckily the line moved quickly and there were still a few tickets available when we reached the front.

Sophie glared at her ticket as if it were an electric eel. "Question. What in god's name are we doing at a wheelchair basketball tourney? And don't give me this new experience crap."

Sophie and I shuffled inside along with the rest of the crowd. "A friend of mine is playing."

"A friend? I know all your friends and none of them are in wheelchairs."

Ignoring her, my gaze darted around the huge facility as I pretended to search for our seats. Two teams were already on the court warming up.

The power and strength the players displayed was incredible. It was like they floated on air, gliding and spinning across the shiny hardwood as they passed and shot the ball. The chairs were different than what I'd seen Hart use on a daily basis. The framing was more intricate and colorful. The footrest consisted of one solid bar across the front with straps across the upper thighs as well as the calves. In addition to the front casters and large side wheels, which were angled in toward the player, there was a caster wheel in the back. The chairs looked lightweight and lower to the ground, which appeared to aid in speed and agility.

I recognized the team jerseys at the farthest end of the court. Within a second, I spotted him. His biceps flexed and relaxed as he pushed across the floor. Black fingerless sports gloves covered his hands. As the ball barreled toward him, Hart released his grip from the wheel. In one smooth continuous motion, he skidded across the court, caught the ball, and shot.

Nothing but net.

A sense of pride and admiration for my new friend washed over me. Hart was an impressive example of strength and courage, not just as a man but as a human being. I thought about the questions he asked me last night. I gave up on my dream so easily just because Will deemed it to be stupid and unnecessary. Our hearts were already separated and soon we would be physically as well. I couldn't blame Will any longer for my apprehension. Hart's life had been shattered by his accident as well as the death of his mother. He managed to rebuild and reinvent himself in the face of seemingly insurmountable odds. All I had to do was push myself to take a step out my comfort zone.

Sophie popped my arm, jolting me from my thoughts. "Earth to Bryson."

"Let's go find our seats," I said.

She looked down at her ticket and then up into the stands. "Jesus Christ, Bryson. These are in the nosebleed section."

I tugged on her arm, pulling her toward the stairs. "That's all they had left."

Before hitting the first step a vaguely familiar voice hit my ears.

"Bryson, baby! I knew you couldn't stay away from me." Doug shoved his way between me and Sophie, draping his meaty arms over each of our shoulders.

Sophie grunted, ramming her elbow into the side of Doug's ribs. She then grabbed his wrist, twisted, and shoved it behind his back. "On your knees motherfucker!" Doug dropped to the ground wincing in pain. "Bryson, go get security now!"

Waving my hands in the air, I yelled, "Sophie, stop! I know him!"

She tightened the twist.

"Ow!" Doug groaned.

With a firm grip on Doug's arm, Sophie said, "You're kidding?"

I shook my head. "We met this weekend."

Sophie refused to loosen her hold. "Is this . . ." She glanced down. ". . . Why we're here?"

"No," I said.

She took a few more seconds deciding whether or not she was ready to release Doug back into the world. After what felt like several hours, she finally relented and let him go.

Doug stood rubbing his arm. "You're lucky you're a girl, otherwise your ass would be mine." Rolling his shoulder backward and forward, his gaze dropped to Sophie's ass. "Damn, I would so like that ass to be mine."

Peering at me over Doug's shoulder, Sophie pleaded, "Angel Fish, please."

Out the corner of my eye, I noticed someone walking toward me. I turned to find Colin with Ronnie only steps behind.

"Hey, lady," Colin said, coming in for a hug.

"Hey!"

Even though we'd just met and spent a brief amount of time together, there was a familiar warmth and kindness about Colin that made me feel comfortable.

Ronnie, who looked to be still in recovery mode from his bachelor party, sent a smile and a wave my way.

Gesturing, I made quick introductions. "Sophie, this is Colin, Ronnie, and you've met Doug."

Sophie politely smiled and nodded toward Colin and Ronnie. With crinkled nose and squinted eyes, she begrudgingly acknowledged Doug.

Colin shifted his gaze toward the court. "Hart didn't mention you were coming today." "It was kind of a last-minute thing." The nervous tickle in my throat caused a slight shake in my voice. "He doesn't know I'm here."

Continuing to look straight ahead, Colin nodded as if to let me know he had no intention of outing me.

Suddenly, the booming voice of Doug broke through the air. "Hartford!"

I snapped my head toward Doug as he raised both hands high and pointed to me.

My gaze darted to the court in time to see Hart turn, wearing a big smile. Our eyes locked and his expression went blank. He was so distracted by my presence that he didn't see the ball flying through the air until it bounced off the side of his head. My muscles flinched, my mouth dried up, and my stomach bottomed out. I couldn't tell if he was annoyed, angry, or happy to see me standing courtside with his friends.

Admittedly, I hadn't thought my plan through in detail. I'd gotten as far as sitting in the stands watching the game. Whether or not I was going to reveal myself to Hart had still been up in the air until a second ago. It was stupid of me not to think the guys would be here to support their friend.

With my back to the court, I grabbed Sophie's hand, and tugged.

"Let's get out of here," I muttered in her ear.

Sophie was in mid-turn when his deep rasp cut through the noisy crowd.

"Bryson?"

I froze, closing my eyes and tightening my grip around my best friend's hand. To her credit Sophie acted unfazed as she waited for my next move.

Since disappearing in the crowd was out, I let go of Sophie and turned to face Hart.

"Hi!" My pitch skyrocketed up eight octaves.

"Way to look alive out there, man," Ronnie said, joking.

Never taking his eyes off me, Hart ignored his friend's comment.

"What are you doing here?"

Fidgeting with the end of my sleeve, I said, "I wanted to come see you." He just kept staring at me. "And I brought Sophie." I pulled her beside me.

Sophie raised her hand and gave a slight wave. "Hi."

I thought I detected a weak smile and a small tilt of his head in acknowledgment. But the movement was so imperceptible it was hard to be sure. The only thing that was definite was Hart's gaze stayed on me. His odd reaction led me to believe this was a monumental bad idea. From Hart's perspective, I was probably coming off a bit stalkerish, inserting myself in his life uninvited.

Finally Hart found his voice and said, "The game's about to start."

Taking in a deep breath, my chest and ribs felt like they were being squeezed. "Good luck."

A quiver began to brew and was headed straight to my bottom lip. I didn't want Hart to know how upset I was by his reaction. It wasn't his fault. It was mine. I shouldn't have come, or at the very least, I should have asked him if it was okay.

With pinched brows, Hart shook his head as the edges of his lips drifted into a grin. "I'm glad you're here."

All the air and anxiety left my body. "Really?"

"You're my good luck charm." He winked, rolling backward until forced to turn away.

A warm sensation spread throughout my body as I watched Hart join his teammates for the start of the game.

Cupping his hands on either side of his mouth, Doug yelled, "Kick some ass, Hartford!"

"What just happened here?" Sophie asked.

The buzzer sounded, the opening tip-off performed, and the game started.

Tears of relief and happiness seeped from behind my eyes. Trying to keep my emotions a secret, I quickly wiped them away before anyone noticed. Ronnie was several steps away watching the game. Doug's focus was split between Sophie's ass and her chest. Colin's eyes zeroed in on the court action but he seemed to be getting closer to me.

When we were shoulder to shoulder, he asked, "You okay?"

I glanced over at him. "Yeah." The word came out as half sigh, half whisper.

Colin still didn't look at me. "I've known Hart my entire life."

"He mentioned you guys had been friends since you were kids."

"You're the Bryson from Garrison." My widened gaze shot to his profile. "Yesterday, when you appeared in the office doorway and I saw the look on Hart's face, I had a hunch it was you." I was stunned into silence. "When he said your name then I knew for sure you were the girl from senior year."

I attempted to blink my confusion away. "Hart told you guys about me?"

"Hart talks to me. He doesn't tell those other guys everything because . . . well, you've met them."

A slight chuckle escaped me.

"So, what has Hart said about me?"

His bright green eyes met mine followed by a sweet grin. "Bryson, there's a reason why Hart confides in me."

"Because you're like a vault?"

"Exactly."

"Can I ask you one question?"

"You can ask but I can't promise I'll answer." His grin faded as he turned back to the game.

I appreciated Colin's honestly and was glad Hart had a loyal friend like him.

"What caused the accident?"

"A broken heart."

A stab of jealousy pierced the center of my chest. I had no right to feel this way. But the idea of Hart being so tangled up in another girl that their breakup caused him to lose control bothered me. Since I got the impression from Colin I had one shot at getting a little information, I stayed quiet. After a few seconds of us watching the game, he elaborated.

"Hart's mom was diagnosed with ovarian cancer the year we turned sixteen. She was the cool mom of our group." A wistful tone laced his words. "Hart took care of her, going to every doctor's appointment, chemo treatment, and even physical therapy sessions. They were trying to keep her strength up as long as possible."

As I listened it was like a bubble formed around Colin and I, blocking out everything and everyone except Hart. I watched as he whipped around the court, living his life to the fullest. My vision got blurry with misty eyes.

"That's why he chose PT as a career," I whispered loud enough for Colin to hear.

"Yeah. He started taking college level courses the summer before junior year. He was a mad man. I don't know how he did it. Hart got it in his head that if he could keep her strong, she'd last long enough until they found a cure. By the end of junior year he'd enlisted their neighbor, Miss Polly, to cook three meals a day even though by that time his mom was barely eating. When she was admitted into the hospice house, Hart had to go live with his dad."

"His mom died the day of the motorcycle accident, didn't she?"

When Colin didn't answer, I knew I was right.

"In a single day everything was ripped away from Hart. His control, his ability to walk, and the one person he loved more than anything in this world. It left him completely broken. His dignity and self-confidence took a massive hit. For a while I was afraid he'd give up and not make it."

It was hard for me to imagine a different Hart other than the confident and self-assured one I'd experienced. The snap of my heart breaking echoed in my ears knowing how much he'd struggled.

"He fought long and hard to get back control." There was a slight quiver in Colin's voice.

This glimpse into Hart's past helped me better understand the way he operated. His directness, the orderliness of his home, the aversion to relationships, and the Amber arrangement. Even the questions he asked me last night about why I wasn't following my passion.

I suddenly felt Colin's eyes on me.

Facing him, I said, "Thank you."

"Bryson, Hart's a good man. He's guarded but not impenetrable. I don't know all the details of your situation."

"I'm getting a divorce and forming a new friendship."

He gave me a knowing smile. "Call it what you will. But the way he looks at you . . . I just don't want anyone to get hurt."

And with that, the bubble popped and Colin turned his full attention back to the game.

I wasn't sure how to feel after our talk. Part of me wanted to enjoy the fact that those closest to Hart had noticed something between us. That this pull, this attraction wasn't my overactive imagination. The other part of me couldn't ignore the concern in Colin's last comment. I didn't blame him for looking out for his best friend. In fact, I liked him even more for it.

The roar of the crowd caught my attention. I'd been so focused on what Colin had to say that I hadn't been keeping track of the score. Sophie and I never went up to our seats in the nosebleed section. Since the game held little to no interest, she spent most of her time on the move dodging Doug. Ronnie left early to meet Julie, his fiancé, for an appointment with someone who had something to do with their wedding. Colin and I stayed put courtside.

The Steelers ended up winning the tournament. I beamed with pride, watching the fans crowd around congratulating Hart and the team. Not wanting to distract from his moment, I decided to quietly slip out. I'd give him a proper congratulations tomorrow when I saw him at the rehab.

Sophie was relatively closed lip as we walked back to the car. She really was an amazing best friend. She knew when I needed an ear to listen, a shoulder to cry on, or a moment of silence. But I knew this wouldn't last long and her curiosity would get the better of her.

She waited until we'd pulled out of the parking lot before firing off her first question.

After applying a fresh coat of lip gloss, Sophie ran her fingers through her hair and flipped the visor back up. "So, you wanna talk?"

"Not really."

"Good then I will."

I cut my eyes in her direction and gripped the steering wheel.

"I'm pissed off at you . . ."

"For what?"

"Um . . . for lying to me, for taking me to a basketball game, for making me walk across gravel in these fabulous heels, for Doug . . ."

"You can't blame me for Doug."

"I can and do."

I simply shook my head.

"For not telling me how into Hart you are." Crossing her arms, she snapped. "I thought we were best besties."

"We are."

"And he's obviously into you."

I glanced over at her. "You think?"

A smile started to creep over my face.

"Puul-lease. I craved a cigarette and a shower after the credits rolled on the eye porn matinee y'all performed. Although the shower may have been brought on by how icky that Doug guy made me feel."

"If it helps, he seems pretty harmless."

"It doesn't."

I chewed on my bottom lip for a few seconds before apologizing. "I'm sorry. If I'd told you where we were going you wouldn't have come and I needed you for moral support."

"I've never seen you look at anyone the way you were looking at Hart. I felt like a peeping Tom watching the two of you." She paused, leaning her head against the headrest. "God, I wish you had dumped Slimy Bastard right after prom."

"I can't go back and change the past."

"If you had taken a chance with Hart back then things might be different now."

I sniffled as tears formed. "Maybe I'm being given a second chance to make things different."

Sophie shifted in her seat, turning toward me. "Bryson, you know I love you and your happiness means the world to me."

"But . . . ?"

"You're gonna make me say it?"

"I think you're going to have to."

She took in a deep breath. "You need to leave Hart alone."

"You were the one touting what a good candidate he'd be for my transition guy." I tried to keep my voice steady.

"That was before seeing the way you look at him and before I knew he was . . ."

My throat thickened as a few tears spilled over. "Say it."

Sophie blew out a loud breath. "Before I knew he was *disabled*. Happy?"

I dug my fingers into the steering wheel. My pulse went from normal to warp speed as heat flushed through my body. Sophie wasn't a cruel person but there was a patronizing and dismissive tone in her voice when she said the word *disabled*. What infuriated me the most was her lack of effort to see the man in the chair.

"I never thought of you as being close-minded. There's so much more to Hart." I choked back a sob.

Sophie placed her hand gently on my shoulder, causing a stream of tears to run down my cheeks. "I know there is but it's a big part of him." She paused. "You're vulnerable right now. He's given you some much needed attention and he's safe."

"Safe? What's that supposed to mean?"

Her hand dropped. "Not many women want the added pressure of being a nurse to a guy like Hart."

I pulled into my driveway and jerked the car into park. My blood boiled at Sophie's assumptions.

"You are so out of line right now," I growled through clenched teeth.

"I'm sorry. I don't mean to sound harsh."

"Hart appreciates me and encourages me. I feel worthwhile when I'm around him."

Sophie brushed the hair back from the side of my face. "Don't lose yourself in this guy just because you're scared to be alone."

A mix of angry, hurt, and disappointed tears ran down my cheeks.

Whipping my head around, my gaze seared into her. "Scared to be alone? I've been alone for the last year. Wait, I take that back. I've been alone for the last ten years. Every time Will left me at a party or forgot about me all together." I paused, took a deep breath, and tried to compose myself. "Do you have any idea what it felt like to watch him go in his office each night knowing he'd rather spend time with a stranger than me? Every time that door closed I was alone. And I was alone throughout our entire relationship because I was the only one in it. So don't you dare insinuate that the only reason I'm drawn to Hart is because he's safe and I'm scared."

Sophie wiped away the tears that had trickled down her face. "You need to think clearly about the good and the bad of the situation. I just want you to be happy."

"Then be a friend and let me figure out what makes me happy. Hart and I just got reacquainted. We're friends. Period."

"That's not how it looked to me."

"It doesn't matter how it looked. I'm well aware of my situation. Besides, Hart doesn't do romantic relationships."

Cupping the side of my face, she said, "Why do I get the feeling he'd make an exception for you? Bryson, I'm afraid you're going to fall hard and hurt yourself."

Sophie and I hugged before she left. The pain from her words was still fresh but I knew deep down they were coming from a place of love and concern. She had much more experience when it came to dealing with men and the potential feelings involved. She'd seen firsthand how this past year affected me and was trying to protect my heart.

I headed to my bedroom to change into more comfortable clothes. As I pulled on the black yoga pants, my mind floated to the conversation with Colin. I couldn't decide if he was for or against my friendship with Hart. But his concern was clearly evident. I shoved my arms into the long sleeves of the white T-shirt Sophie's brutal honesty echoed in my ears. As I slipped into my socks, I thought about Hart dealing with all the obstacles and pain he's had to endure for most of his life. I'm sure he had lots of people over the years telling him he wouldn't achieve his goals and dreams because of the wheelchair. He stayed true to himself and created a life worth the effort.

I was a grown-ass woman and tired of others dictating what I should and shouldn't do. Making me feel guilty for taking a stand, telling me my dream was stupid, that I didn't have enough experience, or that I should give up the one positive thing in my life.

Fuck that.

I went downstairs to Will's office, sat at the desk, and fired up my laptop. I revised my resume, wrote a new cover letter, and googled Charleston caterers. It didn't matter whether or not they were looking to hire. What mattered was that they knew I was ready to take hold of my dream and just needed a chance. Most of the resumes were sent via email while a few others were slipped into envelopes. By the end of the night every caterer in the Lowcountry had been checked off my list. Tilting back in the brown leather chair, I felt a sense of pride and accomplishment wash over me. And I couldn't wait to share it with Hart the next day.

chapter Eighteen

"Lunch is awesome today, babe." Will shoveled another forkful of red rice and sausage into his mouth.

Sitting in the chair next to the bed, I looked at my phone while halfway listening to him. I'd been checking my emails all morning. More than half of the resumes I sent out last night already had responses. All the emails basically said they were fully staffed at the present time but would keep my resume on file for the future. I tried not to get too disappointed. It was a shot in the dark. Besides I still had the resumes I'd sent through regular mail. I probably wouldn't hear anything back from them until next week at the earliest. The point was, I was taking action, making my own decisions, and moving toward something I wanted. All I needed was for that one person to give me a chance.

"Babe!"

My head popped up at the sound of Will's voice. "What?"

"I was giving you a compliment."

"Oh . . . thanks." My gaze and voice lowered a bit. "And by the way, I don't think it's a good idea for you to call me babe."

Tensing my muscles, I braced myself for his reaction. When it didn't come, I looked back at Will eating.

"Did you hear me?"

He swallowed his mouthful of food. "No."

I squared my shoulders and cleared my throat. "I said, stop calling me babe."

"I've called you babe the entire time we've been together."

"We're not together anymore."

He dropped his fork and pushed the hospital bed table away. "That's not my fault."

My shoulders slumped forward as I tried to hide my eye roll. "Will, let's not do this, please. When are you going to accept the fact that we're done?"

Will raked both hands over his face and into his hair and linked them behind his head. "I'll give up porn and go to counseling with you. And I'll limit my time on Virtual Life. You might even want to try it. We could do it together."

"My god, are you that afraid of disappointing your parents?"

He let out an exacerbated huff as his hands fell to the bed. "It's embarrassing."

I nodded. "It's also too late."

Will's dark brown eyes appeared even darker when he stared at me. "You'll lose everything. The house, the car, the savings. There's no way my parents' lawyers will let you get your hands on any of it. They'll have you out of the house so quick it'll make your head spin."

His words came out in a matter-of-fact tone. I knew a long time ago I wouldn't be able to stay in the home I helped create and loved. I'd come to terms with that. What surprised me was how willing he was to step aside, let his parents take over, and leave me with nothing. I'd been with him every day since the accident. I'd hoped when the time came to do the paperwork, Will would remember that I kept my end of the promise. I put my life on hold and kept secrets from my family thinking it would make the whole process go smoothly. But Will wasn't a man of character or integrity. He was a little boy who packed up his toys and left when he didn't get his way.

I stood, yanked my purse over my shoulder, and walked out of the room without saying another word.

Once in the hallway I shut my eyes and took in several deep breaths. I was angry at myself, at Will, and at the complete loss of control I felt in the moment. Will had the upper hand. He caused the downfall of our marriage and I was going to be paying for it. Tears pricked behind my eyes. I hated that whenever I got angry the tears flowed. And I had already passed furious. I needed to hold it together at least until I was safe in my car.

I'd just turned the first corner when I heard my name.

"Bryson."

I teetered on whether to stop or pick up my pace. Not wanting to weigh Hart down with my problems, I decided getting to my car was the best course of action.

My feet moved faster. I wanted it to seem as if I hadn't heard Hart call my name, not that I was running away from him. Before I knew it he was by my side, keeping the pace. He weaved through three wheelchair patients parked in the middle of the hall and swerved around a couple of nurses to avoid any casualties.

Hart's gaze swung from me to the route ahead. "I looked for you after the game."

"I had to run some errands. By the way, congratulations. You were incredible." There was an obvious quiver in my voice.

The traffic was lighter as we headed down the last hallway before the exit.

Hart's arms and chest were pumping hard. "You think you could slow down a little?"

I shook my head. "I have to go."

Reaching out, his warm hand captured mine, stopping me in my tracks. "Hey, look at me."

My chin was already trembling as I looked down at his concerned blue-gray eyes.

"Let's go to my office," he said, not letting go of my hand.

"Hart, I don't want to bother you."

He didn't respond. He just kept guiding me toward his office. Once inside, he closed the door, rolled to his desk, and pressed the intercom. Hart continued to hold my hand and gaze.

"Trish."

"Yes, Hart?"

"Hold my calls and I'm not to be disturbed until I give you the word."

"Will do."

With his other hand, Hart angled one of the chairs in front of his desk toward me. "Sit down and talk to me."

My chin lowered. "I should go and let you get back to work."

The slight squeeze of my hand caused my eyes to shoot up. Without another word, Hart led me to the chair and I sat.

Facing me, he positioned himself to the side of the chair, bringing us less than a foot apart. I took a deep breath, inhaling his spiciness. The first week around Hart I noticed how his eye color changed from blue to gray depending on the color shirt he wore. The heather gray dress shirt he had on today made his eyes appear smoky gray.

"What or who made you cry?" His deep voice vibrated from the back of his throat, sending chills through my body.

I looked down at the armrest where our hands were still joined together. Hart mindlessly laced his fingers through mine.

I sniffled as my other hand fidgeted with the hem of my shirt. "It's stupid but when I get angry the floodgates open."

Keeping my hand hostage, he shifted, pulling a handkerchief from the front pocket of his black dress pants. It was such a gentlemanly move that you didn't see often practiced in my generation. Just like using the word 'lovely'. Raising his hand, Hart dabbed my cheeks before turning the cloth over to me.

"Okay, what or who pissed you off?"

My lips turned up into a weak smile. "Have you ever given someone the benefit of the doubt and then realized they never deserved it?"

"Will?"

I gave a slight nod and pulled my hand away. "I don't want to waste your time whining about what an asshole my soon-to-be ex is being."

Hart glanced down at his lonely hand. When he looked up there was a hint of disappointment in his expression.

"Bryson, any time spent with you is not a waste."

Hart's sweet words caused more tears to flow, which I quickly wiped away with his handkerchief.

"Besides, friends are supposed to be there for one another. I consider us friends."

"Yeah . . . friends," I whispered.

We stared at each other for . . .

One Mississippi.

Two Mississippi.

Suddenly, my cellphone blared to life, breaking the Mississippi spell. Shoving my hand inside my purse, I pulled out the phone and turned down the volume. I didn't recognize the number that appeared on the screen.

I flashed another shy smile and said, "Excuse me for a second."

A small grin ghosted over Hart's lips as he nodded.

I clicked to answer the call and brought the phone to my ear.

"Hello."

"Bryson Walker?" The bluntness of the gruff voice took me off guard.

It then occurred to me that they used my maiden name. All the resumes I'd sent out I used Walker instead of Forsyth. More than likely the call was another rejection but I was excited to get it anyway.

"This is she."

"My name is Nancy Baldwin. I own and operate Good Eats Catering. You emailed me a resume."

With wide open eyes I looked at Hart. "Yes."

"Can you come in this afternoon for an interview?"

Adrenaline pumped through my veins. "Yes."

"Around three?"

My hand trembled. "Yes."

"You know where we're located?"

The tremble migrated to my chest. "Yes."

Hart's grin grew with each yes.

"Do you know any other words beside yes?"

I tried to keep my voice steady. "Yes, ma'am. I mean, I know lots of other words."

"Good to hear. I'll see you at three."

"Thank you so much for calling."

Click.

I lowered the shaking phone. "I got an interview . . . with a catering company . . . today."

Hart's face lit up. "Congratulations!"

"I'd been thinking about those questions you asked me. Yesterday when I got home, I revised my resume. Then sent one to every caterer in town. I wanted to tell you . . . I was going to tell you today but then Will happened and . . ."

He touched my chin with the tip of his index finger. "Don't talk about him right now. Enjoy your moment."

The simple gesture got me lightheaded. I wasn't sure if Hart moved or if it was me leaning in but we seemed closer than before.

"I'm so proud of you, Bryson."

Those few words coming from Hart were all it took for my brain to take a hike. Scooting to the edge of the chair, I flung myself at him, my hands slipping around his neck. Hart's strong arms wrapped around my torso. His large hands skimmed up my back and pulled me against his chest. I wanted to saw the stupid armrest off the chair so I could get even closer to him. Holding on tight, I melted into the sensation of his body.

The rough prickle of his beard grazed my neck as he angled his head toward me. If his scruff was that close then his lips couldn't have been far behind. My body was firing on all cylinders with just the thought of Hart mouth touching my skin. Inhaling a slow deep breath, he pressed his chest against mine.

Was he smelling my hair?

There was a slight groan in the back of Hart's throat before he lifted his head and pulled away.

He was so smelling my hair.

Leaning back, I let my hands slide over his shoulders and down his toned chest. We were almost nose-to-nose. Our eyes locked. Hart's left hand came into view and gently brushed the hair off my cheek. His fingertips took their time outlining the shell of my ear as he tucked the strands behind it. His gaze dropped and lingered on my lips while his fingers traveled down my jaw. Working overtime, my lungs tried to grab what little oxygen was left in the room. I didn't want him to stop touching me. In fact, I wanted more of him touching more of me.

The tip of Hart's tongue rolled over his bottom lip before his hand fell away. When his gaze worked its way back up to mine there was a look of surprise mixed with caution.

With a husky voice, Hart said, "You better go get ready for your interview."

"I guess so." The words came out all breathy.

Sitting all the way back in his chair, Hart pushed away from me, putting more distance between us. As I was wiping away a few stray tears, I heard a beep and then Hart's voice.

"Trish, I'm taking calls and my door is open."

"Got it," she responded.

Clutching my purse in one hand and Hart's handkerchief in the other, I stood and walked toward the door.

"Bryson."

I turned to face him. "Yeah?"

"You're going to do fantastic at the interview."

We exchanged smiles. I held up his handkerchief. "I'll wash this and bring it back tomorrow."

"No rush."

Pausing, I took a deep breath. "Hart, thank you."

"For what?"

"For today and . . . um . . . I wouldn't have this interview if you hadn't . . ."

He raised his hand, interrupting me. "I believe in you, which is the easy part. You're the one who had the courage to take the first step."

I had to get out of there before the tears cranked back up or I crawled in his lap and kissed him unconscious. Luckily, Hart's intercom beeped, snapping some sense into my head.

"Hart, you have a call on line two."

With my hand on the doorknob, I said, "I'll see you later."

"I want a full report on the interview."

We swapped smiles one more time just before Hart picked up his phone and I walked out the door.

On the drive home I made a concerted effort not to overthink the moment in Hart's office . . . or the way he looked at me . . . or how his body felt . . . or that he smelled my hair. Instead, I was going to soak up the feeling of the moment and the excitement of getting the interview.

Lying awake last night, I thought about what to wear in case by some miracle I did get an interview. I chose my black and white Houndstooth pencil skirt, a black long-sleeve silk blouse, and my black leather boots. Makeup was subtle, hair was down, and jewelry was minimal. The look was simple, classic, professional, and sophisticated without being snooty.

Good Eats was one of the most popular and well respected caterers in Charleston. Over the years I'd sampled their food at several weddings and parties. It was out of this world delicious. They prided themselves on southern charm and elegance with a Lowcountry flare.

I was a half hour early for the interview. After my monosyllabic performance on the phone, I didn't want to come off as psychotically eager. So I sat in my car trying to think up possible questions I might be asked and calming my nerves. Several times I thought about calling Hart just to hear his warm encouraging voice. Lucky for him, we hadn't exchanged numbers.

Fifteen minutes before the interview was set to start, I walked toward the building with my head held high, shoulders back, and an ounce of confidence I'd somehow held on to. The bell over the door jingled as I entered the lobby area. The walls were a bright white with black framed photos of special events they'd catered and awards they'd won. Other than a few chairs lining one wall and the high counter on the other wall, the place was sparsely decorated.

Out of nowhere a voice yelled. "Be right with you!"

My gaze darted around hoping to find where the voice was coming from. I noticed behind the counter, on the far left, was an open door. I stayed put until the voice told me otherwise. After a few minutes a pair of powder blue pants and a bright orange flowered shirt with matching Crocs came bursting through the door. The small lady who looked to be in her early sixties with frizzy salt-and-pepper hair barreled toward me.

"You Bryson?"

I headed over to her, extending my hand. "Yes."

Bryson, enough already with the monosyllabic answers.

"I want to thank you again for giving me this opportunity."

The lady's dark gaze slid down behind her dark framed glasses. I followed her gaze to our still shaking hands.

Flashing her a weak smile, I let go. "Sorry."

"I'm Nancy Baldwin." She turned and headed toward the door she came out of. "Come. I'll show you around."

I followed her into a huge white room divided into different prep areas. At the far end was the kitchen with two stoves and a bank of ovens taking up the majority of one wall. Another wall housed a walk-in freezer and refrigerator. Long work tables, shelves, and rolling racks filled the space. Everything was top of the line, stainless steel, very organized, and spotless.

"No one's here because we close on Mondays." She walked toward a small desk tucked away in an empty corner and waved me over. "Come on."

The few minutes I'd been around Nancy I could already tell she walked to the beat of her own drummer.

"Sit," she said, pointing to the fold-out chair across from her desk.

I sat.

Grabbing what I assumed to be my resume, Nancy tilted her chair back and read over it.

Her eyes focused on the paper. "By the looks of it, you don't have any experience."

I swallowed hard. "I realize I don't have much on my resume."

"Not much? You got nothing."

My throat felt thick as I blinked away the moisture in my eyes.

"You're how old?"

"Twenty-seven."

"And never held a job?"

Running my tongue over my dry lips, I said, "No ma'am."

"This says you graduated two years ago. Whatcha been doing?"

"I got married."

"So why a job now?"

"I'm getting a divorce." I paused feeling the need to add more details. "We were together for ten years."

"You have an MBA. Why do you want to work at a catering company?"

"A couple of years ago I discovered my passion for food and cooking. I love that I can be creative and also challenged by it. When I'm in the kitchen I feel peace and contentment. Like I was born to be there."

My head was swimming so much, I had no idea what I'd just said. Looking over her glasses, Nancy gave me an approving nod.

She looked back at my resume, then at me, then back at the resume.

I could tell she was on the fence about me. I had one shot to push her over to my side.

"I know my resume, for lack of a better word, sucks. I've been cooking for just two years. And the only people who've eaten my dishes have been family and a few close friends. But I'm loyal, dependable, and even though you can't tell by my resume, I'm a hard worker. Mrs. Baldwin . . ."

"Ms."

"Ms. Baldwin, I've got the drive and eagerness to learn. All I need is that one person to give me a chance to prove it."

She was silent for an extraordinarily long period of time. Placing my resume back on the desk, she leaned forward and looked me straight in the eye.

"It doesn't pay a lot."

"I don't care. What I learn from you will be invaluable."

"The position is for a prep cook." I nodded. "Weekends are a must and during the busy season we work very long hours." I kept nodding. "As you get familiar with things, you'll be asked to assist at events as well."

"It all sounds great."

My body vibrated with excitement. I couldn't believe that I had just gotten a job doing what I loved to do. What was even more incredible was the fact that I kept my nerves in check and didn't ramble incoherently. Hart was going to flip when I told him I got the job. The realization that he was the first person I wanted to share the good news with flashed across my brain.

Nancy pushed away from her desk and stood. "You start next Monday. You'll get the complete and detailed tour and we'll get all the paperwork out of the way."

I sprang from the chair and thrust my hand toward her. We shook.

"Thank you so much. I can't tell you how excited and grateful I am that you're willing to take a chance on me. I promise you won't regret it."

I followed Nancy's gaze as it dropped down to our still shaking hands.

I let go.

chapter Nineteen

I practically floated across the parking lot and into my car after leaving the interview. Nancy wasn't just giving me a job. She was giving me the opportunity to prove to myself and others that I had something worthwhile to offer. And even though I wouldn't be able to live the life I was used to on what she was paying me, for the first time in my twenty-six years I felt self-reliant and proud.

I was too excited to go home and wanted to celebrate. Calling my parents or Ryan was out. Too many questions would be asked about why I'd gotten a job in the first place. I had already kept the divorce a secret and tonight was not the time to drop that little morsel on their plates. I almost called Sophie but remembered she'd left for a few days on a business trip. Besides, I wanted to see the look on her face when I told her.

With my options dwindling, Hart popped back into my head. Who was I kidding, he'd been popping up since before I left Good Eats. It was no big deal that he was the first person I thought of to share my great news with. He'd inspired me to reach for my dreams and we had become friends. What worried me was how much I *wanted* to share my great news with him. I was so tied up in getting ready for the interview, it left little time and brain power for me to think about that moment in Hart's office. Until now. Just the thought of his arms around me, the look in his eyes, and the touch of his fingers on my skin caused goosebumps to scatter over every visible surface of my body and a few that could not be seen by the naked eye.

The next thing I knew, my car was pulling into the rehab parking lot looking for Hart's car. When it wasn't in its usual spot, I glanced at my watch, realizing it was past office hours. I wondered if stopping by his house would be overkill. He did say he wanted a full report. And his house was on my way home so it wasn't as if I'd be making a special trip. I'd stay long enough to tell him my news and leave. Just a friend stopping by to update another friend.

As I got closer to Hart's house, I saw his car in the driveway. Another car was parked on the street between his place and Miss Polly's, making it hard to tell which one of them had a visitor. The sun had almost set so the front porch and house were lit up. I pulled in behind Hart's car. Hesitating for a few seconds, I reconsidered my friendly drop by. In all likelihood, I'd see him tomorrow at the rehab and could tell him then.

Screw it.

I got out of my car and headed up to the porch. There was all kinds of fluttering going on inside my chest, my stomach, and various other regions of my body. My finger hovered near the doorbell as I listened to my heartbeat pounding in my ears. I closed my eyes and pushed.

Clicking paws across hardwood accompanied by the excited bark of Butter came toward me. It sounded so clear and loud, I thought she'd run up on the porch. Looking to the left then right, I found no Butter. A loud thud from the other side of the door caused me to step back. I then noticed all the windows at the front of the house were open. In Charleston, there was a very short period of time during the year in which the weather was perfect and windows could be left up. The first weeks of fall were one of those times. Butter continued to bark and the door remained closed. My finger was poised to ring the bell one more time but I stopped myself, figuring it would only upset Butter more.

I headed down the steps and back to my car when a thought occurred to me. What if Hart wasn't answering the door because he was hurt? What if he slipped and hit his head while transferring from his chair to the sofa or his bed or any number of other places. His car was here and there were lights on in the house. It was obvious he was home. Maybe Butter's barks were actually cries for help.

Remembering the layout of the house pretty well from the other night, I headed around to the side where I thought the bedrooms were located. The pointy heel of my boots sank in the ground, causing me to stumble toward the first open window. The blinds were open enough for me to tell the room was dark and empty. As I backed away a muffled sound caught my attention.

Wobbling toward the next window, I could see the blinds were down but the lights were on. Another muffled sound, like a moan seeped out. I stepped closer. Laying my palms flat against the house, I craned my neck and tried to peer through the slats.

"My pussy is hot for you, baby." A female's groan assaulted my ears.

Holy shit! Legs get movin'.

But they wouldn't budge.

"Stop talking." Hart's familiar rasp punched me in the stomach.

"You've never complained about my mouth before."

There was a moment of silence followed by Hart growling. "Fuck it."

"What's wrong with you tonight?"

"Just leave."

"But we haven't . . ."

"Amber, get the fuck out. I don't need you."

"What about my . . ."

"Money's on the dresser."

Heels clicked accompanied by some unidentified rustling.

"Thanks, baby. I'll be at the club if you change your mind. I'll even give you a little discount since this visit was a bust."

It took my brain a few seconds to defrost before realizing my car was still in the driveway. Staggering back from the house, I turned and was just about to run when a set of tiny white teeth stopped me.

"Hey, Honeybun," I whispered.

The white puff of fur vibrated as a low menacing rumble shook of out her.

I took a step toward freedom. "Shh . . ."

Still vibrating, Honeybun took a step toward my ankle.

The slam of a door caused my gaze to shoot to the street just in time to see Amber walking past my car. She was so focused on looking at her phone, she didn't even notice. Her bubble-butt got into the mystery car and drove off.

Turning my attention back on the beast in front me, I tentatively stepped to the side, hoping Honeybun would feel less threatened. Before my foot hit the ground a barrage of yip-yaps flew out of the round white puff like a twenty-one gun-salute. I froze. My only hope was that Hart had gotten so used to the noise, he turned a deaf ear on the little bitch. Simultaneously, Miss Polly's voice filled the air as the front of her house lit up.

The sweet old lady appeared at the end of her porch, frantically clapping her hands. "Honeybun, stop that right now and get back in this house."

The puff shot me one final yap before turning and running up on the porch.

Holding my breath, I stayed as still as a statue until Miss Polly went inside her house.

"Bryson, is that you?" she said, leaning slightly over the porch railing.

Fuuuuuck meee!

"Hey," I croaked.

"My heavens, what are you doing out here?"

Think, think, think.

Stepping slightly forward, I kept my voice low and lied. "I was driving by on my way home and I noticed your beautiful rose bushes. I love roses . . . all kinds. I just had to get a closer look."

Her face was in shadow so I wasn't able to tell by her expression whether she believed me or not.

"Come inside for a little bit."

"I really should be going."

She turned and shuffled toward her door, scolding Honeybun for her great escape. I could have and should have just gotten in my car and gone home, putting this asinine move behind me. But I found myself walking up to Miss Polly's porch and into her house.

"Honeybun you've been such a bad girl." Closing the door, she smiled at me. "She must have snuck out when I was sweeping out front."

"She's a really good watch dog."

"Come in the kitchen."

I followed her through a large living room and into the bright yellow kitchen.

Miss Polly pointed to the small café type table by the window. "Have a seat."

Realizing my car was still in Hart's driveway, I said, "I can't stay."

She reached in the cabinet and pulled down two plates. "Hart brought over some of that delicious fried chicken I told you about."

The little lady wasn't exaggerating when she said Hart piled it up high. There must have been two birds perched on the plate set on the countertop.

"Thank you so much but really I can't . . ."

She handed me the plate of fried chicken. "Now go put that on the table."

I did what I was told and sat down.

Miss Polly walked over with our two plates and a roll of paper towels under one arm.

She placed a couple of pieces of chicken on a plate and handed it to me with a smile. "Hart was going to eat with me but he had something come up at the last minute."

He had something come up, alright.

I sunk my teeth into a drumstick and tasted the best thing I'd ever had in my mouth. Just the right amount of buttermilk batter coated the chicken. It was crisp and seasoned to perfection. Underneath, the chicken was tender, moist, and melted in my mouth.

I closed my eyes, and a slight moan escaped me. "Mmm . . . this is amazing."

"I told you." She tore apart a wing. "Now, why don't you tell me why you were lurking in my yard?"

I sputtered and coughed as a piece of chicken lodged in my throat. Miss Polly got up and brought me back a glass of water. A couple of sips later the chicken was free.

"I told you." Bringing the innocence up a notch in my voice.

She sent me a warm grandmotherly smile as she sat back down. "No one looks at roses in the dark, dear."

Busted.

There was no getting around the fact. No matter what story I came up with I had a feeling this little old lady would know I was full of crap. I had to come clean.

My gaze focused down on the piece of chicken I was picking apart. "I got some great news today. I wanted to tell Hart and since I don't have his phone number, I thought I'd drop by but . . ."

"Something came up?" I glanced up at the knowing twinkle in her eye. "I love that boy as if he were my own grandson. When his mom passed I just wanted to wrap my arms around him and not let go until all the pain disappeared. Then there was the accident. After his body recovered he filled his heart and life with work. Hartford has achieved so much. But he's still lost and searching. With your help, I think he might just find what he's been looking for."

This being only the second time I'd been in her company, I wondered where this was coming from.

"It's complicated."

She reached over and placed her hand on mine. "Matters of the heart usually are."

"He seems to have his life arranged the way he prefers."

"Hartford's a good man. And a good man always prefers a woman of quality over a common whore, dear."

She gave my hand a couple of pats and then returned to her plate of chicken.

After sharing my great news with Miss Polly, I helped her clean up our fried feast. I thanked her and my lucky stars that there were no signs my car had been discovered. I drove home with a belly full of goodness and a head full of scrambled thoughts.

In a short period of time my friendship with Hart had grown more than I expected. He felt familiar and new all at the same time. It was as if he saw the real me and not the scared girl who spent the last ten years accepting what others thought of her as the truth. Hart challenged and believed in me. He was interested in what I had to say. And he made me laugh. I felt lighter and stronger around him. I wanted his friendship. I needed his friendship. But my attraction to him clouded everything.

Needing a little breather to clear my head, I avoided Hart for the next few days. I parked in a different spot, came in through the back entrance of the rehab, and did a lot of dodging around corners when I spotted him in the hallway. Not having Hart be a part of my day made everything feel mediocre. But the sinking feeling I experienced when I heard him and Amber scared me. There was a huge amount of self-doubt that I was able to stay unaffected by his relationship with her or any other woman he had an arrangement with. After a little distance, I felt positive I'd be able to sort out my feelings and the pull wouldn't be as strong.

The entire week I flip-flopped on whether to cancel Hart's cooking lesson on Saturday. By Friday afternoon I felt pretty confident that I had my crush under manageable control. Plus, I needed to test myself to see if I could be around him without falling for him.

Every nerve in my body tingled as I pulled into the driveway. Staring at the house, I filled my lungs with steady breaths in hopes of calming the jitters. After a couple of unsuccessful attempts, I finally mustered up enough courage to get out and unload the car. I took the bags with the gift and the surprise up first, setting them by the door. With my purse and tote slung over my shoulder, I grabbed the other two bags loaded with groceries and headed up the steps. I inhaled one last deep breath and pushed the doorbell.

Within seconds the door swung open revealing Hart in a pair of well-worn jeans and a crisp white T-shirt with matching socks. He must have just taken a shower because his hair was damp. The way the T-shirt stretched across his chest had my body throbbing in areas I didn't even know existed. Add to that how happy he looked to see me and I was a goner.

So much for distance. Epic fail.

Butter slipped out the door, her fluffy tail swishing back and forth as usual.

"Hey, sweet girl." I squeaked.

Her big snout nudged at my leg a couple of times until the lure of something greater caught her attention. She tentatively sniffed the bag with Hart's gift and then plunged her head all the way in.

"Butter. No." Her floppy ears bolted from the bag, bouncing back into the house without argument. "Hey," Hart said, his eyes were lit bright blue.

"Hey." Gushed out of me. "Are we still on for the lesson? Because if this isn't a good time or you're tired from the day we can always reschedule . . ."

"Br . . ."

"Don't feel obligated to go through with it if you don't feel up to it."

"Brys . . ."

"I mean, it's no big deal. I can go back home. I only live fifteen minutes away and everything will keep in the fridge for several days . . ."

I was well aware of my sudden onset of verbal diarrhea but it was beyond my power to stop it.

"Bryso . . ."

"I was going to call you and check to see if you were still in the mood. Then I remembered I didn't have your phone number."

Reaching out, Hart grabbed my wrist. "Bryson!"

My body jerked with electricity as his skin touched mine.

"Breathe, Bryson." My chest visibly collapsed. "I was running a little late and just got out of the shower."

"That's okay, I can wait until you're ready." I didn't move.

The corners of his mouth twitched into a grin. "You can come in. You don't need to stay out on the porch."

I shook my head, my face pinching together at my stupidity.

"Let me help you bring some of this stuff in."

"I've got it."

Hart cocked a golden blond eyebrow at me and I knew immediately there was no need to argue. Since I didn't want to ruin the surprise, I handed over the grocery bags to him and picked up the others. Holding one bag and placing the other in his lap, he headed toward the kitchen with me following close behind. Butter poked her head around the corner spying on us. While Hart hoisted the bags onto the counter, I sat mine off to the side, keeping them out of the way until I was ready to reveal what was inside.

"Was there anything left in the store once you left?" He teased.

I started unpacking the groceries. "A couple of things."

Our audience quickly lost interest, trotting away and curling up on her bed in the corner.

"How much do I owe you for all of this?"

"Nothing."

"Bryson . . ."

"This is my treat." I insisted. "Unless of course you don't want to bother with it. You can be honest. I won't be upset. I was going to call you but I didn't have your number . . ."

Hart grabbed my elbow, bringing a halt to the unpacking and the babbling.

He looked up at me with soft eyes. "You already told me that."

My cheeks flushed with warmth. "Sorry."

"First things first. You're staying. Hand me your phone."

He held up his hand. I placed my phone in the center of his palm. As he entered his number, Hart's gaze darted from me to the phone. A second later his cellphone on the coffee table rang.

"Now, you can explain why you've been avoiding me all week."

A knot formed in my stomach as I returned to the grocery bags. "I haven't been avoiding you."

"Bullshit." Hart wrapped his fingers around my wrist, pulling me toward the living room area. "Sit," he said, indicating the large gray leather ottoman. I sat, bringing us eye-to-eye. "Talk to me."

His expression was full of concern, not anger. I didn't want to lie to him but I couldn't tell him the truth either. So I settled for somewhere in the middle.

Tearing my gaze away, I said, "I thought I was being a pest. You know, dropping by your office every day and bothering you with my problems."

He stared at me for a long time, trying to figure out whether I was being honest.

"I don't believe you."

"Well, you can believe what you want." I was going for nonchalance but it sounded more defensive.

"When you didn't come back after the interview, I assumed it didn't go well. The next day I roamed the halls, hoping to see you. I even glanced in Will's room. I was concerned about you."

This guy was killing me.

A pang of guilt hit my chest. I should have stopped in his office the next day and told him. I looked up. My fingers itched to run down his chiseled jawline. Balling my hands into fists, I pressed them into my thighs in an effort not to act on my urge.

"I'm sorry." I paused and contemplated my next words. "Hart, my life is in a bit of a mess right now and it's going to get even messier once the divorce starts. I like being around you and your friendship is very special to me. But I don't want to intrude on your life or put you in the middle of anything." My gaze dropped as I tried to keep the quiver out of my voice.

I had never felt as vulnerable as I did in that moment. My emotions had been all over the place since the first day I saw Hart at the pool. I'd been overthinking and letting other people get in my head. Trying to distance myself was a bust. Seeing him after four days just intensified my reaction. I wanted him in my life in some capacity. If that meant I had to ignore my feelings and his arrangements, then I'd just have to suck it up.

Placing his index finger under my chin, he tilted my gaze up to meet his. "You're not intruding. I like having you around too. And your friendship is very special to me."

I wasn't aware tears had flooded my eyes until I felt the trickle of water down my cheek. My hands flew to my face. I was so embarrassed. The mood was too heavy and needed to be redirected.

Wiping the tears, I said, "God, it must be my time of the month."

An insulting chauvinistic cliché but effective.

Deep laughter burst out of Hart. "You're something else."

"Okay, enough of this Hallmark Lifetime Kumbaya stuff." I raked my hands over my face one more time, catching any stray dribbles before slapping my thighs. "And by the way, I got the job."

As if coming in for a hug, Hart leaned forward, then stopped. His eyes flashed with hesitation. Placing both hands just above my knee, he gave each a squeeze followed by a slight rub. My skin was burning through my jeans. Seriously? Did he actually think a knee squeeze 'n' rub would be less arousing than a hug?

Dimples popped on either side of his mouth. "Congratulations. I knew you'd get it."

"Thanks. It's nice to have you in my corner."

Someone. I should have said it's nice to have someone in my corner.

"It's an awesome corner to be in." His gaze drifted down to my lips as his thumbs glided back and forth over my knee.

I tried to clear my throat. Thank god the abrupt noise caused Hart's gaze and hands to fall away.

243

Wiggling in my seat, I said, "We better get to the lesson."

"Yeah. By the looks of that haul you brought, I got a lot of learnin' to do."

Standing, I held up my index finger. "But first . . ." I walked to the kitchen, reached in the bag from Bake House Bakery, and returned to Hart's side. "Ta-da!"

A big grin along with confusion broke across his face. "You got me a cake? For what?"

"At first it was just to celebrate your tournament win. Now it's pulling double duty with my news." When he didn't respond my nerves kicked in along with more babbling. "I'm not very good at baking so I got it from my favorite bakery. I didn't plan it out very well. They were slammed and weren't able to decorate it. I ended up doing it myself. The orange and black Reese's pieces are supposed to make it look like a basketball."

Glancing down at the cake a sudden wave of embarrassment hit me.

I put the lid back on the box and said, "It looks awful. Like a kindergarten art project but it'll at least taste good."

"I can't believe you did this." He looked genuinely moved by my small gesture.

"We don't have to cut into it tonight. If you'd rather share it with your team or someone else. It's only a nine-inch cake, so it wouldn't feed everyone but I could get you a bigger one. I wasn't sure what flavors you liked so I went with classic vanilla cake with buttercream frosting."

Touching the side of my leg, Hart looked up and caught my gaze. "Stop talking. Vanilla's my favorite. I hate chocolate. And I'm only sharing this with one person."

"Me?"

A chuckle rolled out of him as his head shook. "You are something else."

"In a good way, right?"

His expression turned serious. "In a perfect way."

Flutter.

Tingle.

Flutter.

We simultaneously stammered incoherently as we pulled our gaze apart.

Rolling into the kitchen, Hart said, "Let's cut into that bad boy."

I placed the cake back on the counter. "Oh no. You get cake after the cooking lesson."

"You're gonna be a hardass about this, aren't you?" He teased, slouched in his chair.

"I promise it'll be fun." I finished unpacking the ingredients. "Okay, first I'll need . . ."

"Hold that thought."

Grabbing a wine glass from the cabinet and bottle of red from the countertop rack, Hart poured me a drink.

"A man after my own heart." I inhaled the aroma before taking a sip.

"I may not know how to cook food but I do know how to heat things up." He winked.

I slapped my hand over my mouth trying to stop the spew of wine. "It almost rained red wine up in here."

While I continued getting everything ready, searching for pots, pans, and utensils, Hart headed over to the stereo. Within seconds the surround sound filled the room with a smooth and silky male voice I didn't recognize. The style was different from today's auto tune pop music. It reminded me more of old school R&B.

"I like it. Who is that?"

"Leon Bridges, "So Long," Hart said, getting a beer from the fridge.

From the first time I saw him, I pegged Hart as a hard rock/heavy metal kind of guy. I remembered how shocked I was at prom when he knew the song we danced to was, "The Way You Look Tonight" by Tony Bennet. Hart was unexpected, then and now.

The combination of several sips of wine and the slow sexy music had my hips swaying as I unwrapped the Italian sausage. Reaching for the large pan, I caught Hart staring, the bottle of beer hovering in front of his lips. The image of me crawling into his lap, his arms sliding around my waist, and our lips pressed together had me heating up. As I bit down on my lower lip, Hart's gaze followed. His chest pumping harder with each second that ticked by.

I blinked, forcing my attention back to the task at hand. "We better get a move on or we'll starve."

Hart cleared his throat. "Yeah."

"While I uncase the Italian sausage, I need you to dice the onion and fine mince the garlic."

"I recognized the words sausage, onion, and garlic in that sentence."

"Wow, you really are a virgin."

"I wouldn't go that far." He took another swig of beer.

I pulled out my set of knives from my tote and grabbed the bamboo cutting board near the stovetop.

"You travel with your own knives?"

"Chefs always work with their own knives. Not that I'm an actual chef."

"You are, you just don't have the title yet. And remind me never to piss you off."

Holding up the onion, I instructed. "You're going to peel and medium dice this."

"I think I can handle that," he said, putting down his beer.

I handed over my chef's knife. "Be careful with this, it's ridiculously sharp."

"Ah, you care about me."

"Blood would ruin my knife."

As I finished getting all the meat out of the sausage casing, I gave a sideways glance at Hart. He'd gotten the onion peeled and was slicing it into big chunks. I stopped what I was doing and washed my hands.

"You're doing a good job." My eyebrows drifted up my forehead as I plastered an encouraging smile on my face.

"You're a liar." He teased and handed me the knife.

"We are gathered here tonight to teach and learn."

Leaning in, I placed my hand over Hart's hand holding the onion. The air around us shifted. The side of my arm brushed against his, causing his body to jerk. Hart rolled his shoulders back and forth in order to shake off his reaction.

"Curl your fingertips under just a little bit so you don't cut them off. Like this." Pressing gently, I guided his hand into position. "Take the tip of the knife and slice about a half inch in."

"Like this?" He fumbled a little as he stabbed the onion.

Reaching across his chest, I placed my other hand on top of his hand holding the knife. His lips were only a hairsbreadth from my cheek as he peered over my shoulder. The clean scent of his freshly washed hair was intoxicating.

"More like this." I was like his shadow as we made the first cut together. "Got it?"

"I think I need you to show me again." His voice was even deeper and raspier than usual.

We repeated the movement.

"One more time," he whispered.

Out the corner of my eye, I glanced at him grinning. My knees were on the verge of collapse. I was two seconds away from melting into a puddle on the floor. If Hart didn't get it this time, I was going to have to cut the onion myself.

He turned toward me, which put his lips right at my ear. "Last time. I promise."

I applied slight pressure to his hand, making the final slice into the vegetable.

Straightening up, I said, "I think you've got it."

He looked up at me with those damn sexy blue-gray eyes. "Can I work for extra credit?"

I put all my effort into ignoring his flirting. "Once you finish that, you place the knife parallel and slice through, giving you a nicely diced onion."

He followed my instructions and finished. "Do I get an A?"

I glanced at his work. "A-plus! Now peel and dice the garlic into tiny pieces."

"I'm on it, teach."

As Hart made quick work of the garlic, I finished with the sausage. I drizzled a little olive oil in the pan as it came up to temperature. Once the oil was heated I tossed in Hart's perfectly diced onion and garlic. Using a spatula, I pushed the ingredients around the pan while sipping wine.

Hart grabbed another beer from the fridge. "Exactly what are we making?"

"My famous spaghetti sauce."

"Why don't you just buy it in the jar?"

"Shut your mouth, man! There's no substitute for making it from scratch." I grabbed the plate of sausage and dumped it in the pan, breaking it into small pieces with the spatula. "Smell that." I waved my hand over the pan, spreading the spicy aroma around the room. "It's happiness, joy, and contentment all at once."

"You really love cooking." He smiled.

"I do. It makes me feel cozy and warm." My face scrunched up realizing how silly my words sounded. "It's stupid, I know."

"No it doesn't. It sounds like a lady who's found her passion in life. What other passions do you have, Bryson?"

"You'll have to stick around and find out."

Maybe I need to slow down on the wine sipping.

Once the sausage was done, I drained it and set it to one side. I then tossed the ground meat in the same pan. As the meat cooked, I grabbed the big bag that had Hart's other surprise.

"I'm about to introduce you to your new best friend," I said, pulling out the box with the new crock pot in it.

"What?"

"This is your new crock pot. I got it in stainless steel since you seem to love grays and blacks." I beamed with excitement.

"Bryson, you didn't need to do all this."

"I wanted to."

"Why?"

"Because you're my friend."

"I'd be your friend even if all you knew how to do was order takeout."

I turned to place the gift on the counter and to hide my flushed cheeks. Hart was being sweet but I had the feeling I'd let my eagerness take over and stepped out of bounds.

A large hand on the small of my back caused me to look in Hart's direction. "Thank you." We exchanged smiles. "So, what am I supposed to do with that pot of crock?"

"We're going to take all the ingredients and put them in the pot. Let it cook overnight and tomorrow you just have to boil the pasta, make a salad, and garlic bread. It's so easy. Plus, you'll have leftovers that can go in the freezer."

"We're not eating this tonight?"

I shook my head.

"Then that means you'll be back tomorrow."

I opened my mouth to respond when the doorbell rang. Butter bolted off her bed, galloping toward the door.

"I have no idea who that could be." Hart rolled away.

"It's probably the pizza I ordered," I said, setting up the crock pot.

Hart returned a few minutes later with pizza in hand and a dog nose following closely behind.

He slid the pizza on the counter. "Bryson, you're killing me."

Hart watched closely as I added the meats, a can of diced tomatoes, tomato paste, basil, parsley, salt, pepper, a couple of tablespoons of brown sugar, and a splash of the red wine to his new toy.

"Now what I'm about to show you is top secret. You must swear to carry it to the grave."

"Scout's honor." He crossed his heart.

From the last bag I pulled out a bottle of original Kraft barbeque sauce.

"What are you gonna do with that?"

"It's my secret sauce ingredient."

"You're shitting me?"

With the most serious expression I could muster, I said, "I am not shitting you."

The wine and beer had us buzzing a little more.

Hart craned his neck as I tipped the bottle over. "How much of that are you putting in?"

"I never measure it. Sometimes you have to feel your way."

"Feeling my way is my favorite pastime."

He grabbed another beer, my glass, and the bottle of wine before heading to the sofa with Butter trailing.

I covered the crock pot and flipped it on. "Plates?"

"Second cabinet on the right."

I found the plates with no problem, snatched a couple of napkins, and the pizza and took a spot on the sofa. Butter sat patiently, her caramel eyes focused as I dished out the pizza. I glanced up at Hart refilling my wine glass. In that moment there was nowhere else I'd rather be than right here, with him, doing this. Sophie warned me to be careful not to put my heart at risk for falling. But you can't see a fall before it happens and when it does, it's too late.

chapter Twenty

"What caused your divorce?"

"Wow, you don't believe in easing into things, do you?"

"I believe in easing into some things," he said, cocking an eyebrow along with one corner of his mouth.

Hart and I settled back and got comfy. He was still in his wheelchair while I sat on the sofa, shoes off, with my legs curled under me. I wiped my hands with the napkin before reaching for my wine and taking a sip.

"I had a miscarriage and things snowballed after that." My vision blurred as my eyes began to mist. I shook my head trying to compose myself. "Sorry."

Hart handed me a fresh napkin. "You have nothing to be sorry about."

I dabbed underneath each eye. "I guess some things you never get over."

"My mom used to tell me, you can get past the death of a loved one but you never get over it."

I stared into his soft eyes. "She was a wise woman."

Hart broke the connection and reached for his slice of pizza.

"I also found out he never loved me." The words came out blunt and unemotional.

Hart put down his slice of pizza. "I find that hard to believe."

"Well, it's true. That and his propensity for skanky whores."

Picking up his beer, he leaned back and took a swig. "By definition aren't whores skanky?"

"Not technically. A whore can be sophisticated like your high-priced call girls or the housewives of . . . pick your city. A skank on the other hand is sleazy and unpleasant but doesn't necessarily open her legs up for business."

He held up his beer like he was making a toast. "I stand corrected. Well, I sit corrected."

His joke caught me off guard for a second but it didn't make me uncomfortable.

With pursed lips, I tilted my head to the side. "That was a really bad joke."

"Come on, it wasn't that bad."

"It was pretty bad."

"So, if he never loved you why the marriage?"

"And we're back on topic," I said, raising my glass in the air.

"You don't have to talk about it if you don't want."

I hadn't said much to Hart about my marriage. The main reason being I didn't want to waste our time together talking about Will.

"I was perfect for the role of wife according to his parents. Good girl from a good family with just the right amount of humility. It's all about appearances with the Forsyths. Since Will's older brother, Alex, was and continues to be a huge disappointment, all the expectations were put on Will. He loved being the number-one son and all the perks that came along with it, including being handed the family business. All he had to do was keep up appearances."

The room fell silent as Hart stared and I took one long sip of wine.

"Did you love him?"

"What is it they say? Hindsight is twenty-twenty? Part of me loved him and the other part loved everybody's idea of him. Have you ever done something just because it's easily accessible? Everyone talks in your ear, telling you this is the direction you need to go. There's nothing wrong with the direction except you just don't want to go that way. But you're young and don't trust yourself enough to step out on your own because you've convinced yourself that everyone else has the right answers."

Looking at Hart, he'd not taken his eyes off of me the entire time. My gaze roamed over his lifeless legs and the straps holding them in place. I swallowed the lump in my throat as tears bubbled up behind my eyes. I felt like a whiny brat.

Running my fingers underneath my eyes, I said, "I'm sorry."

"For what?"

"For moaning about the dumbass choices I've made in my life. Compared to what you've had to endure and overcome . . . I have no right to complain."

"It's not a contest to see who had the hardest life, Bryson."

I stared into a pair of steady, intent eyes without a single hint of contempt for my complaining.

"Why didn't you ever ask me out in high school?"

The corner of his mouth quirked up. "The line was too long."

Sniffling, I ran my napkin under my nose. "That's such bullshit."

"Why didn't you ever talk to me after our dance?"

I hesitated several seconds trying to decide if I was ready to admit the truth.

"You scared me," I whispered.

"Looks like we had a lot in common."

We locked eyes as the air in the room thickened. Soft piano notes trickled around us followed by the deep raspy voice of Rod Stewart singing his rendition of "The Way You Look Tonight". When the song drifted into recognition, I thought of my moment with Hart all those years ago and all the moments we'd missed since then. It took every ounce of strength I had to not let sobs of regret pour out of me.

I tore my gaze from his and slid to the edge of the sofa. "I better get this cleaned up."

"Don't worry, I'll take care of it."

Hart moved forward at the same time I stood. My head went fuzzy as the room blurred, causing me to sway toward the end of the coffee table. Hart reached for my hips as I staggered back and onto his lap.

His protective arm snaked its way around my waist, pressing my back to his hard chest. "Whoa! Are you okay?"

"I must have drunk a little more than I thought."

Shifting, I made an unsuccessful attempt at standing.

"I've got you," he whispered in my ear.

The rough tip of his scruff grazed the shell of my ear, prickling all the way down to the spot just below my lobe. Heat roared through my body as his warm breath coated the back of my neck. A layer of goosebumps covered in tingles replaced my skin. Every one of the sensations intensified and culminated between my legs. I clenched my core, hoping to dull the vibrations taking over me.

The soft touch his lips settle in the crook of my neck. Instinctively, I tilted my head to the side, wanting his mouth to continue its trip over my skin. As I melted deeper into Hart, his arm loosened and fell away. My throat tightened with a scream or a sob, I couldn't distinguish which was trying to push its way up and out.

Twisting my body, I shifted my legs to the side, bringing us face to face. My chest brushed lightly against his. We were so close the airspace between us was practically nonexistent. Somehow the scent of pizza, beer, and spices complemented one another and were more intoxicating than the wine. My lips parted at the touch of his breath. Slow and steady, I inhaled as much of him as my lungs would hold. Neither of us said a word as we got lost in the other.

As the music continued to swirl around us, the wheelchair slowly moved away from the sofa and began to gently sway from side to side to the song . . . our song. The movement was almost undetectable. Hart's eyes seared into me as if I was the most incredible sight he'd ever seen. I was utterly spellbound.

Raising his hand, he gently brushed away a stray strand of hair off my cheek. "My god, you're beautiful." His voice was low and full of awe. "And I'm not just talking about your eyes or your lips or even all the amazing soft curves of your body."

I blinked back more tears. It had been such a long time since I felt wanted and admired. Abruptly, we stopped dancing and Hart closed his eyes, breaking the connection. His chest lifted, filling with oxygen as he pulled back.

"Are you okay? Did I do something wrong?" The words shook with panic.

His eyes shot open overflowing with conflict. "Bryson . . . we shouldn't . . ."

I tried to hide my hurt and disappointment but a tear escaped before I was able to rein it in. "I understand."

"What do you understand?"

"Nothing. I was lying before."

Cupping the side of my face, his thumb moved over my cheek, wiping away the tear. "Bryson, you're special and deserve someone who can offer you the complete package. I don't want you to get hurt."

I didn't want to beg or plead, trying to convince him to do something he wasn't into. But I'd reached the point of no return and needed Hart in every sense of the word.

"I'm a big girl, not expecting anything more than what you want to give. It could be as simple as two friends helping each other out."

His eyebrows furrowed. "What are you talking about?"

"I need a transition guy. Just someone to have fun with, no pressure. And you don't do relationships. We'd be perfect together if you think about it."

"Oh, I've thought about it." He peered into my eyes, trying to make sure I knew what I was getting into.

I wasn't exactly sure myself. It was as if my need for Hart possessed my body and was running the show. My brain had shut down and desire was doing all the talking and not considering any of the consequences.

"I can't make promises," he said.

"I'm not asking for any."

Hart's hand slowly traveled up my thigh and hip, stopping where the top of my jeans met the bottom of my chocolate brown wrap shirt. The tips of his fingers played with the edge of the hem as he held my gaze.

He leaned in, his voice deep and husky. "Bryson, is your marriage really done?"

Inching closer, I whispered, "Everything but the paperwork."

"Slide your hands up my chest."

I inhaled and followed his instructions. My gaze dropped as I pressed my palms flat against his toned stomach. After a few seconds of hesitation, Hart covered my hands with his and began guiding them up. I felt every ripped muscle, smooth plane, and deep indention that made up his torso. He sucked in a sharp breath as my palms moved over his already hard nipples, causing my gaze to shoot up. Hart picked up on the flash of uncertainty in my eyes.

"We don't have to go through with anything," he said, letting go.

My hands stayed glued to his chest as I dipped my chin. "My . . . um . . . experience is severely limited . . . in all areas. Even kissing . . . I won't be as good as Amber."

Lifting my chin with his index finger, Hart leaned in and whispered, "Shh, get her out of your head." He nibbled down my cheek to my jaw. "I never kissed her. I never kissed any of them."

I was in the midst of being swept away, so I remained still, allowing him to work his way to the spot under my ear. "None of them?"

A combination moan and huff left me as Hart pulled away.

Cupping both sides of my face, he stared into my eyes. "Never on the lips."

"Seriously?"

Placing a kiss at the corner of my mouth he said, "Seriously."

As Hart continued to explore my skin, my eyes drifted closed.

"It's hard to believe you haven't kissed anyone. I mean, you're twenty-six." My words were coming out part breathy sigh and part moan.

His lips left my skin. "I didn't say I've never kissed anyone. It's just been a long time. A kiss, like the one I'm about to give you, isn't important to a guy unless the girl is."

The pressure and wetness between my legs was getting more intense with each touch of his hand and word out of his mouth. I clenched my knees together and shifted in his lap, hoping to get some relief. Hart smiled, realizing exactly what I was trying to do. We were so close the tips of our noses rubbed. As his hands returned to the side of my face, Hart's fingers slipped into my hair as he pulled me to him. The move was confident and assertive. Like he needed me and couldn't wait any longer.

At first, the kiss was slow and gentle. Hart coaxed my lips open a little more with each touch, until he was fully inside. His tongue was firm as it swirled around mine. My hips began mimicking the rhythm. His hands fell away from my face, traveling down my back and underneath my shirt. My palms roamed over his broad shoulders. They were solid and strong, like they were able to handle anything. When my fingers melted into his blond hair, a deep growl rumbled from the back of his throat.

As if we had read each other's minds, we both broke the kiss at the same time. Without a word, I was the first to raise my arms as Hart peeled off my shirt, tossing it to the side. The look in his eyes at the first sight of my bare skin and lace-covered breasts was a cross between pure awe and unadulterated hunger. The corners of my mouth drifted up as I took a few seconds enjoying the way his eyes felt on me. Feeling bold, I placed my hands on either side of Hart's jaw, lifting his face to a deep kiss. I kept the kiss going as I grabbed the hem of his T-shirt and slid it up, breaking the kiss just before the shirt slipped over his head. Hart's upper body looked more incredible than it had felt under my hands. It was toned, hard, muscular, and powerful.

Suddenly, one of his arms wrapped around my waist. Forcefully he tugged me to his chest, our bodies and lips crashing into each other. The skin-on-skin contact sent an explosion of chills up and down my spine. His hand traveled along my ribcage until it was cupping my breast, his thumb gliding over my nipple. Applying pressure to the back of his head, I pulled him farther into my mouth, moaning into his.

Hart pushed on my lower back, gluing me to his chest. We exchanged raspy deep growls, drowning out the music. I was running out of breath but I didn't want to stop. I was afraid if I backed away even for a second that it would all be over. He would have time to think and decide this was a bad idea after all. I'd never wanted anyone as much as I wanted Hart.

Gasping for breath, he pierced me with his gaze and said, "Are you sure about this?"

My chest rose and fell in heavy rapid pumps as I nodded my answer.

I started to stand but Hart's arm tightened around my waist, holding me in place. I gazed into his heat filled eyes assuring him I wasn't moving. My lips made good use of their free time, traveling up and down Hart's neck as he rolled us into his bedroom.

Entering the room, Hart took me over to the nightstand where I flipped on the lamp. An amber glow filtered through the lampshade, casting shadows over our bodies. Using his fingertips, he caressed from my cheek and down to my neck. His gaze closely following the movement of his hand. As he reached my bra, his breathing visibly picked up speed. My body trembled at the feel of his rough fingers sliding down my strap and gliding across the top of my breasts, tracing the lacey outline.

Hart's gaze lingered on my mouth before traveling up to my eyes. The expression on his face caused the throbbing between my legs to intensify.

He looked as if all of his dreams were about to come true. Leaning in, he nipped at my bottom lip twice, sucking on it hard before diving full throttle into my mouth. I sunk my fingers into his hair and gave it a gentle tug, eliciting a deep moan.

He pulled back, panting. "I want you to stand, unbutton your jeans and push them down your thighs slowly."

I nodded. "Okay."

I eased myself off his lap. It wasn't until I was standing in front of him that it dawned on me, I hadn't considered the logistics of Hart and me having sex. I knew of his arrangements with the other women over the years, so I assumed he was able to have sex in the normal way. I started to ask but then thought better. I felt safe with him and trusted him to guide me. I bit the inside of my cheek in order to guarantee I kept my mouth shut.

Hart watched intently as I lowered my zipper. As his gaze focused on my striptease, mine stayed glued to him. His Adam's apple bobbed up and down with each hard swallow. His breathing sped up the farther my pants slid down my thighs.

"Step out of them," he said.

I did, leaving me in the middle of the room in only my black lace bra and matching boy short panties. His gaze moved with meticulous precision up my leg, his hands clenching and unclenching the higher he looked.

"Rub your tits slowly."

His request caused my knees to buckle. Whenever Will used the word tits, and he always used it, it sounded crude and trashy. But coming from Hart's mouth coupled with the way he was looking at me made it hot.

My eyes closed as I massaged each breast slowly, throwing in a nipple pinch here and there. Sighs and groans seeped out of me. One hand began sliding down my body toward the top of my panties.

"Stop touching yourself," Hart growled.

My eyes shot open with the bark of his order. He didn't sound angry. He sounded like a man who was on the verge of losing control and was trying to hold on to it. A surge of power overtook my body, knowing I'd affected him this much.

"Bryson, I need a few minutes. I'll be right back." He headed toward the bathroom.

"What should I do?"

"Wait."

With Hart out of the room my head had a second to clear. Suddenly, I was very aware of standing almost completely naked in the middle of his bedroom. Not only had I exposed myself to another man for the first time, I touched myself for him. Will asked me all the time to do that in front of him but I never did. I always thought of it as seedy and dirty. But I felt sensual and sexy doing it for Hart.

Minutes later the bathroom door opened and Hart rolled out. He was completely naked except for a towel draped over his lap. My gaze floated over his bare upper body. It had only been out of sight for a short time but long enough for me to miss it. I would never get tired of staring at his muscles or his eyes or his lips. I didn't know what I expected his legs to look like. Frankly, I hadn't given them much thought until this moment. They looked like normal legs, bent as any other pair of legs would be while sitting down. They didn't match the musculature of his upper body, obviously, but they didn't appear mismatched either.

I stood in silence as Hart moved toward the bed. He looked at me like a starving man.

Extending his hand to me, he said, "Come here."

I walked to him, slipping my hand in his. He tugged on my arm, bending me forward, and captured my lips.

He ended the kiss but kept his lips connected to mine. "You're incredible."

"So are you."

"I'm going to sit on the edge of the bed."

"Do you need my help?"

He shook his head. "Just stand there and continue to take my breath away."

Flutter.

Tingle.

Melt.

Hart aligned himself on the side of the bed as closely as possible. He pulled the comforter back and reached for two of the large pillows, stacking them against the huge solid mahogany headboard. He locked the wheelchair and placed his hands on either side of his thighs. In one impressive fluid motion Hart hoisted himself onto the bed. The towel stayed in place.

I waited for his instructions while he unlocked the chair and pushed it closer to the nightstand. Hart slid his hand under his right knee, moving it an inch to thc side. He looked up at me, gauging my reaction to his immobile extremities. I don't know what he saw in my expression but whatever it was made him smile, which gave me a thrill. With a simple tilt of his chin, I knew he wanted me to come to him. When I was close enough, he took my hand, lacing our fingers together.

Starting at my feet, Hart's gaze slowly moved up my body, blazing a trail of heat. He took in every inch of me, lingering on my legs, my stomach, my chest, my collarbone, neck, and lips until finally reaching my eyes.

"Kneel in front of me," he said.

He helped me down as I positioned myself between his legs, sitting back on my heels. Hart cupped the side of my face, running his thumb over my cheek. I closed my eyes, melting into the center of his palm.

"Bryson, look at me." My eyes opened. "I don't want you to do anything you're not comfortable with. Do you understand me?"

"Yes." I paused. "Just remember I've not been with . . . I don't want to disappoint you."

"You're lovely and sexy. You could never disappoint me. I'm going to take care of you. You trust me?"

"Completely." The word came out as more of a sigh.

Hart transformed me into a complete puddle on the floor. I had to fight the urge to jump on him. Leaving my face, his hands moved down my neck to my shoulders, sliding down the straps of my bra.

I slowly ran my palms over his thighs. "Can you feel this?"

"No but I can see it."

For the briefest moment, there was a hint of sadness in his eyes. The Hart I'd been privy to was always strong and in control, having adjusted to his situation with complete confidence. He worked hard to achieve his goals and didn't let his disability hold him back from living a full life. But for that brief moment, I got a glimpse of a Hart who still mourned the loss of his legs. As I blinked back tears the urge to wrap myself around him and never let go washed over me.

If I could just rewind time and go back to that night, I'd do things differently. I hated that I wasn't by Hart's side for the most devastating time of his life. I wanted to give him back his legs and his mom. I wanted to take away all his sadness. My heart and body ached and I was powerless to do any of it.

Pushing off my heels, I rose up, bringing us face to face. I shut my eyes hoping to keep the tears from falling but it was too late. The warm touch of Hart's lips pressed against my cheek.

"Hart, I wish . . ."

Keeping his lips on my skin, he whispered, "There's nothing you can do to fix it."

My hands slipped into his hair as his face burrowed in the crook of my neck. "I want to make you happy." I sighed. "Tell me how."

"You already know how. You've been doing since that day at the pool."

Hart slipped his hands behind me and unhooked my bra. The release along with the feel of his skin moving over my body caused a shiver to run from my head to my toes. I took a deep breath before letting my bra fall away. Raising his hand, Hart palmed one of my breasts as his thumb glided over my hard nipple.

Leaning in painstakingly slow, he let the anticipation and my temperature spike. Then in a flash, he lunged forward, taking my bottom lip in his mouth and sucked. The slight pressure as his teeth grazed my lip sent high-voltage shockwaves through me. My fingers clenched, digging into his shoulders. As he continued to work my mouth, he cupped my ass and pulled me closer. The second my hard nipples hit his hard chest I thought my head was going to explode.

Feeling the twitch of his erection against my stomach, I broke the kiss, gasping for air. "I want to touch you."

"Stand up. When I tell you, I need you to grab my ankles and put my legs on the bed."

I nodded and stood. Placing his hands on either side of him, Hart tilted his chin up to signal me. As he pushed himself up to the head of the bed, I took his ankles and placed his legs stretched out in front of him.

Holding out his hand, he said, "Come here."

I slipped my palm into his and he tugged me forward. His face was at eye level with my chest. As if he were licking a decadent dessert, his tongue glided back and forth over my nipple before taking as much of my breast into his mouth as possible. My knees trembled to the point of exhaustion. Squeezing my ass, he kept me from collapsing.

His eyes peered up at me. His gaze locked with mine as he slowly let my tit slide out of his mouth. I gasped for air as my fingers dug into his skin. A deep chuckle vibrated against my stomach.

"Straddle me," he commanded.

I placed my hand flat on the mattress, testing its stability. I climbed up, swung my leg over Hart, and positioned myself on his lap. His hands were in perpetual motion, gliding over my thighs, hips, ass, and back.

I kissed him and whispered against his mouth, "Let me see you."

He nipped at my bottom lip, giving me silent permission to remove the towel. The feel of his hard dick between my legs caused my body to quake. He gripped my hips as they began to rock back and forth. The friction was exquisite. Hart's gaze swung from my eyes to my bouncing breasts. I let my head fall back as the first wave of pleasure washed over me.

"Stand up," he said.

"What?"

"Stand over me."

"Hart . . ."

"Do it. I promise you won't regret it."

I took hold of his hand and he helped me steady myself as I stood with my feet planted on either side of his hips.

Rubbing his hands along the back of my legs, he said, "Grab hold of the headboard." I looked down at him, questioning. "Do it."

I did as I was told.

My body jolted when his lips skimmed my inner thigh, alternating between nibbles and licks until reaching the top. With his face nuzzling between my legs, his fingers hooked around the top of my panties and slid them down. The combination of the silky lace and Hart's strong hands gliding over my skin had me seconds away from detonating.

Holding me steady, Hart placed wet kisses along my other inner thigh and mumbled, "Lift your left leg." I did, stepping out of my panties. "Now the right."

My mind and body were aching to be consumed by him. I didn't just want Hart inside of me, I needed him inside of me. Seconds later my wish came true.

Hart's lips grazed my hipbone, kissing their way to between my legs. His tongue slowly licked from back to front before pressing flat against my center. A bolt of electricity broke through my total body vibrations. I hung on to the headboard as my knees shook. He spiraled his tongue into me, bringing me to the brink of insanity. I was in sensation overload, unable to process it. Shifting, I tried to catch my breath and my bearings. But Hart had such a tight grip on my ass, I was completely immobile. His tongue flicked in and out, each time pushing deeper and deeper.

Gasps, moans, and several cries of "Oh my god, Hart!" filled the room. My head was spinning so rapidly I was surprised anything remotely coherent came out of me.

I rested my forehead against the headboard as my vision blurred. I blinked several times hoping for clarity. When that didn't work, I thought focusing on something different would help. I glanced down.

Bad move.

The site of blue-gray eyes peering up from between my legs while he sucked me off was my undoing. I squeezed my eyes closed. As my legs gave way, Hart's massive arms wrapped around the back of my thighs. His tongue remained relentless, alternating between licking, sucking, and pushing farther inside as my body convulsed in pleasure. I sank my fingers into his hair and rode the longest and most intense orgasm I'd ever experienced in my life.

My body continued to spasm as Hart slowed down the pace, placing gentle kisses everywhere his lips could reach.

His nose glided over the bend at the top of my leg. "Are you okay?" The deep rumble of words sent a chill through me.

"I . . . I . . . uh . . . what the fuck was that?"

His laughter had my core vibrating.

Holding onto the edge of the headboard, I picked up my wobbly left leg and stepped over Hart. He held my hand as I lowered to the bed. When I was safely beside him, I blinked several times trying to clear my blurry vision. My entire body felt as if it were floating above the bed. Once Hart was in view, I noticed his scruff was wet with me. From deep down in the pit of my stomach hot energy surged giving my desire a second wind. I wanted him to feel how much he meant to me.

I cupped his face and drew him to me, devouring his mouth. Shifting forward, I brought my leg over and straddled him. His big hands ran up and down my back, setting my spine on fire. Both our moans got louder as I pushed deeper into his mouth. If it had been humanly possible, I would have disappeared completely inside of him. The feel of his hard dick rubbing between my legs only spurred me on.

Hart broke the devouring, gasping for air. "Nightstand. Top drawer. Loose." The words came out stilted like a caveman.

I reached over, opened the drawer, and fumbled for what felt like a condom. Hart took it from me.

"Are you okay with me putting it on for you?"

"I'm more than okay with it," he answered.

I tore open the foil packet and slid the condom out. Glancing up at Hart, I gave him what I hoped was a sexy smile. By the return look he gave me, I'd say mission accomplished. His hands continued to roam over every inch of my body. The breath audibly caught in his lungs as I slowly rolled the condom down. Placing my hands on Hart's shoulders, I raised up on my knees.

I'd been so swept away by everything that I hadn't thought about how it would be to have a new man inside of me. I expected to be nervous or even scared but I wasn't. And even if I didn't want to admit it, deep down I knew the reason was because this wasn't just someone new, this was Hart.

Hart nuzzled into my breasts as I lowered myself onto him.

Perfect fit.

With our foreheads resting together, my hips slowly rocked.

"Is this okay?" I whispered.

Even though it was apparent Hart could definitely have an erection, I didn't know what level of feeling he had.

"You're perfect," he said, pulling me to his mouth.

I couldn't help but notice that he emphasized I was perfect.

The pressure soared as he throbbed inside of me. His fingers dug into my hair as mine planted themselves on his broad shoulders. I picked up speed, sliding up and down. While he was deep inside me, I did a slight roll of my hips that caused his head to drop back and his face to squeeze tight. A deep guttural moan rumbled in the back of his throat before his arms tightened around me and several intense jerks took over his body. The feel of Hart climaxing under me sent me over the edge. I thought the previous orgasm was intense but it didn't compare to the one happening wrapped in his arms.

I pulled Hart to my chest, his arms enveloping me as the sporadic jerks slowly faded, replaced by steady trembles. We stayed in this position until the air transformed our hot sweaty bodies into quivering masses.

"You're shivering," he mumbled against my neck.

Neither one of us attempted to move. He reached for the comforter and pulled it over my back, cocooning us in our own little world. We spent several minutes exploring each other's bodies.

My fingertips traced the outline of the black tribal tattoo wrapped around his bicep. "What does this symbolize?"

"A drunk night out with the guys." He chuckled.

"And here I thought it had some deep spiritual meaning behind it."

He placed a soft kiss on my collarbone. "Sorry to disappoint."

"You haven't disappointed me." I tossed him a shy smile.

I directed my attention to the series of tattooed numbers. "Now these can't be the result of a drunken night."

His thumb was mindlessly making circles at the small of my back. "It's the directional coordinates for Charleston. It reminds me that no matter where I'm at or what happens, I can always get back home."

Staring into his smoky eyes, my fingertips prickled as they ran down the scruff peppering his jaw. I wanted to be Hart's home. The safe person he turned to for strength, comfort, and support. I wanted to tell him that no matter what happens or where he finds himself, I'd always be here for him. But instead I bit down on my bottom lip, stopping the words from pouring out. We were just two friends helping each other out.

His gaze roamed to every corner of my face. "What?"

"What, what?"

"There's something rolling around behind those gorgeous eyes."

Yeah, I think I'm falling in love with you.

Tears pricked the back of my eyes.

I wanted to play it cool. Like a modern, free Carrie Bradshaw kind of woman. But I wasn't any of those things.

Panic flashed across Hart's face. "Bryson, why are you crying?"

Shaking my head, I brought my fingers underneath my eyes, wiping away the tears that had a mind of their own. "Ugh, I'm sorry for being such a girl."

Hart moved in so close that there was no space between us. "You being a girl is one of my most favorite things about you."

"Thank you for making me feel worth the effort."

He pressed his lips to mine and whispered, "I hate that motherfucker for not being the man you deserved." He paused, uncertainty crossing his face as he struggled whether to say his next words. "Bryson, from our very first moment you stole my breath and I've been trying to catch it ever since."

I choked back a sob. "No one has ever said anything that beautiful to me before."

"Well, the next guy who's lucky enough to have your heart better or I'll kick his ass."

A large lump formed in my throat. Hart wanted to bring me back to the reality of our arrangement by making sure I knew he was only temporary.

I'm a true believer that we each have a soulmate. That one person you connect with on such a deep level that no words come close to describing it. I used to think Will was that person but I was so off track. Looking into his loving eyes, I knew without a doubt Hart was my soulmate. He was the person I was put on earth for. But just because that person exists somewhere out in the world doesn't always translate into them being with you. People consider finding their soulmate to be the ultimate challenge in life. The challenge was not in the search. The challenge was being brave enough to let them into your life.

chapter
Twenty-One

I floated slowly into consciousness. Turning on my back, I lifted my arms over my head stretching like a lazy cat that had been lying in the sun all day. The fatigue in my muscles was matched by the soreness. I pulled the soft comforter under my chin and snuggled back into the warm sheets. As my mind drifted, the memory of last night shot through me like a bolt of lightning. The looking, the touching, the dancing, the kissing, and the sexing.

One eye squinted open, widening with each roll as it took in my surroundings. I was at Hart's house, in Hart's room, lying in Hart's bed naked . . . I ran my hand over cold empty sheets . . . without Hart. Inhaling a deep breath, I prepared myself for my very first walk of shame. I raised my arms above my head, stretching all the kinks out of my body from one of the most amazing nights of my life. Hart's hands never left my skin as I curled into his side, lulling me into the land of dreams with his touch.

Sliding off the bed, I snatched up my clothes and darted into the bathroom. Since I wasn't exactly schooled in the art of the morning after, I figured a quick and clean getaway was best. I set about to multi-task. As I took my morning pee, I slipped into my underwear and clothes. Then I headed toward the sink to splash cool water on my face. I sucked up enough courage to take a quick glance in the mirror.

Oh, not a good look.

My makeup was completely gone and my hair looked as if I'd stuck my finger in a light socket. I combed my fingers through the mess of twisted strands a few times, making it somewhat presentable. I grabbed one of the small disposable plastic cups that sat on the side of the sink and drank twenty of them, one right after the other. My gaze darted around looking for mouthwash or toothpaste but there wasn't either beside the sink. I had to do something. My mouth tasted like a cat had curled up and died in it overnight.

I hated to rummage through any of Hart's personal items but I had no choice. The second I opened the medicine cabinet I saw everything I needed for oral hygiene. Raising my hand to the toothpaste, my gaze inadvertently shifted to the right. I quickly shut my eyes and closed the cabinet but it was too late. I'd already seen the prescription bottle of Viagra.

After Hart told me the level of his injury, I did some research on spinal cord injuries. I wanted to know what he'd gone through and would have to deal with for the rest of his life. When the topic of sex scrolled across the screen, I couldn't help but skim over the information. Depending on the level and whether it's complete or incomplete, people with spinal cord injuries can lead healthy and satisfying sex lives. They just need a little help. If I didn't believe it when I read it, I sure as hell believed it now after last night.

I squeezed a little of Hart's toothpaste on my finger and sucked on it. I placed it back where I'd found it, eyes focused straight ahead.

Now for the hard part.

Cracking open the door slightly, I listened for any noise indicating Hart was near.

Silence.

My shoes and purse were the only other items I needed and they were still in the living room. A sense of deja vu hit me.

Note to self: Next time I get drunk and naked at Hart's, deposit all personal items in one spot.

I headed for the bedroom door, placed my hand on the knob, and inhaled a deep breath. Easing the door open, the delicious aroma of spaghetti sauce coming from the kitchen slapped me in the face as I heard the rumble of low voices coming from down the hall.

Voicessss . . . with an *s*! My first sexual experience as a single woman was really going well. Top notch.

Nudging my ear in the small crack between the bedroom door and the doorframe, I hoped to make out who the voices belonged to.

"It's nice to know you didn't drop off the planet."

I was almost positive that was Colin talking. Out of all the guys, I'd had the most interaction with him. There was no response to his comment followed by nondescript rustling noises.

"You want some coffee?" My body tingled to the deep rasp of Hart's voice.

"Nah, I'm good."

"What did I do to deserve this early morning unannounced pleasure?" Hart sounded half joking and half annoyed.

"After you cut our tennis match short yesterday without explanation and never answered any of my texts or calls last night, I got worried," Colin said.

"If you were that worried why'd you wait until this morning to check in?"

"Well, asshole, I drove by last night and saw you had company."

No response.

The faint sound and smell of coffee brewing wafted down the hallway.

"And since there's an extra car parked in your driveway, I'm guessing you still have company."

Still no response.

"Isn't that Bryson's little red car?"

"Yep."

"What are you doing, dude?" Colin's tone was serious.

"I'm trying to have coffee and a piece of cake."

I smiled hearing that Hart was eating the cake I brought him.

"You know what I'm talking about."

"No I don't." Hart snapped.

"She's married."

"They've been separated for almost a year and are getting a divorce."

"Okay, let me put it this way." Colin paused. "Bryson's not like the whores you pay to suck your dick."

That was harsh.

I could feel the tension between the two friends and I wasn't even in the room.

After several seconds, Hart said, "Colin, you're my best friend. More like a brother, really. But if you ever use those words in the same sentence as her name again, I will fucking punch you in the nuts and roll over your dick."

"Does she know?"

Do I know what?

"There's nothing for her to know."

Colin chuckled sarcastically. "Really?"

"We're just two friends helping each other out for a little while."

Even though that was the deal Hart and I agreed to last night, his words still punched me in the stomach.

"I'm concerned you're going to get in over your head and one or both of you will get hurt."

"I got it under control."

"I hope so. But when the girl of your dreams comes back into your life, control is the last thing you've got."

What the what?

"You don't have to worry about me, Colin. This thing with Bryson is temporary."

My throat and chest tightened.

"Okay. I need to get going."

The sound of heavy footsteps moved across the hardwood floor and stopped.

"By the way, when did you become Betty Fucking Crocker?" Colin said.

"You should realize by now I'm a man of many talents."

"I know you are. I'll let you get back to one of them now."

The next sound was the front door closing.

My head was still spinning like a whirly bird in fog from the events of last night. Add to it the conversation I just eavesdropped on and I was on course for a crash landing. I pushed my analytics aside for the time being. I needed to get out of there, clear my head, and think about what Colin said.

As a warning to Hart of my impending approach, I jiggled the doorknob loudly. Then for extra security, I cleared my throat the entire way down the hallway.

I found Hart in the kitchen finishing off his piece of cake. He had on the same jeans from last night but the long-sleeve T-shirt was black. As I entered, his gaze immediately shot to mine.

"Did you enjoy it?" I asked.

His eyebrows spiked into his forehead as his jaw went slack. "I . . . uh . . . I thought you were able to tell when I . . ."

"The cake. I was talking about the cake."

"Oh. Yeah. The cake is awesome. And good morning."

For some reason my cheeks flushed with warmth. "Good morning."

Maybe it was because I'd just overheard things I wasn't supposed to but there was a weird vibe between us. As I slipped into my shoes, the clank of a dish being placed in the farmhouse sink startled me. I turned toward the noise.

"Listen, I've got some errands to run and then I usually take Butter to the dog park. You're more than welcome to stay and have coffee . . . cake. Whatever."

"No, that's okay. I need to get home anyway." Glancing down, I fidgeted with the strap on my purse. "Take a shower. Get redressed. Maybe grab some toast or something. Pay a few bills. Take some time to get good and nervous for my first day of work tomorrow. I should probably stop by and see Will too. I mean . . ."

"Bryson, are you okay?"

My head popped up at the sweet tone of his voice. "Yeah . . . I'm . . . uh . . . I'm goood."

I'm so not good at this.

With knitted brows, I said, "I'm not sure what the proper protocol is after what we did last night. Which was anything but proper, if you know what I mean."

God, why do I even bother opening my mouth?

The right corner of Hart's mouth twitched as he worked to suppress a smile.

"Well, you go about tackling that long laundry list you just recited and I'm going to run my errands."

"Okay . . . okay . . . sounds like a plan. I guess I'll see ya when I see ya." The decibels of my voice increased with each word.

"I'll see you out," Hart said as he moved toward the front door.

The words didn't come out as dismissive but my ears heard them that way. I didn't know what I was expecting. Last night we were so connected and in tune with each other. I had to keep hammering it in my head that we were both adults who had agreed, in a slightly buzzed state, to help each other out. I wanted a safe person who I trusted to introduce me to new experiences and Hart wanted to save a few bucks by having a free fuck buddy.

He opened the front door, leaving enough room for me to step out onto the porch. As I got to the first step, Hart's words stopped me.

"Hey, Bryson . . ."

"Yes?"

"What time are you coming over tonight for spaghetti?"

I whipped around with a toothy smile on my face. "Whatever time is good for you?"

Deep dimples popped on either side of his sexy grin. "How about five? I don't want to keep you out too late the night before your new job."

My insides lit up with excitement as I stood at the top of the steps beaming. Hart's chest trembled with a chuckle when I remained glued to the spot staring, smiling, and shining.

"I guess I better run and get my stuff all done before our dinner . . . at five o'clock."

"I'll see you then." He winked.

My gaze lowered and I took one step down. "Five o'clock."

"Five o'clock."

His cheeks reddened the longer he held his grin.

"Okay, I'll see you then." I forced myself not to look back at him until I made it to my car.

Standing between the car and the open door, I glanced at Hart, who was still watching me, and gave a slight wave. He stayed in the doorway until I pulled out of his driveway and headed down the street. Once I was safely out of earshot, I screamed with delight. It was like being a teenager again who'd just been asked to the prom by the hottest boy in school. Except that we had already kissed and had mind-blowing sex.

Fifteen minutes later I was pulling into my driveway. I bounced my way into the house and up the stairs to my room. I couldn't believe how light and fluffy I felt. I headed into the bathroom and turned on the shower. As I waited for the water to heat up, I stripped down to my bra and panties. Realizing I'd not checked my cellphone since last night before going over to Hart's, I went into the bedroom and fished out my phone from my purse.

I hesitated before swiping to unlock the screen. It was a silly reaction but once I swiped the screen, I'd be letting the real world in. I'd already had a little taste of it this morning with Colin's reaction to me being at Hart's. Filling my lungs with an impressive amount of oxygen, I swiped my finger across the screen.

There were several missed calls and voicemails from Sophie, one from my mom, and a string of texts from Will that I didn't even bother to read. I typed a quick reply to Sophie.

Me: *When are you going out of town?*

Sophie: *Hello stranger. I leave for Portland on Wednesday.*

Other than making an appearance at the rehab and dinner with Hart later, I had the rest of the day free. I wanted and needed some time with my best friend to play catch up.

Me: *How about lunch?*

Sophie: *Sounds good. Where were you last night?*

Me: *How's 12:30ish? I'm going to check on Will first.*

Sophie: *Yeah 12:30ish. What were you doing last night?*

A chill ran through my body thinking about what I'd done last night. I shook my head free of the thoughts. If I didn't, I'd get nothing done today.

Me: *All will be revealed soon enough. See you at Tommy Condon's.*

Sophie: *Closed lip biotch.* □

I was definitely sharing my new job news with Sophie today. I was still on the fence on whether or not I was ready to tell her about me and Hart. I'd have to play that by ear. My hope was that when she heard about mine and Hart's arrangement she'd be happy for me. I just had to convince her that I had my emotions in check even though I wasn't exactly positive I did.

Before jumping in the shower I typed a quick text to Will.

Me: *Be there in a little while.*

Without waiting for a response, I plugged the cellphone into the charger and went to take my shower.

An hour and a half later I was walking into the rehab center smiling, feeling sexy and confident. At first it shocked me thinking that one night could change the way I felt about myself so drastically. But I knew it wasn't just one night of sex. Each moment I spent with Hart moved me closer toward the person I wanted to become. The way he looked at me, touched me, spoke to me, listened to me, treated me, and believed in me was what caused the change in me.

Will couldn't see an inkling of my newfound happiness. I needed to keep that under wraps for now and remain the same old Bryson. Attempting to tone down the sexy, I kept it casual, with my black leggings, sage green and cream floral print long shirt paired with my sage green long cardigan, a knit cream scarf, and black pseud short boots. The outfit said inconspicuous but cute.

The closer I got to Will's room my pace slowed and dread replaced all the good feelings. I hovered outside of his door for a few minutes, holding on to the new me a little longer. I was so lost in the Hart effect that I jumped out of my skin when I felt a hand on my shoulder.

"Whoa! I didn't mean to scare you." Andrea, one of the weekend nurses, chuckled.

"I'm so sorry. My head was in the clouds."

"I can imagine it probably is."

My eyebrows knitted together slightly thinking that was an odd response.

She gave me a knowing look. "You're a lucky girl."

I got a tickle in my stomach and throat. "Really?"

I'd heard office gossip spreads like wildfire but how on earth would anyone here find out about last night. The only people who knew were me, Hart, and Colin. Colin didn't work here. And Hart would never let it slip. Could this woman see the sex on me?

"And even if I hadn't heard it through the grapevine, I could tell something was up just by looking at you."

"Really?" My voice cracked.

"You look gorgeous as usual but there is an extra glow radiating off of you today. Must be happiness."

Suddenly my cute infinity scarf was choking the breath right out of me. "This sweater and scarf combo is pretty hot. I don't know what I was thinking wearing it. It's not that cold outside. You're probably just seeing the sweat popping up on my skin."

Andrea's face squished together in disgust.

"Yes . . . Well, I'll let you get to your fella."

She gave me a knowing look before walking away. I shook off the weird exchange and headed into Will's room.

He was sitting on the side of his bed, his back to me, dressed, with a pair of crutches leaning beside him. I stood in the doorway for a second staring at him. Our years together flashed across my mind. I remembered sitting behind him in tenth grade algebra daydreaming what it would be like to date *The Will Forsyth*. Back then there was a sweet innocence about him. I wondered when the change occurred. Maybe that Will never existed and it was the eyes I looked through that made him into something he never was.

He must have sensed my presence because without looking around, he said, "Did you hear the good news?"

I walked farther into the room, placing the bag of Chinese take-out from Red Orchid on the hospital table at the foot of the bed. "No. What good news?"

Will looked at me, his eyes crinkled with a smile. "I'm getting sprung."

"When?"

"Today."

My stomach plummeted as my thoughts spun out of control. For all intents and purposes, Will and I were still legally married. His doctors and all the rehab staff, except Hart, saw us as a happily married couple. They'd release Will, assuming he'd be going home to the house we once shared.

His gaze followed me as I walked to the chair across from him and sat. "We need to talk."

"What's there to talk about?"

"I think it's time to tell everyone the news."

"I just got off the phone with my mom right before you came in."

Finally.

He turned toward the take-out bag. "I'll eat once we get home."

"What?"

"The discharge papers should be here in about a half hour. You need to go ahead and pack up all my things."

I jumped from the chair and quickly walked to the door and closed it. With one hand on my hip, I ran the fingers of my other hand through my hair while taking in several deep breaths. Once I felt centered and composed, I went back to face Will.

"We need to tell both sets of parents we're getting a divorce."

He blew out a frustrated breath. "Bryson, you promised to stay with me until I fully recovered. I'm doing well enough to leave this fucking place but still need you with me. I'm nowhere near ready to be by myself."

"I got a job and start tomorrow. I won't even be home," I blurted out.

His dark eyes zeroed in on me. I couldn't tell if he was shocked or pissed.

"A job? Why?"

"Because I'm trying to move on with my life, Will. Please don't make this harder than it already is."

"You have little to no skill set and you've never made an important decision in your life. You've always had a safety net, first your daddy and then me. We both know you'll never make it on your own, Bryson."

I stared over his shoulder as I tamped down my anger.

Keeping my voice strong and steady, I said, "When I heard you'd been in an accident my first thought was, please god let him be okay. It would be so easy to hate you, Will. But I don't. I don't hate you. We've both wasted ten years living a lie. You can have the house, the cars, and the money. I don't care if I walk away from this marriage with nothing more than my dignity but I am walking away."

My gaze seared into his long enough to communicate my nonverbal fuck you. I turned on my heels and walked out the door with my head held high. The sense of relief and empowerment propelled me down the hall. Before leaving the rehab I made a pit stop at the nurse's station to give them the address of where Will would be spending the rest of his recovery . . . his parents.

Once in my car I sent a quick text to Sophie.

Me: *Sorry but I need to cancel lunch.*

Sophie: *You okay?*

Me: *Better than okay. I'll explain later. I love you.*

Sophie: *Love you too.*

I scrolled through my contacts and clicked on the number I needed.

"Hello."

"Hey, Mom."

"Hey stranger."

"I know. Sorry about that. Are you and Daddy going to be home for the next few hours?"

"Sure. All we have planned today is yard work."

"Okay, I'm headed your way."

"Wonderful. I know you've been busy with Will but I feel like I haven't seen my sweet girl in such a long time."

I swallowed the large lump in my throat as I blinked back tears. "I love you, Mom."

"I love you too, Bryson."

I wasn't sure how I was going to live on my own and was scared my parents would be disappointed in me when I told them about the divorce. But I couldn't control anyone or anything except myself and my actions. As I pulled out of the parking lot, I knew I was capable of handling whatever came my way.

chapter
Twenty-Two

The conversation with my parents was full of tears, hugs, and understanding. They reiterated over and over that they'd support me no matter what and that their only concern was my happiness. Mom said she'd fill in Ryan and a few close family and friends on the situation. After the emotional visit I headed home for a bit of a breather before my dinner with Hart.

As I walked toward the house, my eyes soaked in the beautiful southern porch. Strangers driving by would think the people living just beyond the threshold had a perfect life. They'd never guess how much turmoil swirled within the walls. They wouldn't see the loss of commitment and trust. They wouldn't hear the demeaning and humiliating words or the sobs that filled the air. No, they'd look at the outside and wish they were inside. A weak smile crossed my lips as I realized that the porch had done its job well.

Entering the house I thought about how Will and I breathed life into every nook and cranny. We took our time making sure the tiniest details were exactly the way we wanted. Our dreams of raising a family and spoiling grandkids. I dropped my purse on the small foyer table and wandered the downstairs. I passed the home office, the two guestrooms, the family room, the kitchen. Without our dreams the house felt new, like a blank canvas. Just like I did.

There was no better way to end a day than with Hart. As I walked into his place I swooned and laughed at the sight of him trying to open the can of refrigerated breadsticks with a knife while Butter looked up licking her chops. It was a good thing I stopped by The Bread Shop for a loaf of fresh garlic bread.

Since he seemed so determined with the project, I helped him get the can of dough open, forming it into something resembling breadsticks, and into the oven. After that, I insisted on making the salad and cooking the pasta while he stuck to pouring the wine.

Sitting at his table, our plates piled high with the dinner we'd made together, Hart raised his bottle of beer. "We make a pretty good team."

His words caused my stomach to flutter.

I held up my wine glass and we clinked. "Yeah, we do."

I watched over the brim of my glass as Hart twirled the spaghetti around his fork and slipped it between his lips. I swallowed hard as he slowly pulled the fork from his mouth, remembering how he looked up at me last night as my breast slowly slid from his mouth. His eyes closed as he moaned with a look of pure pleasure crossing his face. A loud sigh drifted out of me.

Hart opened his eyes, aiming them directly at me. "Do I have sauce on my face?"

I shook my head. "No. I'm just thoroughly enjoying your foodgasm."

"Wait till we have dessert," he said, winking.

We ate in comfortable silence for a few minutes before I shattered the mood.

"Will was released today." I blurted it out in such a random manner.

Hart sat back and took a swig of his beer. "So, he's back home."

He tried to hide it but I could tell his jaw was clenched and his grip had tightened around the bottle.

"When the girl of your dreams comes back into your life, control is the last thing you have."

"He'll be at his parents' house for the rest of his recovery." Hart visible relaxed. "I told my family about the divorce today. I guess the next step is to lawyer up."

Reaching over, Hart took my hand in his, running his thumb over my knuckles. "You okay?"

I gave a slight nod. "It's weird. For the last several months I struggled to picture my life without Will. I was never able to get a clear view of what it would look like. The only thing I could see and feel was my fear. I thought about all the things he handled in our marriage. The boring stuff like fixing things around the house, taking the cars in for repairs, and finances. Nothing I couldn't learn but it was just easier to let him take care of it. The picture is still a little hazy but the fear is gone. I have a lot to learn and I'll make mistakes but that's okay. I'm going to be okay."

Hart gave my hand a gentle squeeze. "I'm so proud of you, Bryson."

I swallowed the lump in my throat. "I have you to thank for a lot of it. You have no idea . . . you've given me the strength and courage to believe in myself and take control of my life."

Hart let go of my hand and backed away from the table, moving closer to me. Placing his hands on either side of my face, he sank his fingers into my hair as he pulled me to his mouth. The kiss was slow, deep, passionate, and left me breathless. Once it broke, Hart ran the tip of his nose along mine before our foreheads came together. The words I love you pushed against my lips but I bit down on the inside of my cheek to keep them from breaking through.

After his breathing went back to normal, Hart gave me a quick peck on the lips and said, "That's what friends are for." I bit down harder on my cheek, focusing on the pain as my heart slowed. "I want to give you something."

I narrowed my eyes and pursed my lips, not letting on how his words affected me.

"Not that. At least not right now," he said, taking my hand and pulling me up from the chair.

With a mischievous glimmer in his smoky eyes he rolled backward, leading me to the sofa.

"Sit. I'll be right back."

Hart headed down the hallway toward his bedroom while Butter slinked up in front of me looking for a head rub. As I looked into her warm caramel eyes, I wished I was a dog. Life would be less complicated.

Butter hopped up wagging her tail at the sound of Hart coming back into the room. As he rounded the sofa, her wet black nose sniffed at the large white box with red ribbon he was carrying. He held out the box to me. My gaze bounced from it to his excited expression.

"Open it." The hint of a smile crossed his lips.

"What is it?"

"If you open it you'll find out."

I was in such shock that when I reached for the gift, it looked more like I was picking up a bomb. Setting the large box on the coffee table, I pulled at one end of the ribbon, causing it to twist undone. Before lifting the lid, I glanced at Hart. His excitement from earlier seemed to have morphed into nervousness.

Tilting my head, I said, "Nothing's going to pop out at me, is it?"

"Nothing from the box."

I took off the lid, placing it to the side before separating the red tissue paper. My chest tightened as I slowly ran my fingertips over the material. Biting my bottom lip, I tried to stop the tears from coming but it was useless.

"Bryson?"

I looked at him, with a continuous stream running down my cheeks and choked out. "I c-c-an't be-lieve you did th-is."

Reaching inside, I pulled out the white chef's jacket with my name embroidered in black over the pocket.

"I guessed at the size. If it doesn't work for you I can take it back."

My head kept shaking back and forth. "When did you have time to do this? I just told you about the job last night."

Grinning, he said, "I told you this morning I had errands to run."

"I don't know what to say."

"You don't have to say anything. Your reaction is more than enough."

Without another word, I folded the jacket and placed it back in the box. I got up and crawled into Hart's lap. Not wasting any time, my fingers dove into his hair as I devoured his mouth, my tongue swirling and pushing in as far as it could go. Loud deep moans echoed in the room as his fingers dug into my hips. Heat radiated off our bodies, filling the air to the point of suffocation. As much as I tried, I couldn't seem to get close enough. I fisted his gray crewneck, tugging him to me. His hands traveled up my sides, settling on either side of my face. I tore my lips away from his, letting them lick and bite their way over his neck to behind his ear.

"Thank you," I whispered then nipped at his earlobe. "It's the sweetest most thoughtful thing anyone has ever done for me."

His hand made its way south, sliding up to my inner thigh. "You deserve it. You deserve everything."

"I love it."

I love you.

I yanked the bottom of his shirt as high as I could before Hart's hand stopped me.

His voice was low and husky. "It's getting late." I froze. "You need a good night's sleep before your big day tomorrow."

Rejection invaded my stomach, causing it to harden and feel hollow as I removed my lips from his skin.

I angled myself away from him, dropping my head. "Yeah, you're right. I'll head out after I clean up."

I attempted to stand but Hart's arm snaked around my waist, holding me in place.

"Bryson, look at me." When I didn't, he added. "Please."

I blinked several times, pushing back the tears before gazing into his concerned eyes. "Sorry, I'm just nervous about tomorrow."

Brushing the hair away from my face, he placed a soft kiss on my cheek. "You're going to do great."

"Thanks."

"Go on home and get a good night's sleep. I'll clean up."

I wondered why Hart was being so persistent with trying to get me to leave. The hollow feeling in my stomach moved to my chest as I gathered my things. I gave Butter one last pat on the head before going to the door.

"Good luck with tomorrow and call me. I want to know how things went," he said, quickly glancing down at his watch.

"The place is closed on Mondays so all I'll be doing is filling out paperwork and getting familiar with the equipment and procedures."

He took my hand and caught my gaze. "I still want to know how your day went." I turned to leave. "Bryson, are you sure everything's okay?"

I needed to get out of there. If he asked me one more time if everything was okay I was going to blow and pummel him with questions. I couldn't act like a suspicious jealous girlfriend because I wasn't his girlfriend. He didn't owe me any explanation on how or with whom he spent his time with.

I plastered a fake smile on my face and tried to sound nonchalant. "It's all good. I'll see ya when I see ya."

I turned on my heels and sprinted to my car. Hart stayed in the doorway as I pulled out of the driveway. As I passed Miss Polly's house another car turned down the street headed in my direction. I didn't pay it much attention when it drove by. Glancing in the rearview mirror I stopped breathing as the car pulled into Hart's driveway. I pressed the gas pedal, whipped around the corner, and headed home.

He's a nice guy being nice.

Just two friends helping each other out.

"When the girl of your dreams comes back into your life, control is the last thing you have."

My head was screaming that Hart wasn't doing anything wrong but I didn't have the stomach to watch Amber get out of that car and walk into his house.

Two more weeks passed with no contact from Will whatsoever. I knew he couldn't have been back at work yet but his salary was direct deposited in our joint account like always and the bills got paid like always. Sophie kept pushing me to find out what was going on with him. I planned on doing just that but wanted to get used to being a part of the workforce before tackling anything else. It's easy to be brave when you're just thinking about doing something. It's a whole other ball of wax when you actually take action and do it.

Things with Hart were perfect, except for me falling in love with him and his commitment to our deal . . . kind of. He called a few minutes after I got home the night he gave me the chef's jacket, making sure I was safe and that my nerves weren't getting the best of me. We stayed on the phone until the sound of his voice had me so relaxed I drifted off to sleep. If he'd been with Amber or anyone else, my well-being wouldn't have crossed his mind.

It's highly possible I misinterpreted his actions and the car I thought I saw pull into his driveway. The car could have been lost and was turning around or I mistook a neighbor's driveway for Hart's. Either way he spent the rest of that night with me even if it was only his voice. I hated that my mistrust of Will bled into my relationship with Hart. Not that it was a relationship in the boyfriend/girlfriend sense, I kept telling my heart.

The more I was around Hart the more I wished I'd listened to Sophie years ago. If I'd taken her advice and taken a break from Will, I'd have a wider frame of reference when it came to how guys operated. As it stood right now, I couldn't figure out if Hart was confusing or I was just confused. Adding sex into the mix wasn't what baffled me. There was no question Hart and I had chemistry and craved each other. In fact, having sex with him was the least confusing part of the situation. It was the time before and after we were in his bed . . . or in his chair . . . or on his sofa . . . or in his car. Then there was that time in his shower with the handheld showerhead and loofah. Oh . . . and the time he had me lying naked across the conference table in his office . . . his tongue and hands were truly magical. Anyway, it was what happened between our sexy times that I couldn't wrap my head around.

Will was never affectionate with me unless it led to sex. Even when we first started dating he rarely held my hand. Hart treated me in a very loving way. I melted with each sweet kiss and light touch. The way his eyes roamed over my body when I was fully clothed caused goosebumps to appear on every inch of my body. And when he talked, I swooned at least five times from his words no matter how long the conversation lasted. Without Hart knowing, I caught him looking at me on several occasions. The struggle was evident in his eyes, especially those times when he thought I was asleep and he was safe from being discovered. I'd read enough romance novels to know all these things added up to a boyfriend. But for every boyfriendy move he made, a "friend" comment usually followed, "that's what *friends* are for," or "I care because you're my *friend*." Sometimes I thought he was trying harder to convince himself of this more than me.

My first day at Good Eats went well. Nancy had me fill out all the necessary paperwork. I felt stupid when I had to ask her which box to mark indicating how much I wanted taken out in taxes. She answered, never blinking an eye at the fact that a twenty-six-year-old grown woman didn't know how to fill out a simple form. I spent the rest of the day learning how to operate the equipment, who was in charge of each area, and a more detailed description of what I'd be doing.

My second day at Good Eats was like jumping into a fire. There were three big luncheons we were catering. I breathed a sigh of relief when Nancy first told me I'd be on salad prep until I was actually on *salad prep*. Things started out okay but quickly turned as the hustle and impatience increased in the kitchen. There were a few times I thought I'd been hired by Chef Gordon Ramsey instead of the little petite gray-haired lady. That morning was a chaotic blur but everything got out on time and the clients were happy. And I guessed Nancy was happy too because she's let me come back every day for the past two weeks.

"Bryson!"

My name shot across the kitchen as I was finishing up cleaning for the day. It was past nine o'clock and I was the only other person here besides Nancy, who was sitting at her desk in the corner of the giant space. She had a nice office separate from this area but rarely used it, preferring instead to huddle in the corner for some reason. Her gaze remained focused on a big book in front of her as she held an envelope in the air. I dried my hands on the white towel I had slung over my shoulder as I walked toward her.

Standing in front of her desk, I fidgeted with the hem of my chef's jacket waiting for her to speak. Even after being around her for two weeks, sometimes ten hours a day, Nancy still intimidated me. She may have been only five feet four but her personality was a solid six five.

Not looking up, she waved the mystery envelope in the air. My mind raced with possibilities of what was inside it. Maybe I made a mistake on a form and needed to redo it. Maybe it was payday. At the moment my nerves were taking over and I couldn't remember if it was. Maybe it was a reprimand. Three strikes and I'm out. Off the top of my head I couldn't think of anything major I'd done wrong. Or maybe it was a pink slip. Never having a job meant never having been fired. So I didn't know for sure if a pink slip was pink or even came in a white envelope that Nancy was still waving in the air. I swallowed hard, took a step forward, and reached for the envelope.

Since she never looked up, I assumed she wasn't in the mood to explain what this was, so I kept it short and sweet. "Well, goodnight."

The hand that had been holding the envelope popped up and gave a slight wave. I slowly backed away, clutching the paper to my chest. My heart pounded as I grabbed my coat and purse and headed to my car. Before pulling out of the parking lot, I stared at the envelope, debating whether to open it now or wait until I got home.

Screw it.

I flipped on the car light. Running my nail along the seal, I sliced open the envelope. I took a deep breath and pulled out the piece of paper. A huge smile spread across my face as I blinked back tears while looking at my very first paycheck. The amount wasn't a lot but I earned every penny of it and it was all mine. Last week I'd taken enough money from mine and Will's joint account to open my own checking account. Knowing I'd be putting my own money into my own account gave me a sense of overwhelming pride. And the first person I wanted to share the news with was Hart.

By the time I'd gotten home it was almost 10 o'clock. I decided telling Hart my great news would have to wait until the next day. He was at work by 8 a.m. during the week so I didn't want to bother him in case he was asleep. I'd already eaten dinner at Good Eats, one of the perks of working at a catering company, so I headed up to my bedroom.

I glanced at the clock. Maybe he was still awake. I'd just tell him my news and say goodnight. He usually tried to get to bed by ten though. I plugged in the cellphone and placed it on the nightstand. Biting my lower lip, I stared at the phone, teetering between to call or not to call. I texted him earlier today about me working late. Maybe he's up waiting for me to call.

I didn't want to come off as a clingy girlfriend because I was neither clingy nor his girlfriend. But the fact was, over the last few weeks I ended each day listening to Hart's voice, whether I was in his arms or in my own bed. Tonight was the first time I'd worked late and I was jonesing for some rasp. So more than wanting to share my news, I was afraid I wouldn't be able to fall asleep without hearing him.

Taking the TV remote in my right hand, I crawled into my unmade bed, and snuggled down into the sheets. Aiming the remote, I flipped through the channels, hoping to distract my thoughts. As I glanced at my phone the fingers of my left hand twitched so I switched the remote to my left palm in order to keep it busy. One more flip around the channels then I was giving up and going to sleep . . . at least I was going to try.

By 11 p.m., with nothing holding my interest on the TV, I clicked it off and reached for the bedside lamp when my phone buzzed with a text. The familiar flutter tickled my stomach as the corners of my mouth curled into a smile.

Hart: *Busy?*

Me: *No.*

Almost immediately the cellphone rang and I couldn't press the answer icon fast enough.

"Hi." I sounded out of breath.

"Hi."

"What are you doing up? It's past your bedtime."

"I couldn't sleep." The deep baritone drifted in my ear sending my body into quiver mode.

God, his voice did things to me.

"How come?"

Please say because you needed to hear my voice.

There was a long pause as I heard a deep intake of hesitation. "I wanted to hear your voice."

Even better.

"I wanted to hear your voice too. In fact, I was lying here wondering how I was going to get to sleep tonight without it."

He cleared his throat. "So, you're in bed?"

"Yes."

"Under the covers?"

"My legs are but the rest of me isn't."

"What are you wearing?"

"Are we about to have oral sex?" I blurted out.

"You mean phone sex."

"Right, right, right. Sorry. I've never done it before."

"You wanna?"

"Hell yeah!"

Just the mention of phone sex from that voice had my body burning.

Hart cleared his throat and continued. "I'm about to start the phone sex portion of the call."

I took a quick glance at my phone making sure it was charged enough.

"Good deal. I'm ready to get sexed up."

A deep chuckle rumbled through the phone. "Bryson, you kill me. What position are you in?"

"I'm leaning against the headboard."

"Slide down but don't cover yourself up."

I wiggled farther in the bed. "Okay."

"What are you wearing?"

"I have on pink-and-red striped pj's from Victoria's Secret."

I figured if he knew where my pj's came from it would help with the visualization. Hart drew in a sharp breath on the other end of the phone.

"Tell me what they look like."

"Um . . . well, they're really cute and soft."

"Soft against your skin?"

"Yeah, against my skin." A nervous giggle flew out of me. "Sorry."

"I like making you laugh."

Clutching the comforter, I continued. "The silk felt incredible sliding up my thighs and over my ass."

A low growl hit my ear. "God . . . keep going."

"The shirt has long sleeves and stops just above my belly button. It's kind of tight so I had to undo the first top three buttons to give my ches . . . I mean, my tits more room."

"Are your nipples hard?"

My stomach clenched. "Yes."

"Touch them."

Slipping my hand underneath my shirt, I dragged my nails across my hot skin until I was massaging my breast.

"Are you touching them?"

"Yes." A soft moan escaped me.

Hart swallowed hard. "Think about my fingers pinching your nipples."

I squeezed my knees together. "Oh."

"Take your shirt off."

"I have to put the phone down for a sec."

"Put me on speaker."

Laying the phone on my pillow, I sat up in bed. I peeled the shirt over my head and tossed it to the side. I nestled down deep into the bed, bringing the comforter over my head like Hart had done the first night we were together. His heavy breathing coming from the other end caused my core to tighten as I wiggled with need.

"I'm back," I whispered.

Wasting no time, he commanded. "Suck your index finger into your mouth."

I brought my hand to my mouth and did as he instructed.

"Close your eyes. Picture my tongue sliding in and out of your mouth while my hand glides up your inner thigh."

A low and long moan seeped out of me.

"Fuck." He breathed. "Run your wet finger down to your tits. God, I love having your tits in my mouth, Bryson."

I love the way my name rumbled out of his mouth. My back arched off the bed.

"Do you like when I lick you?"

I wiggled like a worm, hoping for some friction. "Mmm . . . Yeees!"

"What's your favorite thing for me to lick?" he asked through a ragged breath.

"Everything!"

Another deep growl vibrated through the phone. "You know what my favorite thing is?"

"No." I whimpered.

"When my face is buried in your hot pussy."

It felt like a river between my legs. "Hart, I'm wet and . . ."

I needed relief and soon. I knew all I had to do was to touch myself and I was off to the races. But for some unexplained reason I knew it wouldn't be as satisfying unless Hart told me to do it. So I waited.

"Do you feel me sucking you dry?"

A yell flew out of me as I fisted the sheets.

"Hart . . ."

"Slip your little finger into your soaked panties and slide it into that pussy I can't get enough of."

I wasted no time in carrying out his orders. My back sprang off the bed as my finger sought relief between my legs. I exploded in an instant, screaming his name. A loud growl roared from the speaker as I heard Hart come.

Gasping, he said, "Bryson, the sound of you coming is so fucking hot."

Still riding the pleasure wave, the only responses I was able to give him at that moment were gasps, some moans, whimpers, and an occasional "oh god."

"When can I see you?" Raw desire laced his words.

"Give me a sec to calm down. I'm all a buzz." That raspy chuckle that I never got tired of vibrated in my ear. "To-to-morrow?"

"I hope I can make it until then."

"I hope I can function until then." I sighed. Through my haze it occurred to me what I wanted to tell him. "Hey, I got my first paycheck today!"

"How'd it feel?" I could hear the smile in his voice.

"Incredible! Not as incredible as this little chat tonight but incredible nonetheless."

Laughing he said, "God, I love you . . . o . . . odels."

My eyes widened as I bolted straight up in bed. "What?! You love what?"

"Yodels. Drakes Yodels. You know the delicious chocolate snack cake with cream inside."

"What do Yodels have to do with anything?"

"Bryson, fucking you wears me out, in person or on the phone. I gotta keep up my strength."

My entire body flinched. I knew Hart was shocked that he let *I love you* slip and was trying to cover it up. Just like when he throws out the *just friends* comments. He wants to make sure I remember what this was between us. Temporary fuck buddies. But the tone in his voice reminded me of Will's. I always felt degraded and cheap with Will's version of dirty talk. With Hart, those same words made me feel sexy, wanted, and cherished until this moment.

I took a deep breath and tried to keep the tremble out of my voice. "It's late. I better let you go."

Hart was quiet for such a long time I thought he'd hung up.

"Uh . . . I'm really proud of you, Bryson."

Swallowing hard, I barely choked out. "Thanks."

"Fuck," he muttered under his breath followed by another long pause. "The . . . um . . . first paycheck is . . . congratulations."

This was the first time I'd witnessed Hart being at a loss for words.

I sniffled as I ran my finger over my cheek, wiping away the trickling tear. "Goodnight, Hart."

"Will I see you tomorrow?"

"I don't know," I whispered.

He blew out a frustrated breath. "Goodnight, Bryson."

I laid the phone on the nightstand. Flopping back on the bed, I pulled the comforter over my head before letting the sobs take over. With lightning speed, I'd gone from being unbelievably happy to feeling like shit. How did I get here? I'd worked hard to keep my feelings under control. But falling for Hart had been effortless and moving on from him was going to be impossible.

chapter
Twenty-Three

The pain I experienced during my marriage was nothing compared to the pain I'd been in the past three days. It made me sad to think a guy I'd basically known for a few months had more of an impact on me than the guy I'd spent ten years of my life with. But it was true. I hated to admit it because of the years spent with him and the commitment I made to him, but Will never had all of my heart. Just like I had no frame of reference for a failed marriage, I had no frame of reference for what it felt like to be truly connected and in love with someone . . . until Hart.

At one time Will gave me butterflies in my stomach, flutters in my heart, and tingles everywhere else. But everything lacked the heart-stopping, breathtaking intensity that consumes your entire being when you connect with your soulmate. In the short time Hart had been in my life, my heart had stopped and my breath had been taken every time I thought about him or saw him or touched him or heard his voice. I'd already spent a decade of my life with a man who never wanted me, for me. I knew I couldn't move on with Hart, who was scared of making a commitment to me. But just thinking about it was ripping me to pieces.

I forced myself not to contact Hart after our late-night phone-capade. It was excruciating not hearing his rasp or being in his arms. But the worst thing was not seeing his name pop up on my phone screen. I guess I wasn't worth the effort after all. My new daily routine consisted of crying my eyes out before work, work, and coming home, not sleeping after Nancy forced me to leave work. There were many upsides to working for a caterer. One of which was we were busier toward the end of the week and the weekends.

My self-imposed Hart blackout started on Thursday, making it easy to completely immerse myself.

For the next three days with the help of my special cocktail of coffee and Red Bull with a splash of Red Bull, I was the first to arrive in the morning and last to leave at night. To her credit, Nancy never pried into why I'd started spending my entire life at the catering company. She just let me get lost in the food. During the holidays, Nancy operated the business seven days a week. The slower times of the year she preferred to close on Sundays and Mondays unless a huge high-profile event had been booked. Our busy season was only a couple of weeks away. While all my co-workers were relishing the calm before the storm, I was dreading the next two days off.

I spent Sunday morning cleaning the entire house. Like a madwoman, I scoured the place from top to bottom. When I was done with the house, I decided to go for a run. I wasn't a runner but had heard it helped clear your head. I made it halfway down the street and realized why I wasn't a runner. I hated it. Besides, I kept thinking how fun it would be to have Butter run alongside me. That led to Hart thoughts.

I was getting so desperate for a distraction that I almost texted Will to see if he wanted to discuss the divorce settlement. He was another guy I'd had no contact with recently. There had been a few texts back and forth about setting up a time to meet or at least talk on the phone but nothing ever came of it. I wasn't sure why he was dragging his feet. I assumed he'd accepted the fact that we were over and he'd told his parents the news. I found it strange and a little unsettling being in divorce limbo. In one of his texts he promised his salary would continue to go into our joint account and we'd discuss the house soon. I decided replacing one stress for another wasn't a good idea so I pushed Will and the divorce to one side.

By late afternoon I was climbing the walls. I couldn't stay here for one more minute twiddling my thumbs. The more I twiddled the more my mind drifted straight to Hart. I grabbed my phone and texted Sophie.

Me: *You home?*

Sophie: *Yes! Got in late last night. Leave again on Wed. Was about to check on you.*

Me: *I'm off today and tomorrow. I need to get out of the house. Wanna have dinner? Catch a movie? I could just come over if you're tired. Maybe we could do something tomorrow too.*

I babbled even in my texts.

Sophie: *My, my, aren't you full of options. Pack a bag. We're havin' us a good old fashion SLEEPOVER!*

Me: *Be there within the hour.*

Sophie: *The wine be a chillin'.*

I smiled reading her text. Leave it to my best friend to make me feel good, even if it was only for half a second.

Between her traveling, my job, and time with Hart, Sophie and I hadn't been able to spend any quality girl time together. We called or texted every day but it wasn't the same as being face to face. Sophie kept trying to get me to Facetime and I always made some lame excuse not to. I could control my voice better than my expression, which made it a little easier to convince her I was happy and all was great. I kept the subject of Hart to a minimum with her. Since the basketball game she told me on a semi-regular basis her fear that I would lose myself in him. She about went ballistic when I told her Hart and I were sleeping together. That was when she knew for sure I was going to get hurt. I hated when she was right.

The second my foot hit the porch Sophie's front door swung open. A flurry of dark curls whipped around my face as she pulled me into a hug.

"God, I've missed my girl," she squeaked.

"I've missed you too. It seems like two years instead of two weeks."

Sophie pulled out of the hug. Keeping me at arm's length, she eyed me. "What happened?"

I plastered on a fake smile and said, "Pfft, nothing's happened. It's just . . . um . . . I've missed you."

"Bryson Grace Forsyth, soon to be Walker again, you are the suckiest liar in all the land."

Dammit! All it took was one look at my face and I was busted. I kept the fake smile on as my eyes misted over.

Taking my hand, she tugged me into her house. "Come on, let's get started."

Sophie had all the required items for an adult sleepover ready on the coffee table—pizza, wine, chocolate, and a sappy rom-com movie. Funny how the same things that are meant to make us happy are also used to try to mend a broken heart. We changed into our pajamas and met back in the living room. I pulled the soft blanket from the back of the sofa and made myself comfortable at one end while Sophie took a spot on the floor close to the coffee table and bottle of wine.

As she poured our first glass, I lifted the top of the pizza box and peered in. I hadn't eaten much since Thursday. We were drinking so I thought I needed to at least attempt to get something in my stomach. Reaching for a slice, I suddenly felt queasy. I slid back on the sofa and let the lid fall.

"So catch me up on work and any juicy gossip," I said as Sophie handed me the glass.

With wine in one hand and a slice of pizza in the other, she positioned herself to face me. "Work is fantastic. My immediate supervisor, Howard, and my married project manager, Larry, both want to have sex with me. Any way you wanna look at it I'm fucked. Done. Your turn."

I took a long sip of wine. "Work is great. Busy." I took another sip. "Nancy kind of intimidated me at first but we're learning each other's groove." I took another sip. "So she doesn't scare me as much anymore." My gaze drifted down on the last few words while I thought of something else to say. I looked back up. "Everyone is really nice and . . . um . . . oh, I got my first paycheck." I re-plastered the fake smile.

Staring up at me, Sophie swallowed her mouthful of pizza followed by a gulp of wine. "Congratulations on all the above. The paycheck, the job, the busy, you and Nancy groovin'. I'm afraid to ask but . . . tell me what or who has you looking as if your world just ended."

"I'm just tired. It's been a busy week at work and . . ."

Placing her hand on my knee, she said, "Bryson."

And that was all it took to get my chin quivering and my eyes blinking.

"Please don't say you told me so." My hand brushed over my cheek, wiping away the first tear that fell.

Sophie gently rubbed my knee. "Give me a little credit. I'm a bitch but not a cold-hearted one."

"I really thought I could do it but . . . um . . . it was so easy to fall in love with him."

"He knew how inexperienced and vulnerable you were. He should have stopped it. Did he hurt you? Because if he did . . . I don't give a shit if he is in a wheelchair. I'm gonna cut his dick off and put it high up on a top shelf."

A chuckle broke through my soft sob. "It's not his fault. He never lied or pretended with me."

"Then what happened?"

"He's scared."

"That's a bullshit excuse. He's a grown-ass man, not some thirteen-year-old pussy. What exactly did he tell you when y'all had the *talk*?"

I cleared my throat and said, "We never had the talk."

She stopped the knee rubbing. "Back up about a half mile."

"The other night while he and I were on the phone the L word slipped out of his mouth."

"Lesbian?" She grabbed her glass and took a sip.

My face contorted. "No . . . love. But he quickly covered it up and started talking about snack cakes."

Sophie pointed her perfectly manicured finger at me. "That right there is why I don't get too involved with the dudes."

"Then he called what we'd been doing fucking." I choked back a sob. "The tone in his voice reminded me of Will and how cheap he made me feel. I know Hart was trying to get back on track and in control but . . . since then I've forced myself to stay away from him."

"So, he's in love with you?"

Sniffling, I nodded.

She sat next to me and draped her arm over my shoulder, pulling me to her side. "And what makes you think that?"

Resting my head on her shoulder, I whispered, "The way he looks at me and touches my soul."

Giving my shoulder a slight squeeze, Sophie pressed her lips to my temple before twisting to face me. "Then what the fuck are you doing here?"

My eyes widened as my jaw went slack. Her reaction caught me completely off guard.

I sat up straight, squaring my shoulders. "What?"

"Bryson, I love three people in this world, my parents and you. Keep that in mind when I say what I'm about to say. You can be such a fucking princess sometimes."

"Why would you say that?"

"Don't forget I love you. The night of prom I saw you dancing with Hart. It was dark but the light from the big tank lit the two of you perfectly. The way he held you and the way you moved together. I knew I was watching the beginning of something that happens once in a lifetime. But because of your fear and self-doubt you let it slip through your fingers in exchange for a safety net."

"Why didn't you say something back then?" I snapped.

"It wouldn't have mattered because back then you weren't a risk taker. Being Mrs. Will Forsyth was planted so deep inside your head you couldn't see the red flags popping up." Her violet eyes seared into mine. "You're an intelligent and strong woman. You never needed that safety net. I've seen the way you and Hart look at each other. You're getting a second chance at your once in a lifetime. If you ask me, it's worth the effort to do whatever you have to do in order to hold on to it. You may not get a third chance."

Sophie was right. I was doing the exact same thing I did ten years ago. Not making the effort to go after what I really wanted and needed.

I lunged forward, wrapping my arms around her neck. "Thank you for kicking me in the ass."

She tightened the hug. "That's what I'm here for."

Shoving the blanket off, I said, "I gotta go talk to him."

"Are you okay to drive?"

I stood. "Yeah. I only had half a glass."

"Then let's get you dressed."

I'd worn my cream cable knit sweater along with a pair of jeans and my black boots over to Sophie's place. She insisted I needed to crank up the look a notch. After all it's not every day you go pour your heart out to your soulmate.

While Sophie was busy grabbing her black sweater dress from the closet, I washed my face and reapplied my makeup, keeping it simple. My eyes were puffy and red but there was nothing I could do about that at the moment. I left my hair down, pulled on the dress, and slipped back into my black patent leather boots.

Checking myself one last time in the full-length mirror, I said, "How do I look?"

"Stunning."

"Liar but it will do."

I spun around giving her one more hug. "Thank you again."

With a slight head tilt, Sophie's dark eyebrows rose as she gave an exaggerated eye roll. "I'm such a romantic. I love you."

"I love you too." I gave her a quick peck on the cheek and headed out the door.

With each turn I made my stomach twisted in knots. Part of me was confident that Hart's feelings were the same as mine. So much so that I could feel the glow radiate off my cheeks. The other part of me feared he would be too scared to take a chance on us.

I glanced at the clock on the dashboard. Even though it was still early in the evening the sun had already set. As I turned onto his street my heart pounded so violently against my chest, it felt like it was on the verge of shattering. Approaching Hart's I saw the house was lit up and his was the only car in the driveway. I blew out an audible sigh of relief.

I pulled in behind Hart's car and killed the engine. As I stared at the house, I had a hard time catching a deep breath. My hands felt as if they were being stabbed by a million tiny sharp pins. I clenched and unclenched my fist several times and then shook out my hands, hoping they'd go back to normal. Every hair on my body was standing at attention. I'd never been this scared or felt this alive in my life. Attempting to take in one final deep breath, I squared my shoulders and got out of the car.

The second my boot hit the ground it was like everything went into super fast-forward mode. In a flash, I was up on the porch and ringing the bell. The sound of excited barking hit my ears before the click of the lock. And then the door opened.

The second my green eyes met his blue-gray ones my lungs filled with all the oxygen necessary. We stared at each other for several seconds not saying a word. I didn't need to hear him say how much he'd missed me, it was written all over his face. Hart angled his chair, making enough room for me to walk past.

Before Hart made it into the living room, I shook my hands out one more time trying to get some feeling back. Butter did her usual five circles around me and then sat. I was patting her head as Hart moved in front of me. He was even more handsome than just a few days ago. The heather gray sweater that stretched across his solid chest had his eyes looking smoky today.

He glanced at Butter. "Someone around here has missed you." His deep rasp filled the air, causing my knees to weaken and my stomach to clench.

The worst part of having a serious conversation was starting it. On the drive over I'd been too consumed by adrenaline and nerves to give words a second thought. I was flying solo without a net.

I gave him a fragile smile as I scratched behind Butter's floppy ear.

Before I could open my mouth, Hart said, "And my dog's missed you too."

Like a fireball, my heart exploded, filling my body with heat. It was my turn to say all the things I came here to say. But for the life of me I had lost the ability to speak. Holding his gaze, I slowly walked to him. Hart shifted his chair, moving closer to me. Bringing my hand up, I cupped the side of his face. My skin prickled at the feel of his scruff. Hart's eyes closed as he leaned into my touch.

"I've missed you so much," I whispered.

Hart grabbed my hips and nuzzled into my stomach. My fingers melted into his blond hair, holding him to me. His head tilted back and his gaze seared into mine as he guided me onto his lap. His grip tightened, pulling me flush against his chest. My hands fell from his hair, sliding down and over his shoulders to his biceps. Our breathing increased and synced.

Hart brought his hand to my forehead and with the tip of his fingers followed the length of my hair. His touch was gentle and careful like I was a rare work of art. His gaze mimicked the trail of his fingertips. As his thumb glided over my bottom lip, there was no denying the love in his eyes. Leaning forward, he pressed his lips to mine and the world disappeared.

His tongue wasted no time slipping between my lips. It was firm and frantic, exploring every inch of my mouth. Resting my elbows on his shoulders, I wrapped my arms around his head, holding it steady while I pushed closer to him. It was as if we were both desperately trying to crawl inside the other. Heavy breathing, growls and moans echoed around the room.

Hart slowed the kiss. He'd pull his lips away then lean back in three times, taking my bottom lip between his teeth each time.

"Stand up," he whispered. His warm minty breath drifted over my cheeks.

I did.

He looked up and our gaze locked. There was something about this position that caused my insides to melt every single time we were in it. It made me feel protected, worshiped, empowered, and hot all at the same time. I didn't know if I pushed my knees together or they collapsed in on each other. Either way, I gripped Hart's shoulders to steady myself. Starting just above where my boots hit the back of my knees, he pressed his large hands flat against my sensitive skin, sliding them underneath the hem of my dress. His hands continued traveling up until they reached my ass. Never once did his gaze drop from mine as he massaged me, his fingers dipping underneath my panties occasionally. My core tightened in anticipation of his fingers inside of me.

"Turn around."

I hesitated. I'd come here wanting and needing some definitive clarity and as soon as I was near him my brain went fuzzy and my body took over. I didn't want to look away but I did because I'd do anything for him.

His hands stayed glued to my skin as I turned, facing away. My dress was lifted up to my hips. Thank god I had on my cute black and white polka-dotted bikini panties. My body jerked forward at the feel of Hart's lips on the small of my back. With a firm grip on my hips, he concentrated his licks and hot kisses in that one area, at times dipping down and nipping at the top of my ass.

"Fuck, Bryson, your ass is a work of art." His voice was low and husky.

"Hart," I moaned as he pushed my dress high and placed feather-light kisses up my spine.

"I've seen a lot of asses over the years. None of them come close to yours. You're perfect."

With every look, every kiss, and every touch I knew Hart loved me. I also knew my heart wasn't able to continue our arrangement as it stood.

Tearing myself from his grasp, I stepped away and spun around to face him. Shock and disappointment covered his entire face.

I looked him straight in the eye. "Have you seen any other asses lately?"

In real time Hart's silence probably lasted only a few seconds but it was long enough for it to wrap around my throat and choke me. Just as his mouth opened to speak, his phone rang on the coffee table. My gaze landed as the screen lit up. I went numb. My eyes stayed glued to the name filling the screen. The ring kept getting louder, echoing in my ears as I watched Hart grab the phone. His gaze remained zeroed in on mine as he placed the phone to his ear.

He cleared his throat. "Yeah? No. I'm sure." His words were clipped and angry.

Hart clicked off the phone and put it back on the table. I couldn't take my eyes off of it, lying lifeless on the dark wood.

"Bryson . . ."

I told myself not to look at him. If I did, I'd fall apart. And I couldn't fall apart.

"You're still seeing her?" My words sounded weak and robotic.

He took in a sharp breath and blew it out. "I don't see anyone. You know that."

I whipped my head in his direction and forced my voice not to crack. "I'm sorry. Let me rephrase. "Are you still fucking her?" I bit down on my trembling bottom lip. "Please, tell me you're not, even if it's a lie."

Hart's knuckles turned white from the vice grip he had on the hand rim of the large side wheels. His neck muscles pressed hard against his skin as he clenched his jaw. Love and detachment struggled to gain control in his eyes.

"I haven't been with anyone since you and I started . . . Bryson, you knew what this was from the very beginning."

My relief was short-lived as a tremor rumbled through my body while I pushed down another sob. "I knew what we said but . . ."

He abruptly spun his chair away from me and growled. "Fuck! I knew this was a bad idea."

"*Us* is not a bad idea."

Hart circled back to face me. "There is no us." His teeth clenched. "I knew you wouldn't be able to handle this arrangement."

"Neither can you!"

With each deep breath his nostrils flared. "What do you want from me, Bryson?"

"The truth!"

"The only reason I started fucking you was because you said that's all you wanted."

I cringed at his crudeness. "What's happened between us is more than that and you know it."

Hart glanced away for a brief moment searching for his next words. The tip of his tongue darted out and slid over his bottom lip. When he turned back to me his eyes were ice cold.

"Don't mistake a great fuck for feelings," he said flatly.

The words cut right through me. I wasn't sure at this point if I was the dumbest person in the world or the most pathetic. My brain screamed to get the hell out of there but my heart wouldn't let my legs move.

"You're full of shit. You come off as this confident, self-assured man who's in control of every aspect of his life. But you can't control who you fall in love with, Hart. From day one there was a spark. I felt it. You felt it. Hell, even Sophie felt it when she saw us dancing ten years ago and again at the basketball game. You don't think I notice whenever I'm around, your eyes light up, your shoulders push back, your chest puffs out, and you sit up taller? When you look into my eyes, kiss my lips, or touch my body you reach my soul. And you can deny it all you want but I know with every fiber of my being that I've reached your soul too. You may be too much of a pussy to admit your true feelings for me but don't you dare reduce our time together to just a great fuck."

It took every ounce of strength I had not to collapse to the floor. I was shocked and impressed that I stood my ground and that those words came out of me instead of tears. I was not going to let another man demean me or my feelings ever again.

"Are you done?"

I nodded. "For the moment."

My eyes could have been playing tricks on me but I thought the right corner of his mouth twitched with the hint of a grin.

"You want the truth? If I could go back to that fucking prom with a different life, I would have never stopped dancing with you." He blew out several shallow breaths. "That first day I saw you at the pool it was as if someone cracked open my chest and I could finally breathe. I hoped you had turned into a bitch since school. But then you opened your mouth and rattled on and on. I knew right then I was fucked and needed to stay away from you. When I found out you were married I relaxed because you were officially off limits. So I figured it was safe. But each time I laid eyes on you I wanted more. Then I found out about the divorce and my safety net completely unraveled." Pausing, his unblinking eyes turned dark gray. "Between my mom's illness and school, I couldn't . . . . You didn't fit into my life back then, Bryson."

I swallowed the lump in my throat and pushed out the words. "I know and it's okay. I understand."

The rise and fall of Hart's chest was steady and deep as he stared at me. His eyes still had the same conflict as earlier along with something I'd never seen before in him . . . regret.

His grip tightened around the wheel as his Adam's apple bobbed up and down several times. "And I don't fit into your life now."

"How can you say that? Everything about us fits together perfectly."

"Why does everyone else see this fucking chair except you?" There was the hint of a quiver in his voice.

Taking a deep breath, I swallowed another sob. "Because I've been too busy falling in love with the man sitting in it."

"Spinal cord injuries take ten years off of life expectancy."

My gaze locked with his as I took one step toward him.

"I have a specific time each day when I go to the bathroom to manually empty my bowel and bladder."

I took another step toward him.

"I'm at a higher risk for blood clots."

Another step.

"The chances of me fathering a child are slim."

Standing directly in front of him, I said, "I know what you're trying to do. But none of that stuff scares me. I still see the strong, intelligent, virile, confident, kind man I love."

I couldn't stand not touching him any longer. Before Hart could respond, I quickly climbed into his lap, wrapped my arms around his neck, and rested my forehead against his. Keeping his hands to the side, his body stiffened.

"You are so lovely, Bryson. You deserved better than Will . . . you deserve better than me." The last few words came out as a whisper."

"You don't get to decide that for me." Linking my fingers together behind his neck, I pulled Hart's lips to mine and placed a soft kiss. "I know you don't love Yodels because you hate chocolate." Another soft kiss. "I'm going to stay in your way and drive you crazy until you let me love you." Another soft kiss, only this time our lips remained together. "You're not getting rid of me, Hart. Deal with it."

His eyes closed for . . .

One Mississippi.

Two Mississippi.

Three Mississip . . .

His left arm snaked around my waist as his right hand traveled up my thigh. Hart opened his eyes a split second before pressing his lips to mine. The rhythm of the kiss was slow and methodical, his tongue moving deeper into my mouth with each swirl around mine. It was a kiss making up for each year we missed being together. It was a kiss taking all the pain away.

Hart broke from my lips, both of us gasping for air. "I love you, Bryson."

It was a kiss welcoming Hart home.

chapter
Twenty-Four

"Hey! That tickles!" I yelled, giggling as my back lurched off the bed.

His fingers wrapped around my ankles, holding my legs in place. "Keep still." Looking up, his golden brows pushed into his forehead at the same time a devilish grin appeared. "God, you're still so wet. Maybe, if I blow on it . . ."

Hart was leaning against the headboard, shirtless and in black sweat pants. I was stretched out across the bed wearing one of his white T-shirts. The acoustic version of "Latch" by Boyce Avenue swirled in the air. With my feet resting just below his smooth chest, Hart swept the deep dark red polish over my nails.

Lifting up on my elbows, I eyed his handiwork, wiggling my second toe. "I think you put a little too much polish on that one."

"Bryson, please, my mother was a painter. Artistic talent oozes from every pore of my body."

Intently focused on the task at hand, he paid meticulous attention to each brush stroke. Hart looked hot doing pretty much anything but this was definitely a contender for the top five.

A shiver ran through my body as I flopped back onto the bed. "I stand corrected, Rembrandt."

A stream of warm breath drifted over the top of my foot, causing me to squirm a little. I had dreamed, wished, and prayed about the moment when Hart admitted he loved me. But the dream didn't hold a candle to the real thing. Now that I had a frame of reference for what a true connection and being in love with someone really felt like, there was no turning back.

Hart Mitchell had set the gold standard that no other man would ever be able to achieve.

My gaze drifted up to the large painting hanging above the bed. I'd stared at it several times before, always getting lost in the beautiful blend of blues, greens, oranges, and yellows. I still wasn't able to shake the feeling that I'd seen it or something similar to it.

"All done," he said, placing the bottle of nail polish on the nightstand.

I lifted my feet straight up in the air, checking the final product. "They look gorgeous. Thank you, Remy."

Hart grasped both ankles, pulling my legs down toward his chest, causing my head to pop up.

"Where do you think you're going?" He planted my feet back on his chest. "These babies have to dry completely before you start moving around or you'll ruin my masterpiece."

I relaxed back onto the bed. "Yes, Master."

"Say that again."

"Yes, Master?"

"It's got a nice ring to it. We should try it on for size next time I have you service me."

Without raising my head, I grabbed one of the pillows beside me and chucked it at him.

"Hey! Watch the nails!" He laughed.

"I'll Master you only if you Mistress me."

"I could get into that." I heard the smile in his voice.

We were quiet for several minutes enjoying the music and being together. My eyes closed while strong hands massaged up, down, and all around my calves and feet.

"Mmm . . . that feels amazing."

"Glad it meets with your approval, Mistress."

"It *does* have a nice ring to it."

Hart's thumb mindlessly glided back and forth over my ankle as a deep chuckle vibrated from his chest followed by more silence. Just as I was on the verge drifting into an unexpected nap something cold and wet pressed against my arm. Squealing, my eyes shot open as I bolted into a sitting position and tried to yank my feet free. But Hart wouldn't let them budge.

With his head rested back and eyes closed, he said, "Butter, I told you no one wants your toys."

I turned to a pair of liquid caramel eyes hidden behind a large squeaking yellow chicken. Butter dragged the toy over the edge of the bed trying to find a playmate. Two whimpers slipped before the bird dropped. Her long pink tongue unrolled from her mouth and hung off to the side.

Tilting my head to the side I gave Butter a smile. "It's okay, girl. Thank you for offering me your drool-drenched toy."

Prancing around in circles, her tail swished back and forth before she flew out of the room.

"Bryson, our kids will steamroll over us if we don't present a united front." He teased.

Curling my toes into his chest, a warm sensation spread throughout my body. I knew he was joking. It was much too early in our relationship to even consider having children. But the fact that he saw a future for us had me floating on cloud nine.

Lying back on the bed, I propped up my head with a pillow and stared at the man of my dreams. "Tell me about your mom."

The corners of his mouth drifted up into a bittersweet grin.

"She was lovely . . ."

My heart skipped a beat hearing him use the same word to describe his mom as he used for me.

With his thumb in perpetual motion, he continued. ". . . And had a quiet strength and peace about her. Even during difficult times she found something to be grateful for."

"Colin said she was the cool mom of the group."

His eyes opened, filled with love, heartache, and a hint of surprise. "When did you and Colin talk?"

For a brief second a twinge of panic hit my stomach. Maybe I shouldn't have revealed I'd been talking with his friends about his life.

"We were just shooting the breeze during the basketball tournament."

He tipped his chin up acknowledging my answer.

His expression hardened slightly. "She and my dad divorced when I was six. He went off to do his thing, which included a new wife and kids. So it was pretty much just me and Mom."

"Did you have any type of relationship with your dad?"

"He'd send the obligatory Christmas and birthday presents. But he wasn't very giving of his time."

"I'm sorry," I whispered.

I hated that Hart's dad basically dumped him and his mom for a new shiny family. My parents had been married for years. My dad had more in common with Ryan since both of them loved sports and fishing. But he still made it a point for us to have father-daughter time even if that meant putting on a big flowered hat and attending a pretend tea party. It was hard for me to fathom a father not wanting to take part in his child's life even after a divorce.

Each time Hart talked about just his mom, his expression softened. "Don't be. Between my three uncles, Mom made sure I had strong male role models in my life. Hell, she even acted as assistant coach for my little league soccer team. She didn't know the first thing about the game. But she was always there cheering me on."

"Was she always an artist?"

He nodded. "An extremely talented one."

"Her work is beautiful."

"Yeah it is. She was also one of the lucky ones being able to actually make a living doing what she loved, running the Hope Mitchell Gallery downtown."

"That's impressive."

"Things were going really good until they weren't."

It had been ten years since his mother's death but the pain rolled off of his body as if she'd died yesterday.

"My mom used to tell me, you can get past the death of a loved one but you never get over it."

Hart glanced away for a moment, blinking. I placed my hand on his thigh and gave it a slight squeeze. When he didn't react, it dawned on me it was because he couldn't feel the comfort I offered. Then it was my turn to blink back tears.

"She went in for a routine checkup and . . . um . . ." He cleared his throat. ". . . Was already stage three." His voice cracked and my heart broke.

I sat up, wanting to wrap my arms around him, but he pressed my feet into his chest even more. Leaning back, I supported myself on my outstretched arms and listened.

Hart's gaze focused on his thumbs that were still gliding slowly over the top of my ankle. "After three years, five surgeries, and so many rounds of chemo, I lost count, the doctors told us they'd exhausted every possible treatment. At the time it was hard for me to wrap my head around what was going on. I didn't understand how they could just give up on her." Hesitating, he looked at me with tear-glazed eyes. "She was my mom."

A steady stream of tears rolled down my cheeks as I swallowed a sob. I didn't know who needed my arms around his body more, Hart or me. I wriggled my legs trying to set them free but Hart held on.

"Because it was just the two of us, the doctors along with my dad thought it was best if I went to live with him while Mom was admitted to the hospice house. It felt like this stranger wanted to plop me in the middle of his new life, expecting me to fit in. But Mom wanted to stay home for as long as possible and I was determined to make that happen. She'd give me some type of signal when she was ready to leave."

Hart was even stronger than I initially thought. As I looked at him, I said a little prayer to his incredible mom, thanking her for raising this incredible man.

"I don't know what I would have done without Miss Polly. She and I worked out a pretty tight routine. She stayed with Mom during the day while I was at school. She kept the place spotless. Always washed, ironed, and put away the laundry. She even ironed the sheets because Mom liked them that way."

Hart took in a deep breath and continued. "When I was a kid, every morning after I left for school, without fail, she went into her home studio to create. She always said it was the second love of her life next to me." He paused again, reining in his emotions. "Even during the roughest chemo treatments she still wanted to paint. It was like oxygen to her. As she became weaker, I'd set up her canvas, paint, and brushes just the way she liked them and helped her to the studio. Then one day I had set everything up and went to get her. I walked into her room and she was still in bed, which was unusual. That day she told me she didn't feel like painting. And I knew that was the signal."

Wiping my tear drenched face with my palms, I pleaded. "Hart, let go."

The second he loosened his grip, I scurried to the head of the bed next to him. Pedicure be damned. Curling my arms around his head, I brought him to my chest and slowly combed my fingers through his hair. Hart's arms snaked around my waist and tightened. His body didn't shake but I could feel the dampness of tears on my shoulder. We stayed in this position for a long time, neither of us saying a word or making any attempt to move.

Not only did this man have strength of character but also presence of heart. He wasn't afraid or embarrassed to show his feelings for the ones he cared for. Although, I got the distinct impression that opening up and making himself this vulnerable was reserved for only a few select people, namely Colin and now me. I was honored and grateful to be added to the list.

With his arms still wrapped around my body, Hart lifted his head. The tips of our noses stayed connected. I cupped the side of his jaw, pressing my lips to his. A small knot formed in my stomach. If I hadn't been such an idiot back in high school I could have at least formed a friendship with Hart. I hated myself for not being there for him.

"I'm sorry I wasn't there for you during her illness and the accident."

"You don't have to apologize, Bryson. Everything happens for a reason, even if we never understand the why." His nose trailed up and down mine. "She really wanted to meet you." His warm breath wafted over my lips as the words came out like a loud whisper.

Pulling back slightly, I squished my eyebrows together. "What?"

"What?"

Sniffling, I composed myself. "You said your mom really wanted to meet me."

"You caught that, did ya?"

I've witnessed Hart's intense gaze, sexy grin, flirty winks, his caring and loving eyes, and his drop dead, don't-fuck-with-me look. But the expression on his face was a new one and out of this world adorable. He looked like a boy who'd just got caught with his hand in the cookie jar.

"Yeah, I caught that. Care to explain?"

He glanced down for a second. When he looked back up, a sexy grin coupled with soft eyes made an appearance.

"I love you, Bryson," he said, just before pressing his lips against mine. His tongue lightly flicked between my lips, trying to coax them apart.

My mouth flattened into a straight line as I brought my hand up and pressed it on Hart's forehead. "You think you can distract me with your sexy mouth?"

Goose bumps popped up along my skin as his hand tickled up my thigh and slipped under the T-shirt. "I was going to let my fingers take a crack at it too."

The aforementioned fingers were about an inch away from their final destination.

I glued my knees together. "Explain, please."

He removed his hand and leaned back. "Mom's biggest fear was that I'd be lonely after she was gone. She knew the guys, my uncles, and even my dad would be there for me. But at some point people go back to their everyday normal lives. She was a romantic and thought if I had someone special by my side I'd never be lonely. So I kind of told her you were my girlfriend. You gotta understand . . . I would have told Mom anything to give her peace of mind so she wouldn't worry about me, even if it was a lie."

I couldn't keep the smile off my face.

"It really wasn't that far from the truth. I wanted you, and you definitely played a starring role in a lot of my wet dreams."

I slapped his arm. "Hart!"

He grabbed my wrist and placed a kiss in the center of my palm.

Narrowing my eyes, I said, "That's why you showed up at the prom . . . because your mom wanted you to go."

"That and I wanted to see you . . . and dance with you at least one time."

My chest tightened. That brief moment was the only time Hart and I danced before he lost the full use of his legs. By the look in his eyes he was thinking the same thing.

"She loved Tony Bennett and got the biggest smile on her face when I told her we danced to him. Of course I left out the part about your humongous nipples."

I raised my hand to slap his arm again but he grabbed my wrist, tugging me to his chest.

"In fact, that painting . . ." Tilting his chin, he indicated the giant painting above his bed. ". . . Was inspired by the prom story. It was the last work she completed." A hint of sadness clouded his eyes but was gone in a flash.

"It's the aquarium," I said, twisting my body to gaze up at the painting. "Every time I looked, it felt familiar but I couldn't figure out why." Shifting, I grabbed the headboard and pulled myself up to get a closer look at the Hope Mitchell original.

As I stared at the painting for the umpteenth time it came alive with memories. "I can see it so clearly now. All the different hues of blues, greens, and yellows whooshing around this section . . ." I waved my hand over the area. ". . . Looks like the bottom of the sea. And right up at the top . . ." I stretched my arm, pointing. "See how the color intensity gets weaker until nothing is left but bright white like the sun crashing into the surface of the water." Concentrating on the very middle of the canvas, I saw something I'd never noticed before. It was so faint and blended in seamlessly that at a quick glance it was easy to miss. "There's a couple dancing."

Looking down I was met with smoky blue eyes filled with love and desire. Hart's hand traveled up my left calf, sending a shiver through my body. His rough beard pricked my sensitive skin as his lips grazed over my right upper thigh, placing soft wet kisses along the way. His left hand continued its trek up, roaming over my cotton panties. My body buzzed with anticipation. Light kisses alternated with the feel of his scruff-covered cheek gliding between my inner thighs. I closed my eyes and let my head loll back. Sliding his hands down to the back of my thighs, he spread my legs apart before pushing his face between them.

"Hart." I sighed.

"Hmmm?"

The deep rumble of his answer vibrated against my core, causing my knees to buckle. Hart's right hand shot up, palming the right side of my ass as he held me steady.

I dug my fingers into the dark wood and moaned. "Oooh, god."

Hooking his fingers around the top of my panties, he slipped the cotton over my ass and down my legs.

"Keep talking," he mumbled before plunging tongue first inside of me.

Me: *Hey, it's been a month and a half. We need to talk and iron out details.*

Will: *I'm swamped at work. Be able to take time after the holidays. Salary will still go in joint account, bills will be paid.*

Me: *I appreciate that. I'm busy with work too but we really need to get the papers drawn up and move forward.*

Will: *After the holidays.*

"Exactly what are we doing here?" Sophie's face scrunched up as she eyed rows of camping, fishing, and hunting gear.

It had just turned midnight and was officially Black Friday. Sophie and I had been going out on Black Friday since we were fifteen. When we first started the tradition we didn't have any money so we weren't interested in the sales. We just thought it was cool to be at the mall late at night/early in the morning, whichever way you wanted to look at it.

"I told you Hart and his friends are going on their annual fishing trip in a couple of weeks. And I wanted to put his Christmas present together and give it to him before they go so he can use it."

"Let's get crack-a-lackin' and get this over with. The Coach store is calling my name."

I checked my list then scanned the signs at the front of each aisle, hoping for some direction. I wasn't a very outdoorsy person. I liked being outside when the weather was nice and I loved going to the beach. Sitting around the pool with a glass of wine always interested me. But growing up around my dad and brother who were big into camping and fishing, I'd picked up a few knowledgeable tidbits. So I wasn't at a complete loss in a store like this.

As we headed down the first aisle, passing rack after rack of fishing vests and waders, I beamed with excitement. For weeks I'd been busting at the seams to go shopping for Hart's first Christmas present from me. Work had been crazy busy for the past three weeks and was only going to get crazier with Christmas and New Year's approaching. Nancy closed Thanksgiving and Christmas but that was it. I had to be at work by 8 a.m. So this would be the only chance I'd have to shop for Hart.

"Why don't you just order this stuff online?" Sophie whined.

"Because I want to pick out each thing myself and hold it in my hand to make sure it's exactly right."

"Okaaay . . . what are you looking for?"

"I decided to get a bunch of small fishing items and put them in a Yeti cooler."

"What's that, some kind of Star Wars thingy?"

Ignoring her, I pushed my cart farther down the aisle.

"So, what's the fo-wun-wun on the Slimy Bastard situation?"

"Nothing new to report. He doesn't want to talk until after the holidays."

"Fuck that. You need to go ahead and hire a lawyer, get the papers drawn up and serve his ass. And I swear to god, Bryson, if you don't ask for what you're entitled to I won't be your friend anymore."

"You're lying."

"True. But you get my point. Too bad you don't have evidence of him sliding his sausage into some skank's biscuit."

My face crinkled. "Where the hell do you get these phrases from? Besides, he's held strong in his denial of having sex the old-fashioned way with other women."

"He's a liar."

"Maybe. But I'd like to hold on to that one belief he wouldn't do that to me."

Sophie was right about going ahead and getting a lawyer. I had to think of what was best for me. I just felt if Will and I could meet and discuss the details first before getting lawyers involved, it would make the process less complicated.

As we rounded the corner a giant wall of camouflage barreled toward us, almost knocking Sophie over.

"Whoa! Excuse me, darlin'," the giant bear of a man drawled, as he placed his large hands around Sophie's shoulders and steadied her.

Sophie pushed her index finger into the center of the bear's chest and said, "Next time watch where you're going, Grizzly Adams."

A big toothy grin appeared from behind his bushy beard. Sophie was average height at 5'7". Grizzly had to stretch to at least 6'4". It was pretty comical to see a little thing like her threaten a giant.

"It won't happen again. Scout's honor." He winked and headed in the direction we'd just come from.

Sophie's gaze followed Grizzly all the way down the aisle. "Hmm . . . strong hands. Long fingers. Nice ass. Maybe there's something to the great outdoors after all."

Spotting my biggest item, I squealed and pushed my cart forward. "There it is!" I sucked my lower lip between my teeth and studied my options. "I know what size but not which color. Oh, maybe the pretty light blue one. It matches Hart's eyes."

"Uh-huh, cause that's what all the dudes look for when purchasing their caveman crap."

I gave her a sideways glance. Using the self-portrait feature on her iPhone as a mirror, Sophie adjusted a wide brim bush hat in pink camouflage, cocking it to the side of her head.

"I could totally pull this off, don't you think?"

"I'm getting the white cooler."

As we made our way around the store collecting the other items on my list, Sophie spotted Grizzly several times. Her flirting got bolder with each sighting. I was happy she found something to occupy her time while I got the rest of Hart's gift. I paid for my stuff and was waiting at the entrance while Sophie leaned against the gun counter stroking Grizzly's big long hunting rifle he'd just bought. When her violet eyes flitted in my direction I gave her the wrap-it- up sign.

After Sophie and the bear exchanged goodbyes, she headed toward me, smiling with something clutched between her fingers.

Swaying her hips, sounding like a bratty kid showing off, she sang, "Ah-ha! I got his digits . . . I'm gonna call him . . . he's gonna come over. And. Then. I'll. Climb. Him."

I shook my head and headed out the store.

"I'm here! I'm here!" I yelled, shrugging off my coat as I ran into my mom's kitchen.

She was dropping a stick of butter into the stainless steel mixing bowl. "Well, it's about time. I was getting ready to send out a search party." She turned on the big orange KitchenAid mixer.

Mom and I had planned our holiday cookie baking for this Sunday afternoon. I'd gotten delayed at work and was running an hour behind. I considered canceling but she was the better baker in the family, not me. And what's Christmas without cookies? Plus, between work and my secret relationship, I hadn't seen much of my parents.

I walked up next to her, raising my voice so she could hear me over the buzzing of the mixer. "I'm sorry. I got caught up at work. Whatcha need?"

"Measure out two and one-fourth cups of flour," Mom said, as she creamed together the butter and powdered sugar for our Sands.

Technically, we were making traditional Mexican wedding cookies. But Mom always called them Sands for some reason.

I grabbed the measuring cup, a bowl, the sifter, and the flour then got to work.

She cut off the mixer and scraped the sides of the bowl with a spatula. "So, you're staying busy at work?"

I dipped out a cup of flour and leveled it off. "Extremely. But I love it. I'm learning so much."

"That's great." She flipped on the mixer.

We worked in comfortable silence for several minutes. The quieter buzz made it easier for us to chat and catch up. I was standing a few feet away from her, concentrating on my nut chopping when I felt her eyes on me.

Giving Mom a sideways glance, I asked, "Am I doing it wrong?"

"You're doing a great job. I was just admiring your jacket."

Since I was already late I didn't bother going home to change. I was still wearing my uniform from work, which included black pants and the chef jacket Hart gave me. I hadn't told my parents about Hart. One reason was because I was still legally married and I thought they'd be disappointed in me knowing I'd already moved on from Will. The other reason was, until I knew Will's mind set regarding the settlement, I wasn't going to flaunt my relationship with Hart in front of anyone.

"Thanks."

"You look so good and professional in it. And it even has your name embroidered over the pocket. Did you get it from work?"

I didn't want to lie to Mom. I still felt terrible keeping mine and Will's separation a secret from her and Dad for so long. A lie by omission was still a lie in my book.

I exaggerated clearing my throat. "Mmm-hmm." Quickly followed by a fit of coughing, hoping the phlegmy noise would drown out all other utterances. "Nuts are done!"

"Perfect timing."

Once all the ingredients were mixed we got down to the business of making cookies.

"I ran into Susan Bovair the other day," Mom said, rolling the dough between her palms.

I placed a Sand on the cookie sheet. "That's nice."

"You know her daughter Caitlyn had a baby a few months back."

Scoop. "I didn't know that."

Roll. "They also just bought a new house."

Drop. "Good for them."

I wasn't exactly sure why Mom was telling me about Caitlyn Bovair now Merrick. She knew we weren't friends. Caitlyn had been a bitch since the age of five.

Scoop. "She and her husband . . . you know he's a lawyer . . . moved to one of those very nice older neighborhoods in Mount Pleasant."

For a second my hands stopped making cookies. There were a lot of nice older neighborhoods in Mount Pleasant. The chances of it being the same as Hart's was slim. I scooped, rolled, and dropped as I gave Mom a sideways glance.

"In fact, Susan said Caitlyn told her she saw you coming out of the house across the street from hers."

A knot took shape in my stomach.

Hold it together, Bryson.

Scoop. "Yeah, a friend of mine lives there," I said.

Roll. "Who?"

Drop. "No one you know."

Scoop. "Someone from work?"

Roll. I sandwiched another noncommittal "Mmm-hmm" between a throat clear and cough.

Drop. "It's nice you're enjoying girl time with your new friend."

My cheeks flushed with heat. I was definitely enjoying girl time with my new friend.

Scoop. "One curious thing, though. Caitlyn said she saw you coming out of the house around 7:30 in the morning."

The heat from my cheeks spread to the rest of my body. I dropped my last Sand on the cookie sheet and washed my hands while I thought of a response.

Mom turned to face me. "Bryson?"

Drying my hands with the dish towel, I huffed nonchalantly. "Why does she have her big crooked nose . . ."

"Now you know she had that fixed."

". . . Smashed against the window first thing in the morning. I bet her new neighbors wouldn't be too thrilled to know she was spying on them."

"She was up with the baby and just happened to walk by the window when she saw you come out of that house. Why were you there that time of the day?"

Stalling, I tore the band out of my hair and redid my high ponytail.

"Bryson?"

"Fixing my hair, Mom." I sounded a tad more annoyed than I meant to.

Then I grabbed a bottle of water from the fridge, unscrewed the top, and downed half of it. There was no way around this.

Mom wiped off her hands with the bottom of her apron. "Does it have anything to do with the glow you've been sporting around the last few times I've seen you?"

Dayum, she's good.

I took a deep breath. "I . . . um . . . spent the . . . night at that . . . um . . . house with a friend. A *very special friend* from high school."

I prayed Mom would get my implication and I wouldn't have to actually say the words, *I was in that house having passionate mind-blowing sex with my boyfriend.*

Her light brown eyebrows rose as her green eyes widened mimicking me. "Oh . . . Oh . . ." Her eyes finally flashed with understanding. "Ooooh."

"I'm sorry. I wanted to tell you and Dad but . . ."

She waved her hand in the air to stop me. "Bryson, the only thing your father and I have ever wanted for you and your brother is happiness. Honey, I know this whole Will thing has you all confused . . ."

"Well, it hasn't been easy."

"Your father and I fully support you . . ."

"Thanks."

"And if this is what makes you happy right now then more power to you. You're an adult and your lifestyle is your choice."

"What?"

"We love Sophie . . ."

My face scrunched together. "Excuse me?"

"Although, it's a bit of a surprise. I mean she's always been boy crazy."

"Mom."

"But hey, you could do a lot worse."

"Mom! I need to explain."

She placed her hands on my shoulders. "Honey, I'm your mother. You don't have to explain anything to me."

"Oh but I think I do."

"Deep down there was always a part of me that knew."

"What did you know?" My voice squeaked so high with confusion I didn't recognize it. This conversation had traveled way out into left field and I needed to get it back on track. "Mom, sit down, please."

I sat across from her at the small round kitchen table. "Sophie and I are not a couple."

"Oh, I just assumed when you said a *very special friend* from high school . . ."

Each of my facial features scrunched up—my eyebrows, my nose, my mouth. "So me being in a lesbian relationship with Sophie was your go-to thought?"

"Well, Bryson, I'm sorry. But you have to admit you never had a lot of friends." She snapped.

"Okay, I'll give you that one." I paused for a second collecting my thoughts. "His name is Hart Mitchell. He was in my senior class. The day Will was admitted to rehab, I ran into Hart. He's director of the physical therapy department." I inhaled as much oxygen as my lungs would hold for this next part. "Hart and I struck up a friendship and as time went on it developed into something more." My eyes misted. "What I have with Hart is different . . . I'm different. He's helped me find my confidence and strength. And gave me the courage to go after my dream. I'm in love with him, Mom."

I searched her eyes for a reaction.

"First your marriage and now this. Why do you feel the need to keep things about your life from me and your father?" Her tone was more hurt than mad.

I gazed down at my fidgeting fingers as I swallowed the lump in my throat. "I was scared you'd be disappointed in me for failing at my marriage and falling into a relationship before the divorce was final."

Mom was silent for several seconds, then said, "Did I ever tell you about Eddie Marlow?" A soft chuckle slipped from her lips. "Everyone used to call him Pickles."

"Why Pickles?"

She cocked one eyebrow. "Don't ask. Eddie was the boy I dated before your father."

This shocked me.

"But I thought you and Daddy were high school sweethearts."

"I started dating Eddie when we were sophomores. Our parents were very close and really wanted us to be a couple. Your dad's family moved to Charleston the summer before our junior year." A wistful expression drifted over her face. "The first time I saw the new boy in the school cafeteria my heart stopped for a second. When it started back up the pounding was so intense I almost fell over. Long story short, your father and I became close friends, nothing more. He was very respectful of mine and Eddie's relationship. We were almost inseparable. The day after graduation Eddie took me out to dinner and proposed."

A slight gasp escaped me.

"As I watched him get down on one knee, I grabbed his arm and stopped him. After Eddie dropped me at home, I got in my car and went over to your dad's. When he opened the door, neither of us said a word. We just looked into each other's eyes and the rest, as they say, was history. Bryson, the who and when of falling in love is unpredictable. But when you find that special person, the being in love is inevitable. I am extremely proud of the woman you've become. Don't ever doubt that."

I stood behind Mom. Leaning forward, I wrapped my arms around her and rested my chin on her shoulder.

"I love you," I whispered.

She patted my arm. "I love you. And this young man of yours better be damn grateful to have you in his life."

"He tells me he is all the time."

Mom cleared her throat and stood. "Well, these cookies aren't going to bake themselves."

We broke the emotional moment and got back to work.

I'd been on my feet most of the day, so after the last batch of cookies went into the oven, I sat down at the table for a few minutes. Dad came in, grabbed a soda from the fridge, and stole one of the chocolate-chip cookies cooling. Before he made his getaway, he walked up behind Mom, who was standing at the sink. Dad whispered something in her ear that caused her to giggle then gave her a peck on the cheek before going back to whatever sport he was watching on TV. As I watched my parents interact something dawned on me. Mom had been brave enough to marry her Hart.

chapter
Twenty-Five

Beaming, I bounced with excitement on the sofa as each item was pulled from the large cooler.

"Oh my god, Bryson!" Hart said with astonishment holding up the fishing reel. "It's a Shimano Tekota with 6.1 gear ratio. This is gonna be awesome with my spinnerbaits, jerkbaits, and swimming jigs."

"I have no idea what you just said but . . . Yay!"

"The guys are already jealous that I have the most incredible and beautiful woman in my life. When they find out you gave me this, it's gonna send them over the edge."

Hart looked like a little boy as he dug deeper into his gift. With our relationship on the down low we wouldn't be able to spend Christmas Day together. I would be with my family and Hart would be with Colin's. We decided to celebrate our first Christmas since I wanted Hart to be able to use his gift on the annual fishing trip he took with the guys.

My life was complicated at the moment. But earlier today while I prepared dinner, I looked at Hart as he built us a fire and Butter gnawing one of her presents, and felt blessed. The sound of Hart caused my entire body to heat up with the love.

"Hot damn! A Jig-and-Pig. It's ugly but it catches fish like a son of a bitch." He leaned forward. "Come here. Thank you. The gift and you are perfect." His tongue licked across my bottom lip before sucking it into his mouth.

A moan escaped me as the kiss grew deeper. Our lips stayed connected while I shifted from sitting on the sofa to Hart's lap. After several minutes Hart pulled away coming up for air.

"You haven't opened your present yet," he said, reaching over to grab the silver wrapped box with blue ribbon. "Merry Christmas, Bryson."

I wasn't one of those women who slowly peeled back wrapping paper. I tore into that baby with lightning speed. I lifted the lid to find the most beautiful sterling silver bracelet with two charms. The circular charm was surrounded by blue and green diamonds reminding me of mine and Hart's eyes. The other charm was a sterling silver chef's hat.

"Hart . . . it's . . . it's gorgeous."

"So it meets with your approval, Mistress?" He grinned.

"I love it."

"I'll add to it each year until it's full. Then I'll start another one. And another and another."

Tingles ran through me whenever Hart talked about a future with me.

"It must have cost you a fortune."

"Well, it's actually a gift for both of us."

Narrowing my eyes, my mouth formed into a straight line. "What are you talking about?"

The tip of his nose skimmed down my neck. "I was thinking you could wear the bracelet and nothing else for the rest of our holiday."

"Why Hart Mitchell, are you trying to take advantage of me?"

"Every chance I get."

Suddenly, Hart rolled the wheelchair backward, spun around, and popped a wheelie before carrying me to his bedroom. My high-pitched squeals echoed throughout the house.

Me: *Happy New Year. I hope you had a good holiday. When can we meet to discuss things?*

Will: *I picked up some kind of bug over the holidays. Will let you know about meeting once I'm well.*

And that's pretty much how mine and Will's texts went for the next four months. I was always the one who initiated contact and Will would make up some excuse for not meeting. As the weeks went on his response time to my texts got longer and longer. Sometimes I wouldn't get a response for two weeks.

Hart, Sophie, and my parents all felt Will was avoiding dealing with the situation because he still had hope we could work things out. But he never made any attempt to get in touch with me nor did he come by the house to pick up any more of his clothes. As promised, his salary continued to be deposited so all the bills got paid on time. Nothing had really changed except that we were no longer living under the same roof.

My parents and Sophie felt I needed to go ahead and serve Will with divorce papers. Hart said I should do what was best for me in the timeframe that was comfortable for me. I wasn't exactly sure where my hesitation was coming from. Maybe I still felt I owed it to Will to talk with him first instead of blindsiding him with legal documents. Or maybe it was the twinge of guilt I felt being happy and in love.

I was doing so well at work that Nancy added my recipe for Lowcountry shrimp and grits to her menu options and had put me in charge of a few small events.

Hart and I weren't hiding our relationship but we were definitely keeping it low-key. Having a boyfriend would not go over well if by some chance Will was delusional and thought we might get back together. With each passing day, I fell deeper in love with Hart and we became more and more like a couple.

Squeeze.

Pump.

Squeeze.

Pump.

I tried to keep the rhythm slow and steady but my palms were getting sweaty and kept slipping. My damp face was like a magnet to the chunk of hair I didn't secure well enough in my top knot. It kept falling and obstructing my vision. I puckered my bottom lip and blew out and up, attempting to get rid of the annoying strands. My neck was stiff, my shoulders tight, and my knees were aching from being in this position. But it was all worth it if it made Hart happy.

Cramp.

Cramp.

Cramp.

My body needed a break. I placed the pastry bag half full of the twice-baked potato mixture of mashed potato, butter, sour cream, chopped scallions, and nutmeg on the countertop. Even though the recipe read just to mound the mixture back into the hollowed-out potatoes shell, I wanted to make it a little nicer by piping a simple ribbon design. The guys wouldn't notice it, Sophie might, but Hart would appreciate the extra little effort I made.

Tonight was the first time Hart and I were hosting a dinner as a couple, it was also the first time all of our friends would be together. As an added nerve-wrecker I was having everyone over to my place. Hart hadn't even been here before. The three large steps that led up to the house made the place inaccessible to him and I wasn't strong enough to pull him up the steps. Since the guys were coming to dinner, I thought it was the perfect opportunity to have Hart come here for a change.

I'd been running around all day cleaning and getting the food ready. Sophie and Ronnie's new bride, Julia, both offered to help, but I wanted to do this myself. The menu was simple, steaks on the grill, Caesar salad with homemade dressing and garlic croutons, the twice-baked potatoes, and sourdough bread that I'd made yesterday. Sophie insisted on picking up dessert. Since I was just a so-so baker, I didn't argue.

"Sweetness in the house, bitches!" Sophie's voice rang out through the house.

When she called this morning about bringing dessert, she heard the quiver in my voice and knew I was nervous about tonight. I had to admit, relief settled in my stomach just by the sound of her voice.

"In the kitchen!" As she walked in the room, I stood and picked up the pastry bag, ready to get back to work.

"Where shall I put my goodies?"

Glancing over my shoulder, all I saw were white bakery bags.

I walked toward them in search of my best friend. "What's all this?"

Her head popped out from behind the bags. "I couldn't decide. Everything looked so yummy." She pulled out boxes, announcing what each contained. "I gotcha chocolate-chunk cookies, biscotti, whoopee pies, a dozen red velvet cupcakes, and a pecan pie."

Alison G. Bailey

"There's enough for an army."

"Dammit!" she shouted.

"What's wrong?"

"I forgot the whipped cream for the pie."

I shook my head and walked back over to my potatoes. "Don't worry about it."

"But now the pie will be naked with its nuts hanging out." She fell into a fit of giggles at her own joke.

I couldn't help but join her. "You're pretty proud of yourself for that one."

"Aaah, I am," she said as she headed to the fridge.

Grabbing the bottle of white wine and two glasses, Sophie popped the cork and poured.

Waving an almost full glass in front of me, she said, "Drink."

"I can't right now."

"Bryson?"

"I have to finish this and get it in the oven. I still need to cut up the celery and carrots for the crudités . . ."

"The crud-de-what?"

"Crudités."

"English, please." She took a sip of her wine.

"A veggie tray with dipping sauce."

"Okay, that I understand. I can cut up things and put them on a tray."

"The asparagus, olives, cucumber, and bell pepper sticks are all in baggies in the fridge." My rambling was gaining momentum.

"Okay, I . . ."

"You just need to slice the celery and carrots and put everything on that big red tray over there." I tilted my chin toward the counter across the room.

"I got . . ."

"There's hummus and vinaigrette dipping sauces already in bowls in the fridge. The patio is set . . . I've stocked the metal washtub cooler with beer . . . the wine fridge is full . . ."

"I got it!" Sophie shouted.

"I'm sorry. Maybe a sip of wine would do me some good."

325

"A sip? Hell, chug the entire bottle." She took the pastry bag from my hand and replaced it with the glass of wine. "Uncoil. Why are you so nervous?"

I took a long sip of wine. "I just want everyone to have a good time."

Sophie grabbed the bamboo cutting board, a knife, and the vegetables and set up her work station across the room. "Everyone will have a great time but you need to calm down. You look fantastic, the place looks fantastic, and the food will be fantastic. It's all good."

Tonight was supposed to be casual and fun. Just a bunch of friends getting together to enjoy one another and some good food.

"I know . . . I just . . ."

Sophie's gaze locked with mine. "I don't remember you ever being this way about Slimy Bastard."

I smiled at her nickname for Will.

"Hart's worth all the effort."

Sophie didn't show her emotions easily, so when I saw her eyes mist over, I knew she got it and was happy for me.

"You let him know if he ever hurts you, I'm going to dismantle his wheelchair and shove each part up his ass . . . slowly." Laughter burst out of me. "Never mind, I'll tell him myself." She took a gulp of wine and got to chopping.

I gave her a sideways hug before going back to my potatoes.

My assistant and I worked diligently for the next hour. Appetizers lined the kitchen island, beer and wine were chilled, salad chopped, steaks were marinating. I was putting the finishing touches on the last dessert tray when the doorbell rang.

Looking at Sophie, I took off my apron and ran my hands down the front of me, smoothing out my beige long-sleeve shift dress with black chevron stripes. Hart liked me in anything and nothing at all. But he especially liked it when I wore a dress. I decided to go a little shorter with the hemline tonight and paired it with my brown cowboy boots. After freeing my hair from the pins holding it up, I combed my fingers through it a few times, fluffing it up.

She smiled. "You look gorgeous. Now go open the door for your fella."

I turned on my heels and ran to the front door, slowing my speed the closer I got. Taking in a deep breath, I opened the door.

I was met by one warm sweet smile from Julia and four exaggerated teeth-bearing grins from Colin, Ronnie, Doug, and Hart.

"Hey, baby!" The guys said in unison, as they all brought bouquets of flowers from behind their backs.

Julia stood off to the side smiling and shaking her head.

Laughing, I said, "You guys are crazy."

"Crazy for you, baby." Hart winked.

I stepped to the side to make room for them. "Well, come on in and make yourselves at home. Appetizers are in the kitchen . . ."

Colin entered, handing me his bouquet of wildflowers. "I need food."

"There's cold beer out back by the grill and wine in the fridge."

"I need beer," Ronnie said, tossing me his bouquet of calla lilies.

He was quickly followed by Julia. "And I need wine. Lots and lots of wine."

The three disappeared around the corner.

"Oh and Sophie is in there if you need anything," I called after them.

Turning back toward the door, I was met with a bouquet of daises shoved in my face.

In one continuous stride, Doug walked past me and toward the kitchen. "I need woman."

I peeked through my arm full of flowers to find a still grinning Hart. He looked sexy in a pair of dark jeans and pale blue V-neck sweater with a white T-shirt underneath. The color turned his eyes bright blue.

I beamed. "You wore the shirt I got you."

The only time I'd ever seen Hart in a color was the first day at the rehab when I spotted him going into a staff meeting in a bright blue polo. One day when I was shopping I saw the sweater and it reminded me of his eyes. I bought it unsure if he'd break from the black, gray, and white motif he had going on.

"I'm nothing if not open-minded about the other colors of the rainbow. Besides, my hot girlfriend bought it for me. I figured if I wore it I'd get lucky tonight."

Shaking my head, I blew a few daisy petals out of my face. "The guys didn't have to do all of this."

"Those guys are just pussies with those poor excuses for flowers. Now this is a bouquet of flowers." Hart turned his chair, reaching for something next to the door. When he turned back to me, he held up a huge bouquet of red roses. "Now, this is a bouquet."

I dropped the armful of flowers on the small table in the foyer and went to Hart.

I took the roses, brought them to my face, and inhaled. "They're beautiful but you didn't have to bring me anything."

"What kind of a boyfriend do you think I am?"

I leaned down, my lips hovering close to his. "A perfect one."

"Come here."

"Are you going to stay on the porch all night?"

"You can't blame a guy for wanting to have a minute alone with his girl."

I stepped out onto the porch, closing the door behind me.

Hart took the bouquet and set it down on one of the rocking chairs.

Looking up at me, he took both my hands in his and laced our fingers together. "You seem a little on edge. You doing okay?"

I nodded. "I am now that you're here."

He tugged me forward and onto his lap. Our hands disconnected, allowing mine to slide behind his neck. A few quiet moments were spent exchanging soft kisses.

"You look beautiful," Hart whispered against my lips as the tips of his fingers played with the hem of my dress. "I love the short dress-boot combo."

I brought my forehead to his. "I thought you might approve."

Suddenly, I wished the house was empty and we were alone.

Hart's lips brushed along my jaw to my neck while his hand slipped underneath my dress and headed up my thigh. "What pair are you wearing tonight?" His warm breath tickled the spot just under my ear, causing goosebumps to pop up over my skin.

My hand landed on top of his, stopping its progress. "Hart, our friends are here."

"They can't see us." He tried moving his hand farther up my thigh as he nibbled down my neck.

With my eyes half closed, I sighed. "What about the neighbors? I'm sure Mrs. Ravenel is glued to her front window."

His hand made it to the top of my thigh, his fingertips slipping underneath the bottom of my panties. "Then we shouldn't disappoint."

Just as I was on the verge of getting completely lost in Hart the front door swung open startling both of us. I looked up to find a hands-on-hips, pissed-off Sophie. Over her shoulder I saw the reason for her mood swing. An obviously ass-glaring and wide-grinning, Doug.

"Get in here. I need more layers of buffer between me and this ass," she snapped, pointing her thumb over her shoulder.

Muffling a belch, Doug said, "That's no way to talk about your future sex god."

Hart and I exchanged knowing looks before I reluctantly eased myself off his lap and headed inside. "Alright, everyone stop looking at and calling one another asses."

The three followed me into the kitchen. Hart and Sophie grabbed a couple of bottles of wine while I handed off a tray of appetizers to Doug before meeting the others out on the patio.

Hart handled grilling the steaks while I took care of the other dishes. Each of us checked occasionally on the other to see if any help was needed. It felt as if we'd been hosting dinners for years and had our routine down.

For the most part everyone behaved themselves during dinner. And by everyone I meant Doug and Sophie. Doug did provoke a few eyes to roll, several head shakes, and an actual hiss from Sophie. But he was harmless and to his credit blissfully unaware of our reaction. As a group we all seemed to meld together seamlessly. Not once was there any awkwardness or lulls in the conversation.

A Carolina spring night was just about as good as the world got. Even though the temperatures were beginning to rise during the day, the nighttime still had a crisp cool snap in the air. It was a perfect night for sitting around the fire pit with old and new friends.

After a lengthy discussion among the guys on the proper way to create the ideal fire, we were finally enjoying said fire, drinking coffee, and stuffing our faces with the desserts Sophie brought. "Coming Home" by Leon Bridges filtered through the outdoor speakers. Hart's musical taste had definitely rubbed off on me.

Ronnie and Julia were cuddled up on the double lounger. Colin sat on the stone bench near the fire pit, keeping a watchful eye on the fire.

Sophie and Doug looked like they were playing a game of musical chairs. She'd find a spot. He'd head to the spot. She'd move and he'd follow. After twenty minutes of this it was barely noticeable.

I found myself snuggled underneath a soft fleece blanket on what had quickly become my favorite place to be, Hart's lap in his arms. Will and Hart were as different as night and day in many aspects. One of the biggest differences was how comfortable Hart was showing me affection. Around other people he wasn't shy about holding my hand, giving me a light kiss, or having his arms wrapped around me. It wasn't the icky, doe-eyed type of affection that made others feel uncomfortable. It was easy and natural and I loved it.

While my head rested on Hart's broad shoulder, his arm was wrapped around my waist with his hand slowly moving back and forth over my hip. I was exhausted from the long day as well as my nerves being on high alert. The combination of good food, music, and Hart's rhythmic caress had my eyelids struggling to stay open. Just as I was about to completely disappear into the land of dreams my body jolted.

"For god sake, pull your pants up! I do not want to see your ass or your tramp stamp!" Sophie's screech cut through the air.

"Dudes don't get those. Besides, it's on my hip." Doug corrected her.

"Well, I have news for you. Your ass is taking over your hip region." With her face scrunched up, Sophie timidly leaned toward Doug who was standing next to her. "What is that anyway?"

"A fire-breathing dragon."

"I don't see any fire."

"It's in my pants." Doug grinned.

"You're gross and inappropriate!" Sophie squinted her eyes. "Is that a pink bow on its head?"

Doug pulled up his pants. "Fuck."

All the guys burst out laughing.

"It's Hart's fault."

"Hey man, you're a big boy. You make your own choices," Hart said, his chest vibrating with laughter.

"We were all drunk and we all got one." Colin was the ever-present calming voice.

"I swear to god, you said we were all getting cartoons." Doug said.

"We'd been talking about getting our cars tuned as in tune-up, you idiot!" Ronnie yelled.

"But still . . . Doug, even if we said cartoons, why would you get Hello Kitty?" Hart asked.

Doug's face turned red with annoyance. "That fucking tattoo dude was gunning for me."

"You were trying to pick up his girlfriend." Ronnie chimed in.

"How the hell was I supposed to know that chick belonged to him?"

With the iron poker, Colin stoked the fire. "Well, she had the name Ernie tattooed on both arms and just below her neck. The shop was called Ernie's Tatts and the dude introduced himself as Ernie."

At this point we were all rolling with laughter. I was so tickled, tears streamed down my face.

Hart continued the story. "Dumbass Doug goes back to Ernie and bitches, demanding that the guy cover up the kitty."

"And the dude did just enough to make Doug think he transformed the old tat into a cool dragon. But if you look at it the head on the kitty is still shining through." Colin finished the story.

"How did you find out you could still see the kitty?" I asked.

It was Ronnie's turn to add to the story. "He hooked up with this girl. The next morning he woke up to her talking baby talk to his hip, saying how much she loved Hello Kitty."

"Why didn't you just go to another shop and get it fixed?" Sophie asked.

"Because it hurt like a motherfucker."

Sophie stood and headed toward the house. "Idiot. Bryson, I'm going to clean the kitchen."

"Sophie, I'll take care of that."

"No! I insist."

Like a little puppy Doug followed after her. "If you don't start acting a little nicer to me, there's not a chance in hell you'll get with all this." His hands roamed up and down his body.

"Rest assured, there's no part of your body I want to get with."

The two disappeared into the house.

Stretching his arms over his head, Ronnie looked at Julia and said, "You about ready, hon?"

"Yep, we better go or I'm going to be spending the night."

Ronnie and Colin exchanged glances then tilted their chins.

I was about to stand when Julia stopped me.

"Stay put. We'll see ourselves out, Bryson."

"I'm so glad y'all came tonight."

Julia leaned down, giving me a hug. "Thanks for everything." She patted Hart's shoulder. "You behave yourself."

"That's no fun."

Ronnie gave me a quick peck on the cheek. "Thanks, Bryson."

Colin gave the dying fire one more poke before giving me a hug. "Bryson, thanks for an awesome night."

It was obvious all the guys looked out for Hart and had his back. But it didn't take long for me to figure out Colin was the soft-spoken ringleader. He was the one who made sure things happened like tonight, getting Hart up the steps, allowing us to have a night at my place.

I looked up at Colin with grateful eyes. "Thank you for everything."

He gave me a wink, letting me know he understood what *everything* meant.

"I'm gonna go inside and piss Doug off. Just let me know when you're ready." He told Hart.

As soon as the threesome were out of view, I nuzzled Hart's neck, placing a soft kiss behind his ear.

"I don't want you to go," I said against his skin.

"I wish I didn't have to."

I lifted my head and locked my gaze with his. "My next place is going to be flat as a pancake."

Cupping the side of my face, Hart threaded his fingers through my hair and pulled me into a slow deep kiss. As his tongue swirled and stroked mine a moan escaped me.

He broke the kiss and whispered, "I love you, Bryson."

"I love you with my heart and soul."

"You're always trying to one up me in the romance department."

I chuckled then planted a firm kiss in the center of his mouth.

Hart patted my ass. "I gotta go. Colin and Doug are waiting for me."

I stayed in Hart's lap all the way to the front porch where Colin and Doug were patiently waiting. The guys lowered him off the steps. Wrapping my arms around my body, I leaned a shoulder against one of the porch columns and watched as each guy got into their cars. I hated that so many people had to be involved just for him to come over. Hart maneuvered through life with such ease I forgot sometimes he faced limitations. What looked effortless to the naked eye was in fact anything but that for him.

This house once gave me a sense of comfort and security. I remembered months ago sitting on my bed with papers fanned out in front of me, desperate to figure out how I could financially remain here. Looking at Hart getting into his car, I realized I had those things as long as he was by my side, no matter where we were. And I didn't want to be anywhere he couldn't be.

chapter Twenty-Six

Me: *Hey, It's almost June and we still haven't discussed the divorce settlement. I've been holding off going to a lawyer because I felt it would be better if we discussed details first. I called you last week but it went straight to voicemail. Please respond soon. Will, we both need to move forward with our lives.*

"How long has it been since Mr. Forsyth moved out of the home?"

Shana Rafkin hadn't made eye contact since our initial introduction fifteen minutes ago. The short pudgy blond pitbull of an attorney sat across the dark conference table scribbling notes on her yellow legal pad.

The last text I sent Will had been a month ago and remained unanswered. I was tired of trying to figure out his motives for the avoidance. I needed to move on from the limbo I'd been in the last year and a half.

"Actually we've been kind of living separate lives since last January . . ."

"So January 20 . . ."

"No, he didn't move out then. We basically divided the house in two with him downstairs and me upstairs. I'm not sure why I didn't ask him to move out then. I knew the marriage was over. But you see, Will and I had been together since high school and . . ."

Her dark beady eyes lifted up. "I don't care about any of that. All I need is the date he physically moved out of the home."

I was taken aback by her cold tone and abruptness. I hired this woman because one of Sophie's co-workers highly recommended her. I also thought a woman lawyer would be more sympathetic and understanding. As I stared at Shana I felt my eyes mist over.

Swallowing the small lump that had formed in my throat, I said, "Um . . . well . . ."

"Listen, Mrs. Forsyth, I don't mean to sound blunt or short with you but you're paying me to get you financially divorced from your husband. Use your family, friends, and/or counselor to get you through the emotional aspect."

Squaring my shoulders, the tip of my tongue ran over my dry lips. "Eight months."

She gave me a curt nod, her gaze dropping as she jotted down the information.

"Will this be uncontested?" She glanced up when I didn't answer. "You both agree to the divorce?"

"Will fought it in the beginning. I guess he's onboard now. I haven't heard from him in months."

Scribble. Scribble. "Was there infidelity during the marriage from either of you?"

My chest tightened. "Will had intimate contact with other women online."

"Did he have sex with any of them?"

"Um . . ."

"Mrs. Forsyth, did your husband ever have sexual intercourse with any of these women?"

"Technically no."

Dark eyes shot up at me. "I don't understand."

"They weren't in the same room when they did things to themselves. I mean the women were on the screen or on his phone."

"The court doesn't acknowledge that as infidelity."

"They should. The betrayal hurts just as much," I whispered.

"Be that as it may . . . has your husband ever had real-life sexual intercourse with other women?"

"He's always denied it."

"Do you have any proof to the contrary?"

"No."

The rest of the hour was spent with Shana grilling me about each and every aspect of my financial life with Will. After listening to Sophie for the umpteenth time I had decided to ask for what I was entitled to, half of the profits from the sale of the house, half of Will's pension, and my car. I wasn't asking for alimony and as far as the furniture and other items in the house, I wasn't going to argue over petty things.

Shana capped her pen, closed folders, gathered papers, and fired off information. "It will take about ten days to put the settlement agreement together. We'll email you a copy to go over before sending to Mr. Forsyth. Once you proof the document let us know if there are any changes that need to be made. Hopefully, your husband will sign with little to no argument. After he signs then I'll request a court date. He doesn't have to be there. You'll only be in court for ten or fifteen minutes. You will need a witness to testify that you and Mr. Forsyth have been living apart. This could be a family member or friend, preferably female. The judge will ask you a few questions. Nothing to be nervous about. Not that I think you'll do any of these things but I tell all my client three things. Don't be late to court. Don't bring a new boyfriend or fiancé to court. And don't wear revealing clothes to court. Any questions?"

"Is there a deadline for when Will has to sign the papers?"

Her lips pressed into a straight line. "Unfortunately, no. You can't make someone sign a document. I assume he'll have an attorney look it over. We'll take it from there."

And with that I shook the pitbull's paw and played the waiting game.

Other than the part of my life stuck in the past, the present was incredible and the future hopeful. Will was served the separation settlement document the end of June. Three months passed with summer turning into fall and still no response. It was as if he'd dropped off the face of the earth.

Buzz. Buzz. Buzz.

I heard the faint buzz of my phone. But I wasn't curious enough to open my eyes and find out who was texting me early on a Sunday morning. For the past two days the weather had been rainy and chilly and the forecast was calling for more of the same today. I was too warm and cozy with my back pressed against Hart's warm chest to care about the outside world. A faint smile crossed my lips as Hart's hand slipped under my T-shirt and splayed across my stomach.

"You gonna check that?" he mumbled, his lips brushing over the skin just below my neck.

I wiggled into him as he placed a soft kiss on my shoulder. "Eventually."

Five minutes later the phone buzzed with another text followed almost immediately by ringing. I reluctantly shoved my arm out from underneath the comforter and patted the nightstand, feeling for the annoyance. Blindly swiping the screen with my finger, I squinted one eye open. Seeing the name on the screen caused my lungs to fill with what felt like quicksand. I grabbed Hart's wrist, pulling him closer before opening my other eye and reading.

Will: *Hey, I need to see you.*

Will: *Bryson, we really need to talk.*

Will: *I just left you a voicemail. Call me ASAP.*

For months I tried to make contact with Will. A lawyer had been hired and I was ready to move forward with the divorce. I'd been extremely patient with him, waiting weeks to hear something . . . anything. Never really knowing where his head was at or if he was going to pull the rug out from under me. The fact that he was contacting me out of the blue, along with his persistence, and demanding I respond quickly had me pissed off and scared.

This was the first Sunday I'd had off in three weeks. Since I worked mainly on the weekends and Hart's job was during the week, time together was precious. Our plans for the day had already been set—stay as naked as possible for as long as possible, sex followed by more sex, and keep well hydrated.

I slid the phone under my pillow, slid Hart's hand farther up my body, and got back on the plan. Hart's index finger circled around my nipple painstakingly slow just before his thumb joined in, giving it a quick pinch. Rubbing my thighs together, I rolled my hips and ass against him.

Buzz. Buzz. Buzz.

The muffled text notification did not go unnoticed by Hart.

"Bryson, who's trying awfully hard to get in touch with you?"

"Will," I whispered.

Hart's muscles tensed. "What does he want?"

"He wants to see me."

"About what?"

Turning in his arms, I met questioning eyes. "I don't know. It doesn't matter, though. I'll let my lawyer handle it."

Buzz. Buzz. Buzz

Raising his hand, Hart brushed the hair from my cheek and tucked it behind my ear. "Don't you think you should at least tell him that?"

I hesitated for several seconds as I gazed at Hart, searching for signs of anger or jealousy. All I saw was concern and curiosity.

Running my fingernails over his back, I applied just enough pressure to scratch the surface. "I don't want anything to ruin our plans for today."

His hand roamed down my body, stopping at my cotton panties. "Nothing and no one is going to stop me from tapping your sweet little ass all day." He gave it a deep squeeze.

"Wow, that's the sweetest and crudest thing anyone has ever said to me."

"There's more where that came from, baby." He winked.

Lunging forward, Hart captured my mouth, his tongue making contact with mine immediately.

As he broke the kiss, he sucked hard on my bottom lip, his gaze searing into mine. "Get rid of him so I can commence the tappin'."

As I sat up Hart's hand landed on my lower back, causing a calmness to wash over me while I typed out the text.

Me: *Hey, I'm not so sure that's a good idea. My lawyer can answer any of your questions*

Will's response was immediate.

Will: *I need to talk to you face to face. No lawyers.*

My muscles tensed as an audible sigh left my body.

Propping himself up with his hands, Hart appeared next to me. "Bryson?"

I rolled my head to the side, stretching the stress out of my neck. "He insists we meet. No lawyers."

"What are you thinking?"

"That I wish this was over and done with and I could just move forward with my life . . . with us."

"Will's not stopping any of that from happening." Hart gave my shoulder a little bite.

I glanced over at him. "What do you think I should do?"

I could tell by his expression he definitely had an opinion on the matter but he wasn't going to let me in on it.

"You know I'm here for you and will do whatever you need. But this is your decision."

Looking straight ahead, I said, "I know . . . it's just Will has a way of making me second guess myself."

"Bryson, look at me."

My body twisted in his direction.

Cupping the side of my face, his thumb glided over my cheek. "You're a strong intelligent woman. Will can say whatever he wants but he has no control over you. Trust yourself and do what your gut's telling you to do."

Hart was right. In our short time together, he helped me find myself. He didn't tell me how to act or what to say. He gave me the confidence to believe in myself and my abilities. I was no longer the girl Will could make feel less than. I was a strong independent woman and I wasn't going to let anyone take that away from me.

Me: *Okay but it can't be today.*

Will: *When?*

Me: *Wed at 1 p.m., Olympic Deli.*

So no one felt as if they had the upper hand, I asked Will to meet at a neutral location. The Olympic Deli was a little Greek place that was never overly crowded, so we could have privacy. But there was enough of a customer flow that you wouldn't want to make a scene. Hart wanted to go and hover in the background just in case I needed a dose of moral support and to keep his eye on Will. Hart was confident and secure in himself and our relationship. Jealousy never entered the equation. But he was very protective of me and didn't trust Will. Although I loved him for offering, I had to do this by myself. Part of me didn't want to put him in an awkward situation. The other part of me needed to prove to myself that I was as strong as Hart believed.

The days leading up to the meeting I stayed on edge except when I was with Hart. He was the only person who had the ability to calm my frayed nerves. Different scenarios played in my head about what Will would say and how I'd react. I didn't bother to tell Sophie because I knew she would only add to my anxiety.

After so many months apart it was going to feel strange and difficult to see Will. No matter what caused the end of our relationship, he had played a significant part in my life. I had two goals when the divorce came to an end and all ties with Will were severed. One, was to live a happy and purposeful life with the love of my life. Two, to wish Will the same.

On the day of the meeting I felt surprisingly calm. Before dropping my phone in my purse it buzzed with a text.

Hart: *Hey, Lovely. Wanted to let you know I'm thinking about you and know you're gonna handle things great. I love you.*

The warmth surrounding my heart quickly spread to the rest of my insides. I don't know how he did it but Hart's timing and words were always perfect.

Me: *Hey, Handsome. Getting ready to leave in just a minute. I'll let you know how it goes. Thank you for being in my life. I love you.*

After wiping the goofy grin from my face, I headed toward my front door with purse in hand while pushing my other arm through the sleeve of the brown leather jacket. I was about to open the door when the doorbell rang. Prepared to make a quick excuse and getaway from whoever was trying to sell me something, I opened my mouth and the door simultaneously. Both stayed wide open as I stared at Will standing in front of me.

"Hey," he said in a scratchy voice, a faint grin ghosted over his lips.

Him showing up here unannounced knocked me completely off balance and felt like an ambush.

My grip tightened around the doorknob. "What are you doing here? We were supposed to meet at . . ."

"I know and I'm sorry to just show up like this." He chuckled humorlessly. "Feels pretty weird apologizing for showing up at my own house."

"Will . . ."

"Sorry. I'm not trying to be an ass. I know we agreed to meet on neutral territory but I really need to talk to you alone. Can I come in?"

I hesitated. This was my first test to see if I was the strong intelligent woman Hart kept talking about.

"Please, Bryson."

Without saying a word, I stepped aside and let him in.

I closed the door as Will walked farther into the entryway. He looked like a stranger in a foreign land, out of place in the home he designed and built. Now that the shock of finding him on my front porch had slightly worn off, I was able to take a good look. In all the years Will and I were together, his appearance never really changed. But today he looked older, tired, and sad. I put my purse down and slipped out of my jacket. His shoulders lifted slightly and shook with a chill as a deep cough pushed out of him.

My plan was to hear what he had to say and usher him out of here as quickly. So I surprised myself when I asked, "Can I take your coat?"

"Yeah, thank you." He shrugged off his black wool coat and handed it to me.

He was dressed head to toe in L.L. Bean. Black storm chaser shoes and a pair of black jeans along with the burgundy sweater I'd given him the Christmas before I discovered the Val text. Either the sweater had been stretched out of shape from wear or Will had lost some weight, because it didn't fit as well over his broad chest as I remembered.

I draped his coat neatly over the banister. Standing still, I stared at the man I once thought I'd grow old with as the last of my shock wore off.

Will's gaze frantically darted around the space. "The place looks great, Bryson. I mean, from what I can see of it. Everything running okay?"

"Yes."

"Because I'd be happy to look at anything that needs fixing."

"Nothing needs fixing."

"Did you have the guy come out to do maintenance on the heating and air-conditioning unit?"

"He came out."

We stared at each other across the entryway as the awkwardness thickened. Formality filled the air between us.

Clearing his throat, Will said, "You look great, Bryson."

"Will, what did you want to talk about?"

"Maybe we should sit down."

"Maybe you should just say what you came here to say."

"Okay." His gaze dropped to the floor as he blew out a deep breath. "Okay . . . um . . ." He looked up and straight at me. His expression was flat but his eyes were filled with fear and regret. He chewed on his lower lip, stalling.

"Will . . ."

He freed his lip and announced. "I'm sick, Bryson."

My eyes narrowed. "What are you talking about?"

I flipped through a list of illnesses in my head trying to prepare myself for what he was about to say. Cancer was at the top of the list.

"Shortly after the first of the year I came down with what felt like the flu. You know me, I didn't bother going to the doctor. Figured I'd just ride it out. I started feeling better but not a hundred percent. Work was crazy as usual and things between me and my parents weren't great. They were beyond disappointed when I told them about us. Between the accident, work, and our situation, I thought it was just stress."

"Will, please . . ."

"I'm getting to the point." There was a hint of defensiveness in his tone. "I developed a cough I couldn't get rid of, I was tired all the time, and started losing weight. The end of May I went to the doctor. It felt like they ran every test known to man on me trying to eliminate all the possibilities." He paused. "The doctor finally found out what was wrong."

"What is it?"

He inhaled a deep breath that caught in his throat, causing another cough to blast out of him. "Excuse me."

Pulling a handkerchief from his pocket, Will turned, aiming his cough away from me. I remained silent watching his body convulse with each jolt until finally the raw tear-inducing cough died down.

"Sorry," he said, his tone laced with embarrassment.

"It's okay. Would you like some water?"

"No thank you."

Will's dark brown eyes looked black as he struggled to meet my gaze.

"In July I was diagnosed with Acquired Immunodeficiency Syndrome. I have AIDS, Bryson."

All the blood drained from my body as I stumbled back, knocking into the small table.

AIDS?

I'd prepared myself to hear the word cancer. AIDS wasn't even on my radar. I knew there still wasn't a cure. Since the disease hadn't been in the limelight for a long time, I just assumed people weren't as affected by it as they once were.

AIDS.

Not knowing how to respond, I simply stayed glued to my spot and stared. The longer I looked at Will the frailer he appeared. I wasn't sure if knowing he was sick changed the way my eyes saw him. When I first saw him I could tell he was thinner but now he seemed skinny, even gaunt. On closer inspection, his once full cheeks were sunken in, his jawbone more prominent, and his skin pale. The strong, handsome young man who had lived such a charmed life had been replaced by this fragile stranger.

Will looked lost standing in the middle of the entryway, loneliness radiating off of his body. Regardless of the past, he was still a person. Someone that I cared for and loved at one time. I wrapped my arms around his waist. His body stiffened for a moment before his reluctant arms touched me. Pressing his cheek to the side of my head, his body trembled with quiet sobs.

Keeping my voice steady, I said, "There are a lot of treatments out there now, you know." I had no idea if what I was saying had any merit. I knew very little about this disease. "People live longer with all the advancements in medicine."

Will broke the hug and looked down at me. His eyes had a slight hollowed-out appearance and faint dark circles. My gaze moved past his thinning lips, to his boney chin, and down to his neck. Peeking out from under his sweater I noticed a dark reddish purple spot and another just below his right ear.

Will picked up on my stare. "They're Kaposi sarcoma lesions. I have several more down my back and chest."

"Cancer?"

"Yeah."

"Are they treating it?"

He shook his head slowly. "At this point there's no reason."

"Why not?"

"The lucky ones live longer when diagnosed early." He paused and swallowed hard. "Bryson, I'm not one of the lucky ones. Apparently, I've been carrying the virus around with me for a while."

Like an anvil crashing into the head of a poor unaware cartoon character, the realization hit me. I was so wrapped up and concerned with Will having the disease, I never once considered myself.

I dropped my arms and took a step back. "How long?"

Will's chin drifted down taking his gaze with it.

I forced my body and voice to remain strong as I repeated the question. "Will, look me in the eye and answer my question. How long?"

His dark sorrowful eyes met mine. "You need to be tested."

"It's October." Anger surged through me, causing my body to shake. "You were diagnosed in July. And you waited until now to tell me?!"

Will's gaze dropped as his shoulders slumped forward. "I flipped out when I got the diagnosis. I'm sorry." His voice sounded weak and feeble.

Backing away, my hands balled into fists as my jaw clenched. "You swore over and over that you never stuck your dick into anyone else during our marriage."

"I never cheated on you . . ."

"You did each time you fired up your laptop, went online, and contacted other women."

He stood in silence, not even attempting an explanation.

"Okay . . . okay . . . I never stuck my dick into any other woman until the end of our marriage. I swear to god that's the truth."

A twinge of relief settled in my chest. "By that time we weren't sleeping together anymore."

Glancing away, Will ran his tongue over his dry cracked lips. "The day before you asked me for the divorce and I crashed my car into the side of a building. Remember, I came home early and found you at the pool. You'd been drinking and had on my favorite bikini . . ."

My hand shot up in front of me, stopping Will's trip down memory lane.

A tremor broke through the numbness and consumed me as tears stung behind my eyes. "When did you start hating me so much?"

Taking a step forward, Will choked out. "Bryson, I never hated you."

"You had unprotected sex with someone else and then came home and fucked me!"

His face contorted in pain. "I'm sorry. There's no excuse."

"Who was she?"

His gaze dropped to the floor as if the name was written in the slats of wood.

"Look me in the fucking eye and answer me. You owe me that much." I gritted out.

Will lifted his head and did as I asked. "It wasn't just one. They were random women I met."

"Where?"

Shaking his head, he said, "Different places."

"Where?!" I screamed.

"Bars and online. I don't even remember their names."

My stomach twisted tighter with each of his answers. I was the biggest idiot ever to walk the face of the planet. Each time he said he loved me, each time he said he was working in his office, each time he denied fucking another woman . . . all lies. Over the course of ten years everything out of Will's mouth was a lie.

All the tears, the doubts, guilt, and blaming myself. Feeling worthless, demeaned, and not desirable. Hour after hour of obsessing over what I could do to save the marriage. And still I worked to take the high road and not hate this lying piece of shit.

"How many?"

"Does it really matter?"

"I am three seconds away from grabbing my chef's knife and cutting your fucking dick off. How many whores did you fuck?!" I kept my voice low and threatening.

He took in a ragged breath. "Honestly, I don't know."

"You slimy motherfucker!" My resolve was shattering. Nausea bubbled into my throat, setting it on fire. I closed my eyes and pushed the heels of my hands into them. "I can't believe this is happening."

Dropping my hands, I tightly wrapped my arms around me and doubled over as the sobs took over.

Will stepped toward me. "Bryson . . ."

I whipped my head up and glared at him. "Don't you dare come near me."

He stopped dead in his tracks.

"I understand it's a lot to take in and you have every right to freak out."

"Thank you for being so understanding." I spit out each venom-laced word. I forced myself to straighten up. "I need to sit down," I said, walking in the direction of the kitchen.

I jerked back a stool from the breakfast bar and sat. With my elbows on the marble top, I rested my head in my hands. The sound of shoes hitting wood told me Will wasn't far behind.

In a low husky voice, Will said, "The chances of you being infected are minimal. You were only exposed once."

"Once is all it takes." The words came out flat and robotic.

Out the corner of my eye, I saw Will raise a shaky hand and slide something across the counter toward me. "This is my doctor's card. He's a specialist and can answer all your questions. I'll pay for everything."

Dropping my head between my hands, I looked down at the crisp white card embossed with black lettering. As the card hypnotized me, a faint muffled buzz came from the entryway.

"I'll get it for you," Will said.

A few seconds later Will returned with my purse and placed it in front of me. Shoving my hand inside, I felt around for my phone. I needed something from the outside world to invade the walls of this house. My hand flew to my mouth and more sobs gushed out of me as I read the text.

Hart: *FYI-I'm taking you on a date tonight. Meet me at the Charleston Crab House at 6pm? Followed by a meeting in my lap at 9 p.m. I love you.*

"Hart." His name drifted from my lips.

My body shook as I placed the phone down. I was free falling off of a cliff with no sign of stopping. Knowing there was a chance I was infected devastated me. Knowing I'd exposed Hart killed me. He was an incredible and understanding man but even Hart had his limits. I was going to lose him when I'd just found him.

The sound of the chair sliding across the floor snapped me from my thoughts. I glanced over to find Will sitting beside me.

"I ran into Ryan a few months back. He told me you were with someone."

"He never mentioned seeing you."

"This Hart . . . wasn't that the name of the rehab guy in the wheelchair?"

I looked at him through red swollen eyes. "Hart's the man I love and planned on spending the rest of my life with."

"I don't mean to be indelicate but can he . . . I mean, have y'all?"

I bit down hard on my lower lip and just glared at Will.

"Sorry. Y'all used protection, right?"

The irony of my cheating, almost ex-husband asking this question was not lost on me.

"Yes."

"That's good. The chances are slim to none that he's in any danger. But to be on the safe side he should get tested."

I was physically and emotionally drained. My mind was racing with everything and nothing at all. I felt the touch of Will's cool hand as he placed it on top of mine. I didn't pull away.

"Saying this is overwhelming is an understatement. I understand if you never want to see me again. Please know that I'm here for you." His voice trembled. "Bryson, I'm not asking for forgiveness but I'd sure appreciate the chance to earn it."

At the moment forgiveness was not an option. With one short sentence Will had flipped my life upside down. A life I'd worked hard to create with the man I was born to spend it with. Looking at Will's face coated in dried tears and sweat, I saw a shattered human being. A hint of pity nudged its way between the hate and anger. Logic began to break through my mental hysteria. There was nothing I could do to change the past. All I could do was pray for a future that included Hart.

chapter
Twenty-Seven

Time had become irrelevant as I stayed planted on the stool paralyzed and lost. I knew what I wanted my next move to be but was clueless as to what it should be. Hart filled every corner of my mind, body, and soul. I needed to feel his calming presence and his strong arms around me. I needed to look in his eyes and see that he was confident we would get through this together. I loved us—our conversations, our teasing, our smiles, our laughter, our touching, our silent moments. I loved everything about us and I couldn't say goodbye to us.

The clink of ceramic hitting marble startled me out of my head. A green mug of tea came into view. My gaze darted up to Will standing on the other side of the counter. I hadn't even realized he was still here.

"I thought you might like some tea," he said.

"Could you pass me the sugar and . . ."

"Milk. Two sugars and a splash of milk. I remembered." He pushed the mug closer to me and gave me a weak smile.

I wrapped my hands around the warm mug, seeking any semblance of comfort.

Raising the tea to my lips, I said, "How long have I been sitting here?" I took a sip, closing my eyes as the hot liquid coated my raw throat.

"About an hour. I thought you needed the time and I didn't want to leave you alone."

"I don't know what to do." I felt tears forming but I was too exhausted for them to turn into sobs.

"What do you mean?"

"What now? When I get off this stool what do I do next?"

"I told my doctor I was going to tell you today. He said if we needed to talk, he'd be more than happy to see us and do your blood test."

When you're first faced with a life-shattering event the mind lapses into temporary insanity. At least you hope it's temporary. Delusions were a coping mechanism. Like a flour sifter, they allowed only a few grains of the devastation through at a time. Letting the brain get accustomed to a new reality. At the moment, I was convinced that if I stayed on this stool and in my house, my world would remain in one piece. But slowly reality was seeping through the wire mesh forcing my brain to accept the fact that my life was irrevocably altered.

"Bryson, do you want to go?"

Looking up at Will, I said, "Do I have a choice?"

"I'll call Dr. Rudolph and see if we can come now."

Will walked away punching in the number on his cellphone.

My gaze dropped to my phone still sitting where I'd placed it earlier. I tapped the screen and it came to life with the text from Hart.

Hart: *FYI-I'm taking you on a date tonight. Meet me at the Charleston Crab House at 6pm? Followed by a meeting in my lap at 9pm. I love you.*

The words got blurry the longer I stared. I had to at least answer him before I went to Will's doctor. There was no way I could call Hart. He'd know immediately something was wrong by the sound of my voice.

Me: *I'd love to meet at 6 then in your lap. I love you and miss you like crazy.*

His response was immediate.

Hart: *;-)*

A weak smile drifted over my lips at his use of an emoji. Hart was so not an emoji kind of guy. He was barely a texting guy. Even at a low moment like this with a simple smiley wink face from him, Hart was able to brighten my life. Since my emotions weren't stable enough to talk to him live, maybe hearing his soothing rasp on an old voicemail would give me comfort and strength to walk out the door and deal with the unknown. With my finger hovering over the button, I was just about to press Play when the echo of Will's deep cough interrupted.

"Sorry, I didn't know you were on the phone," he said, coming into the kitchen.

"I'm not."

"Dr. Rudolph can see us in a half hour."

I nodded. "This test . . . what's involved?"

"It's just a simple blood test . . . ready?"

Staring up at Will, I wondered how we'd gotten to this place as my mind drifted back to the first time the football hero asked the quirky girl out.

"Bryson, are you gonna be at the football game tonight?"

With one shoulder pressed against my locker, his chocolate brown eyes gazed down at me. I was in shock that Will Forsyth not only knew my name but was standing right in front of me in the flesh, curious about my Friday night whereabouts.

My stomach felt like it was full of fizzy bubbles. "I don't know. Sophie doesn't like sports and I'm not interested in sitting through an entire game by myself."

"If I convince her to go, would you go? Cause I'd really like you to go to the game."

"Why do you want me there so badly?"

He glanced away for a brief moment as his cheeks pinked up. "Cause you're cute. I like you. And I want to show off in front of you so you'll go to the homecoming dance with me."

With my gaze down, I fidgeted with the corner of my Algebra book. "I'd go to the dance with you, game or no game."

The corners of his lips tugged into a sweet smile. "Are you saying I got no game?"

I giggled at his joke even though I didn't get it.

Pushing off from the locker, he took a step toward me. "I'll see you at the game tonight."

Being this close to him made everything blurry. "That is if you convince Sophie."

Will dipped his head and leaned in closer. "I'll see you at the game tonight."

My heart ached at the lost innocence, the lost years, and the lost dream.

Closing my eyes, I inhaled one final deep breath before sliding off of the stool onto wobbly legs.

"I'll get your jacket." Will offered.

While waiting for him to return, I attempted to strengthen my legs and my resolve. I had to deal with things one step at a time. If I thought of everything at once my brain would flood and my insides would implode. I'd get through the blood test and the appointment. Then I'd figure out how to tell Hart and pray he wouldn't hate me for exposing him to this mess. He'd already had a lifetime's worth of pain. And if I had to walk away in order for him to be happy, then I would walk away.

Will came toward me holding my jacket out for me to slip my arms in. Instead of putting my cellphone in my purse, I kept it clutched in my hand. Hart wasn't able to be with me but his words of love and encouragement were all over my text messages and voicemails. As I approached the front door, I took in a deep breath and tightened my grip, using the phone like a security blanket. Will opened the door and a rush of cold air slapped me in the face.

One Mississippi.

Two Mississippi.

Three Mississippi.

And I stepped out of the door.

The ride to the doctor's office was for the most part done in silence. Will tried to strike up casual conversation a few times in order to get my mind on anything else other than the pink elephant in the room.

Numbness was setting in as I stared at the beautiful historic homes, palmetto trees, and tourist whiz by. My breath stuck in my throat as I realized we were about to pass the rehab center. Shifting my gaze, I focused straight ahead so there was no chance of me spotting Hart's car in the parking lot. As memories of my days roaming the halls flashed through my mind something occurred to me.

Looking over at Will, I said, "Why didn't they find out you had the virus after the accident? I mean, with all the blood work they ran on you in the hospital and at the rehab it seems like it would have shown up."

"HIV testing isn't part of a complete blood count. The patient has to request the test."

"You'd been with those other women by then and you didn't ask for the test?"

"Ignorance is bliss, I guess," Will said, sheepishly.

"Maybe you slept with whoever infected you after we'd been together that last time."

"Not possible."

"How can you be sure? I mean, wouldn't you have gotten sick soon after being infected? Correct me if I'm wrong but you started screwing around shortly before the accident, that would be last spring or summer."

Will tightened his grip on the steering wheel. "You can carry the virus for a while before symptoms show. Besides, I'm positive it was before the accident. I haven't been with anyone physically since then."

In other words he was still cyber fucking. Not wanting to pull at that thread, I turned my head and resumed staring out the window.

When Will mentioned his doctor was a specialist, my imagination conjured up all sorts of images of a doom-and-gloom office with half-dead patients lining the corridors. Ridiculous and illogical, yes, but my mind wasn't exactly working at full capacity.

The building looked like the typical medical facility. The handful of people waiting looked up as Will and I entered the room. An older lady in the corner gave me a warm smile when we made eye contact.

As Will checked us in, I inconspicuously scanned the room. It was hard to believe that the people here had AIDS or HIV. They all looked so normal. The lady with the warm smile looked as if she could be someone's grandmother. Once check-in was done, Will and I found two empty seats tucked in a corner and headed their way.

Will shrugged out of his coat, placing it in the chair beside him. Still gripping my cellphone, I draped my jacket over my arm and hugged it to my chest. As we waited, Will mindlessly flipped through the pages of a magazine. Shifting in my chair, I crossed and uncrossed my legs multiple times, never finding a comfortable position. Finally, I gave up and landed both feet flat on the ground. My gaze darted all around the room as I coiled and uncoiled the strap of my purse around my finger. Every little sound caused my body to jerk.

Leaning toward me, Will asked, "You hanging in there?"

"As well as can be expected." Leaning closer to him, I whispered, "Are you sure we're in the right place? None of these people look sick."

"They may be here with a patient or have HIV. People live healthy and normal lives with the virus, Bryson. When it turns into AIDS is when you're fucked."

I stared into his dark brown eyes flooded with awareness. Will knew the expiration date on his life wasn't something in the far away distance. It was no longer a concept to wax poetic about. It was a hardcore firm reality that kept getting closer with each passing day. With everything I'd been trying to process in the last few hours, the fact that Will was dying never really sunk in. I opened my mouth to speak just as Will's name was called.

A pretty blonde dressed in solid blue scrubs stood in the doorway that led to the exam rooms. "Will, you can come back now."

Will stood first, taking his coat in one hand and extending the other to me. I stared at his outstretched hand for a few seconds before taking the offer. It was like an out of body experience as we let the nurse guide us to exam Room D. I was fully aware of my body moving and where I was. But this wasn't my life, it just couldn't be.

"Jennie, this is my . . . this is Bryson."

"Nice to meet you, Bryson." I gave her a weak smile in response.

Indicating the two chairs up against the wall, Jennie said, "Y'all can take a seat there." Sitting on the round stool with wheels, she rolled over to the desk. "Will, how have you been feeling since your last visit?"

"Not too bad. I think the cough might be a little better. My energy has been low and I'm cold all the time."

I was shocked to hear Will reported his explosive cough was getting better.

She gave him a sympathetic smile and typed something into the computer. "Dr. Rudolph will be in to see you in a few minutes. Is there anything I can get either of you?"

There was a friendly familiarity between Will and Jennie letting me know he'd been a frequent visitor since his diagnosis. The realization caused a lump to form in my throat.

Glancing at me, Will asked, "You want anything, coffee or tea?"

I looked at Jennie and shook my head. "I'm good, thank you."

After one more sympathetic smile she left the room.

"I thought your cough was due to a cold," I said.

"I have spots on my lungs." He tugged the neck of his sweater down, revealing the reddish purple spot. "Same type cancer as this."

Looking away, my eyes filled with tears. I swiped my fingers under my eyes, catching the tears before they fell. Suddenly, the door swung open. A tall, round, balding man in a white coat and wire rim glasses whooshed in like a tornado.

Shoving his hand out, he said, "Will, how ya doing, man?"

Will slapped his palm into the doctor's and shook. "About the same."

"Same is good. Better is better. But we'll take same."

"Dr. Rudolph this is Bryson."

It was my turn to have a hand thrust in my face. "Nice to meet you, young lady. Wish it were at a cocktail party and not here, though."

The amount of energy radiating off this guy was somewhat overwhelming. Words fired out of him at lightning speed. So much so that my brain was constantly playing catch whenever he opened his mouth.

"Me too," I said.

Dr. Rudolph took the seat in front of the computer.

His gaze swung from the screen to me. "I'm not sure how much you know about HIV and AIDS."

"I know the basics, I guess."

"I'm a first-things-first kind of guy. I can give you a bunch of reading material. Hell, you can google the information now. But no sense in getting you all nervous and scared . . ."

Too late, doc.

". . . Until we know for a fact that you're infected. Now, if your blood work comes back positive, you need to realize that it's not a death sentence like it used to be. Sure there are lifestyle changes you'll have to make, precautions, but I repeat, an HIV diagnosis is not a death sentence." He looked me directly in the eye. "Do you understand me, young lady?"

"Yes, sir."

I understood him but the jury was still out on whether or not I believed him.

"I'm going to get Jennie to come draw some blood. We can do a rapid test here in the office that only takes a few minutes to get the results."

This shocked me. I thought I'd be in hell for days or even weeks waiting for the results. Knowing I'd have the answer before I left this office gave me a sense of relief but also terrified me.

The doctor bolted up from his seat. "Okay, let's get this show on the road. Jennie will be right in and I'll see you once I have news."

All three of us exchanged courteous smiles before Dr. Rudolph left the room.

Will and I didn't have a chance to say anything before Jennie reappeared. She meticulously lined up the items needed for the blood draw.

"Bryson, would you roll up your sleeve, please?" Jenni said, as she pulled on a pair of purple latex gloves. "There's a big juicy vein."

I knew she was trying to lighten the mood, hoping her little joke would make me less nervous. It didn't. As the needle pierced my skin, I dug my nails into Will's arm. He took it like a man, not wincing or pulling away.

"There, all done."

I looked over at Jennie as she filled one of the tubes with my dark red blood. Her bright blond hair blurred and the room swayed.

Blink.

Blink.

Blink.

After the third blink, I opened my eyes and the room and Jennie's hair were back to normal.

She secured a Band-Aid over the area and gathered up her supplies. "The test only takes a few minutes. The doctor will be back when he has the results. Can I get either of you anything, coffee, a soda . . .? We also have snacks in the lounge."

For the third time I shook my head at her sweet offer as Will answered, "No thanks. I think we're both good right now."

After Jennie left us alone the room fell silent except for the crackling sound whenever Will inhaled a breath. I realized this was due to the cancer in his lungs, and a knot twisted in my stomach. And with each second that passed Will's fate slapped me in the face.

Without looking at me, Will placed his hand over mine and said in a low voice, "Thank you, Bryson."

"For what?"

"For not acting like you hate me."

"I don't want to hate you, Will. I don't want to hate anyone."

"But you have every right to because of what I've done." He gave my hand a gentle squeeze.

I concentrated on the blank wall in front of me. If I allowed my thoughts to drift to anything besides that plain empty white wall, I'd end up a puddle on the floor. Each time thoughts of Mom, Dad, Ryan, Sophie, or Hart pushed through to my consciousness, I pushed back hard until they disappeared. The last thing I wanted to do was to hurt the most important people in my life. And even though this situation was beyond my control the thought of causing those I loved pain was more than I could handle at the moment.

Both Will and I jumped when the door swung open and Dr. Rudolph appeared holding a piece of paper. He didn't bother to sit down. Instead, he stood in front of us and looked into my panicked eyes.

"The rapid test came back negative," he announced.

An audible sigh of relief gushed out of Will. I sat still as a statue, stunned and grateful. The sound of Dr. Rudolph's deep voice jarred me to attention.

"To be on the safe side, I'm still going to send a sample off to the lab."

"If the first test is negative then why bother to do that?" Will asked.

"Just as a precaution. The lab is equipped to conduct more extensive testing. Those results will take a little longer to get."

My ability to think and speak was gradually returning. "How much longer?"

"A few days to a week. Don't worry, young lady. Today's test is great news."

I nodded with tears filling my eyes.

"I'll call you with the other results." He extended his hand to me. "It's going to be okay." The doctor then shook Will's hand. "I'll see you for our regularly scheduled visit next week unless you need me before hand."

"Thank you . . . uh . . . so much for . . . uh . . . seeing us on such short notice, sir," Will stammered.

"Not a problem."

The second Dr. Rudolph left the room, Will doubled over. With his elbows resting on his knees, his head hanging low, sobs quietly seeped out of him.

"Thank God you're okay," he choked out.

This man who belittled me during our marriage, who cheated on me, who exposed me to a deadly disease was completely broken and my heart hurt for him. What Will said was true, I had every right to hate him but I couldn't. I wasn't going to allow the pain he'd caused to change the person I was. Biting my lower lip, I attempted to stay composed as I placed my hand on his back and slowly rubbed. Will and I stayed like this until he shed his last tear and my heart forgave him.

The ride home was just as quiet as the ride to the doctor's office, only this time I think it was more from pure exhaustion than anything else. We pulled into the driveway and Will walked me to the front door.

"Thank you for taking me today," I said, focusing my gaze down.

"Don't thank me for that."

I glanced up in time to witness a visible shiver run through his body. "It's getting pretty cold. You should go get warm."

"Bryson, I know it's already been a long day . . ." He chuckled. "God, it's only 3 p.m."

My eyebrows knitted together in disbelief. "It feels like midnight."

He chewed on his bottom lip, struggling with whether or not to say his next words. "Can I come in?"

"Will, I'm exhausted and I'm meeting Hart in a few hours. I have to tell him."

"I know but I really need to discuss something with you." There was a pleading in his tone and his eyes.

"Something else?"

"Yeah. It's pretty important."

I hesitated for a minute before giving in. "Okay."

I headed inside, thinking Will was behind me but when I turned around to close the door the foyer was empty. I put my purse down, took off my jacket, and went into the kitchen. As I was heating water for tea, Will entered and placed the black bag he always used for work on the counter. He shrugged off his coat and draped it on the back of one of the stools.

"Tea?" I asked.

Pulling several folders out of his bag, he lined them up along the counter. "Yes, please."

I was in hopes that the divorce papers he still hadn't signed were in one of the folders. "What's all that?"

Sitting down, he answered, "The thing I need to discuss with you."

I placed the two mugs of tea on the counter and sat on the stool beside Will.

"I apologize for dumping all of this on you in one day. It's just I don't have a lot of time to waste."

I couldn't tell if Will had accepted his fate or was terrified of its fast approach. Maybe a little of both.

His gaze lowered. "Bryson . . . um . . . I'm not sure exactly how to ease into this."

Fidgeting, I slid my mug back and forth between my hands. "It's okay, just start."

He glanced up at me for a brief second before his gaze dropped again. "When I told my family about my diagnosis . . . let's just say they've been less than supportive."

"I'm sorry."

"My parents have basically disowned me and my brother won't even take my calls. Can you believe that? He's been a loser all his life and he won't talk to me anymore."

I wasn't that surprised by the reaction of Will's parents. Appearances meant everything to them. You would think the fact that your child was dying would override any moral, ethical, or social issues you had. Alex, on the other hand, was a different story. I would have thought he'd at least be more empathetic to Will's situation.

"And my so-called friends have disappeared."

"All of them?"

I knew that at one time people distanced themselves from those with AIDS but I thought that was a thing of the past now.

"Yeah. So, I'm pretty much riding solo these days." The fingers of his left hand nervously tapped one of the folders in front of him before he pushed it toward me. "After the reaction I got from my parents, I left the construction company. But before I quit, I took half of my stock options and my 401K and rolled it into an individual retirement fund. The cash value of it right now is enough to live very comfortably for years."

I had no idea why Will was telling me all of this.

Folder number two.

"The other half of my stocks, I cashed in and opened up a checking account to pay for my medical bills."

Folder number three.

"I've already made and paid for my final arrangements."

Folder number four.

"Here's all the info on the checking and savings accounts."

Folder number five.

"This is an insurance policy. There's enough money to pay off the mortgage, both cars, and tuition for culinary school."

"Culinary school?"

"I've listed you as the sole beneficiary on everything."

My brain was in information overload. "I don't understand."

His dark eyes watered. "I don't have anybody, Bryson." He paused trying to keep his emotions in check. "My lawyer has drawn up all the necessary documents, like do not resuscitate. But as I get sicker, I may not be capable of making decisions." Will choked back a sob. "I know I deserve to be alone but I don't want to be when I die. It's asking a lot and god knows you don't owe me shit. But please, would you consider staying with me until . . . ?"

I stared at Will completely dumbfounded by his request. "I don't know what to say."

"You don't have to say yes to any of it. Nothing will change as far as my will. You'll still get everything."

My brain began to function again and all the information that had been thrown at me began to make sense. "This is why you didn't sign the divorce papers."

"No one can challenge you on any of this if we're still legally married."

"And by no one you mean your parents."

He simply nodded.

I couldn't believe what he'd done. Even when things were good between me and Will, he was never that thoughtful. I was floored by his generosity and that not only was he providing for me but protecting me as well. All he wanted was what anyone would want, comfort and connection with someone who cared. I wasn't sure what the details of this arrangement would be but my answer was clear.

I placed my hand on top of his. "You won't be alone, Will."

His body visibly relaxed.

"How exactly do we do this?"

His hand flipped over so that our palms were touching. "I was hoping I could move back home."

Jerking my hand from his, I slid off the stool and headed toward the sink. "I don't think that'll work out."

"Bryson, I don't mean to make you feel uncomfortable. I'm sorry for the . . . um . . . thing with the hand. It's just I haven't had a compassionate touch in a long time. I accept that we're over."

I turned to face him. "As far as you moving back in here, I have to think about it and talk to . . ."

"The guy?"

"Hart." I corrected his generic term.

"Hart . . . so y'all are that serious?"

"Yes, I told you earlier."

"I guess it didn't sink in. I don't want to cause any trouble between the two of you."

"I need to talk to him before I can agree to let you come back here."

Will's hand curled into a fist on the countertop. "Fair enough. I understand."

I had no intention of letting Will die alone but having him back under the same roof was essentially like being back together. Hart was my priority and I wouldn't do anything to jeopardize us. I promised Will I'd call within the next two days, once I'd had time to digest everything. I needed to feel Hart's presence and touch, but I was physically and emotionally depleted. My head needed some room to clear in order to process everything and decide how to tell Hart.

Once Will left I changed into my black leggings and Hart's long-sleeve gray T-shirt that I wore the first night I stayed at his place. He caught me eyeing it one morning and when I got home, I found it in my overnight bag. I curled up on the sofa with a glass of wine, grabbed my phone, and pressed his number. He picked up on the first ring.

"Hey." His raspy voice sent a shiver through my body.

"Hey."

"Where are you?"

"At home."

"You standing me up?"

"I need your strong arms wrapped around me."

"That can be arranged. You okay?"

"Yes." I choked back a sob.

"Why are you crying?" When I didn't answer, he continued. "I'm going to see if Colin and Doug can meet me at your place."

"I'm fine . . . really. I'm just exhausted. Can I take a raincheck on dinner and your lap?" I managed a slight chuckle.

"I'll hold you to it. You wanna talk about today?"

Tears trickled down my cheeks. "Tomorrow."

"Tomorrow it is. Go get some rest."

"Don't leave me. I need to hear your voice."

"Okay."

"I love you so much, Hart."

"You're making me a little nervous and I don't get nervous."

"I don't mean to."

"I can be by your side in a flash. Even if the guys can't get me up those steps, I figure out a way."

"You are the most important thing in my life."

"Ditto."

I tugged the fleece blanket from the back of the sofa and snuggled underneath it. "Tell me about your day."

"It was a very exciting day."

I adored how Hart and I read each other, being patient and taking cues as to what the other needed at the time. He wanted answers and deserved them but trusted me enough to wait until I could tell him everything. I closed my eyes and pictured him by my side.

His soothing rasp washed over me. "Mrs. Swenson . . ."

"The lady who always flirts with you?"

"Yes, the ninety-eight-year-old lady who always flirts with me. She tried to set me up with her daughter."

"Is she hot?"

"She's sixty-five." He paused while I laughed. "Although, she is pretty hot."

"Hart!"

I fell asleep to the sound of Hart's voice swirling in my ear and calming each frayed nerve.

The next thing I knew the sun was beaming through the double French doors warming my face. Sitting up, I shook the sleep from my head and walked to the kitchen for my morning brew. Waiting for the Keurig to finish I stared out the window, piecing together the events of yesterday. It was almost unbelievable to me that for the second time in a little more than two years my life drastically changed in just a matter of hours. This was another defining moment. Just as my marriage ending and reconnecting with Hart pushed me toward being the person I always wanted to be, when I walked out of my house today, it was time to show everyone the person I'd become.

chapter
Twenty-Eight

With my fingers curled around the handle of the storm door, I stared straight ahead. My body jerked at the sound of the red front door opening. The second he saw me, Hart's eyes lit up and his dimples popped with a sexy grin.

Between the eyes, the dimples, the grin, the worn jeans, and the way his long-sleeve black T-shirt stretched across his well-defined chest, Hart took my breath away. Everything I ever wanted and needed was right in front of me. And I was scared to death that in a matter of minutes I was going to lose it all for the second time in my life.

"Hey, Lovely."

"Hey." I sighed.

"Why didn't you use your key?"

My gaze dropped as I prepared to lie to Hart for the first time. "I forgot it at home. I need to put it on my keychain."

The truth was, in addition to stalling, I took a spec of comfort in the dimly lit porch that hid my misty eyes and crinkled brow.

He held up a stuffed trash bag. "Good thing I was taking the trash out and found you."

"I would have knocked eventually." A faint humorless laugh escaped me.

Sucking on his bottom lip, his gaze traveled the length of my body. "Are you going to come in or do I need to come out?"

I wanted to answer none of the above. The minute I went in or he came out meant I had to tell him about Will, putting me one step closer to possibly hearing Hart say goodbye. My trembling hand tightened around the bag of crab cakes with remoulade sauce I'd brought from work for our dinner. I'd come straight from Good Eats so I still had on my work clothes underneath the black-and-gray checkered wool coat.

"Get your sweet little ass in this house. You're shivering."

No matter how hard I willed them to move, my black Keds wouldn't budge.

Will had texted me a few times today checking to see if I'd talked with Hart yet. I understood his anxiousness. Will didn't have a lot of time to waste waiting. He'd gotten all the legalities done. Now he just wanted the comfort of knowing he'd be well taken care of by someone who knew him and not a bunch of strangers. And here I was stalling.

"God dammit, Bryson, if you don't get inside right now, I'm going to throw you over my shoulder and drag you in. Don't let the chair fool you." Dropping the trash bag, he thrusted his chair forward.

Loosening my grip around the brushed metal handle, my hand shot up to stop him. Hart blocked the storm door before it swung back and hit me.

"Alright! I'm coming." I stepped inside and reached for the bag of trash beside the door. "I'll take this out."

He clamped his fingers around my wrist and tugged. "Fuck the trash."

Holding my gaze, Hart cupped both of his hands around my icy one. Bringing it to his lips, he blew warming breath over my hand until the iciness melted. His eyes never left mine as he led me to the sofa. Sliding the purse from my shoulder and taking the bag of food, he placed both on the coffee table. He leaned forward, unbuttoned my coat, and slipped it over my shoulders. Next came my chef's jacket, leaving me in the black pants and long-sleeve white Henley. He placed my jackets on the sofa and snatched the soft blanket draped over the back.

Glancing down, indicating his lap, he said, "Sit."

Without protest, I crawled into his lap and nuzzled my cold nose in the crook of his neck. Hart wrapped the warm blanket and his arms securely around my body. We moved over to the fireplace where Butter was cozied up in her bed asleep, never acknowledging our presence. Hart's hand moved up and down my shoulder at a steady rhythm as the flames danced in front of us. I've never been able to explain this unspoken language Hart and I have. With just one look he always knew what I needed even if he didn't know why I needed it.

Placing a soft kiss on my forehead, he whispered, "I missed you last night."

I snuggled closer into his chest. "You have no idea how much I missed you. I'm sorry, yesterday was just draining in every way."

"I'm all ears when you're ready to talk."

We stayed like this for a long time. Hart had been so patient and understanding. I couldn't keep him in the dark any longer. Now was the time to tell him everything that happened and what Will was asking of me.

I raised my head and looked into his concerned eyes. My gaze drifted down to his mouth. Needing one last kiss before all hell broke loose, I leaned in and pressed my lips firmly against his. His mouth opened automatically, giving me unobstructed access. Hart's fingertips came up to my face, brushing my hair back. I intensified the kiss, going as deep as he would allow. A low moan vibrated from Hart just before he pulled away.

Gasping for air, he said, "Talk to me. What went on yesterday?"

I ran my teeth over my numb bottom lip, trying to get the feeling back. As he attempted to steady his breathing, Hart's gaze stayed glued to my mouth. Shaking his head, he tore his eyes from the distraction.

Hart's face twisted into annoyance. "Bryson, I'm a patient man but . . ."

When I finally delivered the news, I employed the ripping off the Band-Aid approach by blurting out the words without forethought. "Will has AIDS."

I waited for the information to sink in before adding to it. Hart's body went rigid as his eyes hardened. The grinding of teeth caused a twitch to develop in his chiseled jaw. His downward glance revealed strained neck muscles with one very large throbbing vein. The only time I'd seen Hart angry was the night of Ronnie's bachelor party when Doug kept hitting on me. But this was different. It was quiet, controlled, and scary as hell. Fury radiated from every pore of his body.

"Are you okay?" The words barely made it through his clenched teeth. His tone was low and menacing.

"Yes. I tested negative and the doctor said there was zero chance you were exposed."

Being in the healthcare field, Hart was up-to-date on the protocol and risk factors of bodily fluid transmitted diseases.

Hart's gaze shifted to something over my shoulder. "How long has the motherfucker known?"

My number one goal was to get the information out as quickly as I could in order to calm Hart down before he exploded.

"In January Will thought he just had the flu. Instead of going to the doctor he decided to ride it out, thinking he'd get better. But he never got back to a hundred percent. Over time he began losing weight, got a persistent cough, and had stomach issues. He blamed it on stress or thought maybe he'd picked up another bug. When it didn't improve or go away he got worried. Then he noticed a dark purple spot on his chest. By the time he got an appointment with the doctor another spot showed up on his neck. It was July by the time he got the diagnosis."

Hart's glare turned on me. "It's the end of October and he's known since fucking July? What if you'd been infected?"

"But I'm not."

"But what if you had been?!" The force of his roar caused my head to slightly tilt back. "This lowlife motherfucker was already showing symptoms. And he let you walk around for three goddam months unaware while he licked his fucking wounds."

Raking both hands over his face and through his hair, Hart laced his fingers together, resting them on top of his head. The biceps in each arm vibrated with rage.

"Will didn't excuse his actions except to say when he got the diagnosis he flipped out. And it took him some time to get his head back on straight."

"When did he start fucking around on you?"

"It doesn't matter. All that matters is that you were never in danger and I'm not infected. We're going to be okay." No longer able to hold back, I let the tears trickle down my eyes. "Please tell me we're going to be okay."

"When. Did. He. Start. Fucking. Around. On. You?" The words seeped through his teeth.

"Toward the end of the marriage. After he recovered from his breakdown, he realized we'd been together one time after he'd been with someone else." I paused for several minutes and waited.

"So he stuck his dick in you knowing full well it had already been in some rancid whore." A tight sneer appeared across his face as he let his arms drop to the side. "Get up."

I hesitated, not wanting to lose our physical connection. But I knew he needed time to process everything. I owed him that time. Reluctantly, I lifted myself off of Hart's lap, hugging my body with the blanket. Making one sharp pivot, he headed down the hallway without saying another word or giving me a second glance. The resounding slam of the bedroom door sent a photo crashing to the ground and Butter seeking refuge in the corner behind a chair.

I was frozen in place. A thousand different scenarios played out in my head before I came over here. But nothing compared to the murderous look in Hart's eyes that I just witnessed.

Patience had never been one of my virtues but I desperately needed to practice it in this situation. Hart wanted to know yesterday what was going on and he waited until I was ready. I had to do the same for him. I unglued my feet from the spot I'd been standing in and walked over to the sofa. As I sat down, Butter poked her head around the back of the chair. Seeing that the coast was clear, she slinked over and hopped up beside me. Laying my hand on her head, I mindlessly stroked her yellow fur and waited.

Suddenly, Butter and I started at the loud crash that blasted from behind Hart's bedroom door. It was quickly followed by a string of curse words and then dead silence. I jumped up as Butter took her place behind the chair. I couldn't stand the wait any longer. I had to make sure Hart was okay. I stepped toward the hallway when the door to his bedroom swung open and Hart rolled out. Standing at either end of the hall, our eyes locked. His expression was blank. My heart sank with the distinct feeling that this was the end.

I didn't move as Hart rolled toward me.

"I'm so sorry." I choked back a sob. "I never meant to drag you into all of this. I love you more than I ever thought possible . . ."

Although there was still a lot of anger brewing in his eyes, they had softened a little. Hart rolled in my direction until he was only two feet away.

"Sit down."

I turned away and started back toward the sofa. Hart grabbed my wrist, tugging me toward him.

"Not in there. Right here," he said, glancing down at his lap.

"I'll understand if you never want to see me again. All I want is for you to be happy and if that means walking away, I'll do it. I'll do anything for you."

He gave my arm another tug. "Bryson, sit down."

Timidly, I lowered myself onto his lap.

When we were face to face, I whispered, "Hart, I don't want to hurt you."

"Then don't ever leave me."

A rush of air and sobs left my body. "I meant what I said, if this is too much, just say the word. I love you too much to put you through this."

Cupping the sides of my face, Hart brushed his thumbs over my cheeks wiping away every last tear.

He brought our foreheads together and said, "Lovely, I'm here. Period."

I threw my arms around his neck and glued myself to his chest as my body convulsed with sobs. Hart's arms encircled my waist and held tight, pressing me into his body.

"Did you really think this would end us?" He whispered into my hair.

"It's hard enough dealing with a soon-to-be ex-husband. I didn't think you'd want the additional headache of him being sick."

"You're worth all the headaches in the world to me."

I wanted to leave the conversation right there with the rest of the night devoted to dinner followed by snuggling up to the man I loved. But I had to tell Hart about Will's request. Neither Will nor I had the luxury of time. I breathed in as much oxygen as my lungs would hold and slowly let it drift out of my body.

"There's more," I said sheepishly, lifting my head to look at Hart.

"You're killing me tonight, Bryson."

Hesitating, I furrowed my brows as I chewed on my bottom lip before dropping the bomb. "All of Will's family and friends have turned their backs on him." I paused. "He's terrified of dying alone. He asked me if I would consider letting him move back into the house."

It was slight but the big vein in Hart's neck throbbed again. "Get up, please."

I stood. "Are you going to scare the hell out of Butter and destroy something else in your bedroom?"

Gripping the wheels, Hart rolled his chair back and forth behind the sofa as if he were pacing. Even under his sleeve I could see his muscles flexing with each push as he worked to keep his composure.

"Hart . . ."

He stopped and raised his index finger, indicating he needed more time. He paced for a few more minutes. His expression remained stoic. Finally he stopped and our gaze locked.

"What does *move back in* mean exactly?"

"He's left everything to me in his will—the house, the cars, the money. There's enough for me to live on for a long time and go to culinary school. This is one of the reasons why he hasn't signed the divorce papers. If I'm still legally his wife then no one can contest the will."

"So he's bribing you to take care of him."

"I think it's his way of trying to make amends."

"And the other reasons?"

"I'll be able to make medical decisions if he becomes unable to . . . and he's terrified of dying alone."

"What did you tell him?"

"That I needed to discuss everything with you first. And if you had any problem with the arrangement whatsoever we'd need a Plan B."

"So, he knows about us?"

I nodded.

"You still have feelings for him."

It was a statement not a question, and it ripped me apart.

"No! Why would you even think that?"

"Because I can see it in your eyes. After everything he's done, you're actually considering letting him move back in and taking care of him."

"It always struck me as odd that on my wedding day, I was more nervous than excited. There was something off. At that time it was too late so I ignored it. I blame Will for a lot, all the lies, the cheating, and generally being a giant asshole. I hate that he took ten years of my life. That he thought so little of me and our marriage. But I can't blame him for everything. I had a secret too. Will never had all of my heart. You did. You do. And will always. He's broken. Call it what you want, guilt, sympathy, or some fucked-up version of loyalty. All I know is I don't want to be . . . I can't be that person who hates so much that I turn my back on someone who, for better or worse, was a significant part of my life. I just don't think he should have to die alone as punishment."

Hart moved over to me. Clutching my hips, he pulled me in closer and nuzzled into my chest. Threading my fingers through his hair, I rested my cheek against the top of his head. We stayed in this position for several minutes before he shifted and looked up at me.

Adoring blue-gray eyes locked with mine. "How do you do that?"

The back of my hand ran down the side of his face. "Do what?"

"Constantly take my breath away."

The next day Hart and I got with Will to iron out details of our arrangement and also for the two men to officially meet. Initially, Will wasn't comfortable with Hart being involved but I told him that was the only way this was going to work. Since there wasn't much of a choice, Will accepted. At times the mood was suffocating. It was as if awkwardness, tension, and anger had a three-way that produced a resentful hate child.

Even though we were still legally married and Will had documented his final wishes, there was still a chance, slim as it may have been, that his parents could contest the will if they knew our reconciliation was for show. Somewhat ironic being that they pushed him into a pretend courtship and marriage. So it was important for me and Hart to keep our relationship quiet.

All of the couples Will and I hung out with prior to the separation chose sides post-separation. And no big surprise they all chose Will. Even though they had all abandoned him once he was diagnosed, if one of them happened to find out we were together for technicality purposes only and mentioned it to Will's parents, things could get ugly. Sophie and Colin were the only two people outside of me, Will, and Hart who knew the reconciliation was just a cover.

Hart didn't like or trust Will, so it was important to him to be there when Will moved his stuff back in. The day was set to take place on the Saturday, two weeks before Thanksgiving. Since it was smack dab in the middle of the busy season at work and I needed the day off, I told Nancy about Will . . . kind of. Keeping it short and sweet, I simply said he was an old friend who was very sick and needed my help.

Other than two suitcases and the black bag he used to carry his laptop, Will didn't have anything else to move in. But by the look of all the help that showed up at my doorstep that morning you wouldn't know that. Besides my protective boyfriend, Colin was there to support Hart and help him up my front steps. Sophie came to hold my hand and make sure everyone played nice. The only problem was she didn't include herself in everyone.

I was coming down the stairs with a clean set of sheets for the guest room when I heard voices coming from downstairs. Facing in my direction, Will stood in the entryway with his two suitcases on the floor beside him. He'd just arrived and was being given the royal treatment by the Hart and Sophie welcoming committee.

Sweeping her hand to her hip in dramatic fashion, Sophie said, "I still can't believe she's letting your slimy bastard ass back in here. I hope you realize how fucking lucky you are."

Will cleared his throat while rubbing the back of his neck. "Bryson always had an incredible heart."

"Goddam right she has. Listen, I'm sorry you're sick. But if you fuck with her in any way, shape, or form I will slowly slice off your dick and balls and shove them up your ass. Then I'll bring my dick-sniffing Rottweiler over here to crawl up your ass and retrieve said dick and balls."

Will stood motionless and silent.

Hart twisted his head from Will to Sophie then back to Will. "What she said, times ten."

Slapping my hand over my mouth, I stifled a laugh. I headed down the stairs, clearing my throat loudly to alert them. Two innocent and one stunned pair of eyes met me as I approached them. As I landed beside Hart, his arm immediately snaked around my waist, his hand resting on my hip.

Giving Will a weak smile, I said, "Hey."

"Hey." He looked at where Hart's hand landed before glancing down at his suitcases. "Well, this is it. I travel pretty light these days."

Sophie leaned toward Will. "You'll be traveling even lighter if you fuck up."

My head whipped in her direction. "Sophie!"

"What?! He knows what I'm talking about." Raising two fingers, she pointed them from her big violet eyes to Will's dark brown ones then walked toward the kitchen.

"Remind me never to get on Sophie's bad side," Hart muttered.

A moment of awkward silence as Hart gripped my hip and glared at Will.

"So, you can put your things in the guest room." I held up the sheets. "These are yours. I'll just put them in your room."

I glanced down at Hart letting him know I was fine before stepping out of his hold. I headed down the hall to the guest room with Will following close behind.

Once inside the room and out of earshot of Hart, Will asked, "Does your boyfriend always have to ball up his fist every time he glares at me?"

Will opened the two suitcases on the bed and unpacked.

Placing the folded sheets on top of the dresser, I replied, "My boyfriend can do whatever he needs to do in order to make this situation bearable for himself."

He stopped unpacking and faced me. "I hear ya. Loud and clear."

"Let me know if you need anything or can't find anything."

"Bryson, I know it's been a while but I did use to live here." He smirked.

"Yeah . . . well . . . I gotta go start dinner. Hart, Colin, and Sophie are staying. You're more than welcome to join us."

"Thanks. I'll consult my dick and balls to see if they feel safe enough to venture out of the room."

A soft chuckle escaped me. "They're just watching out for me."

He nodded in acknowledgment.

I made it to the door before the sound of Will's voice stopped me. "Bryson?"

Standing in the doorway, I faced him. "Yeah?"

"I'm glad you have people like them in your life."

Smiling, I said, "Me too."

I made dinner while Hart, Colin, and Sophie watched a football game. As usual Sophie offered to help and as usual I said no. She didn't push, knowing that being in the kitchen gave me solace. I made an easy roasted chicken and dressing casserole, serving it alongside cranberry relish.

I couldn't tell if being around Hart made Will mad, sad, or embarrassed. Eventually he came out of his room and joined us for dinner. As I dished out the chicken casserole, it crossed my mind how surreal this felt having dinner with my boyfriend and my soon-to-be ex-husband. A knot formed in my stomach the second after the thought flashed across my brain. I'd been referring to Will as my soon-to-be ex while I waited for him to sign the divorce papers. But now with our arrangement he'd become my ex once he was dead.

After dinner, Sophie volunteered herself and Colin for cleanup duty, much to his disappointment. She was one-of-a-kind awesome, willing to cut a dick or scrub a pot all in the name of friendship. Looking exhausted, Will went to his room while Hart and I snuck off to the home office for some alone time.

Hart parked himself beside the overstuffed burgundy leather chair I was curled up in. He sandwiched my hand between both of his. We spent the first few seconds nose to nose just looking at each other. I loved every minute with Hart but some of my favorites were the silent ones when we communicated only through sensations. During these moments our souls connected.

"Stay with me tonight," I whispered against his lips.

"You know I can't."

I was still amazed that there were times when I forgot Hart was in a wheelchair. Months ago one of my big goals was to stay in this house but now I couldn't wait to get out of it and into a place where Hart could come and go freely.

Lifting my hand to his lips, he nibbled on my first finger. "You could come to my place." As he nibbled on my second finger, he gently sucked on the tip, causing goose bumps to ripple over my skin. "Butter would love to have you spend the night." He brushed his lips over my third and fourth fingers.

"I have missed Butter."

"Then it's settled." He leaned in, continuing the nibble fest along my jaw.

My eyes closed as I tilted my head to the side, giving Hart total access to my neck. "Thank you for being in my life." I sighed.

The more his lips traveled over my body the more I wanted to feel his bare skin against mine. Just as I was on the verge of getting completely lost in Hart the clearing of a throat ricocheted off the walls. I looked up to find Will standing at the edge of the room. Not acknowledging our visitor, Hart lowered his forehead on my shoulder.

"Sorry, I didn't mean to interrupt," Will said.

"Can I help you with something?" My voice was husky from the mini make out session.

"I was trying to connect to the internet but you must have changed the password."

My insides cringed remembering how betrayed I felt by Will's online activities.

"The password is butterlover, no space and no caps."

Hart knowingly squeezed my knee.

"Thanks." Will stared at me and Hart for a second longer before turning to leave.

"Oh, Will."

He turned to face me. "Yeah?"

"I'm going to spend the night at Hart's."

"Do you think that's a good idea?"

Hart lifted his head and glared at Will. "It's the best fucking idea anyone has come up with all day."

"I'm not trying to cause trouble. Really, I'm not. It's just that, it's my first night here. It might be better for us to establish a routine in case anyone is watching. After that we can find wiggle room for other things."

"Will, don't you think you're being a bit paranoid and overdramatic?"

"Bryson, my parents were beyond pissed when they found out I'd withdrawn all the money from my 401K. I wouldn't put much past them. Look, I'm not saying this is permanent. I'll be dead soon." He was trying to break the tension but failed miserably.

Hart leaned closer to me. "It's okay."

"No it's not. I don't want you to leave."

"I'm not leaving. I'm just going to my place."

Even though my confidence had been rebuilt on a firm foundation I still had moments of doubts. Hart read me like a book and knew the exact words to say to put me at ease. After Will went back to his room, I said goodbye to Hart, Colin, and Sophie. As I headed upstairs to my bedroom I thought about Hart and Will's day-long pissing contest and wondered if this arrangement would do more harm than good.

chapter
Twenty-Nine

Living with someone after being on your own for months was an adjustment. When that someone was your ex/pretend husband there was just no adjusting to that situation. The first week I found myself forgetting Will was in the house at times. At first I thought I was having some sort of mental hiccup due to stress. I mean, how do you block out another human being living under the same roof? I chalked it up to my brain being full. There's only so much the organ can hold before certain bits of information get lost in the shovel.

My forgetfulness resulted in me being startled twenty-three times week one. The police got involved during episode one. I woke up in the middle of the night to the sound of clinking coming from downstairs. I thought it was someone trying to break through a window. It turned out to be Will hitting the side of the mayo jar with a knife trying to get the last little bit out for his turkey sandwich.

I wasn't trying to avoid Will necessarily but I also wasn't going out of my way to spend time with him either. Even though I worked hard not to have any animosity toward him, at times I struggled. Hart supported me in my decision to let Will come back but he wasn't a fan of the situation which was another reason why I limited time with my new roommate. And with the holidays right around the corner most of my time was spent at Good Eats, so in a way it was all working out.

When Will and I did find ourselves in the same room, we didn't speak much. It always felt like so much needed to be said, that neither of us knew where to start. So we didn't, until we did.

Pinning my hair in a messy up-do, I groggily shuffled into the kitchen in search of my morning fuel.

"Good morning." Will was leaning back against the counter sipping his coffee, already dressed in worn jeans, a white T-shirt under a blue flannel long-sleeve shirt, and a pair of dark brown Rockports.

My insides startled a little at the sound of his voice.

I tied the sash around my robe and headed toward the cabinet to grab a mug. "Good morning."

"I already have one poured for you."

Glancing his way, I saw the ready-made cup of coffee beside him.

I lifted the black gold to my mouth and took a tentative sip. "How did you know I was coming down?"

"I was upstairs and heard you moving around in our . . . I mean, your bedroom. I've been up for hours . . . couldn't sleep."

"What were you doing upstairs?" The words came out harsher than I intended.

"I wanted to look in the second bedroom."

The second bedroom, a.k.a. what would have been the nursery. I'd finally emptied it out months ago. Packing up all the baby's things, I had it repainted to cover up the row of color samples that had lined one of the walls. It was wasted space, really. I never stepped inside and kept the door closed.

"You cleared it out." There was a hint of surprise in his voice.

"The furniture and the things our parents gave the baby are packed away in the attic. All the other stuff I donated."

An awkward silence fell between us. I took a long sip of coffee before going on guard.

"Listen, we discussed ground rules. One of them being space. You have yours and I have mine. There's really no reason for you to be upstairs."

It felt weird telling Will certain areas were off limits to him in his own house. After he moved out it was easy for me to make the transition from this is ours to this is mine. Now that he was back the line was murky. Technically this was still his house. He'd been paying the mortgage while I continued to live in it.

Raising one hand in surrender, he said, "True. I apologize. It was nothing more than a sleepless night and an active mind. I just wanted to see the room one last time."

Will seemed to get over losing the baby with ease a lot quicker than I did. I may have been overly suspicious of his motives. It just seemed odd after all this time for him to act like a heartbroken father. I searched his eyes trying to detect whether or not he was playing the pity card but all I saw was sadness and sincerity.

Another round of awkward silence settled in the air.

I walked to the breakfast bar and chose a peaches and cream muffin from the basket. Nancy encouraged me to practice my baking skills. She had become a great mentor, taking me under her wing and teaching me all aspects of the catering business. Good Eats catered a lot of corporate breakfasts and Nancy was always looking for something to add to that menu. I'd been testing this recipe for a couple of weeks, trying to come up with just the right consistency.

There was a slight tremble in my fingers as I peeled back the paper and tore the muffin in half.

"Bryson, if this is going to be a problem then I'll leave. I don't want you to feel uncomfortable and on guard all the time."

I placed the crumbling muffin on a napkin. "It's just weird having you here like this. We've barely spoken in months and now we're living under the same roof."

"It's not like we haven't done that before," he said, giving me a weak smile.

"It's different now. I'm different now." I tried to keep my eyes focused on him, so he could see my confidence. It lasted for about a second and a half before my gaze fell to the floor.

The room filled with the sound of footsteps coming toward me. Will put his index finger underneath my chin and tilted my gaze up to meet his.

"So am I." His gaze traveled down to my lips.

Turning my head, I pulled my chin away. "Will, don't touch me like that."

He dropped his hand and took a step back. "Sorry, I didn't mean anything by it." Regret filled his eyes. "I wish I would have been the man you deserved."

"Did you ever want to be?"

"I don't think I could be." Pausing for a moment, he collected his thoughts. "I know you won't believe me but I did care for you, Bryson. I still do. The type of person I was . . . am had nothing to do with you." He paused. "I've always idolized my dad. I tried to be the perfect son. The son he deserved. He wanted all A's in school, I got all A's. He wanted me to play football, I played football. He wanted me to take over the company, I was going to take over the company. He wanted me to marry a good girl, I married a good girl. But I was never the perfect son. Alex had his problems but at least he was brave enough to be himself." Pause. "The online stuff was an escape that got out of hand. Men think with their dicks. But it's the lack of character in the man that allows himself to be led by it." He looked at me with watery eyes. "I'm sorry I ever made you feel like you weren't enough because you were. I just wasn't."

Will had never told me he was sorry for his role in our marriage ending. He justified his actions, watering them down and blaming me for overreacting. I hated that it took an illness for him to realize how much he'd hurt me. But I was grateful that he'd found the strength and the perfect words to apologize.

I reached out and took his hand. Giving it a slight squeeze, I whispered, "Thank you."

It made me sad that both Will and I had gotten caught up in the current of our lives. In a sense we'd both been pretending all those years, neither one of us having enough courage to step out of the path we were headed down. Looking back I realized there were several different versions of Will. The version his friends liked. The version his parents wanted. And the version I pretended existed. He was like an actor in his own life. Playing to his audience, giving each what they wanted. But it wasn't real. This disease not only forced him to reflect on his life, it also freed him from the illusion he'd been trying to live.

I tugged on the handle of the storm door but it was locked. Just as I was about to press the doorbell the front door opened revealing everything I ever wanted in life.

Hart flipped the lock on the storm door and pushed it open. "Hey."

"Hey." I sighed.

"What are you doing here? I thought it was girl's night."

Since mine and Hart's schedules were getting even busier, I ended up cutting girl's night with Sophie short. I made it through dinner but thoughts of my boyfriend got the better of me. I missed him and knew I'd never make it through a movie. Thank god Sophie understood and gave me a raincheck.

Winking, I said, "I'm girly enough."

His gaze roamed the length of me, causing multiple vibrations to invade my body. "You are the perfect amount."

"So, what's a girl gotta do to get invited inside?"

"Drop her panties at the door."

My cheeks flushed. "Hart!"

"Bryson! What do you expect? You show up on my front porch looking all sexy in your *wool* coat and little knit hat. Flirtin'."

I tilted my head to the side and gave him my best pouty look. "Are you going to let me in?"

"Are you going to drop your panties?"

God, he makes me happy and hot.

I rolled my eyes. "Not out here. It's like forty degrees. Let me in."

Hart shook his head. "Sorry, rules are rules. Drop 'em or no entry."

Darting my gaze from side-to-side, I made sure Miss Polly wasn't peeking out her window or any of the neighbors were walking by. I blew out a breath. It was a good thing I wore a dress tonight. Looking at Hart directly in the eye, I reached under my coat and slid the dark purple lace down and off.

Dangling the delicate material on the tip of my finger, I said, "Happy?"

Hart's gaze bounced from my face to my lacy drawers. "I will be once you come in here and sit on my face."

My knees caved in toward each other. I wasn't sure if I'd be able to make it inside. Hart had a way of rendering me completely immobile with just a few words. He reached up taking the other end of my panties between his fingers and guided me through the door.

Once inside I couldn't believe what I saw. The room was dark except for the flickering candles covering every flat surface. *Turn Me On* by Nora Jones flowed from the speakers.

"Ho-ow . . . how did you know?" I stammered.

We were still connected by the purple lace between us.

"Sophie ratted you out. She called me after y'all left the restaurant."

"What's all this for?"

Hart's blue gray gaze locked with mine. "Because I'm in love with you."

My chin quivered as my eyebrows squished together. Gulping several times, I tried to keep my sobs down.

A look of horror crossed Hart's face. "Don't cry."

Drawing in a ragged breath, I said, "I can't help it. You're beyond sweet."

"I can dick-it up if you want."

My hands flew to cover my mouth as sniffles, snot, and laughter came out of me.

"I need a tissue or something."

Hart raised the lacy material. "Here."

"Not my panties!"

"Oh . . . yeah." He shoved his hand deep into his front pocket and pulled out a handkerchief. "Use this."

I snatched the cloth from Hart's grip, wiped my tears and blew my nose. I was so overwhelmed with emotion I had no recollection of my clothes and Hart's shirt coming off. In only my matching bra I straddled Hart in his chair. With his hands gliding up my thigh and hips, his tongue explored every inch of my mouth.

He slowly pulled away from the kiss until it was broken.

Taking my hand, he placed it over his heart as he gazed at me intently. "Bryson, do you feel that?"

His heartbeat felt so powerful slamming against his chest it caused my hand to tingle.

"Yes," I whispered.

"Only you do that to me." Leaning in he placed a gentle kiss on my lips but didn't pull away. "And do you feel me between your legs?"

I swallowed hard. "Yes."

"Only you do *that* to me." He paused. "I love you. I only see you. And I'll never give you any reason to doubt me."

A steady stream of tears ran down my cheeks. I was completely speechless. There wasn't a word in the English language that would come close to expressing how much I loved and adored Hart. By the look on his face I knew he understood my reaction.

If going through days of pain, months of heartache and years of disappointment was what had to happen in order to have this incredible man in my life then it was worth every second.

"Bryson, what's the ETA on those mini quiches!" Nancy shouted across the noisy kitchen.

"About five more minutes!"

"Don't give me abouts, give me definits."

"Five minutes!"

The catering kitchen was the busiest I'd ever seen in one day. It was the week before Christmas and we had three big events scheduled for this evening, two holiday parties, and one wedding reception.

Who the hell gets married the week before Christmas?

Nancy was headed to Boone Hall Plantation in Mount Pleasant. Sam, the head chef, was scheduled to be at the Gaillard Auditorium in downtown Charleston, and I was in charge of the wedding reception at Hibernian Hall. This was by far the biggest event Nancy had ever put me in charge of. One hundred fifty guests had been invited to this wedding. Add in the equal amount of plus-ones and a handful of tag-ons, and we're talking three hundred twenty five mouths to feed.

The timer on my phone dinged letting me know Nancy's quiches were ready. I weaved my way through the bustling kitchen to the oven. The delivery van was all loaded up and parked out behind the building. As quickly as possible, I boxed up the tiny appetizers and took them outside. The cold air hitting my face was a welcome relief. The kitchen had to be more than a hundred degrees from the ovens alone. Between that and the human body factor, it felt like the tropics. After loading the boxes into the van, I popped the side of the vehicle, letting Chris, the driver, know he was good to go.

Glancing at my watch, I saw that I had a little breathing room. My crew didn't have to head out to the Hibernian for another couple of hours, allowing me a minute and a half to cool down before going back into the sweltering building. Taking off my white Good Eats cap, I pulled the band out of my messy ponytail and redid it. Just as I was putting the cap back on my phone went off with a text. Usually, when I was working I didn't check my messages until lunch or I was at an event since Nancy preferred to communicate via text.

I shoved my hand in my pants pocket, pulled out the phone and did a quick check. Nancy was the only name not listed in the series of texts. The first one made me smile.

Hart: *Good luck today with the reception. Your sweet little ass is gonna kick ass.*

I couldn't help but send him a quick response.

Me: *Had a minute to check texts. Yours brightened my day. Thank you. I love you. Call you when I'm done.*

Hart: *Love you.*

I planned on leaving the other texts until later but curiosity got the better of me. I quickly scrolled down the screen.

Will, 10:45 a.m.: *Not feeling well. Gonna try to see the doc.*

Will, 11:30 a.m.: *Can't stop coughing. Weak. Dr. R can see me in an hour. Not sure if I can drive.*

Will, 12:15 p.m.: *Coughing up blood. Meeting Dr. R at Saint Francis ER.*

I clicked on Will's number. The phone rang once and then went straight to voicemail. I didn't bother leaving a message. I wasn't sure what to do. I'd noticed over the past week or so, he stayed at home in his room more. Since it was cold and flu season, I assumed he didn't want to expose himself to a lot of people. I talked with him last night and he seemed fine. This morning he slept in so I didn't see him before leaving for work.

Checking the time, the last text was sent twenty minutes ago. However Will was getting to the hospital, it would take him at least twenty minutes from our house. My chest tightened. There was no mention that Will wanted me to meet him at the hospital. Nancy was counting on me. She was high-strung and stayed in a constant state of stress on a slow day. If I told her I needed to bail due to an emergency her head would probably explode. I could make a quick call to the hospital and have one of the nurses get a message to him that I'd be there right after the reception tonight. I thought about calling to see if Sophie was available but then remembered she was out of town. Besides, the arrangement between Will and I was just that, *between Will and I*. It was not my family's or friend's responsibility to pick up my slack.

The hospital was just around the corner, less than five minutes away. Everything was lined up and on schedule for the reception. I could run over, check on Will, and be back in plenty of time to leave for the hall. Heading back inside, I searched for Tommy, my second in command. He'd joined the Good Eats crew the same week I did. Over the past months we'd developed a great chemistry working with each other. Usually he was calm, collected, and confident. When I told him I had to run out for a while his face turned whiter than our chef's jackets. After he recovered from hyperventilating, I left him in charge and headed to the hospital.

Pulling into the hospital, I headed around to the side of the building where the ER entrance was located. Just as I was about to step up on the sidewalk the back doors to an ambulance flew open. I stopped as the EMTs rolled the stretcher out from the back. I tried not to be a rubbernecker and look. I mean, if I were in that situation I wouldn't want to be gawked at. When I glanced away, I heard a familiar cough. I looked over to see a pale Will sitting up slightly under a white blanket with an oxygen mask covering his nose and mouth. The tall, dark, and handsome football hero was gone, replaced by a fragile and scared young man.

The two EMTs briskly pushed the stretcher toward the entrance.

I ran to the stretcher. "Will, are you okay?!"

He looked at me with glassy eyes and my heart broke.

"Ma'am, you need to step to the side." The woman ordered.

Will's body violently jolted forward as a congested cough echoed inside the oxygen mask.

"Is he going to be okay?"

Not slowing down, the male EMT said, "Ma'am, please! Let us do our job."

I followed behind them into the crowded waiting area. Without stopping they rolled Will down the hall, around the corner, and out of sight.

I walked to the check-in desk. "Hi, is Dr. Rudolph here?"

The nurse clicked a couple of things on the screen. "He's with a patient who was just brought in."

"I need to talk with him about that patient."

Her eyes lifted to me as if I were crazy. "And who might you be?"

"I know the patient."

"Are you a close relative?"

I hesitated for a moment, not quite sure how to answer her question. This right here was what the arrangement was all about.

"I'm his wi . . . wife."

The nurses clicked around on her computer for what felt like hours.

"Bryson." The deep baritone of Dr. Rudolph's voice hit my ears.

I turned to his caring expression. "Is Will okay?"

"Let's go where we can talk."

Dr. Rudolph led me down a narrow hallway. We passed several closed doors with signs that read Consult Room. He opened the door to room five, stepping aside to let me in first.

"Have a seat, Bryson." He motioned toward the pair of chairs.

As he took the seat across from me, I glanced at the clock over his head. I had ten minutes to listen to what he had to tell me and check on Will before I had to bolt out of here.

A warm smile appeared across Dr. Rudolph's face. "Will explained your arrangement."

I tried to keep my shocked expression to a minimum. I knew Will had been a patient of Dr. Rudolph's for a while and they had formed a close friendship. I didn't realize how close until now. The first time I'd met the doctor, Will introduced me as Bryson. I wasn't sure at the time he even knew we were married.

"I have to commend you for what you've agreed to do, Bryson. Not many people would be so generous."

"Is Will going to be okay? He didn't appear sick yesterday."

"I don't know how much you know about the disease."

"I've done some research since I found out about Will but I haven't had a lot of time . . . Oh, I did watch that Tom Hanks movie."

I suddenly felt like a heartless idiot, not making the time to find out everything about the disease.

"There have been a lot of strides in the treatment of HIV and AIDS. People are living better and longer. Many lead productive and active lives."

Insert but *here.*

"I've been specializing in this field since the late 1980s. I've seen just about everything there is to see related to the disease."

I snuck another glance at the clock. Eight minutes and counting.

"Has Will explained everything about his situation to you?"

"Obviously, I can tell he's lost weight. I know about the spots on his neck and he told me he had a few spots on his lung."

"In all my years of working with HIV and AIDS, I've never seen a case like Will's. The disease has taken over his body like wildfire. A person in his condition has usually been living with AIDS for several years."

"I'm sorry but I'm not sure what you're trying to tell me."

"Will has pneumonia. His lungs are compromised due to the Kaposi sarcoma, which makes things even worse. I've admitted him. Hopefully he'll be able to go home in the next few days. Bryson, you need to prepare yourself before Will is released. The next two months aren't going to be easy for either one of you."

Two months? I forgot all about the clock on the wall.

I stared at Dr. Rudolph. This was the first time I'd heard an exact number attached to Will's life expectancy. He never spoke in specifics, always saying he had months to go. Months could be an indefinite number. The sound of the deep baritone snapped me into the present.

"Bryson, I'm going to give you some information to look over. It's not just about the disease and the patient but about the caregiver as well.

Since you're Will's only support you need to have a clear understanding of what you're in for."

My eyes misted over as I slowly nodded. "Can I see Will?"

"Sure. We have him on oxygen. He's pretty tired, so not too long of a visit, okay. While you're with him, I'll have the nurse gather that information and it will be waiting for you at the desk out front." He stood. "Bryson, remember Will's not the only one who'll need support."

"Okay." The one word came out in a daze.

Dr. Rudolph guided me to the large room like the one Will was in right after his accident. When the doctor drew back the dividing curtain what I saw shook me to my core. The man lying in the bed was a stranger. His dark brown hair and eyes were similar to Will's. His nose, cheeks, mouth, and jawline had only a hint of familiarity. Clear tubes connected him to the bags of fluid and medicine hanging above, as monitors beeped in steady rhythm.

Only a matter of hours separated the last time I'd seen him until this moment. I couldn't wrap my head around how his appearance had changed. Turning his head, his glassy gaze met mine briefly before drifting closed. My throat constricted as I tried to swallow the lump that had formed. Tension built between my eyes, as a piece of my heart completely shattered. Then it dawned on me that what had changed so drastically in Will's appearance was the vulnerability that poured out of his eyes. He was no longer the boy I'd dated, the man I'd married, or someone who betrayed me. He was now a fragile and scared twenty-eight-year-old who needed compassion and kindness.

I felt a hand on my shoulder just before Dr. Rudolph's voice filled my ears. "We sedated him so he could get some rest. Apparently he's had a lot of sleepless nights lately."

As I over to Will's bedside, his lids groggily opened halfway and looked up at me. I tried hard to keep my expression pleasant, wanting to give him hope that things weren't as bad as he might think. A faint smile ghosted over his pale lips as recognition filled his eyes.

"Hey," he whispered through the oxygen mask. His voice was so weak the word was barely audible.

"H . . . ey . . .," I stammered.

Raising his right hand slightly off the bed, Will motioned for me to lean in closer. I did.

"Reception."

It took me a second but then realized he was referring to my work.

"What about it?" I said.

"Get out of here and go to work."

I choked back a sob. He knew how important the reception was to me. The day Nancy assigned it to me, I was beside myself happy. After work I went home to change before going to Hart's. When Will asked me how my day went, I told him about the event and that it was my chance to really prove myself to Nancy. Looking in from the outside, no one would realize what a huge moment this was in mine and Will's history. It was the first time that he put my needs before his own.

I swallowed hard and said, "I'll be back as soon I can get away."

He shook his head. "Rest. I'll still be here in the morning."

Just then my phone buzzed. As I went to turn it off, I glanced down and saw a string of panicked texts from Tommy wanting to know where I was.

Placing my hand on top of his cold one, I gave Will a warm smile. "I'll be back soon, okay."

Will nodded and closed his eyes. Before leaving, I studied the lines and wrinkles of his face. The disease had accelerated the aging process, turning months into years. My phone buzzed again jarring me into action. I reluctantly backed away from Will's bedside, my eyes staying focused on him, until I had to turn and leave.

I hit the hallway running, making a quick stop at the nurse's desk to pick up the information Dr. Rudolph wanted me to read. As I sprinted out to my car, I called Tommy to let him know I was on my way. He picked up immediately.

Before he said the first word, I blurted out, "I'm on my way!" Gasping for air.

"Oh my god, Bryson! I'm about to have a heart attack! I've literary aged ten years. I'm so stressed out!"

Tommy could be a bit over dramatic.

"Calm down. I'm sorry. I'll be there in four minutes."

I ended the call, tossing my phone on the passenger's seat. Driving back to work, I took several deep breaths, attempted to clear my mind and focus on the task at hand. If today was any indication of what's to come I prayed that I'd be up for the challenge.

chapter Thirty

'Twas the night before Christmas and all through the house nothing was stirring, not a mouse, not me, nor even a spoon. Between work, visiting Will, and spending time with Hart, I was completely exhausted. From the moment I woke up my body was in constant motion. At night when I tried to go to sleep, my head would spin with everything I needed to do for the next day. I tried hard to stay present and focused on the task in front of me but half the time I didn't know which end was up. I was stretched in all direction, doing everything but not to the best of my abilities.

Nancy was so impressed with the job I'd done on the wedding reception she put me in charge of even larger events. The confidence she had in me was a huge ego boost. Too bad I was too tired to enjoy it. Since the hospital was right around the corner from work, I stopped in to see Will whenever I got a chance. I'd neglected my family and Sophie for the past month opting instead to grab what little free time I had with Hart. Recently my time with him had been relegated to phone calls and texts. He was understanding but it was wearing on him and me. Hart was my safe place, my strength, and the calming force in my life. I missed seeing him, kissing him, lying next to him. I missed us.

There weren't enough hours in the day, days in the week, or weeks in the month to make it all work. My stress level was off the charts. I was so overwhelmed with everything going on, my mind went blank when it came to figuring out how to divide up my holiday. I wanted to spend it with Hart but I couldn't take him to my parents since our relationship had to stay a secret. I ended up lying to Mom, Dad, and Ryan, telling them what I had with Hart turned out to be just a fling. It physically hurt me to say he and I had broken up. Soon after telling them, Will moved back in. Three sets of eyebrows raised when they found out.

In the blink of an eye, Christmas Eve had arrived.

The tradition in my family had always been to have a casual dinner Christmas Eve and attend midnight Mass. Desperately needing alone time with Hart, I bowed out of the tradition. I explained to Mom I thought I was coming down with a bug and needed to be completely rid of it before Will would be allowed to come home. She understood, telling me to go straight to bed. Instead, I went straight to Hart's.

With my purse in one hand and Hart's gift in the other, I ran toward his house. I couldn't get up the steps fast enough. The second my foot hit the porch the front door swung open. Butter came bounding out barking and wagging.

Taking my wrists, Hart tugged me just inside the door and into his lap. My purse and his gift fell to the floor as our lips got reacquainted. Butter barked her way inside as Hart rolled us backward farther into the house, pushing the door closed with a tap of his footrest. Once safely out of sight of the neighbors our hands had a free for all. Hart fumbled with the big buttons on my coat. Finally freeing all of them he shoved the heavy wool off my shoulders as I pulled my arms from the sleeves. His hands ran across my thighs, over my ass, and up my back, while mine alternated between his torso, arms, and hair. Finally, we both came up for air.

With our foreheads resting together, our chests pushed against each other as we gasped for a breath. Hart's hands continued traveling the same path over my body only this time slowly. My fingers stayed deep in his hair. I just wanted to feel him—his presence and love. We stayed in this position for several minutes. The only sounds in the room were our heavy breathing, Butter's distant panting, and the holiday music playing.

Suddenly, the smell of pork and candied sweet potatoes filled my senses.

"You cooked?" My brows knitted together, as I remembered Hart's last attempt at a meal.

"I haven't seen you in a week . . ."

"Eight and a half days."

"I haven't seen you, kissed you . . ." He nibbled my lips. ". . . Or touched you . . ." His hand grazed my inner thigh. ". . . In eight and a half days and that's the first thing out of your mouth?"

"Well, your tongue has been in there since I came through the door."

The tip of his tongue rolled over his bottom lip as his gaze bounced from my mouth to my eyes. That move. Got me. Every time. My hips wiggled in his lap. Hart ran his nose along mine, then to my cheek, my jaw, finally landing at the spot just below my ear. With my lips parted and my eyes half closed, I breathed in the clean spicy scent of Hart. I was primed and ready for us to continue our make-out session when I felt a cold snap where his lips had been. My nipples hardened at the vibration of Hart's chest as a deep chuckle rumbled out of him.

Opening my eyes, I said, "Dude, you left me hanging. That's not a very Christmassy thing to do."

His gaze pierced my eyes. "What I'm thinking about doing to you is not very Christmassy either."

My cheeks flushed with heat as I gave him a shy smile. "Really?"

With a raised eyebrow, he said, "Really. But first we eat." He gave my ass a playful pop. "Up, up."

I had offered to cook tonight but Hart refused. He seemed really excited to do this for me and I was very touched so I didn't argue. But as memories of his prior attempt at a meal flooded my mind I wished I had at least brought some backup food.

Taking my lower lip between my teeth, I reluctantly climbed off his lap and followed him into the kitchen. "So, *you* cooked."

"Sure did," he said, swinging around the corner toward the oven.

"Food?" I put as much sarcasm in the one word as possible.

"Being a smartass is not very Christmassy either."

Hart cracked open the oven door, checking whatever delicacy he had roasting. Lifting the lid off one of the pots on the stove, he stirred the mystery content a couple of times and popped the lid back on. He was very secretive and very cute. I stayed planted at the edge of the kitchen so as not to interfere with the master chef, but my curiosity was craning my neck wanting a sneak peek.

"Can I help with anything?" I offered.

He reached into the cabinet and came up with a wine glass. "Just sit down and look beautiful."

Pulling out one of the barstools, I sat at the counter that divided the kitchen from the main living room, and enjoyed the show. The sound of Tony Bennet singing "I'll Be Home for Christmas" filled the room.

"I have a gift for Miss Polly. Don't let me forget to take it next door," I said.

"You'll have to hold on to it until after the New Year. She's on a cruise with her family. An early Christmas gift from her daughter."

"Sweet."

Hart moved around the kitchen with such ease. He was in a pair of black jeans and matching sweater. The color brought out the darker tones of his dirty blond hair. Each time he reached for something the sweater stretched across his broad shoulders and toned back, causing tingles to pop up in all my hidden places.

I caught a flickering out the corner of my eye. When I turned to see what it was my breath was stolen. Right then I knew I didn't care if this meal tasted like dirt and rocks, I was going to eat every last morsel and pretend it was the best thing in the entire world. The table had been set for two with the works—beautiful white and silver china with crystal goblets, candlelight, and red roses.

With my jaw slack and my eyes wide, I looked at Hart as he grabbed a bottle of wine from the rack.

"Hart . . ."

He cocked an eyebrow. "Yes?"

"The roses, the candlelight . . . it's . . . you're incredible." My eyes misted.

Pouring the wine, he said, "You have very little faith in me as a romantic guy, don't you?"

"No. I have very little faith that I'm worth all of this attention."

He stopped pouring.

His gaze snapped up and zeroed in on me. "I thought we were past all that. You are worth everything to me. I don't want to hear you talk about yourself like that anymore."

Hart was always strong in his convictions. He didn't feed my insecurities like Will had, he starved them every chance he got. That was one of the many things I loved about him.

"Thank you for loving me."

Offering me the wine glass, he held my gaze. "It's my favorite part of life."

"Mine too." I grinned, taking the glass.

We stared at each other for a few seconds before Hart abruptly announced. "Barbaresco!"

Laughter flew out of me. "Excuse me?'

"The wine."

"My favorite!"

"I know all your favorites, baby." He winked.

"I've got one helluva boyfriend."

Focusing on the sexy man in front of me, I let the wine do its thing. This was the first time since Will came back into my life that I felt completely at ease and relaxed. I pushed the thought of him to the side before guilt settled in. I didn't stop by the hospital after work today. Will understood but I still felt horrible. I'd neglected Hart so much lately, I was determined not to let anything get in the way of our night together.

I took in a deep relaxing breath, inhaling the saltiness of the pork mixed with the sweetness of the potatoes. As the aromas swirled around me, something smelled familiar. I took another sip of wine and tried to place it. The sound of the kitchen timer going off caught my attention.

"Lovely, you mind getting the roast out of the oven?"

Setting my wine down, I hopped off the stool. "Finally, you're letting me help."

I slid my hands into oven mitts and pulled down the oven door. Heat and spices slapped me in the face. Peering in, I couldn't believe my eyes when I saw the beautiful crown roast. Tapping the oven door closed with my knee, I placed the roast on top of the marble countertop. Turning around, I accidentally knocked into Hart, causing the gravy in the gravy boat he was holding to splash all over his sweater.

"Oh god! Is it hot?! I'm so sorry!" I yelled, reaching for the gravy.

Hart placed the boat on the counter. "Bryson, its fine. Just a little spilled."

"Let me wet a paper towel and I'll wipe it off."

"It's no big deal. I got it."

Ignoring him, I ripped off a paper towel from the holder and ran it under warm water. I leaned forward and wiped the splattered gravy off of his sweater. The wine and his nearness had my head all fuzzy. And it didn't help that he was nibbling my earlobe as his hands roamed their way under my green knit dress, up my thigh and to my ass. I was so glad I'd worn the dress and black patent leather boots.

I giggled. "How can you expect me to work under these conditions?"

"Focus," he whispered, tickling my neck with his lips.

I wiped the last gravy spot off and playfully shoved him back. "Now, now. You went to all of this trouble to make a wonderful dinner and set a gorgeous table. We can't let it go to waste."

His head fell back as a low groan escaped him.

As I tossed the paper towel in the trash, I glanced down and discovered the main ingredient in Hart's dinner. Picking up the familiar container by my fingertips, I turned toward him and cleared my throat. When he saw what I was holding his brows rose and he shot me a pair of blue-gray innocents.

"Seriously, Hart? You had the dinner catered by the same company I work for?"

He flashed his megawatt smile. "Only the best for you, Lovely. It was Nancy's idea . . ."

Hart met Nancy when he picked me up one day for lunch and they hit it off immediately. Both knew a lot of the same people in town and Hart had been to many events catered by Good Eats. I never defined my relationship with Hart to Nancy. But by her knowing looks it was obvious she could tell we were more than just friends.

Hart continued. " . . . She told me to stick everything in the oven for a half hour to keep it warm and make the place smell good. I was gonna come clean but she said chicks love guys who can cook."

Standing next to him, I laced my fingers through his hair. "I already love you despite the fact that you are a horrible cook."

He grasped my hips and looked up. "I wanted to impress you."

"You do all the time."

Bringing my lips to his, my plan was to give him a soft sweet kiss and get back to our dinner. It didn't take long for the sweet kiss to turn hot. I guess that's what happens when you don't see the love of your life for eight days straight. Although, Hart and I could spend 24/7 together and I'd still want to devour him every chance I got. His firm tongue pushed its way into my mouth without apology as he squeezed my ass. God, I loved it when he acted like he couldn't get enough of me.

Hart tore his lips from mine and nuzzled into my chest, giving my nipple a quick bite through the material. I braced my wobbly knees against the side of his chair as my palms roamed over his biceps and shoulders.

Resting my cheek on the top of his head, my eyes closed and I got lost in the feel of him. "God, I've missed your lips."

"They've missed you," he mumbled against my body.

The bottom of my dress slid up my leg just as a kitchen timer blared, jolting me and Hart from the moment.

Clearing his throat, Hart said, "Dinner. We have dinner."

I stepped back, smoothing my dress down. "Yeah, dinner."

After we cooled down a bit, Hart and I worked perfectly together to get the food on the table. As I sat across from him, I couldn't believe how blessed I was to have been given a second chance at a life with him. And I would never take Hart or our time together for granted.

Taking my hand in his, Hart placed a kiss in the middle of my palm. "You are hands down the best gift I ever got."

My entire body flushed with heat. Gazing over at Hart, I felt the water rising in my eyes.

Giving my hand a squeeze, he said, "There's no crying at Christmas."

I tried to cover up my sniffling with a small laugh. "I just get overwhelmed with how much I love you sometimes."

"I know the feeling." He paused right before a sexy gin appeared. "You have no idea what you were up against. You just edged out the electric blue BMX bike I got on my tenth birthday."

"Wow, thanks. Well, my pale yellow Easy Bake Oven doesn't hold a candle to you."

"Merry Christmas, Bryson."

"Merry Christmas, Hart."

"Let's eat!" He announced.

Nancy was a true artist. Each bite of roast melted in my mouth. Pairing it with the Barbarsco made me want to cry tears of joy.

Hart lifted his glass, letting it hover in front of his mouth. "Did you see Will today?"

I stopped eating but kept my gaze down, not wanting him to see the guilt in my eyes. "No. Work was crazy and I needed to go home and get ready to come here. I texted him and he said he was feeling better. He might get to come home next week."

A funny feeling spread across my chest. Other than having a baby, there was no good time to be in the hospital. But there was something especially lonely about being in one during the holidays. People should be with those they love, not cooped up staring at sterile white walls.

A spurt of air hit my face snapping me out of my head. Hart finished blowing out the other candle.

"What are you doing?"

With his plate on his lap, he rolled away from the table. "Packing up the food."

My stomach twisted. The last thing I wanted to do was to ruin this night for us. We deserved time together.

I pushed away from the table and followed him into the kitchen. "Why? We're not done eating."

"We'll finish at the hospital." He tilted his chin toward the cabinet. "Paper plates are in there."

"Hart . . ."

He stopped what he was doing. "Bryson, no one should be alone on Christmas Eve."

I leaned over, took his face between my hands, and kissed him hard. His hands came up and buried deep in my hair.

"You're a good, good man, Hart Mitchell," I whispered against his lips.

"Was there ever any doubt?" He grinned.

"Not in my heart and soul."

Hart and I packed up the food and corked the wine, putting all of it in the rolling cooler along with paper plates, napkins, and silverware. I lifted the caramel cake, which was also from Nancy, and placed it in one of my grocery totes I'd left here. As I pulled on my coat, a thought occurred to me that could derail our spreading of joy and good food.

"What if the night nurse won't let us bring the cooler in? They can be pretty strict."

As Hart tugged his black knit cap down over his blond hair I chuckled to myself. In all black he looked like a sexy spy or a burglar.

"We'll be fine. The ladies know me." He winked.

"I bet they do. But as charming and sexy as you are, I don't think it will work in this situation. The night nurse on duty this week has been a guy."

"What's his name?"

"Chad."

Flashing me a lopsided grin, Hart said, "We'll be fine."

Since it was the holidays the hospital was quieter than normal with only a skeleton staff. Once the nurse's station was in sight Hart told me to hold back with the cooler while he took the tote. I found the perfect spot by the fake Christmas tree in the corner, allowing me to be close enough to hear the conversation without being noticed. Sweet as you please, Hart rolled right up to the desk with tote in lap.

"Merry Christmas, buddy." Hart smiled.

Dark-haired, portly Nurse Chad's seafoam green eyes lit up like twinkling stars.

Chad shifted his gaze from side to side, making sure no one was within earshot. "Well, look who the cat dragged in, Hottie McGee."

"How's it going, Chad?"

"Much better now," he said flirtatiously.

The Hart effect was in full swing.

"I'm here to see my friend Will Forsyth. Wanted to bring him some holiday cheer."

It might have been my imagination but it sounded like Hart choked a little on Will's name. The fact that Hart was doing this made me love him even more, which I didn't think was possible.

Craning his neck, Chad peered over the desk. "Whatcha packing?"

"A few snacks."

Fiddling with the top button of his shirt, Chad said, "Hmm . . . now Hart, you know the hospital frowns upon outside food or drink being brought in. Especially on this floor. There are some very sick people up here."

Hart lifted the cake out of the bag and placed it on the desk right under Chad's nose. "I'd sure like to share some of the holiday with you too, Chad."

Chad's cheeks glowed redder than Rudolph's nose. His gaze swung between the cake and Hart. Honestly, I couldn't tell which he wanted more.

"It is the holidays. And since the patient is doing better, I see no harm."

Hart reached for the cake. "You're the best, dude."

Gripping the other side of the cake plate, Chad said, "You can leave this here."

"No problem."

Hart tossed Chad a lazy grin as he rolled back away from the desk. Tilting his head to the side, he gave me the signal to join him. As I scooted past the nurse's station, a glaring pair of seafoam green eyes followed me.

"Hart, don't forget to come see me later for a little something sweet." Chad scrunched up his face in my direction.

Free and clear, Hart and I headed down the hall toward Will's room.

"That guy's a piece of work. He actually gave me the stink eye."

"You're adorable when you're jealous, Bryson. You have nothing to worry about. Chad's too much man for me."

"Ha-ha."

Once standing outside Will's room, I looked over at Hart. "You sure you want to do this? You don't have to."

"Yes I do. It's important to you so it's important to me. The fact that I think he's a fucking bastard is beside the point."

I kissed his lips before giving the door a light knock.

Will's muffled cough filtered through the cracked door. "Come in."

Poking my head in, I smiled and said, "Merry Christmas."

At first I couldn't tell if Will was shocked or confused. My guess was a little of both.

Will's voice had gotten a little stronger but was very hoarse and scratchy. "H-ey. What are you doing here?"

I pushed open the door revealing my cohort. "We're here to celebrate Christmas with you."

Will's gaze shifted to Hart, causing his expression to go slack.

"Merry Christmas, motherfucker," Hart said sarcastically.

The tension in the air was stifling as the two men locked in a staring contest. Time stood still and I stayed put, waiting to see if Hart and I were even staying. After a few moments, the edges of Will's mouth twitched until a full-blown laugh erupted. Blowing out a deep breath, my body felt weightless. It had been such a long time since I shared anything positive with Will.

With the tension lifted, Hart and I slipped into the room and set up the feast.

Pressing the button on the side of the bed, Will sat up and watched in astonishment. "What is all this?"

"Christmas Eve dinner," I explained, clearing off the hospital table to make room.

Like a well-oiled machine, Hart unpacked the cooler, handing off each item to me. I dished out the food while Hart poured a small amount of wine into the plastic hospital cups.

"I can't believe you're here," Will said with a slight shake in his voice.

I divvied out the silverware. "You can thank Hart. If it wasn't for him you wouldn't be about to sink your teeth into this deliciousness."

Will's head jerked in Hart's direction. "Really? How's that?"

"The dude at the desk has a hard-on for me." Hart blurted out.

More laughter filled the room. I won't ever stop being amazed by Hart. The way he was handling this situation was beyond anything I could have expected. Just the fact that he offered to come and spend time with my ex spoke volumes about the type of character he possessed and the depth of his love for me.

Raising his plastic cup, gazing at me, Hart toasted. "To love, life, and happiness."

Warmth started in my cheeks and spread the entire length of my body as I took a sip of wine.

"I'd like to add to that toast if you don't mind," Will said.

With my gaze on Hart, I searched for any signs that indicated he thought Will was stealing his thunder. Catching the subtle glint in his eyes, I knew he was fine. "Sure."

All three of us raised our cups once more.

Grateful dark brown eyes looked directly at me and Hart. "To friendship, generosity, and kindness."

"Cheers!" We said in union.

The dinner conversation was fairly benign—holiday memories, football, and basketball took up most of the talk. It was as if we'd all taken a silent vow not to delve into any explosive subjects. After the food was gone we were all too full to bother with dessert or dealing with Chad. The guys watched ESPN while I cleaned up. They made random comments here and there but for the most part were quiet.

Even though I was exhausted and craved alone time with Hart, I was in no rush to end the night. Our visit seemed to really help Will's spirits. It was no secret this would more than likely be the last holiday he would see so it needed to be a happy one. I curled up in the recliner draping an extra blanket over me. My eyelids drifted down as ESPN faded into the background. The next thing I knew the raspy deep voice of the man I loved swirled in my ears.

"Not a problem," Hart said.

"I mean it. Coming here tonight was very generous of both of you. I know Bryson's being pulled in all directions."

My eyes stayed closed and my ears open.

Hart cleared his throat. "She's a strong woman."

"Yeah, she is." Pause. "Bryson said you went to high school with us."

"Just senior year."

Cough. Cough. "Funny, I don't remember you."

"You were busy getting hit in the head with a football. Besides, we didn't exactly run in the same crowd."

"I know but Bryson and I did. All of our friends were the same for the most part. It's just odd she remembered you well enough to recognize you at the rehab after all these years."

Hart was silent for a long time. When he finally responded there was tension in his tone. "Look, Will. I'm sorry you're sick. No one should have to go through this disease. But you and I will never be friends. I tolerate you because you're in Bryson's life. I'm here for her. Period."

"Are you in love with her?" Will asked with a slight tremble in his voice.

"Yes."

"Then you better be good to her or I'll come back and go all poltergeist on your ass."

The sounds of Sports Center replaced the tense voice. Snuggling deeper into the chair, I faded back to dozing with a smile on my face, feeling loved and protected.

chapter Thirty-One

"Bryson!"

I bolted straight up in bed at the sound of Will's strained voice coming over the baby monitor.

Will was discharged three weeks ago on New Year's Day. With his immune system being so compromised the pneumonia took a big toll on his body. His cough had gotten deeper, his body was weaker, and his appetite was almost nonexistent. With each day that passed he seemed to be spending more time in bed. While in the hospital Will noticed the vision in his right eye had deteriorated, another side effect of the disease. He was able to get around the house on his own and take care of himself. But with the loss of vision and his weak body driving had become a thing of the past. Nancy had been kind enough to work my schedule around any doctor visits Will had since I was his driver now. Will put on a brave face, claiming to be feeling better and stronger. But I couldn't see any evidence of it.

I shook the sleep from my head while tossing the blanket off of me. After work I had come up to my room to change clothes. Before heading downstairs to make a dinner Will probably wasn't going to eat, I lay down on the bed. Apparently my body needed the rest because an hour later, I was startled from a deep sleep by Will's call. Looking down, I checked to make sure I had indeed already changed into my pair of navy blue sweatpants and gray sweatshirt.

For some reason as I ran out of the room I took the baby monitor with me. It had been one of the gifts my parents had bought when I was pregnant. I was able to donate the things Will and I had bought for the baby, but I kept everything both sets of grandparents bought. When Will came home from the hospital this time, I thought we could put it to good use in case he needed me during the night. Moans and a coughing fit blared through the tiny speaker as I descended the stairs.

I headed into Will's room without knocking. He was sitting on the side of the bed hunched over with his hands gripping the edge of the mattress. The brown long-sleeve crewneck his body once filled out, hung loosely to his skeletal frame.

"Sorry, I didn't get here quicker. I fell asleep," I said, as I squatted in front of him.

His face was beet red while his lips were faintly tinted blue due to his uncontrolled coughing.

"Do you want me to get your oxygen?"

Raising his index finger, he shook his head in response. Will's poor lungs had been beaten up so much between the cancer and the pneumonia that Dr. Rudolph put him on oxygen. At first Will argued with the doctor, not wanting to be tethered to the tank, but breathing won out. He still used it only as a last resort.

After several deep inhalations through his nose, Will's breathing regulated and the coughing subsided.

Lifting his gaze to mine, he said, "I wanted to take a shower but I was having a hard time standing and then the fucking coughing started."

"I've told you over and over to call me when you need to get up. You're not steady enough on your feet yet to be trying it on your own."

The whiny Will from the rehab had disappeared and in his place was the stubborn Will. When Dr. Rudolph ordered a walker and a wheelchair on discharge from the hospital, Will was not happy and refused to take them. Without Will knowing, I went back the next day to pick up both items and stored them in the large hallway closet. Better to be safe than sorry. I understood where Will was coming from. AIDS was stripping everything from him little by little and he was determined to put up a fight to the end.

"I'm not a baby, Bryson."

"Then stop acting like one and ask for help."

"Would you please help me into the bathroom so I can take a shower?" Standing, I teased. "See, that wasn't too difficult."

As Will draped his arm around my shoulders, I wrapped mine around his waist and lifted. Gripping my shoulder like he was hanging on for dear life, Will and I slowly made our way toward the bathroom, each step harder than the last as his energy level dwindled. Once inside, I helped him lower onto the shower seat we'd gotten the second day he was home from the hospital. His legs weren't strong or steady enough to risk standing in a shower.

Turning on the water, I aimed the handheld showerhead away from Will. "I'll get the water going so it can heat up."

Will nodded without looking toward me.

I gathered the shower gel, shampoo, washcloth, towel, and a pair of pajamas, placing everything on the small portable folding table we'd set up.

"Do you want your shaving kit?"

Will shook his head.

"Do you need me to help you get undressed?"

Dark brown tear-filled eyes looked up at me. "I need help standing to get my pants off."

"Okay, I'll pull you up and then you can steady yourself on my shoulders, while I slide them down."

Will put his hands in mine and I tugged him into a standing position. Once he felt secure enough, I undid his jeans. His body tensed and his fingers dug into my skin as I pushed the denim and his boxers down to mid-thigh. Easing Will back down, I squatted and gently tugged his jeans and underwear off. As I looked up, I caught tears running down his sunken cheeks. His dignity was being ciphered off a little more each day. I wasn't sure whether or not to say anything. I didn't want to make him feel even more self-conscious but I also didn't want him to feel less than the person he was.

"Thank you, Bryson."

I stood and folded the pair of jeans. "No problem."

"I don't deserve your compassion but I need you to know how much I appreciate it."

Swallowing the lump in my throat, I said, "I know. I'm glad I can be here for you."

A faint smile ghosted over his thin lips.

"I'll go get supper ready. Call me when you're done or need anything."

He simply nodded as he wiped his tears.

Pulling the door shut, I caught Will taking off his shirt. My hand flew to my mouth as an audible gasp escaped me. Thank god the shower drowned it out enough so he didn't hear. I'd felt how thin Will had gotten whenever I helped him walk but to see it was another thing. The once athletic body had been eaten away. His shoulder blades were bony and protruded out so far they looked as if they could cut through his skin. And there had to be at least a dozen or more Kaposi lesions scattered up and down his back.

Tears stung the back of my eyes as the tightening in my chest grew so intense it shattered my heart. I wondered what went through Will's mind when he looked in the mirror. He seemed more interested in making amends rather than sharing his feelings about what was happening to him. As his body weakened, I saw the fear in his eyes strengthen. But at this point, I couldn't tell if Will was afraid of dying or living.

"Bryson!"

My body jumped, causing the spoon to slip from my hand and into the big bowl of chicken salad I was mixing. I looked up to find Nancy standing in the doorway of her office, glaring at me, pointing at me, summoning me. My mind quickly flipped through possible reasons as to why she was pissed off at me. Nothing obvious was popping up at the moment.

"Bryson!" Nancy's voice bounced off the walls.

"Coming!" I quickly covered the bowl of chicken salad.

Wiping my hands with the rag, I hurried across the room and into Nancy's office.

She was sitting behind her desk looking intently at the computer. "Close the door and sit down, please."

Behind the gruff intimidating exterior Nancy was a caring and good-hearted person. A year ago she was the only one willing to give me a chance to prove myself with this job. She'd become a bit like a second mom to me. But there were still times when she scared the shit out of me.

I lowered into the chair across from her and fidgeted with the hem of my chef's jacket.

Nancy swiveled her chair in my direction, her dark frames pushed halfway down her nose.

With her brows perched high on her forehead, she peered over her glasses at me. "Bryson, do you think I'm harder on you than the others around here?"

Wetting my dry lips, I wondered if this was a trick question. "Um . . . I'm not sure I'd say harder . . . but . . ."

"I am. I am harder on you. And do you know why?"

I figured silence accompanied by a shoulder shrug was the best response.

Nancy pulled off her glasses and placed them in front of her. "It's because I see an enormous amount of potential. You've been with me for quite a while now and look how far you've come. No longer are you this timid little girl who had never held a job before. You're an incredibly talented culinary artist."

I could sense a huge "but" in my near future.

"It's because of those talents along with your drive and perfectionism that I've put you in charge of some of my most coveted events. It's also why I'm about to rip you a new one."

The lump in my throat fell to my stomach like a boulder. Again my mental flip book was coming up empty as to what this could be about.

"The Virginia Hamilton funeral was at one o'clock today."

The Hamilton family was a big name in town and one of Nancy's biggest clients. Miss Virginia was the matriarch of the family who'd lived a long happy life. After her huge funeral service at Saint John's the family was having an equally huge reception at the church hall.

"Yes and the van was packed and went out by 11 a.m."

"Oh the van got there on time. I got a call from Mr. Hamilton. He said that although his ninety-five-year-old mother did enjoy football, he didn't find the Super Bowl party set up an appropriate theme for her funeral!" She yelled the last few words.

Puckering my lips, I pushed them out and I blinked in confusion. Nancy stared, waiting for my fog to clear.

Holy shit! I sent the wrong van to the wrong address.

My mouth dropped open and my eyes doubled in size. "Nooo!"

A sarcastic Grinch-like smile crept across her face. "Yes."

I slapped my hand over my mouth. "Oh my god, Nancy! I'm so, so, so sorry. That means the Howy's Super Bowl party . . ."

"Will be enjoying a variety of tea sandwiches and petit fours."

"Oooh," I groaned, dropping my chin to my chest.

"Bryson, you know how fond I am of you."

Sensing the "but" was about to make an appearance, I looked up and braced myself.

"But here comes the ripping. Where the fuck was your head?! These are two of my biggest clients! Their referrals alone are gold."

"I'm sorry." Tears played at the back of my eyes. Nancy wasn't a fan of weakness so I did my best to stay dry.

"Because of your screw-up I'm going to have to issue a refund. And on top of that the money spent on product is a complete loss. And don't even get me started on how unprofessional we appeared."

I bit down on my quivering lip, desperately trying to keep my emotions in check.

"Nancy, I know there's no excuse but things have been stressful in my life lately. Juggling work and personal stuff has been difficult. I'll pay you back. I promise." A few tears had seeped out and trickled down my face.

"I don't pay you enough for you to pay me back," she said.

Swiping my fingers under my eyes, I wiped the tears away. "Are you going to fire me?"

Nancy leaned back in her chair, staring at the quivering mess in front of her. "How's that friend of yours doing?"

"He's gotten worse, weaker and . . . um . . . weaker."

As Nancy listened her expression softened with the look of understanding in her eyes.

"Do you have any help?"

"Hart offers all the time. It's just he and Will don't really like each other so it's awkward. And my parents and my friend Sophie said they would help but . . ."

"You can't do this alone, Bryson."

"The thing is . . . it was my choice. I don't want to disrupt everyone else's life. It's not fair."

"So instead you're going to run yourself ragged taking care of him and working full-time. And what about Hart? How does he fit into all of this?"

"Unfortunately, not very much at the moment."

My chest hurt thinking of how all of this was affecting mine and Hart's relationship. He was a good and patient man. But everyone had their limits. Since Christmas, even when we did manage to spend time together I was either preoccupied with thoughts of Will or exhausted, falling asleep on him. I certainly wasn't contributing to our relationship.

Leaning forward, Nancy rested her forearms on the desk and said, "I'm not going to fire you but I am ordering you to take a leave of absence."

I felt as if I'd been gut punched. Leave of absence sounded like a fancy and less brutal way of saying I was fired. This job meant the world to me. It was a foot in the door to my dream career. With my work history and a recommendation from Nancy I could pick whatever culinary school I wanted to attend after Will . . .

"Nancy, please. I know I fucked up royally. I think if I get a couple of good night's sleep under my belt I'll be as good as new."

"Bryson, this isn't up for discussion. You're no good to me here unless you're a hundred percent. Right now you can't be that. I promise you, your job will be here when things settle down."

I should have felt relief and gratitude but I didn't. My stomach twisted in knots just like it used to when Will told me I couldn't do this or that. I knew it was a knee-jerk reaction and had more to do with me than with what Nancy was saying. Still it made me feel as if I'd failed.

I left Good Eats that afternoon with Nancy's reassurance that I could come back and pick up right where I'd left off. All I needed to do was say the word. I knew deep down she would be true to her promise but there was still a twinge of doubt. I'd worked hard to grow more confident and let my talents shine. With the help of this job and Hart I felt secure and on a solid foundation. But with one misstep I let the old me creep back in and I hated seeing her again.

The second I walked in the house a strange feeling washed over me. There was an eerie stillness that hung in the air. Sitting my purse down on the small foyer table, I slipped out of my brown leather jacket and placed it on the coat hook. On my way home I had texted Will so he wouldn't be surprised to see me so early in the day but I didn't hear back. I took a deep breath as I walked into his room. Since his last stint in the hospital my greatest fear was that I'd come home and find that he'd passed away alone. When my gaze hit the empty bed, I blew out a deep breath.

Noticing the bathroom door was slightly ajar, I walked over and gave it a soft tap. "Will, are you in there?"

No response.

Being more forceful with my knock, the door opened wider. If it hadn't been for the odd sensation in the pit of my stomach I would have searched the rest of the downstairs first before invading Will's privacy and possibility of embarrassment by walking in on him in the bathroom.

Closing my eyes, I pushed the door the rest of the way. "Will, are you okay?"

Still no response. I tentatively squinted my eyes open. They quickly widened at the sight of Will lying on the tile floor with blood spattered around his lifeless body. My heart thudded out of my chest as panic took over. Everything slowed except my heart rate and my breathing. I felt as if my feet were buried in quicksand as I ran over and fell to my knees. Even though I didn't have any cuts or open areas on my hand, I was extremely careful when placing my finger on the side of his neck. A weak pulse existed. Shoving my hand in my front pocket I pulled out my cellphone and called 911.

"911, what's your emergency?"

"I found my hus . . . my husband unconscious on the floor of the bathroom. There's blood."

"Ma'am, what's the address?"

"555 Cypress Point."

"Okay, an ambulance is on its way. You said there was blood?"

"Yes. Coming out of his mouth like he'd coughed it up. It looks like he may have been going to the bathroom when this happened. His pajamas are around his knees and there's blood in the toilet."

"Is he still breathing?"

"Yes, barely."

"The ambulance is turning onto your street right now."

"I also need to let you know . . . my husband has AIDS."

As I waited for the EMTs to arrive, I knelt beside Will and stroked his hair. I wanted so badly to clean him up so no one would see him this way. Just asking me for help was a blow to his dignity. I couldn't imagine what it would do to him if he knew strangers were about to see him at his lowest moment. I vowed to myself right then I would spare him the details of today.

The loud banging propelled me up and to the front door. Swinging open the door, I found three burly men on my porch.

"Ma'am you called 911?" The black-haired man said.

Stepping to the side, I let them in and then guided them to Will. "Yes, he's back here."

I wrapped my arms around my body and stood off to the side as the EMTs did their job. The two older looking dark haired men tended to Will. After checking his vitals, they lifted him onto the stretcher, his body limp like a ragdoll. The younger redheaded man cleaned up Will's blood, going through the meticulous protocol used when dealing with an AIDS patient. The air turned into disinfectant, stinging my nose with each breath.

"Ma'am!"

My gaze snapped to the dark-haired man with bright green eyes as he pulled off his blue latex gloves, tossing them in the special bag marked hazardous material. I assumed by his sharp tone he'd been trying to get my attention for several seconds.

"I'm sorry," I said, barely able to get the two words out.

"You can follow us to the hospital." He then turned, joining his partners as they pushed Will out of the room.

Snatching my purse and jacket off the table, I followed closely behind. Even though I knew exactly where they were headed, I didn't want to lose sight of them . . . of Will. He needed to know he wasn't alone.

It felt like it took an eternity to get to the hospital even with the roaring sirens and the traffic parting like the Red Sea. Without wasting any time, the EMTs got Will out of the ambulance and inside the ER. The hospital staff immediately went into action, rolling Will through the large double doors to the back and out of my sight. I stood staring at where

Will disappeared to until bumped by the rush of staff members in route to another patient.

A myriad of horrible thoughts ran through my mind. Was today the day? Even though Will said his parents disowned him, shouldn't I call them? I couldn't imagine a parent not wanting to know when their child was dying no matter what had taken place in the past. My thoughts were too jumbled. My heart was pounding at the speed of hummingbird wings, causing my head to swim and feel lightheaded. I sat down in the first empty seat I saw. Staring blankly straight ahead a wave of loneliness washed over me. I felt like I should be doing something or calling someone. But there wasn't anything to do or anyone to call. I was the only one in Will's life and would be the only one during his death.

A tremor hummed through my body, quickly turning into shakes and then sobs. Burying my face into my hands, I tried to be as quiet as possible. I don't know how long I stayed like this before I thought my name had been called. Using the back of my hand to wipe my tears, I looked toward the nurse's station. A pretty blonde gave me a warm smile as she walked from behind the desk toward me.

"Are you Bryson Forsyth?"

"Yes. They just brought my husband in." My throat was sore and raw from crying.

"Dr. Rudolph wanted me to take you to one of the consult rooms."

I'd only been in those rooms one other time and that was when the doctor prepared me for the months ahead. The knot in my stomach told me this wasn't a good sign. The nurse led me back to the same consult room I'd been in before. When she opened the door I was surprised to see the doctor already waiting for me.

"Hello, young lady," the doctor said, as he stood like a gentleman.

The nurse quietly closed the door, leaving me alone with a concerned looking Dr. Rudolph.

"Bryson, have a seat."

"Is Will okay?" I blurted out even before I was in the chair.

Dr. Rudolph took the seat across from me. "You know I'm not a beat-around-the-bush kind of guy. I don't have time for that nonsense." He paused. "The Kaposi tumor in Will's right lung has gotten much larger.

That's why he's coughing and out of breath a lot of the time. It also explains the blood coming from his mouth. Obviously, the pneumonia didn't help matters. The tumor in his abdomen and liver . . ."

"Wait, I thought he only had them in his lungs."

"He didn't tell you?"

My eyes glazed over as I stared at him.

"The tumor in his abdomen has tripled in size since his diagnosis. The other blood you saw was due to this tumor. And there are multiple small tumors in his liver. We've stopped the bleeding but Will lost a lot of blood. I'm going to admit him for at least a couple of days." He paused, looking down at his wringing hands. When he looked up, his grim expression slapped me in the face. "Bryson, I'm going to recommend Will be admitted into The Hospice House after I discharge him."

"Why?"

It was a stupid ridiculous question and I couldn't explain what made me ask it.

"You know why, young lady."

I bit down on my trembling lip as I held back a sob. "He's only twenty-eight. Twenty- eight-year-olds aren't supposed to die."

"AIDS is merciless. It rolls through a person's life like an armored tank, mowing down everything in its path. And even though we've made strides in treatment and life expectancy, we haven't found a cure and we haven't eradicated the stigma. There are still a lot of people out there who believe if you get it, you deserved it. I've been in this field for twenty years and have seen thousands of patients from all walks of life. Some were nicer than others. But none of them deserved it."

My vision was blurred but I thought I saw Dr. Rudolph's warm eyes fill with tears.

Leaning forward, he took my hand in his. "Will was one of the lucky ones because he had you. You need to know that what you did, opening your home and your heart, gave him extra time."

"Thank you." I choked out.

He patted my hand and stood. "I'll get everything set up with hospice and get the information to you."

Before opening the door, Dr. Rudolph turned to me and said, "I hope one day my son is lucky enough to find a lovely young lady like you, Bryson."

Will was heavily sedated and would be for the rest of the night so Dr. Rudolph ordered me to go home and get some rest. Explaining I wouldn't be able to be there for Will if I ended up making myself sick. I did as he ordered.

When I got home I stripped out of my clothes and took a shower. The hot water loosened the tense muscles of my neck and shoulders. Stepping out of the shower, I wrapped a big towel around my body, dried my hair, gathering it up into a top knot. I took a pair of panties from my dresser and slid them on under the towel. I was walking around like a zombie, not quite aware of my actions, which explained what I did next.

I went into my closet and rummaged through the box in the very back against the wall. I found Will's high school football jersey. Dropping the towel, I pulled the jersey over my head and down my body. I hadn't thought of the jersey in years and had forgotten it was still here until tonight. I walked back into the bedroom, pulled back the comforter, and crawled into bed. As I was plugging in my phone, I glanced down. There were missed texts from Hart, Sophie, and my mom.

Hart: *Bryson, I haven't heard from you today. Is everything okay? I love you.*

Mom: *Bryson, sweetheart, I haven't seen or heard from you for several days. Is everything okay? I love you.*

Sophie: *Bryson, I'll be back in town this weekend. We're doing a girls spa day. Don't fight me on it. I'm worried about you. I love you.*

Bryson! Bryson! Bryson!

Ignoring all of them, I set the phone on the nightstand, grabbed the edge of the comforter, and pulled it over my head. I just wanted to disappear for a while and go back to a time when the biggest problem in my life was which pair of jeans I was going to wear to the football game.

Worry and guilt had me tossing and turning all night. I worried that Will would pass away before I got to his side. I felt guilty that I didn't return any of the texts or calls from yesterday, especially Hart's. By morning my brain was exhausted and needed a rest, some type of distraction for a little while. I pulled on a pair of black leggings along with socks and my black

Nikes. The sun was just coming up as I headed downstairs to the kitchen in hopes of finding a moment of peace.

After flipping on the Keurig, I lined up all the ingredients for a frittata and got to work. I was just about to slice into my first pepper when the doorbell rang. Glancing at the clock on the stove, I couldn't imagine who'd be coming by this early in the morning. I washed my hands and headed toward the door. Not thinking to look who it was first, I opened the door, surprised to find Hart. My mouth watered at how handsome and powerful he looked in his black suit, dark gray shirt with matching tie, and shiny black dress shoes. He must have a meeting with corporate later.

As I stared into his beautiful eyes, I wondered how he managed to get up the steps. Then I glanced toward the driveway and saw Colin sitting in the passenger's side of Hart's car.

"Hey." Shock evident in my voice.

"We need to talk."

Stepping aside to let him in, I said, "Does Colin want to come in? It's cold out there. You want some coffee? I just made some."

I closed the door as Hart rolled farther into the entryway.

He faced me. "I can't stay long. I came over to find out if you were okay since I didn't hear back from you yesterday." His words were teetering between relief, concern, and annoyance.

"I'm sorry. I should have called you but . . . Will's in the hospital. I found him yesterday unconscious in the bathroom."

Hart's expression softened as he moved closer to me. "I'm sorry."

"Dr. Rudolph feels Will needs to be under hospice care."

"What can I do?"

"Nothing. There's nothing anyone can do."

Just then I noticed Hart's gaze zeroed in on my chest. I still had on Will's jersey.

Shit.

"What's going on, Bryson?"

Unable to look at Hart, my gaze darted all around. "I-I-I don't know. I've been so tired and stressed. Nancy let me go yesterday because I fucked up two important events. Then I found Will. I've been neglecting you. When we're together I feel guilty because I think I should be with Will.

But when I'm with Will I feel guilty because I should be with you. I don't know why I slept in his old jersey."

I was rambling uncontrollably and couldn't stop. My nerves were completely shot.

"Look at me." Hart commanded.

I was so ashamed at how I was acting I didn't listen to him. "Just give me a minute and I'll go change. I don't even know why I still have this stupid shirt on."

I went to pass Hart when he reached out and grabbed my arm.

"God dammit, Bryson, I said look at me." His tone was strong and assertive.

I looked into steely blue-gray eyes.

"Stop dumping all this guilt on yourself. Let me help you."

I shook my head. "He wants me by his side when he passes."

Hart blew out a sharp breath. "Go deal with what you need to deal with."

My heart sank as tears pooled in my eyes. Even the best man in the world has a limit.

"I don't blame you for pushing me away." I choked back a sob.

"Bryson, I'm not pushing you away. I'm letting you go."

I didn't know if I collapsed or Hart tugged me into his lap.

Cupping my face, Hart brought his lips to mine. He softly kissed each corner of my mouth before placing a firmer kiss in the center of my lips. My arms immediately slid behind his neck and held on tight as my body convulsed in sobs. Hart's strong arms pulled me flush against his chest. I never wanted to let go.

After several minutes, Hart peeled my hands away from his body.

Looking deep into my soul, he said, "I know what it feels like to watch someone you care about die. It's the most frustrating and helpless feeling in the world. It's going to happen. You can't stop it. All you can do is make sure that person knows they mattered. And give them the peace of mind that they won't be looking at strangers when they take their last breath. They'll be looking at someone who loved them."

My heart ached for him, realizing he was referring to his mother.

"I'm not in love with him, Hart. Please don't think it's anything like that. I'm in love with you." I couldn't get the words out fast enough.

"I know you are. And god help me, I love you so much, Bryson. But you can't help that you care for Will. Your heart and kind spirit are what makes you, you."

"I didn't realize it would be this difficult. I can't lose you, Hart."

"There are two things in life that I'm absolutely, without a doubt, positive about. One is that I'm mind, body, and soul in love with you. And the other is you're never going to lose me." Swiping his thumbs over my cheeks, he wiped away my tears. "Whenever you need a breath, I'm here. You need to focus on one thing. Will needs you right now. Then you and I will continue our forever."

Even though I understood why Hart was, in a sense, putting us on pause, it didn't make the pain any less as I watched him and Colin pull out of my driveway.

Hart knew exactly how the remainder of Will's days would play out and what an emotional toll it would take on me. Hart had already lived through the experience with his mother.

"You didn't fit into my life back then, Bryson."

Hart Mitchell was the very essence of what a real man should be. He was intelligent, strong, confident, caring, generous, kind, and all mine.

chapter
Thirty-Two

I navigated the car down a winding road lined with large bare Bradford pear trees. Even though the bright green leaves and white blossoms were still months away from appearing on the branches, the entrance was still pretty and impressive. Driving farther onto the property we discovered a large pond to the left surrounded by weeping willow trees and carved wooden benches. The entire grounds had been designed to allow the natural peacefulness to shine. The building had just come into view when Will reached over and touched my elbow.

"Could you pull over for a second?" His voice was gravelly, each word ending in a breathless whisper.

There wasn't much room on the side of the long winding driveway but I managed to pull far enough over not to block another vehicle from passing. I killed the engine. We sat for several minutes in silence. There was no need for me to ask Will why he wanted to pull over. I knew why. Will had accepted his fate but that didn't mean he had to like it or be in any rush to meet it.

On discharge from the hospital Dr. Rudolph made arrangements for Will to be transported via ambulance to the hospice house. Will refused, insisting he wanted me to drive him here today. He was holding on to as much normal life as possible while he was still able to grip.

"I guess this is it," he said, staring straight ahead, his body tense.

I didn't know how to respond. I wasn't even going to try to imagine what was going through his mind at this moment. A few more minutes of silence passed as we stared at the pale yellow building where he'd be spending his final days.

"I could turn this baby around and get the hell out of here." I cringed at my poor attempt at lightening the mood until I heard a chuckle next to me.

"God, if only doing that would change everything." More silence. I wasn't budging until Will gave me the signal. "Have I thanked you today, Bryson?"

Over the last week Will's memory had taken a hit. Once his sedation was tapered way back he was alert but then I noticed him asking the same questions or making the same comments. As the week went on his brain had more periods of fuzziness. I asked Dr. Rudolph about it. He looked at me with warm eyes and said, "It's just part of the process."

It was very important to Will that I knew how appreciative he was of me. He was either thanking me for everything or asking me if he had thanked me.

"Yeah, back at the hospital you thanked me."

"Good. I don't ever want to forget to do that."

"Don't worry. You don't."

A few more minutes passed. I was beginning to think I actually did need to turn the car around and head back to the hospital or our house. Medically Will might be ready for this but it was obvious mentally he wasn't quite there yet.

"I realize we need to move this along," he said.

"No hurry. I'll do whatever you want, when you want."

"I'm not fooling myself. I know I'm not going to get better. It's just once I go through those doors, that's it."

There wasn't one word I could think of that would give him lasting comfort and I wasn't going to insult him by spouting platitudes. Unless you have walked the same mile, you have no right telling another how to feel, especially at a time like this.

"Do you remember Herbert Young?" I said.

"Vaguely."

"He was an old man that went to Saint Mary's. I remember going to midnight mass with Mom, Dad, and Ryan. I think we were juniors at Garrison. Anyway, it was the first time Father Batron asked for everyone to please pray for Herbert Young who was in hospice care. Every Sunday after that, Father would say the same thing, please pray for Herbert Young who was in hospice care. For two years everyone prayed for Herbert Young who was in hospice care."

Out the corner of my eye I saw Will's shoulders shake with a chuckle. Taking in a deep breath his lungs crackled, straining to suck in the air. As his chest deflated a loose cough burst out of him, followed by another. And another. And another. And another . . .

Once recovered, he said, "Okay. Let's do this."

Reaching over, I placed my hand on top of his and gave it a slight squeeze before starting the car.

I pulled the car into the empty parking space that was closest to the entrance. Will and I exchanged brief looks before I got out of the car and pulled his wheelchair from the trunk. Even though it was only a few steps to the entrance, Will's body wasn't cooperating much these days. With my assistance, he was able to transfer in and out of the chair but that was about all he could handle before getting worn out.

Pushing through the main entrance door felt as if we'd just entered a luxury hotel where we were spending the weekend. Other than the sign out front that read Hospice House, you'd never know this was a place where people came to spend their final days. The color scheme was a mix of neutral earth tones—greens, creams, and browns with pops of vibrant bright reds and oranges. A cozy seating area made up of two cream-colored leather sofas and two red high-back chairs sat in front of a wall of floor-to-ceiling windows. A large multicolored floral arrangement sat in the middle of the coffee table.

The lady at the desk introduced herself as Grace. As she guided Will through the admissions process I could tell why she was the first point of contact here. Just her presence made you feel relaxed. A picture of Hart holding my hand, calming my nerves, flashed across my mind.

Grace treated Will with dignity and respect. Never speaking to him with a conceding tone or offering a disingenuous smile. After a few forms were signed, Grace escorted Will and I to his room.

More floor-to-ceiling windows lined one side of the hallway we turned down. They looked out onto a meticulously manicured garden full of a variety of blooming pansies, Gerber daisies, holly berry, and several evergreens. More cozy sitting areas similar to the one spotted on the drive in were scattered around.

Grace pointed out all the pertinent areas—dining room, lounge, library, and family room complete with play area for children. My chest tightened at the thought of a child visiting their parent here. These rooms were mostly used by the families, but occasionally, a patient having a good day would use them as well. I thought about Hart coming here to see his mother and the tightness in my chest strangled me.

With each turn we made we moved further into tranquility. It dawned on me as we rounded the final corner before Will's room. This wasn't a place where people came to die. It was a place where people came to say goodbye. Before entering his room, I looked down at Will and noticed his shoulders had relaxed. A warmth washed over me knowing the peaceful place had already started doing its job.

The decor of Will's room kept in line with the rest of the hospice house. The walls were sage green complimented by dark wood furnishing. The bed was positioned to have maximum view out the large picture window. There was a seating area in the far corner with a red recliner and chocolate-brown sofa. A flat screen TV was housed in an ornate wardrobe against the opposite wall from the bed. The bathroom was large and equipped for wheelchair accessibility. Grace gave us a packet of information, a quick rundown of when meals were served, and which staff member would be with Will tonight. She then left us alone to settle in and absorb the new surroundings.

"It's a really nice place, Will."

"Yeah." He agreed as his hollow eyes scanned the room.

"Will you be okay here for a few minutes while I go grab your suitcase?"

He nodded slightly. "Bryson, have I thanked you for everything today?"

Tears threatened behind my eyes. I thought it was hard watching this once strong athletic young man physically wither away but it didn't compare to witnessing the deterioration of his true self.

I cleared my throat. "Yeah, you did."

Tilting his chin up, Will said, "Good. I don't ever want to forget to do that."

My legs couldn't get me down the hallway fast enough, taking each turn as quickly as possible. Once I was safely outside and in my car I let the sobs and tears flow. I didn't want to show my weakness in front of Will. I just needed a minute and a deep breath.

After pulling myself together somewhat, I picked up my phone. I scrolled to the number and clicked the call icon.

He picked up before the first ring had a chance to finish. "Hey." Hart's rasp warmed every part of my soul.

I hadn't seen him since that morning at my house. It was beyond difficult not being around him every day but I understood his motives. I loved him even more for how selfless he was.

"Hey. Are you busy?" I said.

"Never too busy for you."

I stayed quiet for several minutes in order to steady my voice. I didn't want it to become a habit that every time we spoke I cried.

I swallowed hard. "I needed to hear your voice."

"I'm glad you called. How are things?"

"I'm sitting outside of the hospice house right now. It's a really nice place." My voice cracked.

"You can do this, Bryson."

"I hope so."

"I know so. And if you need me, I'll be there in a flash."

"I miss you."

"Good. Prepare yourself because when you're ready I'm going to be on you for the rest of your life."

Warmth spread throughout my body. "Tell me about your day."

"Let's see . . . I had an eighty-eight-year-old great grandmother grope me."

I chuckled. "Seriously?"

"Yep. Slid her hand right up my thigh and gave me a squeeze and a wink. She was so pleased with herself I didn't have the heart to tell her I couldn't feel her advances."

Laughter flew out of me. "Oh my god! That's hilarious. I'm thinkin' I may need to come down there and school some biotches about keeping their hands off my man."

"You're adorable when you're claiming what belongs to you."

The corners of my mouth tugged into a smile. "I love you."

"Till the end of time," he said.

I always knew Hart's voice had magical powers. Never was I more convinced than in this moment. In less than five minutes he'd managed to lighten my heart and mood.

"I guess I better let you get back to work. I need to get Will's things put away."

"I love you, Bryson."

"I love you too, Hart." I choked on a sob.

"I'm here, Lovely, 24/7/365."

I nodded even though he couldn't see me. "I'll talk to you soon."

A heavy sigh drifted through the phone before I ended the call.

I wiped my tear-stained face as best I could, grabbed Will's suitcase, and headed back inside.

Social Withdrawal

Initially, Will was interested in talking with the staff. On day two he actually felt strong enough for me to take him on a mini-tour down the hall to the family room. After that day he never wanted to leave his room. He still interacted with the nurses but by the end of the week even that faded into courteous quietness. Dr. Rudolph came several times. I never thought this was unusual since Will was his patient. Then one day Will's nurse Tricia asked if we were related to the doctor since he was visiting so much. Will seemed to really enjoy when Dr. Rudolph came by. I had to wonder if this was because he missed his own father.

Mom, Dad, and Ryan came by one evening. It was awkward on so many levels. For one, all my family knew was Will and I had reconciled after a yearlong separation. I never went into specifics on how we ended up getting back together. I figured the less said the better, especially since it was all a lie. Two, most people are uncomfortable around death and my family was no exception. Both Will and I appreciated their effort, though. Even Sophie stopped by and true to her form, she didn't hold back or wear kid gloves around Will. I think he enjoyed her visit most of all.

To say I was shocked and appalled by the way the Forsyth family acted would be an understatement. Neither Will's parents nor his brother made any attempt to contact their son and brother.

One evening I broached the topic, asking if he wanted me to reach out to them. He was pretty adamant in his response.

"Are you sure you don't want me to call to at least feel them out?"

Will was already in bed while I was curled up in the recliner with a blanket tucked under my chin. There was a well-stocked DVD library just down the hall from Will's room. He surprised me tonight after dinner with the movie. He'd looked up *Fried Green Tomatoes* online.

Apparently he didn't bother reading the description because he thought it was about cooking. When he asked one of the nurses to see if the library had it, he had no idea he was committing himself to a chick flick.

"I'm positive."

I sat up, twisting my body toward him. "I understand where you're coming from. I just don't want you to have any regrets because you didn't tie up any loose ends."

I brought up the idea for Will, not for his family's sake. I wanted him to be at peace with everything.

Looking over at me, he said, "The only loose end I gave a shit about tying up was with you." He laid his hand, palm side up, across the bed.

Reaching over, I slid my hand into his and gave it a slight squeeze. Our gaze locked for several seconds. An unspoken understanding passed between us. Will appreciated what I was trying to do and I knew to let it go.

Surrender

Once Will was admitted into hospice care, I spent a total of two nights in my own bed before I began staying overnight with him. Our house was only twenty minutes away but a life could change during that short drive. And if I were being honest, saying goodbye those couple of nights was hard for both of us.

I was coming out of the bathroom after changing into Hart's gray long-sleeve T-shirt and my navy blue sweatpants, a.k.a. my pajamas. Will was leaning against the padded headboard watching the late news. Grabbing my blanket and pillow, I curled up on the small sofa. As I was setting the alarm on my phone for the morning, I saw my nightly text from Hart. We made it a point to talk on the phone or text at least once a day. Tonight's text had a photo attached. My finger hovered over the icon for a few seconds, nervous to see what the photo was of. I didn't need to be getting all hot for Hart with Will only a few feet away. Finally, I opened up the message and a huge smile crossed my face. The photo was of Hart and Butter attempting a selfie with the text, we miss you and love you. I immediately replied.

Me: *Ditto. Y'all both look gorgeous.*

As I plugged my phone in and slid it on the small table beside the sofa, I caught Will staring at me.

"What?"

Pointing the remote at the TV, he turned down the volume. "Text from Hart?"

My gaze dropped. I felt a twinge of guilt in my chest. I didn't want Will to see the happiness in my eyes.

"Bryson, does he make you happy?"

I hesitated before finally looking at him. "Yes."

"He loves you very much."

"Will, I feel kind of weird discussing Hart with you."

"Did you know he stops by here almost every night?"

My expression went slack. "What are you talking about?"

"The second night I was here, he stopped in late. You were at home. I don't think he'd planned on talking to me but I happened to be awake. Still not quite sure how he talked fuck-face Estelle . . ."

My hand flew to cover my mouth. "Oh my god, Will! That's a horrible thing to say."

"What?! Her face is always scrunched up like someone's giving it to her in the back."

I bit the inside of my cheek to stifle a laugh. "Be that as it may, you shouldn't call her that. It's not nice."

"Fine. I don't know how he talked Estelle into letting him through that time of night."

The corners of my mouth drifted up into a smile. "Hart has ways. Also his mother had been a patient a long time ago. Maybe Estelle was here then."

"It wouldn't surprise me. Estelle looks like she's been around a looong time, squared."

I shook my head as my curiosity soared to the moon wondering what a conversation between Hart and Will looked like.

"He claimed to be checking up on me but I could see the disappointment in his eyes when he realized you weren't here. I made a point the next night to stay awake to see if he came. He did. He stared at you for a minute and then left. The times I've been awake, he catches my eye, nods, and leaves."

"So y'all never talk?"

"Not since the first night. He asked how I was handling things. It was brief."

"I talk or text with him every day. He never mentioned coming by here."

"I think he just needs to see for himself that you're okay."

Clutching the blanket to my chest, I closed my eyes, determined not to get weepy.

"He's a good man, Bryson. He's the man you deserved all along."

That night I stayed awake to see if it was true. Around 11 p.m., I thought I heard the quiet creak of the door. Peeking out from underneath my blanket, I saw him. Hart had the door opened halfway as he stared at me, making sure I was okay, and then left. Just like Will said.

Loss of Appetite

"Stop treating me like a fucking baby!"

"If you'd stop acting like one then I would. Just eat a couple of spoonfuls. You love butterscotch," I said, holding the spoon of pudding to his mouth.

Will turned his head away, refusing to take even one bite. "Give the dying man a break! I don't want any."

"Will, the only thing you've had in the past two days is half of a turkey sandwich and a cup of coffee. You have to eat."

Turning, he glared at me. "Why?"

"They'll stick a feeding tube in you if you don't start eating."

"Bryson, stop it! I don't feel like eating and there's not going to be a feeding tube."

Tears pricked behind my eyes. I knew he was right. Food had always been my way of showing people how much I cared. Will's eating had begun slowing down when he was admitted to the hospital for pneumonia. But at least he was still eating. Over the last two days his appetite had been a no show.

Sinking the spoon back into the bowl of pudding, I placed it on the nightstand. I walked to the large picture window. Wrapping my arms around myself, I stared out at the small duck pond. A few ducks were scattered in and around the water as a white egret took off into the sky.

It's hard to describe how the mind works when you watch a person go through the dying process, especially someone you care about. I've witnessed firsthand the weight loss, the lesions, the coughing, the blood, the frailty, and weakness. I know Will's death will come sooner rather than later. But there's a small corner of my brain that believes if he could just hang on a little longer they'd find a cure.

"Hart got it in his head that if he could keep her strong, she'd last long enough until they found a cure."

Colin's words echoed in my head. I'd been so focused on Will's peace of mind I'd pushed mine to the side. By the time a cure was found, if a cure was found, Will wouldn't be here to reap the benefits. And no amount of pudding was going to change that fact.

Weakness and Fatigue

By the time we entered into week two, Will was too weak to get out of bed. He spent most of the day in a deep sleep. When he was awake he remained groggy for the most part. There were moments of lucidity but they were few and far between. No longer able to control his body or bodily functions, he started wearing adult diapers and the nurses were taking care of all of his needs.

Repositioning the recliner closer to the bedside, I turned it to face Will. Late one afternoon while Will was sleeping, I sat watching him. No thoughts of the past, present, or future were in my head. I just quietly concentrated on Will.

The sunlight shining through the window cast a warm glow over his pale skin. His dark hair was thin and brittle with a hint of gray. It looked like someone had taken their thumbs and pushed his eyes farther into his head. His cheeks were nonexistent, the bones merely there to give the skin something to hang on. The once chiseled jawline was so frail the slightest touch seemed like it would have caused it to shatter. And the mountain of blankets swallowed up his skeletal frame making it look even smaller.

This Will looked nothing like the old Will. The new Will was humble, honest, remorseful, apologetic, and kind. Maybe I hadn't been completely fooled by his act all those years after all. That somehow I saw glimpses of this new Will inside the old one. The Will who appreciated me and thought I deserved the best. The Will who supported my dreams of culinary school. The Will who, in his own way, did love me.

Clearing his throat, Will began. "I, Will . . . I mean, William, take you, Bryson, to be my wife. I promise to be true to you in good times and in bad, in sickness and in health. I will love you and honor you all the days of my life."

The love and sincerity in his voice was overwhelming, causing my eyes to fill with tears.

I swallowed hard and tried to hold down the emotions that kept trying to bubble to the surface. "I, Bryson, take you, William, to be my husband. I promise to be true to you in good times and in bad, in sickness and in health. I will love you and honor you all the days of my life."

And in the end the new Bryson was able to let the new Will know he wouldn't be alone all the days of his life.

Confusion

"Ooohhh . . ."

I startled awake at the sound of a loud long moan. I looked over to find Will on his back, thrashing his head back and forth. I jumped off the sofa and ran to his bedside.

Sitting, I placed my hand in the middle of his chest, rubbing slow small circles, and said calmly, "Will, it's okay. I'm here. Try to relax." I paused, hoping my words and touch penetrated his fog of confusion. "Remember how much you loved playing football? You were such an awesome player." The thrashing slowly subsided as I continued to rub Will's chest. "Even I knew how good you were and I'm clueless about all of that stuff. Our first date was at one of your games."

"Homecoming." The faint hint of the word swirled in the air for a split second before vanishing.

I thought my mind and ears were playing tricks on me as I looked down at Will.

With his head turned toward me and his eyes closed, Will whispered, "First official date."

A lump formed in my throat. "You're right. I always considered the game you asked me to come to as our first date."

Placing his hand over mine, Will stopped the slow circles. And just like that he was back. Gently, I lowered down on the bed next to Will, our hands still joined together on his chest.

"You had to bribe Sophie to go with me because I wasn't going to go by myself. She never did tell me what you offered her."

"Fifty bucks." I could barely hear him.

"Wow, I had no idea I was worth that much."

"Priceless." He sighed.

Tears pooled in my eyes as I whispered into Will's ear, "Thank you."

Will's eyes opened halfway, his gaze drifting up to the ceiling. Raising his anorexic hand off mine, he pointed in the air at no particular thing.

"I need my uniform cleaned. What time is the game tonight?" He mumbled.

With tears trickling down my face, I kept my voice steady and answered. "It's at seven o'clock. They always start at seven o'clock."

And just like that he was gone.

Goodbye

The stillness in the air was overwhelming and uncomfortable. I shifted in the recliner from side to side while mindlessly flipping through a cooking magazine in the dimly lit room.

"Bryson." Will's voice was barely above a whisper.

The past two days Will had been in and out of consciousness. Most of the time he was so out of it, mumbling incoherently and then drifting back to sleep. But on rare occasions the old Will would show back up.

I closed the magazine and leaned forward. "Hey, sleepy head. I had no idea I was so boring."

The corners of his mouth twitched up like he was trying to smile.

Will's body had wasted away to almost nothing. There wasn't a bone on him that wasn't protruding through his pale sallow skin. More Kaposi lesions had developed, an especially large one had invaded his right eye, causing complete loss of vision.

"Have I thanked you today?"

"You sure have."

"Tell me about your day." He strained to get the words out.

The truth was my day could be summed up in a word. Sitting. But Will liked to hear what was going on outside of these walls so I started making up things based on actual events that had happened. Just not recently.

Smoothing out his top sheet, I said, "I got up and out early. I had to go to the grocery store before I came here. When I was taking the groceries out of the car, Mrs. Ravenel came over wanting to know where I'd been since she hadn't seen me lately."

"Nosy old broad." Will joked.

"Pretty much."

"What else?"

"Oh, I got response letters from both Johnson and Wales and The Art Institute about my application."

I'd actually received the letters the week before Will was admitted to hospice.

"Don't leave me hanging."

"I got accepted to both culinary programs."

"Never doubted it for a second." The loud wheeze escaped him as he inhaled a shallow breath. "Bryson, promise me . . ." Another loud wheeze choked him.

My entire body seized up as tears spilled over and down my face.

Will forced his lids up and aimed his gaze directly at me. ". . . You'll go get your happily ever after. You deserve it."

Placing my hand over Will's heart, his chest stilled as life slipped from his dark brown eyes.

"I promise," I whispered between sobs.

I don't know how long I stayed in that position before feeling the light touch of a hand on my shoulder.

"Mrs. Forsyth, do you need anything?" I don't even remember alerting the nurse that Will was gone.

I swept my hands over my face, wiping away the tears. Standing, I looked at the pretty redhead with the sympathetic green eyes. I shook my head and without a word walked out of the room.

With my gaze focused on the floor in front of me, I made my way down the hallways. Each turn brought my mind, body, and spirit to numbing exhaustion. As I rounded the last corner, my gaze drifted up to a pair of blue-gray eyes.

"How?"

Shaking his head slightly, Hart said, "Something in my soul told me you needed me."

My footsteps sped up. In one continuous motion I landed in Hart's lap and my arms securely wrapped around him. With my face buried deep in the crook of his neck, I held on tight as we rolled out the door and into our *forever*.

According to the U.S. Centers for Disease Control and Prevention (Last updated March 2016)

More than **1.2 million** people in the United States are living with HIV infection.

It is estimated that almost **1 in 8** (12.8 percent) don't know they are infected.

From 1981 to 2013, an estimated **1,194,039 people in the United States had been diagnosed with AIDS. Of those, 658,507 have died.**

An estimated **50,000** new HIV infections occur in the U.S. each year.

At the end of 2011, **23 percent** of all people living with HIV in the United States were women.

The vast majority of newly diagnosed HIV-positive women contracted the virus through heterosexual sex.

Women account for **1 in 5** new HIV diagnoses and deaths caused by AIDS.

Twenty-five percent of them are between the ages of **13 and 24.**

That means at least one teenager or young adult in this country is infected with HIV every hour of every day.

epilogue

I stood in front of the giant wall of glass. The fake sunlight shimmered down through the water, bouncing off the yellow, green, and pink coral. The blue glow of the tank gave the dimly lit room a romantic dreamy feel.

"Bryson!"

I turned around to a power-walking Tommy headed straight toward me with arms a-flailin'.

"Oh my god! The entire line has come to a grinding halt because of that old lady.

"Miss Polly?"

"She won't leave the mini fried chicken and waffles station."

Placing my hands on his shoulders, I said, "Tommy, calm down. Simple solution."

"You want me to kick her to the curb?"

My face scrunched at his suggestion. "She's eighty years old."

"I think I can take her."

"Go in the kitchen and grab a platter. Pile it high with chicken and take it to Miss Polly's table."

"I would have thought of that eventually. Please don't consider my momentary lapse in judgment as a reflection on my ability to be in charge of this event."

"You're doing a great job. The place looks fantastic and the food is mouthwatering."

"Thanks, boss." He spun around and power-walked away.

It's been three years since Will died and so much has changed. Not a day goes by that I don't think of him and thank him for what he did for me in the end. His will was so airtight his parents never bothered to contest it.

I graduated from The Art Institute of Charleston with a degree in culinary arts. With the experience I gained working for Good Eats I was able to earn my degree in half the time it usually takes. Last year Nancy wanted to step back a little from the catering business to enjoy her grandchildren. She offered me a partnership in the company. Not only was I following my dream, I'd also been able to use my MBA degree after all.

As my gaze scanned the room a smile crossed my face. Everyone I loved was gathered together to share this incredible moment.

"Hey, let's dance."

My gaze shifted to a pair of twinkling blue-gray eyes.

I chuckled. "Who do you think you are ordering me to dance with you?"

Grinning oh so sexily, Hart extended his hand. "Your husband, Mrs. Mitchell."

I slipped my hand in his and melted into his lap. With my palms flat against his toned tuxedo clad chest, they traveled up over his shoulders to the base of his neck. Hart rolled us onto the dance floor as the smooth voice of Tony Bennett singing "The Way You Look Tonight" flowed from the speakers.

"Have I told you how hot you are in your classic black tux, Mr. Mitchell?"

Hart leaned forward, placing his lips against mine and whispered, "Have you seen my lovely wife? She's uber hot. I had to up my game."

My dress was pretty awesome. The floor-length champagne chiffon skimmed over my skin and wrapped around my body, gathering at my hip with elegant crystal beading. Hart was a big fan of the backless aspect of the halter top.

Hart asked me to marry him a year ago. Well, I should say Hart and Butter asked. Somehow he convinced me that camping would be fun. One weekend last fall we packed everything and went to the mountains of North Carolina. The first night while we snuggled up by the fire Hart called Butter over. The ring was dangling from a red ribbon tied around Butter's neck. It was perfect.

We kept the ceremony small, inviting just close friends and family. As for the reception, there was never any question it would be held here at the aquarium. Ballroom B was smaller and more intimate than the one the prom was held in. The tables were scattered on one side of the room, dressed in white linen with deep red rose centerpieces. The food, catered by Good Eats, thank you very much, was set up in the far left corner. In the far right corner was an easel with a white spotlight shining down on the painting Hope Mitchell created after hearing the prom story. It was a nice way to honor Hart's mother and feel her presence. And the tank wall made for a gorgeous backdrop for the dance floor.

I pressed my cheek to his scruffy one and laughed. Glancing up, I caught Mom and Dad at one of the tables. Dad was holding an endless supply of tissues while Mom ruined her makeup.

Closing my eyes, I got lost in the song, the sway, and the sensation of Hart.

One Mississippi.

Two Mississippi.

Three Mississippi.

"Bryson!" The loud shrill whisper of Sophie cut through the air.

Hart and I looked up just in time to see Sophie circling us with Doug hot on her heels.

Rotation one. "Get away from me. I'm not going to tell you again."

"Good. I'm sick of hearing it. Stop fighting it. Give in to the urge."

Rotation two. "The only urge I have is to punch you in the neck."

"How'd you know I liked it a little rough?"

Suddenly, she stopped, turned on her heels, and got right up in Doug's face. "I swear if you don't stop it, I'm gonna have to . . . to . . ."

"Have to do what?"

"Fuck you."

"Man, I hope the rest of you is as filthy as your mouth."

Sophie's shoulders slumped as she rolled her eyes. "Oh gawd. Come on. I gotta get drunker than I am now. Like a lot, a lot more."

On her way to drinking herself into the hooking-up-at-a-wedding cliché, Sophie passed Ronnie and Julia slow dancing and shaking their heads in unison.

Standing off to the side, Colin held a glass of champagne and joked. "She's gonna have to suck down the entire bar to stomach you."

"She can suck anything she wants as long as I'm one of the suckees." Doug said over his shoulder as he weaved his way through the tables in search of Sophie.

Hart and I looked at each other, exchanging brow-lifting expressions. Our cheeks reconnected. His right hand landed on the bare skin at the small of my back while his left hand worked the wheel as we danced to our song at our wedding.

When I was younger I thought I had a clear vision of what the perfect guy would look like. But the perfect man isn't the one with dark hair or blond hair. He doesn't have a specific eye color. He's not tall or short with washboard abs and bulging biceps.

The perfect man is the one who gives you strength, encouragement, and love. He builds you up and holds you up. He protects you while giving you room to grow as a person. He desires you and lets you know just how special and lovely you are. He appreciates your intellect and opinions. He supports your dreams. And he's the one you can cry in front of and laugh out loud with.

"I love Yodel you, Bryson." His rasp had every inch of my body, heart, and soul tingling.

I tightened my hold. "I Yodel you, Hart."

And in the end we lived happily ever after.

Thank you for taking the time to read my book. I'd really appreciate it if you could take a few minutes to leave an honest review on Amazon.

note from the author

One of my top goals in writing is to portray characters and situations in a relatable and realistic manner. I do extensive research on every aspect of the story down to the tiniest of details. While the sequence of Will's illness is realistic I took creative license in the timeframe the disease took over.

acknowledgements

Since the first day I told my family I'd written a book they have encouraged me every step of the way. During the writing of The Dance I went through a couple of health related issues. If it weren't for the love and support of my family you wouldn't be reading this book. No words will ever express adequately how grateful and blessed I am to have them in my life.

My incredible beta team, Beth Hyams, Concepcion Capon, Jennifer Mirabelli, Kim Bias, Tabitha Willbanks, and Tammy Zautner. You ladies are the cream of the crop. Thank you for your generosity of time and all the honest feedback you give me. I don't know what I'd do without you.

Linda Roberts (editor), hard to believe this is our 4th book together. Thank you for making me and my words look even better than I do.

Murphy Hopkins (cover designer, Indie Solutions), thank you for another gorgeous cover, teasers, and ads. I don't know how you decipher my babbling but I'm glad you do.

Abigail Marie, (photographer, Nonpareil Photography) your artistry never ceases to amaze me.

Elaine York, (formatting), thank you for your patience, understanding, and for making the inside of The Dance all pretty. It was a great experience working with you for the first time and I look forward to many more projects.

Nina Grinstead, (Gossip Girls PR), what can I say. From the moment we met I knew we'd be friends. Your love and friendship mean the world to me.

Emily Smith, (Gossip Girls PR), thank you for keeping me on track and calm. Knowing you were at the helm made my life so much easier.

Thank you Sandra Sipple and Hayden (her son) for answering all my questions. The information you gave me made Hart's character come alive.

Tricia Zoeller (friend/sounding board/talker down off ledge). I will never be able to thank you enough for the hours you listened and gave me your honest thoughts. You challenged me with a new perspective and set me on a better track.

Flavia Viotti and Meire Dias, (agents at Bookcase Literary Agency), it's been an exciting year ladies and a lot of it is because of your hard work. Thank you for your continued belief in me and my writing.

Bloggers, you work tirelessly for the love of reading. I feel very blessed that so many of you have chosen my books to review and then spread the word to your readers. I appreciate you more than you know.

Readers, I could not do what I do without you. The love and support you've given me over the years has been mind-blowing. Whenever I feel like giving up on this writing thing it's you guys who remind me why I do it. I will never take you for granted and will always strive to give you the quality of stories you deserve.

Christopher and Dana Reeves Foundation, thank you for all the information you sent me regarding spinal cord injury.

about the author

Alison was born and raised in Charleston, SC. She attended Winthrop University and graduated with a major in Theater. While at school Alison began writing one-act plays, which she later produced.

Her debut novel, Present Perfect, is an Amazon and International bestseller. The novel won Best Book at the 2014 Indie Romance Convention Awards. Both follow-up novels in the Perfect Series landed on many Best Of Lists for 2014-2015. Stop!, Alison's first YA novel was named one of the top YA novels of 2015.

connect with the author

Website: www.alisongbailey.com
Facebook: www.facebook.com/AlisonGBaileyAuthor
Twitter: www.twitter.com/AlisonGBailey1
Instagram: www.instagram.com/alisongbailey
Pinterest: www. pinterest.com/alisongbailey/present-perfect-by-alison-
g-bailey/
Goodreads: www.goodreads.com/author/show/7032185.Alison_G_
Bailey

Playlist: open.spotify.com/user/1244737523/
playlist/1J85KbZ6b3zYUliFF7K3JJ

recipes

Swiss Chicken

Ingredients:
6 boneless skinless chicken breast halves (1-1/2 pounds)
1 can (10-3/4 ounces) condensed cream of chicken soup, undiluted
1/2 cup white wine or chicken broth
6 slices Swiss cheese
1 cup crushed seasoned croutons

Directions:
1. Place chicken in a greased 13-in. x 9-in. baking dish. In a small bowl, combine the soup and wine or broth; pour over chicken. Top with cheese and sprinkle with croutons.
2. Bake, uncovered, at 350° for 35-40 minutes or until chicken juices run clear.
Makes 6 servings.

Zucchini Pie

Ingredients:
4 cups sliced thin zucchini
8 oz canned crescent rolls
10 oz package of shredded mozzarella cheese
2 eggs
1 medium onion chopped
½ cup butter
2 Tbsp parsley
½ tsp salt
¼ tsp pepper
½ tsp garlic powder

½ tsp basil

½ tsp oregano

Directions:

1. Melt butter in a large skillet.

2. Add zucchini and onion. Cook 10 minutes or until zucchini is somewhat limp.

3. Add seasoning to zucchini and onion.

4. In medium bowl mix the eggs and cheese.

5. Remove zucchini and onions from heat.

6. Add egg and cheese mixture to skillet, mix well.

7. Separate crescent rolls, place in a 9-inch pie pan, form into crust.

8. Pour zucchini and cheese mixture into crust.

9. Bake 375 degrees for 20 minutes.

10. Remove from oven and let stand for 5 minutes. Slice and serve.

Serves between 5-6

Serving suggestions: Great with cooked apples.

Best Ever Chicken Salad

Ingredients:

4 cups cooked chicken, cubed

1 cup celery chopped fine

1 1/3 cups mayonnaise

2 Tbsp Durkee's sandwich and salad sauce

2 tsp lemon juice

½ tsp pepper

Salt to taste.

Directions:

1. Boil chicken, cube and measure.

2. Mix all ingredients together and let stand for several hours before serving.

Serving suggestions: Add in 1 cup red grapes cut in half and 1 cup of pecans.

Crockpot Spaghetti

Ingredients:

1 lb of ground beef or Italian sausage or ½ a lb each

4 Tbsp extra virgin olive oil

3/4 cup finely chopped onion

2 cloves garlic, peeled and minced

2 1/2 lbs ripe plum tomatoes

Salt

Pepper

Fresh basil, minced (about 10 leaves)

1 bay leaf

Barbeque sauce

Directions:

1. Bring a pot of water to a boil.

2. To prepare the tomatoes, cut steams. Drop tomatoes into boiling water for 2 to 3 minutes or until you see the skins begin to slip off.

3. Transfer the tomatoes to a colander in the sink and run cold water over them until they are cool enough to handle.

4. Peel off the skins and cut tomatoes in half.

5. Cut out the core and scoop out the seeds.

6. Coarse dice tomatoes.

7. In a saucepan, heat the olive oil over medium heat until sizzling, then cook the onion, stirring often, until it is soft and translucent.

8. Add the garlic and cook a minute or two just until fragrant.

9. Add meat to skillet and cook until done, no longer pink. Drain.

10. Transfer all meat, tomatoes, salt and pepper, bay leaf, salt, pepper, and as much barbeque sauce as you like to a 3-quart crockpot.

11. Set on low for 7-8 hours.

12. Stir in fresh basil just before serving.

Serving suggestions: Your choice pasta. Can substitute jar sauce for tomatos.

Lowcountry Red Rice

Ingredients:

1 can tomato paste

1 ½ to 2 cans (tomato paste can) of water

2 onions, chopped fine

3 tsp salt

2-3 tsp sugar

4 strips of bacon, cubed.

8 Tbsp bacon grease (Yes, you read that right)

2 cups white rice

A good dash of pepper

Directions:

1. Fry bacon, remove from pan, sauté onions in grease.

2. Add tomato paste, water, sugar, salt, and pepper to pan of onions. Cook slowly (about 10 minutes) until mixture measures 2 cups.

3. Add mixture to rice in the top section of rice steamer.

4. Add ½ cup additional grease. (You read that right as well)

5. Steam for half hour.

6. Add crumbled bacon and stir with a fork.

7. Cook an additional 30-45 minutes.

Serves 6-8

books by
Alison G. Bailey

Present Perfect (Book #1)

Amazon (http://tinyurl.com/km2b3bn)

Audible (http://tinyurl.com/prjuacn)

Past Imperfect (Book #2)

Amazon (http://tinyurl.com/pumtvb8)

Presently Perfect (Book #3)

Amazon (http://tinyurl.com/oxrrhpe)

The Perfect Box Set

Amazon (http://tinyurl.com/mavdtuf)

Stop!

Amazon (http://tinyurl.com/jzg0592)

Read all of Alison's books FREE with Kindle Unlimited

For additional information on spinal cord injuries and HIV/AIDS visit

Christopher and Dana Reeves Foundation
https://www.christopherreeve.org/

Amfar
http://www.amfar.org/

Made in the USA
Lexington, KY
23 March 2018